Honoré de Balzac was born at Tours in 1799, the son of a civil servant. He spent nearly six years as a boarder in a Vendôme school, then went to live in Paris, working as a lawyer's clerk then as a hack-writer. Between 1820 and 1824 he wrote a number of novels under various pseudonyms, many of them in collaboration, after which he unsuccessfully tried his luck at publishing, printing and type-founding. At the age of thirty, heavily in debt, he returned to literature with a dedicated fury and wrote the first novel to appear under his own name, *The Chouans*. During the next twenty years he wrote about ninety novels and shorter stories, among them many masterpieces, to which he gave the comprehensive title *The Human Comedy*. He died in 1850, a few months after his marriage to Evelina Hanska, the Polish countess with whom he had maintained amorous relations for eighteen years.

Marion Ayton Crawford taught English Language and Literature in the Technical College at Limavady, Northern Ireland until she died in 1973. She translated five volumes of Balzac for the Penguin Classics: *Cousin Bette*, *Domestic Peace and Other Stories*, *Eugénie Grandet*, *The Chouans* and *Old Goriot*.

ST. PAUL'S SCHOOL LIBRARY
LONSDALE ROAD, SW13 9JT
WITHDRAWN

WITHDRAWN

Honoré de Balzac

COUSIN BETTE

PART ONE OF
POOR RELATIONS

TRANSLATED BY
MARION AYTON CRAWFORD

W
S P S
L

G21919.

PENGUIN BOOKS

PENGUIN BOOKS

Published by the Penguin Group
Penguin Books Ltd, 27 Wrights Lane, London W8 5TZ, England
Penguin Putnam Inc., 375 Hudson Street, New York, New York 10014, USA
Penguin Books Australia Ltd, Ringwood, Victoria, Australia
Penguin Books Canada Ltd, 10 Alcorn Avenue, Toronto, Ontario, Canada M4V 3B2
Penguin Books (NZ) Ltd, Private Bag 102902, NSMC, Auckland, New Zealand

Penguin Books Ltd, Registered Offices: Harmondsworth, Middlesex, England

This translation first published 1965
3 5 7 9 10 8 6 4

Film and TV Tie-in edition published 1998

Copyright © M. A. Crawford, 1965
All rights reserved

Printed in England by Clays Ltd, St Ives plc
Set in Monotype Garamond

Except in the United States of America, this book is sold subject
to the condition that it shall not, by way of trade or otherwise, be lent,
re-sold, hired out, or otherwise circulated without the publisher's
prior consent in any form of binding or cover other than that in
which it is published and without a similar condition including this
condition being imposed on the subsequent purchaser

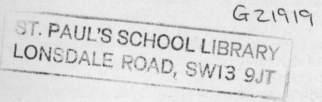

GZ1919

ST. PAUL'S SCHOOL LIBRARY
LONSDALE ROAD, SW13 9JT

INTRODUCTION

As the dedication makes clear, this novel is one of a pair entitled *Poor Relations*, which were conceived and written practically simultaneously, in less than a year, between 1846 and 1847; the other is *Cousin Pons*. In spite of its speed of production, *Cousin Bette* is a deeply considered book, the fruit of a life-time of thought and experience, and a culminating point in Balzac's chronicle and analysis of Revolutionary, Napoleonic, Restoration, and later times, in his novel-sequence *The Human Comedy*. The main action takes place between 1838 and 1846, and is thus brought up to date, to the time when the novel was being written. The scene throughout is Paris.

Paris was then the capital of a rapidly changing France, in an age when the modern world as we know it was coming into existence, with the construction of railways, the expansion of industry and trade, the growing power of international finance and of the Press. The period saw the beginning of the French colonial adventure in Algeria. It was the age of the middle class. Louis-Philippe, 'the bourgeois king', brought into strictly limited power by the middle-class revolution of 1830, ruled a nation of highly acquisitive and politically and socially ambitious individuals.

The book depicts these changes vividly, through the eyes and lives of two generations. The older characters remember the glories of the Imperial past, the exhilaration of life under Napoleon, the circumstances in which their careers were made through unprecedented opportunities grasped then, the brilliance and lavish display of the First Empire society in which they played their part; their eyes are still dazzled. The younger generation have a different conditioning, a new outlook, different aims. It is evident that to Balzac, in comparison, the present was a mean and sordid age, carrying the seeds of disaster in its breaking up of the social framework, and its selfish and philistine money-grubbing. It is worthy of note that Karl Marx considered Balzac's characters the prototypes of the bourgeois society that came into existence later – after Balzac's death in 1850 – under Napoleon III.

The novel, for Balzac, always had a complex function. *Cousin Bette* is, among other things, a serious investigation of the Paris *demi-monde*. Because of its enlargement of the scope of the novel, and in particular its objective gaze at vice and crime, it has been hailed as the first volume of French fiction of the naturalistic school, later to be established by the works of the Goncourt brothers and Émile Zola. It has the purposes of the kind of inquiry with which modern Government Commissions have lately familiarized us, as well as those of the modern documentary film. It is also, plainly, an ancestor of the modern thriller.

There is nothing heavy or dull about this serious work. In reading it one occasionally remembers that Balzac had adapted the *Contes drolatiques* of Rabelais. Shakespeare, Molière, and Racine, three dramatists, are progenitors whom he invokes in the book; and brilliant scenes of comedy, irony, and high tragedy, although quite characteristically his own, show that he had assimilated something from all three. These scenes succeed one another at a very fast pace, with many changes of points of view and twists of circumstance. The book adds notably to Balzac's gallery of unforgettable characters.

Balzac was always fascinated by the relations between husband and wife, father and children, lover and mistress, between those with material possessions, social status, and close family ties, and those not so endowed, and by the different ways in which emotional life can vary, and is tied up with the individual's everyday existence. These relations and variations are explored and studied here in a way that anticipates Freud.

Many minor characters, set in their proper environment, help to re-create the richness of life in the capital. Paris is mapped topographically as well as socially: its various groups of upstart tradesmen, politicians, civil servants, bankers, opera singers, courtesans, journalists, artists, money-lenders, Marshals, withdrawn aristocrats, and its colonies of foreigners,

6

Italian stove-fitters and Polish refugees, are seen going about their business, in their natural habitat.

The characters, actively engaged in their trades or professions, naturally discuss the technical questions that interest them, as well as the events and social questions of the hour – all of burning interest, of course, to Balzac himself. These he is able to make interesting to the reader, partly because of their dramatic place in the story, partly historically, because the period saw the rise of so many new ideas and movements that still involve us, partly because some of the questions that he discusses through the characters or in his own person are eternal questions.

The sound of Balzac's voice throughout the book is a unifying factor, but his success in combining very disparate elements to make a satisfying unity is due mainly to the subtle arrangement of the plot. This technical skill is just one respect in which Balzac's genius, after more than sixty volumes of *The Human Comedy*, achieves its full maturity in the book. It is a book in which, in all respects, he is most characteristically and triumphantly himself.

M.A.C.

A NOTE ON MONEY

Money is of considerable importance in *Cousin Bette*; indeed it is the central theme of this portrait of a society given over, in Balzac's eyes, to the feverish pursuit of wealth. It may therefore be of some use to the reader to have a rough idea of comparative values. Professor Hunt, in his biography of Balzac, states that 100,000 francs were equal to £4,000; this would be roughly equivalent in purchasing power to £130,000 today (1986).

To Don Michele Angelo Cajetani, Prince of Teano

I dedicate this small fragment of a long story, not to the Roman prince, nor to the heir of the illustrious Cajetani family that has given Popes to Christendom, but to the learned commentator of Dante.

I owe the revelation of the wonderful structure of ideas upon which Italy's greatest poet built his poem, the only modern poem that bears comparison with Homer, to you. Until I had heard you, *The Divine Comedy* seemed to me a vast enigma, to which no one had found a key, commentators least of all. To comprehend Dante as you do is to be great in his manner; but you find all forms of greatness easy.

A French scholar would make a reputation, be given a Professor's Chair perhaps, and a host of honours, by publishing, as an authoritative work, the improvization with which you whiled away one of those evenings when we were resting after sight-seeing in Rome. But perhaps you do not know that most of our professors live on Germany, England, the Orient, or the North, as insects live on a tree, and like the insect become part of what they live on, borrowing their importance from the importance of their subject.

As it happens, Italy has never yet been exploited in this way by the scholars; and I shall never be given the credit I deserve for my self-restraint as a man of letters. Dressed in your borrowed plumage, I might have been a savant, worth three Schlegels in weight and erudition, and yet I remain a simple doctor of social medicine, a horse-doctor of desperate social ills; if only in order to offer a tribute to my cicerone, and add your illustrious name to the names of Porcia, San Severino, Pareto, Negro, Belgiojoso, which in *The Human Comedy* will represent the close and enduring alliance between Italy and France.

So long ago as the sixteenth century, that alliance was celebrated in the same fashion by Bandello (the bishop who

9

wrote some very diverting tales) in a magnificent collection of stories, from which several of Shakespeare's plays were derived, in some cases entire characters being taken directly from the text.

The two sketches which I dedicate to you represent the two eternal aspects of a single reality. *Homo duplex*, said our great Buffon; why not add *res duplex*? Everything has two faces, even virtue. For this reason Molière always presents both sides of every human problem. Following his example, Diderot one day wrote *Ceci n'est pas un conte*, perhaps his masterpiece, in which he sets the sublime figure of Mademoiselle de Lachaux, immolated by Gardanne, as pendant to that of a perfect lover slain by his mistress.

My two stories are therefore placed together as a pair, like twins of different sex. It is a literary fancy in which one may indulge once, especially in a work which seeks to represent all the forms in which thought may be clothed.

Most disputes are due to the fact that there are many scholars, and many ignorant men, so constituted that they can never see more than one side of a fact or idea; and each man claims that the aspect he has seen is the only true and valid aspect. The prophecy of holy writ is fulfilled: 'God will deliver the world to disputation'. I declare that that line from scripture should oblige the Holy See, in proper obedience to it, to give you two-Chamber government, as Louis XVIII by his Ordinance of 1814 furnished a commentary upon it.

May your wit, may the poetry that is yours, take under their protection the two episodes of *Poor Relations*

By your affectionate and devoted servant,

DE BALZAC

Paris, August–September 1846

COUSIN BETTE

*

Towards the middle of July, in the year 1838, one of those vehicles called *milords*, then appearing in the Paris squares for the first time, was driving along the rue de l'Université, bearing a stout man of medium height in the uniform of a captain in the National Guard.

Our Paris citizens are credited with plenty of mother wit; yet there are some among them who fancy themselves infinitely more attractive in uniform, and think women so simple as to be easily impressed by a bearskin cap and military trappings.

The rubicund and rather chubby face of this Captain of the Second Company fairly radiated self-satisfaction. He wore the aureole of complacency achieved by wealthy, self-made, retired shopkeepers, that marked him as one of the Paris elect, an ex-Deputy Mayor of his district at least. The ribbon of the Legion of Honour, naturally, was conspicuous upon his chest, which was valorously puffed out in the Prussian manner. Proudly ensconced in a corner of the *milord*, this decorated gentleman allowed his glances to rove among the passers-by, who are often, in Paris, the recipients in this fashion of pleasant smiles intended for bright eyes that are far away.

The *milord* stopped in the part of the street that lies between the rue de Bellechasse and the rue de Bourgogne, at the door of a large house recently built on part of the court of an old mansion set in a garden. The mansion still stood in its original state beyond the court, whose size had been reduced by half.

As the Captain alighted from the *milord*, accepting a helping hand from the driver, it was evident that he was a man in his fifties. Certain movements, by their undisguised heaviness, are as indiscreet as a birth certificate. He replaced his yellow glove on the hand that he had bared, and, making no inquiry of the concierge, walked towards the steps leading to the mansion's ground floor, with an air that declared 'She is mine!' Paris porters know how to use their eyes. They never dream of stopping gentlemen with decorations on their chests who are dressed in National Guard blue and walk like men of weight. In other words, they know money when they see it.

This whole ground floor was occupied by Monsieur le Baron Hulot d'Ervy, Commissary general under the Republic, lately senior officer controlling the Army Commissariat, and now head of one of the most important departments of the War Ministry, Councillor of State, Grand Officer of the Legion of Honour, etc., etc.

Baron Hulot had taken the name of Ervy, his birthplace, in order to distinguish himself from his brother, the famous General Hulot, Colonel of the Grenadiers of the Imperial Guard, created Comte de Forzheim by the Emperor after the campaign of 1809. The elder brother, the Count, with a fatherly concern for the future of the younger, who had been committed to his charge, had found a place for him in military administration, in which, partly owing to his brother's services but also on his own merits, the Baron had won Napoleon's favour. From the year 1807, Baron Hulot had been Commissary general of the armies in Spain.

When he had rung, the bourgeois Captain exerted himself energetically to smooth down his coat, which had been wrinkled up both in front and behind by his corpulence. Admitted on sight by a servant in livery, this important and imposing visitor followed the man, who announced him as he opened the drawing-room door:

'Monsieur Crevel!'

When she heard this name, admirably appropriate to the appearance of the man who bore it, a tall, fair, well-preserved woman started, and rose, as if she had received an electric shock.

'Hortense, my angel, go into the garden with your Cousin Bette,' she said hastily to her daughter, who sat at her embroidery not far away.

With a graceful bow to the Captain, Mademoiselle Hortense Hulot left the room by a french window, taking with her a desiccated spinster who looked older than the Baroness, although she was five years younger.

12

'It's about your marriage,' Cousin Bette whispered in her young cousin Hortense's ear, apparently not at all offended by the way in which the Baroness had sent them off, as if she were of little account.

The appearance of this cousin would have afforded sufficient explanation, if explanation were needed, of such lack of ceremony.

The old maid wore a puce merino dress whose cut and narrow ribbon trimmings suggested Restoration fashion, an embroidered collar that had cost perhaps three francs, and a stitched straw hat with blue satin rosettes edged with straw, of the kind seen on the heads of old-clothes women in the market. A stranger, noticing her goatskin slippers, clumsily botched as if by a fifth-rate cobbler, would have hesitated before greeting Cousin Bette as a relation of the family: she looked for all the world like a daily sewing-woman. Before she left the room, however, the spinster gave Monsieur Crevel an intimate little nod, a greeting which that personage answered with a look of friendly understanding.

'You are coming tomorrow, Mademoiselle Fischer, aren't you?' he said.

'There won't be company?' Cousin Bette asked.

'Just my children and you,' replied the visitor.

'Very well, then, you may count on me.'

'I am at your service, Madame,' said the bourgeois Captain of Militia, turning to bow again to Baroness Hulot. And he rolled his eyes at Madame Hulot, like Tartuffe casting sheep's eyes at Elmire, when a provincial actor, at Poitiers or Coutances, thinks it necessary to place heavy emphasis on Tartuffe's designs.

'If you will come this way, Monsieur, we can discuss our business more conveniently here than in the drawing-room,' said Madame Hulot, leading the way to an adjoining room that in the lay-out of the suite was designed for a card-room.

Only a thin partition divided this room from the boudoir, whose window opened on the garden, and Madame Hulot left Monsieur Crevel alone for a moment, considering it necessary to shut both the window and the boudoir door so that no one could eavesdrop on that side. She even took the precaution of closing the french window of the drawing-room, smiling as she did so at her daughter and cousin, whom she saw installed in an old summer-house at the far end of the garden. Returning, she left the door of the card-room ajar, so that she might hear the drawing-room door open if anyone should come in. Moving about the apartment, the Baroness, being unobserved, allowed her face to express what she was thinking, and anyone seeing her would have been quite alarmed by her agitation. But as she crossed the drawing-room to the card-room, she masked her face with that inscrutable reserve that all women, even the most candid, seem able to assume at will.

During these preparations, singular to say the least, the National Guardsman was examining the furnishings of the room in which he found himself. As he remarked the silk curtains, once red, but now faded to violet by the sun and frayed along the folds by long use, a carpet from which the colours had disappeared, chairs with their gilding rubbed off and their silk spotted with stains and worn threadbare in patches, his contemptuous expression was followed by satisfaction, and then by hope, in naïve succession on his successful-shopkeeper's commonplace face. He was surveying himself in a glass above an old Empire clock, taking stock of himself, when the rustle of the Baroness's silk dress warned him of her approach. He at once struck an attitude.

The Baroness sat down on a little sofa that must certainly have been very pretty about the year 1809, and motioned Crevel to an armchair decorated with bronzed sphinx heads, from which the paint was scaling off, leaving the bare wood exposed in places.

'These precautions of yours, Madame, would be a delightfully promising sign for a . . .'

'A lover,' she interrupted him.

'The word is weak,' he said, placing his right hand on his heart, and rolling his eyes in a fashion that a woman nearly always finds comic when she meets them with no sympathy in her own. 'A lover! A lover! Say rather – a man bewitched!'

'Listen, Monsieur Crevel,' the Baroness went on, too much in earnest to feel like laughing. 'You are fifty – that's ten years younger than Monsieur Hulot, I know; but if a woman is to commit follies at my age she has to have something to justify her: good looks, youth, celebrity, distinction, brilliant gifts to dazzle her to the point of making her oblivious of everything, even of her age. You may have an income of fifty thousand francs, but your age must be weighed in the balance against your fortune; and you have nothing that a woman needs.'

'And love?' said the Captain, rising and coming towards her. 'A love that . . .'

'No, Monsieur, infatuation!' said the Baroness, interrupting him to try to put an end to this ridiculous scene.

'Yes, infatuation and love,' he went on, 'but something more than that too, a right . . .'

'A right!' exclaimed Madame Hulot, suddenly impressive in her scorn, defiance, and indignation. 'But if you go on in this strain, we shall never have done; and I did not ask you to come here to talk about something that has made you an un-welcome visitor in this house, in spite of the connexion between our two families.'

'I thought you did. . . .'

'What – again?' she exclaimed. 'Do you not see, Monsieur, by the detached and unconcerned way in which I speak of a lover and love and everything that is most indecorous on a woman's lips, that I am perfectly certain of remaining vir-tuous? I am not afraid of anything, even of incurring sus-picion by shutting myself in this room alone with you. Does a frail woman behave so? You know very well why I asked you to come!'

'No, Madame,' Crevel replied, with a sudden chill in his manner. He pursed his lips and struck his pose.

'Well, I'll be brief, and cut short the embarrassment this causes both of us,' said the Baroness, looking him in the face.

Crevel made an ironic bow, in which a man of his trade would have recognized the affected courtesy of a one-time commercial traveller.

'Our son has married your daughter . . .'

'And if that were to do again! . . .'

'The marriage would not take place,' rejoined the Baroness,

with spirit. 'I have little doubt of it. All the same, you have no cause for complaint. My son is not only one of the leading lawyers in Paris, but a Deputy since last year, and he has made such a brilliant début in the Chamber that it seems likely that he will be in the Government before long. My son has been consulted twice in the drafting of important Bills, and if he wanted the post he could be Solicitor-General, representing the Government in the Court of Appeal, tomorrow. So that if you mean to imply that you have a son-in-law with no fortune . . .'

'A son-in-law whom I am obliged to keep,' returned Crevel; 'which seems to me worse, Madame. Of the five hundred thousand francs settled on my daughter as her dowry, two hundred thousand have gone heaven knows where! In paying your fine son's debts, in buying high-class furniture for his house, a house worth five hundred thousand francs that brings in barely fifteen thousand because he occupies the best part of it himself, and on which he still owes two hundred and sixty thousand francs – the rent from it barely covers the interest on the debt. This year I have had to give my daughter something like twenty thousand francs to enable her to make ends meet. And my son-in-law who, they say, was making thirty thousand francs in the law-courts is going to throw that up for the Chamber. . . .'

'That, Monsieur Crevel, is a side issue, quite beside the point. But, to have done with it, if my son gets into office, if he has you made Officer of the Legion of Honour and Municipal Councillor of Paris, as a retired perfume-seller you will not have much to complain of.'

'Ah! now we have it, Madame! I am a tradesman, a shopkeeper, a former retailer of almond paste, eau-de-Portugal, cephalic oil for hair troubles. I must consider myself highly honoured to have married my only daughter to the son of Monsieur le Baron Hulot d'Ervy. My daughter will be a Baroness. That's Regency, that's Louis XV, that belongs to the Oeil-de-Boeuf ante-room at Versailles! All very fine . . . I love Célestine as a man cannot help loving his only child. I love her so much that rather than give her brothers and sisters I have put up with all the inconveniences of being a widower in Paris – and in my prime, Madame! – but you may take it from me that although I may dote on my daughter I do not intend to make a hole in my capital for your son, whose expenses seem to an old businessman like myself to need some explanation.'

'Monsieur, you see that Monsieur Popinot, who was once a druggist in the rue des Lombards, is Minister of Commerce now, at this very moment. . . .'

'A friend of mine, Madame!' said the ex-perfumer. 'For I, Célestin Crevel, once head salesman to old César Birotteau, bought the business of the said Birotteau, Popinot's father-in-law, Popinot being just an ordinary assistant in the business; and he himself reminds me of the fact, for he is not stuck-up – I'll say that for him – with people in good positions, worth sixty thousand francs a year.'

'Well, Monsieur, so the ideas that you describe as *Regency* are not in fashion now, in times when people accept a man on his personal merits; which is what you did when you married your daughter to my son.'

'And you don't know how that marriage came about!' exclaimed Crevel. 'Ah! confound this bachelor life! If it had not been for my libertine ways my Célestine would be the Vicomtesse Popinot today!'

'But let me repeat, let's have no recriminations over what is done!' the Baroness said, with emphasis. 'We have to talk of the reasons I have to protest about your strange conduct. My daughter Hortense had an opportunity to marry. The marriage depended entirely upon you, and I believed I could rely on your generosity. I thought that you would be fair to a woman whose heart has never held any image but her husband's, that you would have realized how necessary it was for her not to receive a man who might compromise her, and that you would have been eager, out of regard for the family with which you have allied your own, to promote Hortense's marriage with Councillor Lebas. . . . And you, Monsieur, have wrecked the marriage.'

'Madame,' replied the retired perfume-seller, 'I acted like an honest man. I was asked whether the two hundred thousand francs of Mademoiselle Hortense's dowry would be paid. I replied in these words precisely: "I would not answer for it. My son-in-law, on whom the Hulot family settled that sum on his marriage, had debts, and I believe that if Monsieur Hulot d'Ervy were to die tomorrow, his widow would be left to beg her bread." And that's how it is, my dear lady.'

'And would you have spoken in the same way, Monsieur,' asked Madame Hulot, looking Crevel steadily in the face, 'if I had been untrue to my vows for your sake?'

'I should have had no right to say it, dear Adeline,' exclaimed this singular lover, cutting the Baroness short, 'for you would have found the dowry in my note-case. . . .'

And suiting action to words, stout Crevel dropped on one knee and kissed Madame Hulot's hand, attributing to hesitation her speechless horror at his words.

'Buy my daughter's happiness at the price of – get up at once, Monsieur, or I'll ring the bell.'

The retired perfumer got to his feet with considerable difficulty, a circumstance which made him so furious that he struck his pose again. Nearly all men cherish a fondness for some posture that they think shows off to best advantage the good points with which nature has endowed them. In Crevel's case this pose consisted in crossing his arms like Napoleon, turning his head to show a three-quarter profile, and gazing, as the artist painting his portrait had made him gaze, at the horizon.

'Faithful,' he said, with well-calculated rage, 'faithful to a libert –'

'To a husband, Monsieur, worthy of my fidelity,' Madame Hulot interrupted, before Crevel could get out a word that she had no wish to hear.

'Look here, Madame, you wrote asking me to come. You want to know the reasons for my conduct. You drive me out of patience with your airs, as if you were an empress, your disdain and your . . . contempt! Anyone would think I was a black. I tell you again, and you may believe me! I have a right to . . . to court you . . . because . . . No, I love you well enough to hold my tongue.'

'Go on, Monsieur. In a few days' time I shall be forty-eight years old. I am not unnecessarily prudish. I can hear anything you may have to say.'

'Well then, do you give me your word as a virtuous woman – since, unluckily for me, that's what you are – never to give me away, never to say that I told you this secret?'

'If that's the condition of your telling me, I swear not to reveal to anyone, not even to my husband, who it was that told me the dreadful things I'm about to hear.'

'I may believe you, for it concerns only you and him.'

Madame Hulot turned pale.

'Ah! if you still love Hulot, this will hurt you! Would you rather I said nothing?'

'Go on, Monsieur, if it is true that what you say will justify the strange declarations you have made to me, and your persistence in annoying a woman of my age, who only wishes to see her daughter married, and then . . . die in peace!'

'You see, you are unhappy!'

'I, Monsieur?'

'Yes, lovely and noble creature!' cried Crevel. 'You have suffered only too much. . . .'

'Monsieur, say nothing more, and go! Or speak to me in a proper way.'

'Are you aware, Madame, how our fine Monsieur Hulot and I became acquainted? . . . Through our mistresses, Madame.'

'Oh, Monsieur!'

'Through our mistresses, Madame,' repeated Crevel melodramatically, breaking his pose to raise his right hand.

'Well, what then, Monsieur? . . .' said the Baroness calmly, to Crevel's great discomfiture.

Seducers, whose motives are mean, can never understand magnanimous minds.

'Having been a widower for five years,' Crevel went on, like a man who has a story to tell, 'not wishing to marry again, for the sake of my daughter whom I idolize, not wishing to have intrigues in my own establishment either, although at that time I had a very pretty cashier, I set up, as they call it, a little seamstress, fifteen years old, a miracle of beauty, whom I confess I fell head over in love with.

And so, Madame, I even asked my own aunt, whom I brought from my old home in the country (my mother's sister!), to live with this charming creature and look after her and see that she remained as good as she could in her circumstances, which were what you might call ... *chocnoso*? ... improper? ... no, compromising! ...

'The little girl, who plainly had a vocation for music, had masters to teach her, was given an education (she had to be kept out of mischief somehow!). And besides I wanted to be three persons in one to her, at the same time a father, a benefactor, and, not to mince matters, a lover: to kill two birds with one stone, do a kind deed and make a kind friend.

'I had five years' happiness. The child has a singing voice of a quality that would make any theatre's fortune, and I can only say that she is a Duprez in petticoats. She cost me two thousand francs a year, only to develop her talent as a singer. She made me an enthusiast for music: I took a box at the Italian Opera for her and my daughter. I went there on alternate evenings with them, one night with Célestine, the next night with Josépha ...'

'What, you mean the famous singer?'

'Yes, Madame,' Crevel continued proudly, 'the famous Josépha owes everything to me. Well, when she was twenty, in 1834 (I thought I had bound her to me for life and had become very soft with her), I wanted to give her some amusement and I let her meet a pretty little actress, Jenny Cadine, whose career had some similarity with her own. That actress too, owed everything to a protector who had brought her up as a cherished darling. Her protector was Baron Hulot.'

'I know, Monsieur,' said the Baroness calmly, without the slightest tremor in her voice.

'Ah bah!' exclaimed Crevel, more and more taken aback. 'All very well! But do you know that your monster of a husband was *protecting* Jenny Cadine when she was thirteen years old?'

'Well, Monsieur, what then?'

'As Jenny Cadine,' the retired shopkeeper went on, 'like Josépha, was twenty when they met, the Baron must have been playing Louis XV to her Mademoiselle de Romans since 1826, and you were twelve years younger then. . . . '

'Monsieur, I had my reasons for leaving Monsieur Hulot free.'

'That lie, Madame, is enough to wipe out all your sins, no doubt, and will open the gate of Paradise to you,' Crevel replied, with a knowing air that made the Baroness turn crimson. 'Tell that story, sublime and adored woman, to others, but not to old Crevel, who, I may tell you, has roistered too often at two-couple parties with your rascal of a husband not to know your full worth! When he was half-seas over, he sometimes used to reproach himself and enlarge on all your perfections to me. Oh, I know you very well: you are an angel. Between a girl of twenty and you a rake might hesitate, but not me.'

'Monsieur!'

'Very well, I'll stop. But you may as well know, saintly and worshipful woman, that husbands in their cups tell a great many things about their wives while their mistresses are listening, and their mistresses split their sides at them.'

Tears of outraged modesty, appearing between Madame Hulot's fine lashes, stopped the National Guardsman short, and he quite forgot to strike his pose.

'To return to the point,' he said, 'there is a bond between the Baron and me, because of our mistresses. The Baron, like all rips, is a very good sort, really a genial type. Oh I enjoyed him, the rascal! No, really, the things he thought of. . . . Well, no more of these reminiscences. We became like two brothers. The rogue, very Regency, did his best to lead me astray, to preach Saint-Simonism where women were concerned, give me notions of behaving like a lord, like a blue-jerkined swashbuckler; but, you see, I loved my little dear well enough to marry her, if I had not been afraid of having children. Between two old papas, such good friends as we were, naturally the idea couldn't but occur to us of marrying our children. Three months after the marriage of his son and my Célestine, Hulot . . . (I don't know how I can bear to utter his name, the scoundrel! For he has fooled us both, Madame!) . . . well, the scoundrel stole my little Josépha. The

21

cunning devil knew that he had been supplanted by a young Councillor of State and by an artist (no less!) in Jenny Cadine's heart (because her successes were making more and more of a splash), and he took my poor little mistress from me, a love of a girl; but you surely must have seen her at the Italian Opera, where he got her in by influence.

'Your man is not so careful as me. No one twists me round their fingers – I do everything methodically, according to rule. Jenny Cadine had already had a good cut out of him; she must have cost him pretty near thirty thousand francs a year. Well, you had better know that he has completely ruined himself now for Josépha. Josépha, Madame, is a Jewess; she is called Mirah, an anagram of Hiram, and that's a Jewish label to identify her, for she's a deserted child who was picked up in Germany. I have made some inquiries and found out that she's the natural child of a rich Jewish banker.

'The theatre, and above all what Jenny Cadine, Madame Schontz, Malaga, and Carabine taught her about the right fashion to treat old men, developed in that little girl whom I was bringing up in a proper, decent way – not expensive either – the instinct that the ancient Hebrews had for gold and jewels, for the Golden Calf! The famous singer now has a keen eye for the main chance; she wants to be rich, very rich. And she doesn't squander a sou of all the money that's squandered upon her. She tried her claws on Hulot, and she has plucked him clean – oh, plucked isn't the word, you can call it *skinned*!

'And now, poor wretch, after struggling to keep her against one of the Kellars, and the Marquis d'Esgrignon – both mad about Josépha – not to mention unknown worshippers at her shrine, he's about to see her carried off by that Duke who's rolling in money and patronizes the arts – what's he called, now? . . . he's a dwarf – ah! the Duc d'Hérouville. This grand lord wants to keep Josépha for himself alone. The whole courtesan world is talking about it, and the Baron knows nothing at all; for it's just the same in the Thirteenth District as in all the others: the lover, like the husband, is the last to learn the truth.

'Now do you understand my right? Your husband, my

dear lady, snatched my happiness from me, the only joy I have had since I lost my wife. Yes, if I had not had the bad luck to meet that old beau I should still possess Josépha, for, you know, I would never have let her go into the theatre; she would have stayed obscure, good, and my own.

'Oh! if you had seen her eight years ago! Slight and highly-strung, a golden Andalusian, as they call it, with black hair shining like satin, an eye that could flash lightning, and long dark lashes, with the distinction of a duchess in every movement that she made, with a poor girl's modesty and an unassuming grace, as sweet and pretty in her ways as a wild deer. And now, because of Hulot, her charm and innocence have all become bird-lime, a trap set to catch five-franc pieces. The child is now queen of the demi-reps, as they say. She's up to all the artful dodges now, she who used to know nothing at all, hardly even the meaning of the expression!'

As he said this, the retired perfumer wiped away tears that had risen to his eyes. The sincerity of his grief had its effect on Madame Hulot, and she roused herself from the reverie into which she had fallen.

'Well, Madame, is a man likely to find a treasure like that again at fifty-two years of age? At fifty-two love costs thirty thousand francs per annum: I have the figures from your husband; and I love Célestine too well to ruin her. Seeing you on that first evening when you received us, I could not understand how that scoundrel Hulot could keep a Jenny Cadine. You looked like an empress. You were not thirty, Madame,' he went on; 'to me you seemed young; you were lovely. 'Pon my word of honour, that day, I was stirred to the depths. I said to myself, "Old Hulot neglects his wife, and if I had not my Josépha she would suit me to a T." Ah! pardon me, that's an expression from my old trade. The perfumer breaks through now and again; that's what stands in the way of my aspiring to be a Deputy.

'And so when I was done down in such a treacherous way by the Baron – for between old cronies like us our friends' mistresses should have been sacrosanct – I swore to myself that I would take his wife. It was only fair. The Baron would not be able to say a word, and there was nothing at all he could do. When I told you of the state of my heart, you showed me the door as if I were a dog with mange at the first words, and in doing that you made my love twice as strong – my infatuation if you like – and you shall be mine!'

'Indeed? How?'

'I do not know how, but that's the way it's going to be. You see, Madame, an idiot of a perfumer – retired! – who has only one idea in his head, is in a stronger position than a clever man with thousands. I am mad about you, and you are my revenge! That's as if I were in love twice over. I speak my mind to you, a man with his mind made up. Just as bluntly as you say to me "I will not be yours", I tell you soberly what I think. I'm putting my cards on the table, as the saying is. Yes, you'll be mine, when the right moment comes. Oh! even if you were fifty, you should still be my mistress. And you shall, for I don't expect any difficulty with your husband. ....'

Madame Hulot cast a look of such frozen horror at this calculating businessman that he thought she had gone out of her mind, and stopped.

'You asked for it; you covered me with your contempt; you defied me, and now I have told you!' he said, feeling some need to justify the brutality of his last words.

'Oh! my daughter, my daughter!' cried the Baroness despairingly.

'Ah! there's nothing more I can say!' Crevel went on. 'The day Josépha was taken from me I was like a tigress robbed of her whelps. ... In fact, I was in just the same state as I see you in now. Your daughter! For me, she is the means of getting you. Yes, I wrecked your daughter's marriage!... and you will not marry her without my help! However beautiful Mademoiselle Hortense may be, she needs a dowry.'

'Alas! yes,' said the Baroness, wiping her eyes.

'Well, try asking the Baron for ten thousand francs,' returned Crevel, striking his attitude again.

He held it for a moment, like an actor pausing to underline a point.

'If he had the money, he would give it to the girl who will take Josépha's place!' he said, speaking with increasing urgency and vehemence. 'On the road he has taken, does a man stop? He's too fond of women, to begin with! ('There's a way of moderation in everything, a *juste milieu*, as our King has said). And then vanity has a hand in it! He's a handsome man! He'll see you all reduced to beggary for the sake of his pleasure. Indeed you're on the high road to ruin already. Look, since I first set foot in your house, you haven't once been able to do up your drawing-room. The words HARD UP shriek from every split in these covers. Show me the son-in-law who will not back out in a fright at sight of such ill-concealed evidence of the cruellest kind of poverty there is, the poverty of families that hold their heads high! I have been a shopkeeper and I know. There's no eye so keen as a Paris shopkeeper's for telling real wealth from wealth that's only a sham. ... You haven't got a penny,' he said, lowering his voice. 'It shows in everything, down to your servant's coat. Would you like me to let you into shocking secrets that have been kept from you?'

'Monsieur,' said Madame Hulot, who was holding a soaking handkerchief to streaming eyes. 'That's enough! No more!'

'Well, my son-in-law gives money to his father. That's what I wanted to tell you at the beginning, when I was talking about how your son lives. But I'm watching over my daughter's interests. Don't you worry.'

'Oh! if I could only marry my daughter and die!' cried the unhappy woman, her self-control breaking.

'Well, here's the way to do it!'

Madame Hulot looked at Crevel in sudden hope, with such an instant change of expression that it should have been enough in itself to touch the man, and make him abandon his ridiculous ambition.

'You will be beautiful for ten years yet,' went on Crevel, his arms folded, his gaze on infinity. 'Be kind to me, and Mademoiselle Hortense's marriage is arranged. Hulot has given me the right, as I told you, to propose the bargain quite bluntly, and he won't be angry. In the last three years I have been able to make some profitable investments, because my adventures have been restricted. I have three hundred thousand francs to spend, over and above my capital, and the money's yours –'

'Go, Monsieur,' said Madame Hulot; 'go, and never let me see you again. I had to find out what lay behind your base behaviour in the matter of the marriage planned for Hortense. Yes, base,' she repeated, as Crevel made a gesture. 'How could you let such private grudges and rancours affect a poor girl, an innocent and lovely creature? If it had not been for the need to know that gave my mother's heart no peace, you would never have spoken to me again, you would never again have crossed my threshold. Thirty-two years of honourable life, of a wife's loyalty, are not to be razed by the assaults of Monsieur Crevel!'

'Retired perfumer, successor to César Birotteau at the Queen of Roses, rue Saint-Honoré,' said Crevel ironically. 'Former Deputy Mayor, Captain of the National Guard, Chevalier of the Legion of Honour, exactly like my predecessor.'

'Monsieur,' the Baroness continued, 'Monsieur Hulot, after twenty years of fidelity, may have grown tired of his wife – that concerns me, and only me; but you see, Monsieur, that he has preserved some reticence regarding his infidelity, for I did not know that he had succeeded you in Mademoiselle Josépha's heart.'

'Oh! at a price, Madame! That song-bird has cost him more than a hundred thousand francs in the last two years. Ah! you haven't reached the end of trouble yet.'

'We need not prolong this discussion further, Monsieur Crevel. I do not intend to give up, for your sake, the happiness that a mother feels when she is able to embrace her children with a heart uncankered by remorse, and knows that she is respected and loved by her children. I mean to give my soul back to God unstained.'

'*Amen!*' said Crevel, his face distorted by the diabolical bitterness of aspirants of his kind who have failed after a renewed attempt to gain their ends. 'You don't know what extreme poverty is like – the shame, the disgrace. ... I have tried to open your eyes. I wanted to save you, you and your daughter too! So be it! You shall spell out a modern parable of the prodigal father from the first letter to the last. Your tears and your pride affect my feelings, for to see a woman one loves cry is dreadful!' Crevel went on, sitting down. 'All I can promise you, dear Adeline, is to do nothing to injure you, or your husband; but never send anyone to me to make inquiries. That's all!'

'Oh, what shall I do?' cried Madame Hulot.

Until this moment the Baroness had held out bravely under the three-fold torture that the interview's plain speaking inflicted upon her heart, for she was suffering as a woman, a mother, and a wife. As a matter of fact, so long as her son's father-in-law had shown himself overbearing and aggressive, she had found strength in the very opposition of her resistance to the shopkeeper's brutality; but the good nature he evinced in the midst of his exasperation as a rebuffed lover and a handsome Captain of the National Guard turned down released the tension of nerves that had been strained to breaking point. She wrung her hands, dissolved into tears, and was in such a state of dazed exhaustion that she let Crevel, on his knees again, kiss her hands.

'Oh God! where am I to turn?' she went on, wiping her eyes. 'Can a mother see her daughter pine before her eyes and look on calmly? What is to become of this being so splendidly endowed, by her own fine character and by its nurture, too, in her pure sheltered upbringing at her mother's side? There are days when she wanders sadly in the garden, not knowing why. I find her with tears in her eyes.'

'She is twenty-one,' said Crevel.

'Ought I to send her to a convent?' said the Baroness. 'At such times of crisis religion is often powerless against nature, and the most piously brought up girls lose their heads! But do get up, Monsieur. Do you not see that everything is finished between us now, that you are hateful to me, that you have struck down a mother's last hope?'

'And suppose I were to raise it again?' he said.

Madame Hulot stared at Crevel with a frenzied look that touched him; but he crushed the pity in his heart, because of those words 'you are hateful to me'. Virtue is always a little too much of a piece. It has no knowledge of the shades between black and white, or of the compromises possible between different human temperaments, by means of which a way may be manoeuvred out of a false position.

'A girl as beautiful as Mademoiselle Hortense is not married off in these days without a dowry,' Crevel observed, assuming his stiff attitude again. 'Your daughter's beauty is of the kind that scares husbands off; she's like a thoroughbred horse, which needs too much care and money spent on it to attract many purchasers. Just try walking along with a woman like that on your arm! Everybody will stare at you, and follow you, and covet your wife. That sort of success makes lots of men uncomfortable because they don't want to have to kill lovers; for, after all, one never kills more than one. In the position you're in, you can choose one of only three ways to marry your daughter: with my help – but you won't have it – that's one; by finding an old man of sixty: very rich, childless, and wanting children – difficult, but they do exist. There are so many old men who take Joséphas or Jenny Cadines that surely you might come across one ready to make that sort of fool of himself with the blessing of the law – if I did not have my Célestine, and our two grandchildren, I would marry Hortense myself. That's two! The third way is the easiest...'

Madame Hulot raised her head, and gazed anxiously at the retired perfumer.

'Paris is a meeting-place, swarming with talent, for all the forceful vigorous young men who spring up like wild seedlings in French soil. They haven't a roof over their heads, but they're equal to anything, and set on making their fortune. Your humble servant was just such a young man in his time, and I have known some others! Twenty years ago du Tillet had nothing, and Popinot not much more. They were plodding along, both of them, in old Birotteau's shop, with their minds made up to get on; and, as I see it, that determination was worth more to them than gold. You can run through money, but you don't reach the bottom of the stuff you're made of! All I had was determination to get on, and spunk. . . . And now you see du Tillet rubbing shoulders with all the nobs. Little Popinot became the richest druggist in the rue des Lombards, rose to be a Deputy, and there he is, in office, a Minister! Well, one of these *condottieri*, as they call them – freebooters of finance, the pen, or the artist's brush –

is the only hope you have in Paris of marrying a beautiful girl without a sou, because they are game enough for anything. Monsieur Popinot married Mademoiselle Birotteau when she hadn't a penny. Young men of that kind are mad: they believe in love, just as they believe in their luck and their own wits! Look for a man of enterprise and vigour to fall in love with your daughter, and he will marry her without worrying about cash. You must admit that I'm pretty generous, for an enemy, giving you advice against my own interest!'

'Ah, Monsieur Crevel, if only you would be my friend and give up your absurd ideas!'

'Absurd? Madame, don't rush on your own destruction. Consider your position ... I love you, and you'll be mine! I want to say, one day, to Hulot: "You took Josépha from me. Now I have your wife!" It's the old law of an eye for an eye, and I'll stick to my plan – unless, of course, you should become much too ugly. I'll get my way, and I'll tell you why.' He struck his attitude, staring at Madame Hulot.

'You will never find an old man or a young lover either,' he resumed, after a pause, 'because you love your daughter too much to expose her to the little games of an old rake, and because you, Baroness Hulot, sister-in-law of the old Lieutenant-General who commanded the veteran grenadiers of the Old Guard, will never resign yourself to looking for the young man of force and energy where he is to be found; because he might be an ordinary working man, like many a millionaire nowadays who was an ordinary mechanic ten years ago, or a simple works overseer, or an ordinary foreman in a factory. And then, watching your daughter, twenty years old, driven by the urges of youth, capable of disgracing you, you will say to yourself: "Better that I should dishonour myself than that she should; and if Monsieur Crevel is willing to keep my secret, I'll go and earn my daughter's dowry – two hundred thousand francs for ten years' attachment to that old shopkeeper who knows how to get on ... old Crevel!" I am vexing you, and what I say is shockingly immoral, isn't it? But if you had been seized by an irresistible passion, you would be arguing with yourself, trying to think up reasons for yielding to me, such as women always do find when they're in love. Well, Hortense's plight will suggest these reasons to your heart, ways of settling things with your conscience!'

'Hortense still has her uncle.'

'Who? Old Fischer? ... He's winding up his business, and that's the Baron's fault too – he uses his rake on all the cash-boxes within reach.'

'Count Hulot ...'

'Oh, your husband, Madame, has already squandered the old Lieutenant-General's savings; he furnished his opera-singer's house with them. Come now, are you going to let me go without some reason for hoping?'

'Good-bye, Monsieur. A passion for a woman of my age is soon cured, and you will come to see things in a Christian light. God protects the unfortunate.'

The Baroness rose, in order to oblige the Captain to retreat, and drove him before her into the drawing-room.

'Should the beautiful Madame Hulot have to live among worn-out trash like this?' he said. And he pointed to an old lamp, the flaking gilt of a chandelier, the threadbare carpet: the tatters of opulence that made the great white, red, and gold room seem like the corpse of Empire gaiety.

'Virtue, Monsieur, casts its own radiance over everything here. I have no desire to buy magnificent furnishings by using the beauty you attribute to me as "bird-lime, a trap to catch five-franc pieces"!'

The Captain bit his lip as he recognized the expressions that he had used to stigmatize Josépha's greed.

'And all this unswerving fidelity is for whose sake?' he said.

By this time the Baroness had conducted the retired per-fumer as far as the door.

'For a libertine's!' he wound up, pursing his lips smugly, like a virtuous man and a millionaire.

'If you were right, Monsieur, there would be some merit in my constancy, that's all.'

She left the Captain, after bowing to him as one bows to some importunate bore to get rid of him, and turned away too quickly to see him for the last time striking his pose. She went to reopen the doors that she had closed, and did not observe the menacing gesture with which Crevel took his leave. She walked proudly, her head held high, as martyrs walked in the Colosseum. All the same, she had exhausted her strength, and she let herself sink on the divan in her blue boudoir as if she were on the point of fainting, and lay there with her eyes fixed on the little ruined summer-house where her daughter was chattering to Cousin Bette.

From the first days of her marriage until that moment, the Baroness had loved her husband, as Josephine had come in the end to love Napoleon: with an admiring love, a maternal love, with abject devotion. If she had not known the details which Crevel had just given her, she knew very well that for the past twenty years Baron Hulot had been habitually unfaithful to her; but she had sealed her eyes with lead; she had wept in secret, and no word of reproach had ever escaped her lips. To reward her for this angelic kindness, she had gained her husband's veneration, and was worshipped by him as a kind of divinity.

A woman's regard for her husband, the respect with which she hedges him about, are contagious in the family. Hortense thought of her father as a perfect husband, a model, quite without fault. As for her brother, he had been brought up in an atmosphere of admiration of the Baron, in whom everyone saw one of the giants who had stood by Napoleon's side, and he knew that he owed his own position to his father's name and standing, the regard in which his father was held. Besides, the impressions of childhood hold their influence long, and he still feared his father. Even if he had suspected the irregularities disclosed by Crevel, he would have been too respectful to protest, and also he would have found excuses, looking at such lapses from a man's point of view.

But now, the extraordinary devotion of this beautiful and magnanimous woman demands some explanation; and, briefly, here is Madame Hulot's story.

From a village on the extreme frontiers of Lorraine, at the foot of the Vosges, three brothers named Fischer, simple peasants, came to join what was called the Army of the Rhine, as a result of the Republican call-up.

In 1799, the second of the brothers, André, a widower and Madame Hulot's father, left his daughter in the care of his elder brother Pierre Fischer, who had been wounded in 1797 and invalided out of the Army, and had then undertaken some small-scale contracting work for Military Transport, business which he owed to the favour of the Commissary general, Hulot d'Ervy. By a natural enough chance, Hulot, on his way to Strasbourg, met the Fischer family. Adeline's father and his younger brother were at that time employed as contractors for the supply of forage in Alsace.

Adeline, then aged sixteen, was comparable in her loveliness to the famous Madame du Barry, like her a daughter of Lorraine. She belonged to the company of perfect, dazzling beauties, of women like Madame Tallien, whom Nature fashions with peculiar care, bestowing on them her most precious gifts: distinction, dignity, grace, refinement, elegance; an incomparable complexion, its colour compounded in the mysterious workshops of chance. All such beautiful women resemble one another. Bianca Capello, whose portrait is one of Bronzino's masterpieces, Jean Goujon's *Venus*, whose original was the famous Diane de Poitiers, that Signora Olympia whose portrait is in the Doria gallery, and Ninon, Madame du Barry, Madame Tallien, Mademoiselle Georges, Madame Récamier, were all women who remained lovely in spite of the years, their passions, and their lives of excess. There are similarities in their build and proportions, and in the character of their beauty, striking enough to persuade one that there must exist an Aphrodisian current in the ocean of generation, from which spring all these Venuses, daughters of the same salt wave.

Adeline Fischer, one of the most beautiful of this divine race, possessed the noble features, the curving lines, the veined flesh, of women born to be queens. The blonde hair that our mother Eve had from God's own hand, an empress's stature, a stately bearing, an imposing profile, the modesty of a country upbringing – these made men come to a halt as she passed, enchanted, like amateurs of art before a Raphael. And so, seeing her, the Commissary general made Mademoiselle Adeline Fischer his wife forthwith, to the great surprise of the Fischers, who had all been brought up to look up to their betters.

The eldest, the soldier of 1792, who had been seriously wounded in the attack on Wissembourg, worshipped the Emperor Napoleon and everything that pertained to the Grand Army. André and Johann spoke with respect of Commissary general Hulot, a protégé of the Emperor's, and the man, besides, to whom they owed their prosperity; for Hulot d'Ervy, finding them men of intelligence and integrity, had taken them from army forage wagons and put them in charge of important special supplies. The Fischer brothers had done good service in the campaign of 1804. Hulot, after the peace, had obtained for them their contract to supply forage in Alsace, not knowing that he himself would be sent later to Strasbourg, to make preparations there for the campaign of 1806.

For the young peasant girl, this marriage was something like an Assumption. The lovely Adeline passed without transition from her village mud to the paradise of the Imperial Court; for it was at that time that the Commissary general, one of the most trustworthy and most active and indefatigable members of his corps, was made Baron, given a place near the Emperor, and attached to the Imperial Guard. The beautiful village maid had the spirit to educate herself, out of love for her husband, with whom she was quite madly in love. It is easy to understand why, for the Commissary general was a masculine counterpart of Adeline, as outstanding among men as she was among women, one of the elect company of handsome men. Tall, well-built, fair, with blue eyes of a gaiety, fire, and charm that were irresistible, with an elegant and graceful figure, he was remarkable even among the d'Orsays, the Forbins, the Ouvrards, and the whole array of the Empire beaux. He was a man accustomed to making conquests and imbued with the ideas of Directory times regarding women, yet his gay career was at that period interrupted for a considerable time by his attachment to his wife.

For Adeline, the Baron was therefore from the beginning a kind of god who could do no wrong. She owed everything to him: fortune – she had a carriage, a fine house, all the luxury of the period; happiness, for she was openly loved; a title – she was a Baroness; celebrity – she was known as the beautiful

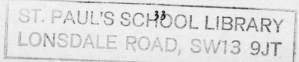
ST. PAUL'S SCHOOL LIBRARY
LONSDALE ROAD, SW13 9JT

33

Madame Hulot, and in Paris! To complete her success, she
had the honour of refusing the Emperor's addresses; and he
presented her with a diamond necklace and repeatedly singled
her out for marks of his interest, continuing to ask from time
to time: 'And is the lovely Madame Hulot still as virtuous as
ever?' in the tone of a man prepared to exact vengeance from
anyone who had triumphed where he had failed.

It does not require much penetration, then, to understand
the causes, affecting a simple, unsophisticated, and magnanimous soul – of the fanatical strain in Madame Hulot's
love. Having once fairly said to herself that in her eyes her
husband could do no wrong, she became, of her own volition,
in her inmost being, the humble, devoted, and blind servant
of the man who had made her what she was.

Note, moreover, that she was endowed with great good
sense, the good sense of the common people, which gave her
education solidity. In society, she was accustomed to talk
little, spoke ill of no one, made no effort to shine. She reflected
upon everything, listened, and modelled herself upon the
women most respected for their integrity and good breeding.

In 1815 Hulot followed the example of Prince de Wissembourg, one of his intimate friends, and became one of the
organizers of that improvized army whose defeat brought the
Napoleonic era to an end, at Waterloo. In 1816 the Baron
was one of the most hated men of the Feltre Ministry,
and was reappointed to the Commissariat only in 1823, when
he was needed on account of the war in Spain. In 1830 he reappeared in the administration as Deputy Minister, at the
time when Louis-Philippe was levying a kind of conscription
among the old Napoleonic adherents. Since the advent to the
throne of the younger branch, which he had actively supported, he had remained in the administration, an indispensable
Director at the War Office. He had already been given his
Marshal's baton, and there was nothing more the King could
do for him, short of making him a Minister, or a Peer of
France.

With no occupation in the years between 1818 and 1823, the
Baron had gone on active service – in a campaign against
women. Madame Hulot dated her Hector's first infidelities

from the final dissolution of the Empire. The Baroness, then, had held for a dozen years of her married life the position of *prima donna assoluta*, unchallenged. She still continued to enjoy the inveterate old affection that husbands bear to wives who have resigned themselves to playing the part of good and kind companions. She knew that no rival would stand for two hours against one word of reproach from her, but she shut her eyes, she stopped her ears, her wish was to know nothing of her husband's conduct outside his home. In the end, she came to treat her Hector as a mother treats a spoiled child. Three years before the conversation with Crevel that has been described, Hortense had recognized her father at the Variétés, in a first tier stage box, in Jenny Cadine's company, and exclaimed:

'There's Papa!'

'You are mistaken, my dear; he is with the Marshal,' the Baroness replied.

The Baroness had certainly seen Jenny Cadine; but instead of being sick at heart when she saw that she was so pretty, she had said to herself: 'That rascal Hector is very lucky.' She suffered nevertheless; she gave way secretly to storms of violent feeling; but as soon as she saw her Hector again, she saw again her twelve years of pure happiness, and was quite incapable of uttering a single word of complaint. She would very much have liked the Baron to confide in her; but she had never dared to let him know that she knew of his escapades, out of respect for him. Such excessive delicacy is found only in girls of noble character sprung from the people, who know how to take blows without returning them. In their veins flows the blood of the early martyrs. Well-born girls, as their husbands' equals, feel a need to bait their husbands, to score off them as in a game of billiards, to make up for their acts of tolerance by biting remarks, in a spirit of revengeful spite and in order to assure themselves either of their own superiority or of their right to have their revenge.

The Baroness had an ardent admirer in her brother-in-law, Lieutenant-General Hulot, the venerable Colonel of the Infantry Grenadiers of the Imperial Guard, who was to be given a Marshal's baton in his later years. This veteran, after commanding from 1830 to 1834 the military region that included the Breton Departments of France (the theatre of his exploits in 1799 and 1800), had come to live in Paris, near his brother, for whom he still felt a fatherly affection. This old soldier's heart was instinctively drawn to his sister-in-law. He admired her as the noblest, the saintliest creature of her sex. He had not married because he had hoped to meet a second Adeline, and had vainly searched for her in twenty provinces during a score of campaigns. Rather than suffer any diminution of the esteem in which she was held by the pure-souled unimpeachable old Republican, of whom Napoleon said: 'That fine fellow Hulot is the most obstinate of Republicans, but he will never betray me', Adeline would have endured far worse pain than that she had just experienced. But this old man, aged seventy-two, broken by thirty campaigns, wounded for the twenty-seventh time at Waterloo, gave Adeline admiration, not protection. The poor Count, among other infirmities, could hear only with the aid of an ear-trumpet.

So long as Baron Hulot d'Ervy was a handsome man, his light loves made no inroads on his fortune; but at fifty it was necessary to propitiate the Graces. At that age, love suffers an old man's change into vice: inordinate vanities become involved in it. At about that time Adeline watched her husband grow unbelievably finicking about his toilet, dyeing his hair and side whiskers, wearing belts and corsets. He was determined to remain handsome at all costs; and this concern for his personal appearance, a weakness which he had once found contemptible, he carried into the minutest details. Finally, Adeline began to realize that a river of gold was being poured out for the Baron's mistresses, whose source was her own home. In eight years a considerable fortune had been dissipated, and so completely that two years previously, at the time when Hulot's son was setting up his separate establishment, the Baron had been forced to admit to his wife that his salary constituted their entire resources.

'Where will this lead us?' had been Adeline's comment.

'Don't worry,' the Councillor of State had replied. 'I shall turn over my salary to you and provide for a settlement for Hortense and our future, by doing some business.'

His wife's profound faith in the ability and outstanding qualities, in the talents and character of her husband, had allayed her momentary misgivings.

And so it is not hard to imagine what the Baroness's thoughts were, and her tears, after Crevel's departure. The poor woman had for the past two years known herself to be living at the bottom of a pit, but she had thought that she was there alone. She had had no knowledge of how her son's marriage had been arranged; she did not know of Hector's liaison with the grasping Josépha; she had hoped that no one in the world knew of her sorrows. Now, if Crevel was talking so freely of the Baron's dissipations, Hector was going to suffer loss of respect and reputation. She had caught a glimpse, through the injured ex-perfumer's vulgarly expansive talk, of the hateful convivialities which had led to the young lawyer's marriage. Two loose young women had been the priestesses of that hymen, first proposed during some drunken revel, in an atmosphere of humiliating intimacy and the degrading familiarities of two tipsy old men!

'He has quite forgotten Hortense!' she said to herself. 'And yet he sees her every day. Will he find a husband for her among his good-for-nothing cronies?'

She was speaking only as a mother at that moment, and the wife's voice was silenced, for she could see Hortense, with her Cousin Bette, laughing the unrestrained laughter of reckless youth, and she knew that such nervous outbursts of mirth were a symptom as much to be feared as the tearful reveries of her solitary rambles in the garden.

Hortense was like her mother in appearance, but her naturally wavy and astonishingly thick hair was red gold. Her dazzling skin had the quality of pearl. It was easy to see that she was the child of a true marriage, of pure and noble love in its perfect prime. There was an ardent eagerness in her face, a gaiety in her gestures, a youthful surge of vitality, a fresh bloom of life, a vigorous good health, that seemed to vibrate in the air about her and emanate from her in electric waves. All heads turned to watch Hortense. When her sea-blue eyes with their clear limpidity of innocence rested on some passer-by, he involuntarily thrilled. Moreover, her complexion was not marred by freckles, which are the price that golden-fair girls often pay for the milky whiteness of their skins. Tall, rounded without being plump, of a graceful physique as noble as her mother's, she merited the title of 'goddess' that the old authors bestow so freely. No one meeting her in the street could help exclaiming: 'Heavens! what a lovely girl!' She was so utterly innocent that she used to say when they came home: 'How can they speak of a "lovely girl", Mama, when you are with me? You are surely so much lovelier than I! . . .'

And, indeed, at past forty-seven, the Baroness might have been preferred to her daughter by those who admire the setting sun; for she had lost nothing yet of what women call their 'good points', by a rare chance – especially rare in Paris, where, in the seventeenth century, Ninon was notorious for a similarly long-lived beauty, stealing the limelight at a time of life when women are plain.

From her daughter, the Baroness's thoughts passed to Hortense's father. She imagined him declining day by day by slow degrees, to end among the dregs of society, dismissed some day, perhaps, from the Ministry. This dream of her idol's downfall, accompanied by a dim prevision of the misfortunes that Crevel had prophesied, was so excruciating that the poor woman lost consciousness and lay in a kind of trance.

Cousin Bette, as Hortense was talking, looked up from time to time to see whether they might return to the drawing-room; but her young cousin was pressing her so closely with teasing questions just when the Baroness reopened the french window, that she did not notice her.

Lisbeth Fischer, five years younger than Madame Hulot although she was the daughter of the eldest of the Fischer brothers, was far from being as beautiful as her cousin; and for that reason she had been desperately jealous of Adeline. Jealousy lay at the root of her character, which was full of eccentricities – a word that the English have coined to describe freakish behaviour in members of distinguished families, not ordinarily used of the socially unimportant. A peasant girl from the Vosges, with everything that that implies: thin, dark, with glossy black hair, heavy eyebrows meeting across the nose in a tuft, long and powerful arms, and broad solid feet, with some warts on her long, simian face: there is a quick sketch of the spinster.

The family, who lived as one household, had sacrificed the plebeian daughter to the pretty one, the astringent fruit to the brilliant flower. Lisbeth worked in the fields while her cousin was cosseted; and so it had happened one day that Lisbeth, finding Adeline alone, had done her best to pull Adeline's nose off, a true Grecian nose, much admired by all the old women. Although she was beaten for this misdeed, that did not prevent her from continuing to tear her favoured cousin's dresses and crumple her collars.

When her cousin's amazing marriage took place, Lisbeth had bowed before her elevation by destiny, as Napoleon's brothers and sisters bowed before the glory of the throne and the authority of power. Adeline, who was good and kind to an exceptional degree, in Paris remembered Lisbeth and brought her there about 1809, intending to rescue her from poverty and find her a husband. The Baron found it impossible to marry off this girl with the black eyes and sooty eyebrows, who could neither read nor write, as quickly as Adeline would have liked. So, as a first step, he gave her a trade: he apprenticed Lisbeth to the Court embroiderers, the well-known Pons Brothers.

This cousin, called Bette for short, had the vigorous energy of all mountain-bred people, and, when she became a worker in gold and silver braid embroidery, applied her capacity for hard work to learning to read, write, and reckon; for her cousin, the Baron, had impressed upon her the necessity of possessing these techniques if she was to run an embroidering business of her own. She was determined to make her way, and within two years she had achieved a metamorphosis. By 1811, the peasant girl had become a passably pleasant-mannered, sufficiently skilled and dexterous forewoman.

Her line of business, *passementerie* – gold and silver lace-work – included the making of epaulettes, sword-knots, aiguillettes, and in fact all the vast variety of brilliant decoration that formerly glittered on the handsome uniforms of the French army, and on civilian dress clothes. The Emperor, with a true Italian fondness of finery, had embroidered gold and silver lace on every uniform in his service, and his empire comprised one hundred and thirty-three Departments. The supplying of these braid trimmings, in the ordinary way to substantial, solidly-established tailoring firms, but sometimes directly to important officials, was good business, a sound trade.

Just when Cousin Bette, the best workwoman in the Pons establishment where she was in charge of the workroom, might have set up in business for herself, the Empire fell to its ruin. The olive branch of peace borne in the hands of the Bourbons alarmed Lisbeth; she was apprehensive of a slump in this trade, which would in future have only eighty-six Departments to exploit instead of a hundred and thirty-three, to say nothing of its loss of clients through the enormous reduction of the Army. Taking fright at the uncertain prospects of the industry, she refused the offers made her by the Baron, who thought her mad. She justified this opinion by quarrelling with Monsieur Rivet, the purchaser of the Pons Brothers' business, with whom the Baron had proposed to set her up in partnership, and she went back to being just an ordinary workwoman.

Meanwhile the Fischer family had relapsed into the precarious situation from which Baron Hulot had rescued it.

Ruined by the disaster of Fontainebleau, the three Fischer brothers had fought with the Volunteer Corps of 1815 with the recklessness of despair. The eldest, Lisbeth's father, was killed. Adeline's father, sentenced to death by a court-martial, fled to Germany and died at Trèves in 1820. The youngest, Johann, came to Paris to entreat the help of the queen of the family, who was said to eat off gold and silver, and who never appeared on public occasions without diamonds in her hair and round her neck, diamonds that were as big as hazelnuts and had been given to her by the Emperor. Johann Fischer, at that time aged forty-three, received a sum of ten thousand francs from Baron Hulot in order to start a small business supplying forage at Versailles, the contract for which was obtained from the Ministry of War by the private influence of friends whom the former Commissary general still had there.

These family misfortunes, Baron Hulot's fall from favour, the knowledge borne in upon her that she counted for little in the immense turmoil of contending people, ambitions, and enterprises that makes Paris both a heaven and an inferno, intimidated Bette. The young woman at that time gave up all idea of competing with or rivalling her cousin, whose many and various points of superiority she had realized; but envy remained hidden in her heart, like a plague germ which may come to life and devastate a city if the fatal bale of wool in which it lies hidden is ever opened. From time to time, indeed, she would say to herself: 'Adeline and I are of the same blood; our fathers were brothers. Yet she lives in a mansion, and I in a garret.' However, year in year out, Lisbeth received presents from the Baroness and the Baron, on her birthday and on New Year's Day. The Baron, who was exceedingly kind to her, paid for her winter firewood. Old General Hulot entertained her to dinner one day a week. Her place was always laid at her cousin's table. They laughed at her, certainly, but they never blushed to acknowledge her. They had in fact enabled her to live independently in Paris, where she led the life that suited her.

Lisbeth was, indeed, very apprehensive of possible restriction of her liberty. Should her cousin invite her to live under her roof... Bette at once caught sight of the halter of domestic servitude. Several times the Baron had found a solution to the difficult problem of arranging a marriage for her; but on each occasion, although the prospect attracted her at first, she soon refused to entertain it, afraid that she might see her lack of education, ignorance, and want of fortune, cast in her face. Then, when the Baroness suggested that she should live with their uncle and look after his household in place of his house-keeper, who must be expensive, she replied that she would make a match in that position even less easily.

Cousin Bette had that kind of oddity in her cast of mind that one notices in people who have developed late, and among savages, who think much but say little. Her native peasant intelligence had, however, acquired through her workshop conversations, in her constant contacts with the men and women of her trade, a Parisian keenness of edge. This young

41

woman, who had a temperament notably resembling the Corsican temperament, in whom the active instincts of a strong nature were frustrated, would have found a happy outlet in protecting some less robust-natured man. In her years of living in the capital, the capital had changed her superficially, yet the Parisian veneer left her spirit of strongly-tempered metal to rust. Endowed with an insight that had become profoundly penetrating, as are all men and women who live genuinely celibate lives, with the original twist which she gave to all her ideas, she would have appeared formidable in any other situation. With ill will, she could have sown discord in the most united family.

In the early days, when she had still cherished some hopes, the secret of which she had confided to no one, she had brought herself to wear stays, to follow the fashion, and had then achieved a brief season of splendour during which the Baron considered her marriageable. Lisbeth was at that time the piquante nut-brown maid of old French romance. Her piercing eye, her olive skin, her reed-like slenderness, might have brought her an admirer in the shape of a major on half-pay, but she was content – so she said, laughing – with her own admiration. She came indeed to find her life a sufficiently pleasant one, once she had eliminated the need to concern herself about material comfort, for she went out to dinner every evening at houses in town, after a day of work that began at sunrise. With dinner provided, she had only her lunches and her rent to pay for. In addition she was given most of her clothes, and many acceptable provisions for her household supplies such as sugar, coffee, wine, etc.

By 1837, after twenty-seven years of an existence largely paid for by the Hulot family and her Uncle Fischer, Cousin Bette had resigned herself to being a nobody and allowed herself to be treated with scant ceremony. She refused, of her own accord, to go to large dinner-parties because she preferred the intimacy of family gatherings in which she had her own importance; and so she avoided wounds to her pride. Wherever she went she seemed to be at home: in the houses of General Hulot, Crevel, the younger Hulots, Rivet – the successor to the Pons brothers, with whom she had made up her differences and who welcomed and made much of her – and with the Baroness. She knew how to ingratiate herself with the servants in these houses, too, giving them small tips from time to time and never forgetting to spend a few minutes chatting with them before going into the drawing-room. The absence of patronage with which she put herself frankly on their level earned her the servants' good will, which it is absolutely essential for parasites to have. 'She's an excellent woman, and a really good sort too!' – that was what everyone said about her. Her willingness to oblige, unlimited when not taken for granted, like her air of friendly good nature, was of course a necessary consequence of her position. She had come at last to understand what life was like in her world, having seen herself at everyone's mercy. In the wish to be generally agreeable, she laughed in sympathy with the young people, who liked her because of that kind of adulation in her manner that always beguiles the young. She guessed and made herself the champion of the things that lay near their hearts; she was their go-between. She struck them as being the best possible person to confide in, since she had not the right to shake her head at them. Her absolute discretion earned her the trust of older people too, for, like Ninon, she had some masculine qualities. As a general rule, confidences are made to persons below one socially rather than to those above. Much more readily than we can employ our superiors in secret affairs, we make use of our inferiors, who consequently become committed sharers in our most hidden thoughts; they are present at our deliberations. Now, Richelieu considered that he had achieved success when he had the right to take part in privy councils. Everyone believed this poor spinster to be so dependent that she had no alternative but to keep her mouth shut. Cousin Bette herself called herself the family confessional. Only the Baroness, with the memory of the harsh usage that she had received in childhood from this cousin, then stronger – though younger – than she, still felt some mistrust. In any case, in shame, she would not have confided her domestic sorrows to anyone but God.

Here, perhaps, it should be remarked that the Baroness's house preserved all its former splendour in the eyes of

Cousin Bette, who was not impressed, as the newly rich ex-perfumer had been, by the signs of distress written on the worn chairs, the discoloured hangings, and the split silk. The furniture with which we live is in the same case as ourselves. Seeing ourselves every day, we come, like the Baron, to think ourselves little changed, still young, while other people see on our heads hair turning to chinchilla, V-shaped furrows on our foreheads, and great pumpkins in our bellies. These rooms were still lit for Cousin Bette by the Bengal lights of Imperial victories and shone with perennial splendour.

With the years, Cousin Bette had developed some very odd old-maidish quirks. For example, instead of following the fashion, she tried to make fashion fit her peculiarities and conform to what she liked, which was always a long way behind the mode. If the Baroness gave her a pretty new hat, or a dress cut in the style of the moment, Cousin Bette at once took it home and remodelled it according to her own ideas, completely spoiling it in the process of producing a garment or headgear reminiscent of Empire styles and the clothes she used to wear long ago in Lorraine. Her thirty-franc hat after that treatment was just a shapeless head-covering, and her dress like something out of the rag-bag. Bette was, in such matters, as obstinate as a mule; she was determined to please herself and consult no one else, and she thought herself charming in her own mode. Certainly the assimilation of the style of the day to her own style was harmonious, giving her from head to foot the appearance of an old maid; but it made her such a figure of fun that, with the best will in the world, no one could invite her on smart occasions.

The stubborn, crotchety, independent spirit, the inexplicable inability to conform, of this young woman for whom the Baron had on four different occasions found a possible hus-band (a clerk in his department, a regimental adjutant, an army contractor, a retired army captain), and who had also refused an embroiderer who had become a rich man since then, had earned for her the nickname 'Nanny', which the Baron joking-ly gave her.

But that nickname applied only to the superficial oddities, to those variations from the norm which, in one another's eyes, we all exhibit within society's conventions. This woman, more closely observed, would have revealed the fiercely ungovernable side of the peasant character. She was still the child who had tried to tear her cousin's nose off, and who, if she had not learned rational behaviour, would perhaps have killed her in a paroxysm of jealousy. She held in check, only by her knowledge of law and the world, the primitive impetuous directness with which country people, like savages, translate emotion into action.

In this directness, perhaps, lies the whole difference between primitive and civilized man. The savage has only emotions. The civilized man has emotions plus ideas. In the savage, the brain receives, one may conclude, few impressions, so that he is at the mercy of one all-pervading emotion; whereas thoughts, in the civilized man, act upon his feelings and alter them. He is alive to a host of interests and many emotions, while the savage entertains only one concept at a time. The momentary ascendancy that a child holds over his parents is due to a similar cause, but it ceases when his wish is satisfied, whereas in primitive people this cause operates constantly.

Cousin Bette, a primitive peasant from Lorraine and not without a strain of treachery, had a nature of this savage kind, a kind that is commoner among the masses than is generally supposed and that may explain their behaviour during revolutions.

At the time when the curtain rises on this drama, if Cousin Bette had chosen to allow herself to be well dressed, if she had learned to follow the fashion – like Parisian women – through every change of style, she would have been presentable and acceptable; but she remained as stiff as a stick. Now, without charm or grace a woman might as well not exist in Paris. Her black head of hair, her fine hard eyes, the rigid lines of her face, the Spanish darkness of her complexion – which made her look like a figure by Giotto, and which a true Parisian would have set off and used as assets – above all her strange clothes, gave Cousin Bette such a bizarre appearance that at times she reminded one of the monkeys dressed up as women that children, in Savoy, lead about on a string. As she was well known in the households connected by family ties among whom she moved, as she restricted her social movements to that circle and liked to keep herself to herself, her oddities no longer surprised anyone and, out-of-doors, were lost to view in the ceaseless maelstrom of life thronging Parisian streets, where it is only pretty women that attract attention.

Hortense's laughter at that moment was caused by a triumph over an obstinate refusal of Cousin Bette's. She had just caught her out in an admission which she had been trying for three years to wring from her. However secretive an old maid may be, there is one emotion that will always make her break silence, and that is vanity! For three years Hortense had been extremely inquisitive about a certain topic, and had bombarded her cousin with questions, which, indeed, revealed her completely innocent mind: she wanted to know why her cousin had not married. Hortense, who knew the story of the five rejected suitors, had built up her own little romance. She believed that Cousin Bette was cherishing a secret passion in her heart, and a half-serious game of attack and riposte had developed between them. Hortense would speak of 'marriageable young girls like us!' meaning herself and her cousin. Cousin Bette had on several occasions retorted provocatively: 'How do you know that I haven't a sweetheart?' So Cousin Bette's sweetheart, real or fictitious, was now a centre of interest and a subject for playful teasing. On Bette's last visit, after three years of this light-hearted warfare, Hortense had greeted her with the words:

'How is your sweetheart?'

'Only middling,' she had replied. 'He's not very well, poor young man.'

'Ah! He's delicate, is he?' the Baroness had asked, with a laugh.

'Yes, indeed. He is so fair. . . . A coal-black creature like me had to fall in love, of course, with a fair man, the colour of moonlight.'

'But who is he? What does he do?' said Hortense. 'Is he a prince?'

'A prince of tools, just as I'm a queen of spools. Can a poor

46

girl like me expect to be loved by a rich man with a house of his own, and money in government stocks, or a duke and peer, or some Prince Charming out of one of your fairy tales?'

'Oh, how I should like to see him!' Hortense had exclaimed, smiling.

'To find out what the man who can love an old nanny looks like?' asked Cousin Bette.

'He must be some monster of an old clerk with a goatee beard!' said Hortense, looking at her mother.

'Well, that's where you are mistaken, Mademoiselle!'

'Ah, then you really have a sweetheart?' exclaimed Hortense triumphantly.

'Just as really as you have not!' her cousin had retorted, apparently piqued.

'Well, if you have a sweetheart, Bette, why don't you marry him?' the Baroness had said, exchanging a look with her daughter. 'It's three years now since we first heard of him, and you have had plenty of time to find out what he is like. If he has remained faithful to you, you ought not to prolong a situation that he must find trying. It's a question of conscience. And then, even if he is young, it is time that you were thinking of providing a crutch for old age.'

Cousin Bette had stared at the Baroness, and, seeing that she was laughing, had replied:

'That would be hunger marrying thirst. He works for his living as I work for mine. If we had children they would have to work for theirs.... No, no, ours is a love of the soul. It costs less!'

'Why do you hide him?' Hortense asked.

'He's not presentable,' replied the old maid, laughing.

'Do you love him?' the Baroness asked.

'Certainly I do! I love him for himself alone, the angel. I have been carrying his image in my heart for four years now.'

'Well, if you love him for himself,' the Baroness had said gravely, 'if he really exists, you are treating him shockingly badly. You don't know what it means to love.'

'We all know that from birth!' said her cousin.

'No, some women love and yet remain egoists, which is what you are doing!'

Cousin Bette had bowed her head, and the look in her eyes would have made anyone who saw it shudder, but she kept her gaze fixed on her reel of silk.

'If you introduced your sweetheart to us, Hector might be able to find him a place, and help him to make his way in the world.'

'That is not possible,' Cousin Bette had said.

'Why not?'

'He's a sort of Pole, a refugee...'

'A conspirator?' exclaimed Hortense. 'How lucky you are! Has he had exciting adventures?'

'He fought for Poland. He was a teacher in the school whose students started the revolt, and as it was the Grand Duke Constantine who placed him there he can't hope to be pardoned.'

'Teacher of what?'

'Art!'

'And he came to Paris after the revolt had been suppressed?'

'In 1833. He had crossed Germany on foot. ...'

'Poor young man! And how old is he?'

'He was only just twenty-four at the time of the insurrection. He is twenty-nine now. ...'

'Fifteen years younger than you,' the Baroness had said then.

'How does he live?' asked Hortense.

'By his talent. ...'

'Ah! he gives lessons?'

'No,' Bette had answered, 'he takes them, and hard ones too!'

'And what's his Christian name? Has he a nice one?'

'Wenceslas!'

'What imaginations old maids have!' the Baroness had exclaimed. 'From the way you talk, anyone would believe that you were telling the truth, Lisbeth.'

'Don't you see, Mama? He's a Pole brought up on the knout, and Bette reminds him of that little amenity of his native land!'

They had all three burst out laughing, and Hortense had

sung: '*Wenceslas! O my heart's dearest love!*' instead of '*O Mathilde ...*', and for a few moments there had been something like an armistice.

'These little girls,' said Cousin Bette next time she came, looking at Hortense, 'imagine that no one but themselves can have sweethearts.'

'Now,' said Hortense, as soon as she and her cousin were alone, 'prove to me that Wenceslas isn't a fairytale, and I'll give you my yellow cashmere shawl.'

'But Wenceslas is a Count!'

'All Poles are Counts!'

'But he isn't a Pole, he's a Li ... va ... Lith ...'

'Lithuanian?'

'No ...'

'Livonian?'

'Yes. That's what he is!'

'But what's his name?'

'Tell me, are you sure you can keep a secret?'

'Oh, Cousin, I'll be dumb!'

'As a fish?'

'As a fish!'

'You swear by your eternal salvation?'

'By my eternal salvation!'

'No, by your happiness in this world?'

'Yes.'

'Well, he's Count Wenceslas Steinbock!'

'That's the name of one of Charles XII of Sweden's generals.'

'That was his great-uncle! His father settled in Livonia after the death of the King of Sweden; but he lost all his money in the 1812 campaign, and died, leaving the poor child, aged eight, penniless. The Grand Duke Constantine, for the sake of the name of Steinbock, took him under his protection and sent him to school.'

'I'll keep my word,' Hortense had said. 'Give me proof of his existence and my yellow shawl is yours! Ah, yellow is a brunette's colour – it does as much for her as cosmetics!'

'You will keep my secret?'

'I'll give you all mine.'

'Well, the next time I come, I shall have the proof.'

'But the proof is the sweetheart,' Hortense had said.

Cousin Bette's fancy had been greatly taken by the wraps that she had seen in Paris, and she had been fascinated by the prospect of possessing the yellow shawl, which the Baron had given to his wife in 1808, and which, in 1830, had passed from mother to daughter, in accordance with the custom in some families. The shawl had become somewhat the worse for wear in the past ten years' use, but the precious web, always kept in a sandal-wood box, seemed, like the Baroness's furniture, unalterably new to the old maid's eyes. So she had brought a present in her reticule that she intended to give the Baroness for her birthday, and that she considered convincing proof of the legendary lover's existence.

The present consisted of a silver seal composed of three figures wreathed in foliage, standing back to back and bearing the globe aloft. The three figures represented Faith, Hope, and Charity. Their feet rested on snarling snapping monsters, among which the symbolic serpent writhed. In 1846, after the tremendous impetus given to Benvenuto Cellini's art by the work of Mademoiselle de Faveau and such artists as Wagner, Jeanest, Froment-Meurice, and wood-carvers like Liénard, this fine piece of work would surprise no one, but at that time a girl with some interest in jewellery could hardly fail to be impressed as she examined the seal, which Cousin Bette handed to her with the words: 'Here, what do you think of this?'

The figures, with their flowing draperies, had the composition and rhythm of the style of Raphael. In execution they suggested the Florentine school of workers in bronze created by Donatello, Brunelleschi, Ghiberti, Benvenuto Cellini, John of Bologna, and their peers. The French Renaissance had produced no more fantastic whimsical monsters than those symbolizing the evil passions. The palms, ferns, rushes, reeds, springing up around the Virtues showed a virtuosity, and a style and taste, that expert craftsmen might despair of rivalling. A ribbon twined among the three heads, and where it appeared between them displayed a W, a chamois, and the word *fecit*.

'Who can have made this?' Hortense asked.

'My sweetheart, of course,' Cousin Bette replied. 'There are ten months of work in it. I earn more by making sword-knots. He told me that Steinbock means creature of the rocks or chamois, in German. He intends to sign everything he makes like this. . . . Ah! your shawl is mine!'

'Just tell me why.'

'Could I buy a thing like this? Or commission it? Impossible – so it must have been given to me. Who would give such a present? Why, only a sweetheart!'

Hortense, with a lack of candour that would have alarmed Lisbeth if she had perceived it, carefully refrained from expressing all her admiration, although she experienced the thrill that people sensitive to beauty feel when they see a master-piece: faultless, complete, and unexpected.

'Certainly,' she said, 'it's very pretty.'

'Yes, it's pretty,' answered the old maid; 'but I would rather have an orange shawl. Well, my dear, my sweetheart spends his time working at things like this. Since he came to Paris he has made three or four trinkets of the same sort, and that's the fruit of four years' study and work. He has been serving an apprenticeship with founders, moulders, jewellers. .|. . Bah! a mint of money has gone on it all. The young man tells me that in only a few months, now, he will be rich and famous.'

'So you do really see him?'

'Well, do you think I'm inventing all this? I was laughing, but I told you the truth.'

'And he loves you?' Hortense asked, with intense interest.

'He adores me!' her cousin replied solemnly. 'You see, my dear, he has only known insipid, die-away women; they're all like that in the north. A young, dark, slender girl, like me, soon warmed the cockles of his heart. But mum's the word! You promised!'

'He'll go the same way as the five others,' the girl said teasingly, still looking at the seal.

'Six, Mademoiselle! I left one in Lorraine who would have fetched the moon out of the sky for me, and still would to this day.'

'This one does even better. He brings you the sun.'

'How can I make money out of that?' Cousin Bette demanded. 'You need to own a lot of land for the sun to be of any use to you.'

Capping each other's pleasantries with nonsense that may be imagined, they had burst into the laughter that had caused the Baroness such poignant distress as she saw her daughter unrestrainedly enjoying the gaiety natural at her age and was forced to think what her future might be.

'But if he gives you jewels that have taken six months to make, it must be because he owes you a great deal?' said Hortense, her mind profoundly exercised by the seal.

'Ah, you want to know too much all at once!' Cousin Bette replied. 'But listen ... now I'm going to let you into a secret.'

'Shall I be with your sweetheart in it?'

'Ah! you would like to see him, wouldn't you? But, you know, when an old maid like your Bette has managed to keep a sweetheart for five years, she has him well tucked away. So you may leave us alone. I don't possess a cat or a canary, you see, or a dog or a parrot, and an old nanny like me needs some little thing to love and make a fuss over; well ... I give myself a Pole.'

'Has he got moustaches?'

'As long as that,' said Bette, holding up a large needle filled with gold thread. She always took her sewing out with her, and worked while waiting for dinner.

'If you keep interrupting me with questions,' she went on, 'you shall not be told anything. Here you are, only twenty-two, and you have much more to say than I have at forty-two, almost forty-three.'

'I'm all ears. I'm as dumb as a doorpost,' said Hortense.

'My sweetheart has made a bronze group ten inches high of Samson tearing a lion to pieces,' Cousin Bette continued; 'and he buried it in the ground and got it covered with verdigris, so that anyone would think that it's as old as Samson. It's for sale as a work of art in one of the antique shops in the place du Carrousel, near my house. If only your father, knowing Monsieur Popinot, the Minister of Commerce and Agriculture, and Count de Rastignac, as he does, would speak to them about this group as a fine antique that he had happened to notice in passing! It seems that the great have a taste for that kind of thing instead of keeping their minds on our sword-knots, and that my sweetheart's fortune would be made if they bought or even came to look at this worn-looking lump of metal. The poor boy declares that the thing would be taken for an antique, and fetch a handsome price. And then, if it was one of the Ministers who took the group, he would go and present himself, prove that he made it, and bays would crown his head! Oh, he thinks no small beer of himself, that young man! He's as full of pride as two new-made Counts!'

'He's Michelangelo over again,' said Hortense; 'and for a lover he has kept his wits. . . . How much does he want for it?'

'Fifteen hundred francs! The dealer can't take less, because he has to have his share.'

'Papa is King's Commissioner at present,' said Hortense. 'He sees the two Ministers every day in the Chamber and he'll arrange what you want, I'll see to it. You'll be a rich woman, Madame la Comtesse Steinbock!'

'No, my young man is too lazy. He spends whole weeks twisting and playing with red wax, and nothing gets done. Ah bah! he spends his life in the Louvre, in the Library, looking at engravings and making sketches. He's an idler.'

So the conversation went gaily between the two cousins. Hortense's laughter sounded forced, for the kind of dreaming romantic love that seizes all young girls had overwhelmed her, love of a stranger, with thoughts crystallizing round some figure cast in the way by chance, like frost flowers forming on straw drifted to a window ledge by the wind. For ten months she had been building up the image of a real person from the stories about her cousin's lover, a fabulous lover, because she believed, as her mother also did, in her cousin's perpetual celibacy; and, a week before, this phantom had become Count Wenceslas Steinbock, the dream had a birth certificate, a mist had materialized as a young man of thirty. The seal that she held in her hand, a kind of Annunciation, in which genius sprang forth like a light, had the power of a talisman. Hortense felt so overflowing with happiness that she grasped at the thought that the legend might be true. There was an effervescence in her blood, and she laughed wildly in order to prevent her cousin from reading her mind.

'Ah, I think the drawing-room door is open,' said Cousin Bette; 'so let's go and see whether Monsieur Crevel has gone.'

'Mama has been very sad ever since the day before yesterday. The marriage that was being discussed must have fallen through.'

'Bah! that can be put right. I can tell you this much – a Councillor of the Supreme Court is the person in question. How would you like to be Madame la Présidente? Well, if it rests with Monsieur Crevel, he will certainly say something to me about it, and I shall know tomorrow whether there is any hope!'

'Cousin, leave the seal with me,' begged Hortense. 'I won't show it to anyone. It's a month till Mama's birthday. I'll give it back to you that morning.'

'No, give it to me now. I must have a case made for it.'

'But I want to let Papa see it, so that he can speak to the Minister with all the facts before him, because people in authority have to be careful not to put themselves in a false position,' she said.

'Well, don't show it to your mother, that's all I ask; for if she knew I had a sweetheart she would laugh at me ...'

'I promise you I won't.'

The two cousins reached the boudoir door just as the Baroness fainted, and Hortense's cry was enough to bring her back to consciousness. Bette went in search of smelling salts. When she returned she found daughter and mother in each other's arms, the mother soothing her daughter's fears, telling her: 'It's nothing: just an attack of nerves. ... Here is your father,' she added, recognizing the Baron's ring. 'On no account are you to mention this to him. ...'

Adeline rose to go to meet her husband, with the intention of taking him into the garden before dinner, meaning to speak to him about the broken-off marriage negotiations, ask him for information about his intentions, and try to give him some advice.

Baron Hector Hulot presented an appearance at once parliamentary and Napoleonic, for it is easy to distinguish the Imperials, men who served under the Empire, by their military erectness, their blue coats with gold buttons, buttoned high, their black silk cravats, and the air of command developed in them by the habitual exercise of despotic authority necessary in the rapidly changing circumstances of their careers. In the Baron, it must be agreed, nothing suggested age. His sight was still so good that he read without glasses; his handsome oval face, framed in black side-whiskers – too black, alas! – had a high colour, with the veining that indicates a sanguine temperament; and his figure, controlled by a belt, was still, as Brillat-Savarin would have described it, majestic. A high aristocratic air and great affability cloaked the libertine with whom Crevel had had so many joyous sprees. He was, indeed, one of those men whose eyes light up at the sight of a pretty woman, who smile at every beautiful creature, even at a passer-by whom they will never see again.

'Did you speak in the debate, my dear?' Adeline asked, noticing that he looked preoccupied and worried.

'No,' replied Hector, 'but I am tired to death of listening to speeches dragged out for two hours before they put the question to the vote. They fight battles of words, with speeches like cavalry charges that fail to scatter the enemy! Words have taken the place of action now, which is not very enjoyable for men who are used to marching, as I said to the Marshal when I left him. But it's quite bad enough to be bored on the Ministers' benches, let's enjoy ourselves here.... Good evening, Nanny! How are you, little kid?'

And he put his arm round his daughter's neck, kissed her and pinched her cheek, drew her to his knee with her head on his shoulder and her beautiful golden hair against his face.

'He is tired and harassed,' Madame Hulot said to herself; 'and now I'm about to add to his worries. Perhaps I ought to wait. ... Are you going to spend this evening with us?' she said aloud.

'No, my dear children. I must leave you after dinner; and if it had not been the day that Nanny comes, and my children, and my brother, you would not have seen me at all.'

55

The Baroness picked up the newspaper, looked at the theatre list, and laid it down again when she had read the announcement of *Robert le Diable* at the Opera. Josépha, whom the Italian Opera had surrendered to the French Opera six months before, was singing the part of Alice. This pantomime did not escape the Baron's notice, and he stared at his wife. Adeline lowered her eyes. She went out to the garden, and he followed her.

'What is it, Adeline?' he said, putting his arm round her, drawing her to him and holding her close. 'Surely you know that I love you more than ...'

'More than Jenny Cadine and Josépha!' she boldly interrupted him.

'And who told you that?' demanded the Baron, releasing his wife and stepping back.

'I received an anonymous letter, which I burned, and it told me, my dear, that Hortense's marriage came to nothing because of our financial difficulties. As your wife, my dear Hector, I would never have uttered a word. I knew of your liaison with Jenny Cadine – did I ever complain? But as Hortense's mother I must not shrink from the truth.'

Hulot, after a moment's silence most painful to his wife in which the heavy beating of her heart could be heard, uncrossed his arms and put them round her, pressed her to his heart and kissed her brow, saying with the intensity of strong emotion:

'Adeline, you are an angel, and I'm a miserable wretch. ...'

'No, no,' answered the Baroness, at once laying her fingers on his lips to stop his denigration of himself.

'Yes, I haven't a sou at this moment to give Hortense, and I feel desperately worried; but since you open your heart to me like this, I can confide in you, pour out troubles that are stifling me. ... If your Uncle Fischer is finding himself in difficulties, it's my fault; he has backed bills of exchange for me for twenty-five thousand francs. And all that for the sake of a woman who deceives me, who ridicules me behind my back, who calls me an old dyed tom-cat! Oh, it's appalling that it should cost more to satisfy a vice than to support a family! And it is impossible to resist. ... I might promise you here and now never to return to that abominable Jewess, and yet if she scrawled me a couple of lines I would go, like a man going into battle under the Emperor.'

'Don't torment yourself, Hector,' said the poor woman, in despair, forgetting her daughter at the sight of tears in her husband's eyes. 'You know, I have my diamonds. You must save my uncle, no matter what happens.'

'Your diamonds are hardly worth twenty thousand francs today. That would not be enough for old Fischer; so keep them for Hortense. I'll see the Marshal tomorrow.'

'My poor dear!' exclaimed the Baroness, taking her Hector's hands and kissing them.

That was all she said in rebuke. Adeline offered her diamonds; the father gave them to Hortense. The gesture seemed to her sublime, and she was completely disarmed.

'He is the master – he has the right to take everything, and he leaves me my diamonds! How noble he is!'

So this woman thought, and indeed she had gained more by her gentleness than another might have done by jealous anger.

The moralist cannot deny that, generally speaking, well-bred people addicted to a vice are much more likeable than the virtuous are. Being conscious of their own shortcomings, they are careful to show a broadminded attitude towards their critics' weaknesses; and so they purchase lenience for themselves, and are considered first-class fellows. There may be some delightful people among the virtuous, but virtue usually believes that it is fair enough of itself to be able to dispense with trying to please. Besides, really virtuous people, leaving hypocrites out of account, have nearly all certain misgivings about their situation. They think that they have had the worst of a bargain in life's market, and their remarks are apt to be charged with acid, in the tone of those who consider themselves not properly appreciated.

And so the Baron, who was reproaching himself with ruining his family, exerted all the resources of his wit and his graces as a charmer in order to please his wife, his children, and his Cousin Bette. When he saw his son arriving with Célestine Crevel, who was nursing a little Hulot, he was charming to his daughter-in-law and plied her with compliments, a diet to which Célestine's vanity was unaccustomed, for never was a daughter of wealth so commonplace and so utterly insignificant. The grandfather took the little boy, kissed him, declared him to be a delight and an enchanting fellow. He talked baby-talk to him, prophesied that this youngster would be taller than himself, slipped in some implied flattery of his son, young Hulot, and returned the child to the stout Norman woman in charge of him. And Célestine exchanged a look with the Baroness that said: 'What an adorable man!' It goes without saying that she stood up for her father-in-law against her own father's attacks on him.

Having shown himself an agreeable father-in-law and a doting grandpapa, the Baron took his son aside into the garden in order to offer some very practical observations about the line to follow on a ticklish issue that had arisen in the Chamber that morning. The young lawyer was filled with admiration by the profundity of his views, and touched by his friendly tone, especially by the note almost of deference which seemed to show a desire, nowadays, to treat his son as his equal.

The younger Hulot was a perfect type of the kind of young man produced by the 1830 revolution; with a mind absorbed in politics, taking his ambitions very seriously and containing them behind a solemn mask, very envious of established reputations, uttering sententious phrases instead of the incisive sallies that are the diamonds of French conversation, but with a self-possessed correctness, mistaking arrogance for dignity. Such men are walking coffins containing the Frenchman of an older France. This Frenchman stirs at times and kicks out against his English envelope, but ambition checks him and he consents to stifle in it. These coffins always go draped in black cloth.

'Ah! here is my brother!' said Baron Hulot, going forward to welcome the Count at the drawing-room door.

He greeted the probable successor of the late Marshal Montcornet warmly, then took his arm and led him into the room with every mark of affection and respect.

This Peer of France, who was excused from sittings of the Chamber by reason of his deafness, had a fine head, frosted by the years, whose grey thatch was still thick enough to show a mark left by the pressure of his hat. Small and stocky and grown lean, he wore his green old age with a sprightly gaiety; and as he preserved an exceedingly active spirit, condemned to idleness, he divided his time between reading and walking. His kind and gentle approach to life was reflected in his pale face, his bearing and his tactful conversation, which was full of good sense. He never talked war or campaigns; he knew himself too great to need a show of greatness. In a drawing-room he confined the part he played to a constant attentiveness to the ladies' wishes.

'You are all very gay,' he said, seeing the animation that the Baron had infused into this little family gathering. 'Hortense has still to be married, however,' he added, noting traces of melancholy on his sister-in-law's face.

'Time enough for that!' Bette shouted in his ear, in a formidable voice.

'That's what you say, you bad seed that refused to flower!' he replied, laughing.

The hero of Forzheim was fond of Cousin Bette, for they had a certain amount in common. He was a man without education, sprung from the people; his courage alone had carved out his military achievement, and his practical good sense took the place of brilliance. Full of honours, his hands immaculate, he was ending his fine life radiantly, surrounded by this family in which all his affections were centred, with no suspicion of his brother's still secret aberrations. No one enjoyed more than he did the pleasant sight presented by the meetings of this family group, among whom no slightest discord ever arose, and brothers and sisters were equally affectionate, for Célestine had been immediately accepted as one of the family. Indeed, the kind little Comte Hulot habitually inquired from time to time why old Crevel was not there. 'My father is in the country!' Célestine would shout. On this occasion they told him that the retired perfumer was on a journey.

Surrounded by this truly united family group, Madame Hulot said to herself: 'This is the surest kind of happiness, and who, indeed, could take it from us?'

Seeing the Baron so attentive to his favourite, Adeline, the General teased him so much about his preference that the

Baron, afraid of appearing ridiculous, transferred his gallantry to his daughter-in-law, whom he always singled out for flattery and attention at these family dinners, for he was hoping through her to bring old Crevel round and induce him to get over his resentment. Any witness of the family scene would have found it hard to believe that ruin was staring the father in the face, the mother was in despair, the son to the last degree uneasy about his father's future, and the daughter busy planning to steal a sweetheart from her cousin.

At seven o'clock, seeing his brother, his son, the Baroness, and Hortense absorbed in their game of whist, the Baron left to go and applaud his mistress at the Opera, taking Cousin Bette away with him. She lived in the rue du Doyenné, and was accustomed to make the loneliness of that desolate quarter a pretext for always leaving soon after dinner. Any Parisian will acknowledge that the old maid's precaution was sensible enough.

The continued existence of the conglomeration of houses running the length of the old Louvre is one of those reassuring defiances of common sense by which the French fondly hope to persuade Europe that Frenchmen have not much intelligence and are not to be feared. We have here, perhaps, hit upon an important principle of international strategy. It will not, certainly, be supererogatory to describe this corner of present-day Paris. Later, it will be unimaginable; and our nephews, who will no doubt see the Louvre completed, will refuse to believe that such an outrageous eyesore should have existed for thirty-six years, in the heart of Paris, facing the palace where during the same thirty-six years three dynasties have received the *élite* of France and Europe.

Beyond the archway leading from the pont du Carrousel to the rue du Musée, anyone visiting Paris, even for a few days, is bound to notice a number of houses with decayed façades, whose discouraged owners do no maintenance work upon them. These are all that remains of an old quarter, in process of demolition since the day when Napoleon decided to complete the Louvre. The rue du Doyenné and the blind alley of the same name are the only passages that penetrate this sombre and deserted block, inhabited presumably by ghosts, for one never catches sight of anyone here. The footway, standing much lower than the pavement of the rue du Musée, comes out on a level with the rue Froidmanteau. These houses, submerged and darkened by the raising of the Square, also lie wrapped in the perpetual shadow cast by the high galleries of the Louvre, blackened on this side by the north wind. The gloom, the silence, the glacial air, the hollow sunken ground level, combine to make these houses seem so many crypts, or living tombs. If, passing in a cab through this dead area, one happens to glance down the impasse du Doyenné, a chill strikes one's heart, one wonders who can possibly live here and what may happen here at night, at the hour when the alley becomes a place of cut-throats, when the vices of Paris, shrouded in night's mantle, move as they will.

The problem the area presents, alarming enough already, becomes frightening when one sees that these so-called dwellings are bounded by a swamp on the rue de Richelieu side, a sea of jostling broken paving-stones towards the Tuileries, small plots and sinister hovels facing the galleries, and steppes of dressed stone and half-demolished ruins by the old Louvre. Henri III and his minions looking for their breeches, Marguerite's lovers in search of their heads, must dance sarabands by moonlight in these barren wastes, dominated by the vault of a chapel still standing, as if to demonstrate that the Catholic religion, so tenacious in France, outlasts everything. For nearly forty years the Louvre has been crying from the open mouths of all the gashed walls, the gaping windows, 'Strike these excrescences from my face!' One must suppose that the utility of this cut-throat place has been recognized, and the need to symbolize in the heart of Paris that intimate alliance of squalor and splendour which is characteristic of the queen of capital cities. Indeed, these stark ruins, in the midst of which the legitimist newspaper contracted the malady of which it is dying, the shocking hovels of the rue du Musée, the boarded enclosure where the street-stall vendors display their wares, may perhaps have a longer and more prosperous existence than three dynasties!

In 1823, the moderate rent asked for rooms in condemned houses had brought Cousin Bette to live here, in spite of the necessity, imposed on her by the isolation of the quarter, to reach home before nightfall. She did not consider this a hardship, in fact, because she had preserved the country habit of going to bed and rising with the sun, a habit which enables country people to make substantial economies in light and heating. She lived, then, in one of the houses that, thanks to the demolition of the famous house once occupied by Cambacérès, now had a view of the Square.

Just as Baron Hulot was setting down his wife's cousin at the door of this house and saying 'Good-night, Cousin!', a young woman, small, slender, pretty, dressed with great elegance and moving in a waft of expensive scent, passed between the cab and the wall to enter the same house. The eyes of this lady, turning simply in order to have a look at her fellow-tenant's cousin, met the Baron's eyes, quite without premeditation; but the libertine experienced the sharp reaction that all Parisians feel when they meet a pretty woman who realizes, as the entomologists put it, all their *desiderata*, and he stood pulling on one of his gloves with a careful deliberation before getting into his cab again, so as to keep himself in countenance and be able to follow the young woman with his eye, a young woman whose dress was agreeably set swaying by something rather different from those hideous and fraudulent crinoline bustles.

'There,' he said to himself, 'goes a charming little woman whom I would be very pleased to make happy, for I have no doubt she would do the same by me.'

When the stranger had reached the turn of the staircase serving the main building overlooking the street, she looked back at the carriage entrance out of the corner of her eye, without actually turning round, and saw the Baron nailed to the spot with admiration, consumed with desire and curiosity. Such a tribute is a flower, and all Parisian women breathe its fragrance with pleasure when they find it in their path. There are women devoted to their obligations, and virtuous as well as pretty, who come home in a bad temper when they have failed to gather their little bouquet in the course of their walk.

The young woman hurried up the staircase. Presently a

second-floor window opened and she appeared, but in company with a gentleman whose bald pate and placid un-wrathful eye showed him to be a husband.

'You could hardly call these creatures lacking in knowing-ness or directness!' reflected the Baron. 'She's doing this to show me where she lives. It's a little too smart, especially in a quarter like this. I had better take care.'

The Director looked up when he had got into the *milord*, and then the woman and her husband abruptly drew back, as if the Baron's face were Medusa's head.

'One would suppose they know who I am,' thought the Baron. 'That would explain the whole thing.'

And when the cab had climbed the slope to the rue du Musée, he leaned out to look back at the stranger again, and found that she had returned to the window. Ashamed at being caught staring at the carriage hood which concealed her admirer, the young woman sprang hastily back.

'I'll find out who she is from Nanny,' the Baron told him-self.

Sight of the Councillor of State's features had startled the couple very much, as we shall see.

'But that is Baron Hulot, my chief!' exclaimed the husband, as he stepped back from the balcony on to which the window opened.

'Well then, Marneffe, can the old maid on the third floor at the far end of the court, who is living with that young man, be his cousin? How odd that we should only have found that out today, and by accident!'

'Mademoiselle Fischer living with a young man!' repeated the civil servant. 'That's just porters' gossip. Let's not speak so lightly of the cousin of a Councillor of State who makes the sun shine and the rain descend at the Ministry. Come on, let's have dinner; I've been waiting for you since four o'clock!'

The lovely Madame Marneffe, natural daughter of the Comte Montcornet, one of Napoleon's most famous lieu-tenants, had been married, with the aid of a twenty-thousand-franc dowry, to a junior official in the Ministry of War. Through the influence of the illustrious Lieutenant-General,

Marshal of France for the last six months of his life, this pen-pusher had reached the unlooked-for position of senior book-keeper in his office; but just as he was about to be appointed head clerk, the Marshal's death had cut off Marneffe's and his wife's expectations at the root. Monsieur Marneffe's means were small, for Mademoiselle Valérie Fortin's dowry had already slipped through his fingers and melted away in paying his debts, buying all the things needed by a young man setting up house, and above all in satisfying the demands of a pretty wife accustomed in her mother's house to luxuries which she had no mind to give up; so that the couple had been obliged to economize in house rent. The situation of the rue du Doyenné, not far from the Ministry of War and the centre of Paris, suited Monsieur and Madame Marneffe, and for the past four years or so they had been living in the same building as Mademoiselle Fischer.

Monsieur Jean-Paul-Stanislas Marneffe was an underling of the type that resists the stupefying effects of routine service in an office by the kind of power that depravity gives. This meagre little man, with wispy hair and beard, his face bloodless and wan, drawn rather than wrinkled, his eyes, with slightly reddened eyelids, harnessed with spectacles, of hangdog looks and still more hangdog bearing, was exactly the type of man who is brought before the police courts on a charge of indecent offences, as everyone pictures him.

The apartment occupied by this couple presented the flashy display of meretricious luxury all too often met with in Parisian homes, in establishments like theirs. In the drawing-room, the furniture covered in faded cotton velvet, the plaster statuettes masquerading as Florentine bronzes, the clumsily-carved painted chandelier with its candle-rings of moulded glass, the carpet, a bargain whose low price was explained too late by the quantity of cotton in it, which was now visible to the naked eye – everything in the room, to the very curtains (which would have taught you that the handsome appearance of wool damask lasts only for three years), everything cried poverty like a ragged beggar at a church door.

The dining-room, looked after incompetently by a single

servant, had the nauseating atmosphere of provincial hotel dining-rooms; everything in it was greasy, ill-kept.

The master's bedroom was more like a student's room, with his single bed and the furniture he had used as a bachelor faded now and shabby like himself; and it was cleaned only once a week. It was a horrible room, in which nothing was put away and old socks dangled from the chairs, stuffed with horse-hair, on whose covers the faded flowers reappeared outlined in dust. It quite clearly proclaimed a man whose home meant nothing to him, who lived outside it: at gaming-houses, cafés, or elsewhere.

The mistress's room was not like the others. There was no sign there of the degrading neglect shamefully evident in the rooms used in common, whose curtains were all discoloured with smoke and dust, in which the child, abandoned apparently to his own devices, left his toys lying everywhere. Situated in the wing of the house facing the street, to one side of the main block on the court of the adjoining property, Valérie's bedroom and dressing-room, with their stylish chintz hangings, rosewood furniture, and velvet pile carpet, were redolent of the pretty woman, one might almost say the kept woman. On the velvet-draped mantelpiece stood the kind of clock that was a fashionable possession at the moment. A well-filled little cabinet for ornaments and richly mounted Chinese porcelain flowerstands caught the eye. The bed, the dressing-table, the wardrobe with its mirror, the *tête-à-tête* sofa, the usual toys and trifles lying about – all bore witness to the affectations or whims of fashion.

Although the luxury and elegance were third-rate and everything was three years old, a dandy would have seen nothing to find fault with in the room, except perhaps that its opulence smacked of the middle class. Yet there was no art or distinction in the furnishing, nothing of the effect which good taste achieves by intelligent selection of possessions. A doctor in social science would have deduced the existence of a lover from some of the useless, highly ornamental knick-knacks, which in the home of a married woman could only have come from the demi-god, whose power is invisible but ever present.

The dinner that husband, wife, and child sat down to – the dinner that had been kept since four o'clock – would have revealed this family's financial straits, for the table is the most reliable thermometer of the fortunes of Parisian households. Soup made from potherbs and the water from boiled beans, a piece of veal with potatoes, swamped in brownish water by way of gravy, a dish of beans, and cherries of inferior quality, all served and eaten from chipped plates and dishes, with forks and spoons of nickel's mean unringing metal – was that a menu worthy of such a pretty woman? The Baron would have wept to see it. The dull carafes did nothing to improve the harsh colour of wine bought by the litre from the wine-merchant on the corner. The table-napkins had been in use for a week. Everything, in sum, betrayed a graceless poverty, an indifferent lack of care for the family on the part of both husband and wife. The most unnoticing observer, seeing them, would have said to himself that the dismal moment had come, for these two creatures, when the necessity of eating makes people look about them for some piece of luck which, by fair means or foul, may be induced to come their way.

Valérie's first words to her husband, indeed, will explain the delay in serving dinner, which had been kept back for her, probably by a self-interested devotion on the part of the cook.

'Samanon will only take your bills of exchange at fifty per cent, and wants part of your salary assigned to him as security.'

Financial distress, which could still be concealed in the household of the Departmental Chief in the Ministry of War, who was cushioned against it by a salary of twenty-four thousand francs plus bonuses, had plainly reached its last stage in the case of the clerk.

'You have *made* my chief,' said the husband, looking at his wife.

'I believe I have,' she replied, without blinking at the expression, borrowed from stage-door slang.

'What are we to do?' Marneffe went on. 'The landlord is all set to seize our things tomorrow. And your father must needs go and die without making a will! Upon my word, those

Empire fellows all believe that they're immortal like their Emperor.'

'Poor Father,' she said. 'I was the only child he had, and he was very fond of me! The Countess must have burned the will. How could he possibly have forgotten me, when he always used to give us two or three thousand-franc notes at a time?'

'We owe four quarters' rent, fifteen hundred francs! Is our furniture worth that? "That is the question", as Shakespeare says.'

'Well, good-bye, my pet,' said Valérie, who had taken only a couple of mouthfuls of the veal, from which the maid had extracted the juices for a gallant soldier back from Algiers. 'Desperate situations require desperate remedies!'

'Valérie, where are you going?' cried Marneffe, moving to stand between his wife and the door.

'I'm going to see our landlord,' she answered, as she arranged her ringlets under her charming hat. 'And you had better try to get on the right side of that old maid, if she really is the Director's cousin.'

The ignorance of one another's social position in which tenants of the same house live is something constantly noted, and shows clearly how people are borne along in the swift current of existence in Paris. It is easy to understand, however, that a civil servant who leaves early every morning for his office, returns home for dinner, and goes out every evening, and a wife addicted to the gaieties of Paris, may know nothing of how an old maid lives on the third floor across the court in their block, especially when the old maid has Mademoiselle Fischer's habits.

The first person to stir in the house, Lisbeth would go to bring in her milk, bread, and charcoal without exchanging a word with anyone, and she went to bed with the sun. She never received either letters or visitors, and was not on neighbourly terms with her fellow tenants. Hers was one of those anonymous insect-like existences to be found in certain houses, in which one may discover at the end of four years that there is an old gentleman living on the fourth floor who once knew Voltaire, Pilâtre de Rozier, Beaujon, Marcel,

Molé, Sophie Arnould, Franklin, and Robespierre. What Monsieur and Madame Marneffe had just said about Lisbeth Fischer they had come to know because the quarter was so isolated and because of the friendly relations with the porters which their financial embarrassment had obliged them to establish, for they were too dependent on the porters' good-will not to have carefully cultivated it. It so happened that the old maid's pride, closed lips, and reserve had provoked in the porters that exaggerated show of respect and cold attitude which spring from an unacknowledged discontent and a sense of being treated as inferior. The porters, moreover, in the case in question, as they say in the law courts, considered themselves just as good as a tenant paying a rent of two hundred and fifty francs. Since Cousin Bette's confidences to her second cousin Hortense were in fact true, one can understand how the portress, gossiping with the Marneffes, might have slandered Mademoiselle Fischer in the belief that she was simply passing on a scandalous piece of news.

When the spinster had taken her candlestick from the hands of the portress, the respectable Madame Olivier, she moved forward to see whether there was a light in the attic windows above her apartment. At that hour, even in July, it was so dark at the end of the court that the old maid could not go to bed without a light.

'Oh, you needn't worry; Monsieur Steinbock is in. He hasn't even been out,' Madame Olivier said to Mademoiselle Fischer, maliciously.

The spinster made no reply. She had remained a peasant in this respect, that she cared little for what people not close to her might say. Peasants are aware of nothing outside their own village, and to her the opinion of the little circle in the midst of which she lived was still the only one that mattered. She climbed the stairs, then, purposefully, to the attic instead of her own apartment. At dessert, she had put some fruit and sweetmeats into her bag for her sweetheart, and she was going up to present them, for all the world like an old maid bringing home a titbit for her dog.

She found the hero of Hortense's dreams working by the light of a little lamp, whose rays were concentrated by passing through a globe filled with water – a pale, fair young man, sitting at a kind of work-bench littered with sculptor's tools, red wax, chisels, roughed out bases, bronze copies of models, wearing a workman's blouse, with a little group in modelling wax in his hand, which he was scrutinizing with the concentration of a poet at work.

'Here, Wenceslas, look what I've brought you,' she said, spreading her handkerchief on a corner of the bench. Then she carefully took the sweets and fruit from her reticule.

'You are very kind, Mademoiselle,' the poor exile replied, in a melancholy voice.

'These will refresh you, my poor child. You heat your blood working like this. You weren't born for such hard work.'

Wenceslas Steinbock looked at the old maid in some surprise.

'Well, eat them,' she said then, roughly, 'and don't gaze at me as if I were one of your figures that you're feeling pleased with.'

This verbal cuff on the ear put an end to the young man's astonishment; for he recognized the voice of the female mentor to whose bullying he was so inured that tenderness from her always took him by surprise. Although Steinbock was twenty-nine, he appeared, as fair men sometimes do, to be five or six years younger; and anyone seeing his youthful face – although its bloom had vanished in the fatigues and hardships of exile – side by side with Mademoiselle Fischer's lean, hard countenance, might have thought that Nature had made a mistake in assigning their sexes. He got up and flung himself into an old Louis XV easy chair upholstered in yellow Utrecht velvet, apparently ready to take a breather. The old maid then selected a greengage and gently offered it to her friend.

'Thank you,' he said, taking the fruit.

'Are you tired?' she asked, giving him another.

'I am not tired with work, but tired of life,' he replied.

'What nonsense you talk!' she said, somewhat tartly. 'Haven't you got a guardian angel to watch over you?' she went on, offering him the sweetmeats and watching with pleasure as he ate them all. 'You see, while I was at dinner at my cousin's I was thinking of you.'

'I know,' he said, turning a look at once caressing and plaintive on Lisbeth. 'Without you I should have died long ago. But you know, my dear lady, artists need some distraction. . . .'

'Ah, so that's what's in your mind!' she interrupted him, sharply, setting her hands on her hips and fixing him with kindling eyes. 'You want to ruin your health in the stews of Paris, and end up like so many artists, dying in the workhouse! No, no, make a fortune for yourself first, and when you have money stacked away you can take your fun then, my child. You will have the wherewithal then, you libertine, to pay for the doctors as well as the pleasures!'

Wenceslas Steinbock took this broadside, delivered with looks that searched him with their magnetic flame, and bowed his head. The most bitter-tongued of Mademoiselle Fischer's detractors, watching even the beginning of this scene, would have acknowledged that the scandalous suggestions of the Olivier pair must be false. Everything in the tone, the gestures, and the looks of these two beings declared the purity of their life together. The old maid evinced the tender feeling of a dictatorial but sincere maternal affection. The young man submitted like a respectful son to a mother's tyranny. This strange relationship appeared to be the result of a powerful will constantly acting upon a malleable nature, upon that inconsistency of the Slav temperament which allows Slavs to display heroic courage upon the battlefield and yet show an incredible lack of resolution in their conduct of ordinary life, a kind of flabbiness of the moral fibre whose causes might well be investigated by physiologists, for physiologists are to politics what entomologists are to agriculture.

'And what if I die before I get rich?' Wenceslas asked gloomily.

'Die?' exclaimed the spinster. 'Oh, I won't let you die! I have life enough for two, and I would give you my lifeblood if it came to that.'

As he listened to that frank, vehement declaration, tears rose to Steinbock's eyes.

'Don't be sad, my little Wenceslas,' Lisbeth, touched in her turn, went on. 'Do you know, I think my cousin Hortense thought your seal very nice. Now I'm going to set about getting your bronze group sold; you'll be able to pay off your debt to me, and do what you like; you'll be free! Come now, smile!'

'I shall never be able to pay off my debt to you, Mademoiselle,' the poor exile replied.

'And why not?' demanded the Vosges peasant, ready to take up the cudgels for the Livonian against herself.

'Because you have not only fed, housed, and cared for me in my need, you have given me strength! You have made me what I am. You have often been harsh, you have made me suffer. ...'

'I?' said the old maid. 'Are you going to start on your usual nonsense about poetry and the arts, and crack your fingers and wave your arms, talking about ideal beauty and all your northern moonshine? Beauty is nothing compared with solid practical common sense, and I represent common sense. You have ideas in your mind, have you? That's all very fine! I have my ideas too. ... Of what use is what's in the head if you don't turn it to practical account? People with ideas don't get on so well as those who have none, but know how to bestir themselves. Instead of thinking of your dreams, you need to work. What have you done while I was out?'

'What did your pretty cousin say?'

'Who told you she was pretty?' Lisbeth instantly took him up, in a tone behind which could be heard the roar of a tigerish jealousy.

'You did, of course.'

'That was to see the face you would put on. You want to go chasing after petticoats, do you? You like women: well, model them, express your desires in bronze; for you'll have to do without your little love-affairs for some time yet, and especially love-affairs with my cousin, my dear boy. She's not game for your game-bag. That girl has to find a husband worth sixty thousand francs a year ... and he's been found. ... Goodness, the bed is not made!' she said, looking across into the other room. 'Oh, poor dear, I've been neglecting you.'

71

And the energetic spinster at once took off her gloves, her cape and hat, and briskly set to work like a servant to make the narrow camp-bed on which the artist slept. The combination of brusqueness, of downright roughness even, and kindness in Lisbeth's treatment of him may account for the ascendancy she had acquired over this man, of whom she was taking complete possession. Life binds us, surely, by both the good and the evil that come our way, fortuitously. If the Livonian had encountered Madame Marneffe instead of Lisbeth Fischer, he would have found a complaisance in his patroness that would have led him into some miry and dishonourable path, in which he would have been lost. He would certainly not have worked, and the artist in him would not have burst the bud. And indeed, even while he groaned under the old maid's bitter tongue and grasping ways, his good sense told him that he should prefer her iron rule to the idle and precarious existence which some of his compatriots led.

Here is the story of the events which brought about that alliance of feminine energy and masculine weakness – a kind of reversal of attributes said to be not uncommon in Poland.

In 1833, Mademoiselle Fischer, who sometimes used to work late at night when she had a great deal of work on hand, at about one o'clock in the morning noticed a strong smell of carbonic acid gas and heard the groans of a man at the point of death. The charcoal fumes and the throat-rattle came from an attic above the two rooms of her apartment. She surmised that a young man who had recently come to the house and rented the attic, empty for the previous three years, was attempting to commit suicide. She rushed upstairs, threw herself against the door, and with her peasant strength succeeded in bursting it open. She found the tenant of the room writhing on a camp-bed, in the convulsions, apparently, of his death-agony. She extinguished the stove. With the door opened, fresh air flowed in, and the exile was saved. Later, when Lisbeth had put him to bed like a nurse, she was able to deduce the reason for his suicide from the extreme bareness of the two rooms of the attic, which contained nothing but a rickety table, the camp-bed, and a couple of chairs.

On the table was the following statement, which she read:

I am Count Wenceslas Steinbock, born at Prelia, in Livonia.

Let no one be blamed for my death; the reasons for my suicide are in these words of Kosciusko's: *Finis Poloniae!*

The great-nephew of a brave general of Charles XII could not beg. A delicate constitution made military service impossible for me, and yesterday saw the end of the hundred thalers with which I came to Paris from Dresden. I leave twenty-five francs in the drawer of this table to pay the rent that I owe to the landlord.

As I no longer have relatives living, my death concerns no one. I beg my compatriots not to blame the French Government. I did not make myself known as a refugee; I did not ask for aid; I met no other exile; no one in Paris knows that I exist.

I die in Christian faith. May God forgive the last of the Steinbocks!

WENCESLAS

Mademoiselle Fischer, profoundly touched by the honesty of a dying man who paid his rent, opened the drawer and saw that there were in fact five five-franc pieces there.

'Poor young man!' she exclaimed. 'And there's no one in the world to care about him!'

She ran down to her room, fetched her sewing, and went back to work in the attic while keeping watch over the Livonian nobleman. When the refugee awoke, one may imagine his surprise when he saw a woman sitting by his bed: he thought he was still dreaming. As she sat stitching gold aiguillettes for a uniform, the old maid had been making up her mind to look after this poor boy, whom she had watched with admiration as he slept. When the young Count was quite conscious again, Lisbeth spoke cheerfully to him and questioned him in order to find out how she might possibly enable him to make a living. After telling his story, Wenceslas added that he had owed his post as teacher to his acknowledged talent for the arts; he had always felt a natural bent towards sculpture, but the time necessary for study seemed too long for a man without money, and he felt that he was not nearly robust enough at the moment to devote himself to a profession demanding manual labour, or undertake large works of sculpture. This was so much Greek to Lisbeth

Fischer. She answered the unfortunate young man by saying that Paris offered so many opportunities that a man who was resolved would always find a living there; men with pluck never came to grief in Paris, provided that they brought with them a certain fund of patience.

'I am just a poor woman, a countrywoman, myself, and I have managed very well to make my own way and earn my own living,' she said in conclusion. 'Listen to me. If you are willing to give your whole mind to working in earnest, I have some savings, and I will lend you the money you need to live on, month by month; but only for living frugally, not for leading a gay life and gadding about the town! It is possible to dine in Paris on twenty-five sous a day, and I will make your lunch with my own every morning. And I'll furnish your room, and pay for whatever apprenticeship you think you need. You shall give me formal receipts for the money I spend for you; and when you are rich you can repay it all. But if you don't work, I shall not regard myself as bound to do anything further for you, and I'll leave you to your fate.'

'Ah!' exclaimed the unfortunate refugee, who was still feeling the bitterness of his first encounter with death. 'The exiles from every country have good reason to stretch out their hands to France like souls in purgatory straining upwards to paradise. Among what other nation could one find help and generous hearts everywhere, even in a garret like this? You shall be the whole world to me, my dear benefactress. I'll be your slave! Be my sweetheart,' he said caressingly, in one of those impulsive demonstrations of feeling so characteristic of Poles, which make people accuse them, quite unjustly, of toadyism.

'Oh, no! I am much too jealous, I should make you unhappy; but I will gladly be something like your comrade,' Lisbeth replied.

'Oh, if you only knew how fervently I longed for any human creature, even a tyrant, who had some use for me, when I was struggling in the empty loneliness of Paris!' Wenceslas went on. 'I wished myself in Siberia, where the Emperor would send me if I returned! Be you my Providence. ... I'll work, I'll be better than I am, although I am not a bad fellow.'

'Will you do everything I tell you?' she asked.

'Yes!'

'Well then, I adopt you as my child,' she said gaily. 'Here I am with a boy who has risen from the grave. Come! we'll begin now. I'm going down to do my marketing. You get dressed, and come to have lunch with me when I knock on the ceiling with my broom-handle.'

Next day, when Mademoiselle Fischer called on the firm who took her work, she made inquiries about a sculptor's profession. By persistent questioning she succeeded in finding out about the studio of Florent and Chanor, a firm specializing in casting and foundry work and the chasing of fine bronzes and silver services. She presented Steinbock there for employment as an apprentice sculptor, which seemed an odd proposition to the partners. Leading sculptors sent their clay models to the firm to be cast; it did not teach the art of sculpture. Thanks to the old maid's stubborn persistence, however, her protégé was in the end taken on as an ornament designer.

Steinbock soon learned to model ornaments, and created new ones, for he had genuine talent. Five months after completing his apprenticeship as an engraver and carver, he made the acquaintance of the famous Stidmann, the principal sculptor working for the Florent firm. By the end of twenty months Wenceslas knew more of the art than his master, but in thirty months the savings amassed by the old maid, coin by coin for more than sixteen years, were completely gone. Two thousand five hundred francs in gold, a sum which she had intended for buying a life annuity, were now represented by what? A Pole's iou! Moreover, Lisbeth was now working as she had worked in her youth, in order to meet the Livonian's expenses. When she found herself with a piece of paper in her hands in place of her gold coins, she lost her head and went to consult Monsieur Rivet, who for the last fifteen years had been the adviser and friend of his forewoman and most able worker. On hearing of this escapade, Monsieur and Madame Rivet scolded Lisbeth, told her she was crazy, abused all refugees whose plots to achieve national independence again were a threat to the prosperity of trade and the policy of peace at any price, and urged the old maid to obtain what in business are known as securities.

'The only security this fellow can offer is his liberty,' Monsieur Rivet said in conclusion.

Monsieur Achille Rivet was a magistrate in the Commercial Court.

'And for foreigners that's no joke,' he went on. 'A Frenchman stays five years in jail and then he gets out, without paying his debts indeed, for only his conscience can force him to do so then and that never troubles him; but a foreigner is kept locked up permanently. Give me your IOU. You must pass it to my bookkeeper; he will have it protested, sue both you and the Pole, and in default of the money obtain a writ of arrest for debt; and then, when everything has been done in proper form, he will sign a defeasance to you. If you do that your interest will run on, and you will always have a pistol to hold at your Pole's head!'

The old maid let herself be advised, and told her protégé not to be alarmed at the legal proceedings, for they were taken only in order to provide security for a moneylender, who would then be willing to advance some money. This yarn originated in the Commercial Court magistrate's fertile imagination. The unsuspecting artist, hoodwinked by his trust in his benefactress, lit his pipe with the stamped papers, for he was a smoker, like all men with worries or unused energies that make them require the effects of narcotics. One fine day, Monsieur Rivet showed Mademoiselle Fischer a file of documents, saying:

'Wenceslas Steinbock is in your hands now, bound hand and foot, and tied up so thoroughly that within twenty-four hours he could be landed in Clichy for the rest of his days.'

This worthy and respected magistrate felt that day the satisfaction naturally resulting from the consciousness of having done a wrong-headed good deed. Benevolence takes so many different forms in Paris, that this odd phrase applies to one of its varieties. The Livonian being now entangled in the toils of Commercial Court proceedings, the next question was how to get payment, for Wenceslas Steinbock was regarded by the successful businessman as a confidence trickster. Sentiment, reliance on a man's integrity, poetry, were in his eyes, in matters of business, *disastrous*. In the interests of poor Mademoiselle Fischer, who, according to him, had been *diddled* by a Pole, Rivet went to see the prosperous firm that Steinbock had recently left. It so happened that Stidmann was in Chanor's office when the embroiderer arrived, to ask for information about 'the man Steinbock, a Polish refugee'. This was the same Stidmann who, seconded by the notable Parisian goldsmiths referred to above, is responsible for the present excellence of French decorative art, which can stand comparison with the Florentine masters and the Renaissance.

'Whom do you mean by "the man Steinbock"?' Stidmann exclaimed jovially. 'Can it by any chance be a young Livonian who was a pupil of mine? Let me tell you, sir, he's a great artist. I think myself a devil of a fellow, so they say; but that poor boy doesn't know that he has the capacity to become a god. . . .'

'Ah!' said Rivet, with satisfaction. Then he went on:

'Although you have a very cavalier manner of speaking to a man who has the honour to be a magistrate of the Seine Department . . .'

'Pardon me, Consul!' interrupted Stidmann, saluting.

'. . . I am very pleased to hear what you tell me,' the magistrate continued. 'It's true then that this young man is capable of earning money?'

'Certainly,' said old Chanor; 'but he will have to work hard. He would have made a good deal already if he had stayed with us. But what can you expect of artists? They have a horror of not being their own masters.'

'They have a sense of their own worth and their dignity,' rejoined Stidmann. 'I do not blame Wenceslas for going off on his own, for trying to make a name for himself and become a great man; he has a right to do so! But it was a great loss to me, all the same, when he left me.'

'There you are,' exclaimed Rivet; 'you see the conceit of these young fellows when they emerge from their tutelary

77

egg. . . . Make an income for yourself first, and look for fame after: that's what I say!'

'Money-grubbing spoils one's hands!' Stidmann replied. 'It's for fame to bring us money.'

'What can you do?' Chanor said to Rivet. 'You can't tie them up.'

'They would gnaw through the halter!' declared Stidmann.

'These gentlemen,' said Chanor, looking at Stidmann, 'may be very talented, but the talent seems to go with a head full of freakish notions. They all spend right and left, keep light-o'-loves, throw their money out of the windows, and have no time to do their work. They neglect their commissions; and so we have to go to workers who are not nearly so good, and *they* make money. Then they complain of hard times, while if they had applied themselves to their work they would have gold by the cartload.'

'You remind me, Papa Lumignon,' said Stidmann, 'of the bookseller who used to say, before the Revolution: "Ah! if I could only keep Montesquieu, Voltaire, and Rousseau properly short of cash, in my garret, with their breeches locked up, what good little books they would write for me and I should make my fortune!" If fine works of art could be turned out like nails, commissionaires would be making them. . . . Give me a thousand francs, and shut up!'

The worthy Rivet returned home, delighted on poor Mademoiselle Fischer's account. She was in the habit of dining at his house every Monday, and he now found her there.

'If you are able to make him work hard,' he said, 'it will turn out better for you than your rashness deserves; you will get your money back: interest, costs, and capital. This Pole has talent, he is capable of earning a living; but lock up his trousers and shoes, prevent him from going to La Chaumière and the Notre-Dame de Lorette quarter, keep him on a leash. If you don't take such precautions your sculptor will be idle, and if you only knew what artists mean by *idleness*! – such horrors, you've no idea! I've just been told that a thousand-franc note may be frittered away in a single day!'

This episode had a disastrous effect on the relationship

between Wenceslas and Lisbeth. The benefactress soaked the exile's bread in the bitter wormwood draught of reproach whenever it seemed to her that her savings were in danger, and she very often believed that they were gone for ever. The kind mother became a cruel stepmother; she rated the poor boy and nagged him, reproached him with not working fast enough and with having chosen a hard profession. She could not believe that models in red wax, small figures, trial designs for ornament, sketches, could be of any use. Presently, reacting against her own harshness, she tried to efface its effect by her concern for the Pole's needs, by kind and thoughtful services. The poor young man, groaning to find himself dependent on this shrew, domineered over by a peasant woman from the Vosges, was disarmed by her affectionate coaxing and her motherly solicitude for his physical and material well-being. He was like a wife who forgives a week's ill-treatment in the caresses of a fleeting reconciliation. In this fashion, Mademoiselle Fischer gained an absolute empire over his spirit.

The love of power which had lain dormant in the old maid's heart developed rapidly. She was able to satisfy her pride and her need to find an outlet for her energy: had she not a creature of her own to scold, manage, spoil, make happy – with no need to fear any rival? The good and evil in her character were equally employed and active. If she sometimes tormented the wretched artist, at other times she could show a delicacy of feeling and a kindness that had the charm of meadow flowers. It was her delight to see that he lacked nothing. She would have given her life for him, Wenceslas was sure of that. Magnanimous like all noble spirits, the poor boy forgot the bad side, the shortcomings of this woman, who, indeed, had told him the story of her life in excuse of her roughnesses, and he constantly remembered only her generosities. One day, exasperated because Wenceslas had gone out for a stroll instead of working, the spinster made a scene.

'You belong to me!' she told him. 'As an honourable man you ought to try to pay back what you owe me as quickly as possible. ...'

The young aristocrat turned pale. His Steinbock blood kindled in his veins.

'God knows,' she said, 'we'll soon have nothing left to live on but the thirty sous I earn, a poor working woman like me. . . .'

In need of money as they both were, provoked by the exchange of bitter words, they became incensed against each other; and then the poor artist for the first time reproached his benefactress for having snatched him from death to make him live a galley-slave's life; worse than annihilation, so he said, in which one at least had peace. And he spoke of running away.

'Run away!' cried the spinster. 'Ah! Monsieur Rivet was right!'

And she explained categorically to the Pole how he might within twenty-four hours be put in prison for the rest of his days. It was a staggering blow. Steinbock sank into a black melancholy and absolute silence.

More than a day later, in the night, Lisbeth, who had heard preparations being made for suicide, climbed the stairs to her pensioner, and presented him with the file of papers and a legal receipt for the money he owed her.

'Take these, my child, and forgive me!' she said, with tears in her eyes. 'Be happy; leave me: I torment you too much. But tell me that you will sometimes think of the poor girl who set you in the way of earning a living for yourself. What can I do? It's for your own sake I am unkind. I may die, and what would become of you without me? That's the reason for my impatience to see you able to make articles that can be sold. I'm not asking for my money for my own sake, believe me! I am afraid of your idleness that you call reverie, of your thinking out of ideas that consumes so many hours while you stare at the sky; and I would like to have seen you develop the habit of work.'

This was said in a tone of voice, with a look, tears, an expression, that went straight to the magnanimous artist's heart. He put his arms round his benefactress, pressed her to him, and kissed her forehead.

'Keep these papers,' he said, almost with gaiety. 'Why

should you put me in Clichy? Don't you see that gratitude makes me a prisoner here?'

This crisis of their secret life together, which had happened six months earlier, had roused Wenceslas to produce three pieces of work: the seal that Hortense was keeping, the group at the antique dealer's, and a beautiful clock which he was now just finishing – he was in the act of tightening the last screws.

The clock represented the twelve Hours, admirably symbolized by twelve female figures whirling in a dance so swift and full of verve that three Cupids, clambering up on a pile of fruit and flowers, could attempt to check only the Hour of Midnight, whose torn chlamys remained in the grasp of the most daring Cupid. This group was mounted on a circular base gaily ornamented with lively fantastic creatures. The time was indicated in a monster's mouth, gaping in a yawn. The Hours carried apt symbolic tokens of the occupation appropriate to each hour.

It is easy to understand, now, the extraordinary nature of the attachment which Mademoiselle Fischer had come to feel for her Livonian: she wanted him to be happy, yet she watched him pining away, growing blanched and sickly in his garret. How this appalling state of affairs had come about may be imagined. The Lorraine peasant watched over this child of the north with a mother's tenderness, a wife's jealousy, and the temper of a dragon. She so arranged things as to make any kind of escapade or dissipation impossible for him through lack of money. She would have liked to keep her companion and victim entirely to herself, well-behaved as he was of necessity; and she did not understand, because she herself had become accustomed to endure any privation, the barbarity of this insane desire. She loved Steinbock well enough not to marry him, and loved him too well to give him up to another woman. She could not resign herself to being only his mother, yet thought herself crazy when the idea of playing the alternative role crossed her mind.

These warring impulses: her fierce jealousy, her happiness in possessing a man of her own, kept this woman's heart in a state of inordinate agitation. She had been truly in love for the past four years, and she cherished the wild hope of making this illogical way of life – leading nowhere – permanent, though its continuance must mean the destruction of the person she called her child. The battle between her instincts and her reason made her unjust and tyrannical. Vengeance was wreaked on the young man for the fact that she was not young nor beautiful nor rich. Then, after each vengeful act, recognizing her faults, she achieved infinite depths of humility and tenderness. She knew how she must sacrifice to her idol only after she had marked her power with axe-blows upon it. The situation, in fact, was that of Shakespeare's *Tempest* in reverse, with Caliban master of Ariel and Prospero.

As for the unhappy young man – a man of high ideals, reflective, with a tendency to indolence – his eyes, like the eyes of lions encaged in the Jardin des Plantes, revealed the desert that his benefactress was creating in his soul. The forced labour that Lisbeth imposed upon him did not satisfy the needs of his heart. His boredom was becoming a physical malady and he was dying without being able to ask for, without knowing how he could obtain, money for the distraction that he often needed. Occasionally, on days of restless energy when the consciousness of his unhappiness aggravated his exasperation, he looked at Lisbeth as a thirsty traveller traversing an arid waste must look at undrinkably brackish water.

The bitter fruits of poverty and of their hermit-like existence in Paris were savoured by Lisbeth as pleasures; and she foresaw with terror that the faintest breath of a love-affair would take her slave from her. Sometimes, as by her tyranny and upbraidings she drove on this poet to become a great modeller of small-scale works of art, she reproached herself with having given him the means to do without her.

The following day, those three existences so different from one another and all so truly wretched, the lives of a mother in despair, of the Marneffe couple, and of the hapless refugee, were all to be affected by Hortense's naïve passion, and by the singular events that were to be the outcome of the Baron's ill-fated passion for Josépha.

*

As he was about to enter the opera-house, the Councillor of State was struck by the somewhat gloomy aspect of the

82

building at the rue Le Peletier entrance, with no gendarmes, no lights or attendants, no crush barriers in evidence. He consulted the poster, and saw a white sticker with the ritual announcement conspicuous across it: PERFORMANCE CANCELLED OWING TO INDISPOSITION.

He at once rushed off to Josépha's lodgings in the rue Chauchat, for like all the singers and dancers attached to the Opera, she lived near by.

'Whom do you wish to see, Monsieur?' the porter asked him, much to his surprise.

'Don't you recognize me?' the Baron asked, in some uneasiness.

'On the contrary, Monsieur, it is because I have the honour to remember Monsieur that I inquire: "Where are you going?"'

The Baron was seized with a mortal chill.

'What has happened?' he asked.

'If Monsieur le Baron went up to Mademoiselle Mirah's apartment, he would find Mademoiselle Héloïse Brisetout there, and Monsieur Bixiou, Monsieur Léon de Lora, Monsieur Lousteau, Monsieur de Vernisset, Monsieur Stidmann, and a number of women reeking of patchouli, all having a house-warming party.'

'But where is ...?'

'Mademoiselle Mirah? I really don't know if it would be right to tell you.'

The Baron slipped two five-franc pieces into the man's palm.

'Well, she's living in the rue de la Ville-l'Évêque now, in a house which they do say the Duc d'Hérouville gave her,' the porter said, in a confidential whisper, behind his hand.

Having obtained the number of this house, the Baron took a *milord*, and was set down in front of one of those pretty modern double-doored houses where everything, even to the gas lamp at the entrance, makes a display of luxury.

The Baron, in his blue coat, with white cravat, white waistcoat, nankeen trousers, shining patent leather boots, well-starched shirt-frills, looked like a belated guest to the door-keeper of this new Eden. His imposing presence, his way of walking, everything about him, seemed to justify this supposition.

The porter rang, and a footman appeared in the hall. The footman, new like the house, made way for the Baron, who said in the voice of a man accustomed to Imperial command, with an Imperial gesture:

'Have this card sent in to Mademoiselle Josépha.'

The shorn sheep mechanically looked round the room he found himself in, and saw an ante-chamber filled with exotic flowers, whose furnishings must have cost at least twenty thousand francs. The footman returned to ask Monsieur to wait in the drawing-room until the party at dinner came in to take their coffee.

Although the Baron had known the undoubtedly extravagant luxury of the Empire, which had created settings – shortlived though they may have been – that had cost fantastic sums, he stood dazzled, dumbfounded, in this drawing-room, whose three windows opened upon a fairytale garden, one of those gardens brought into existence in a month with soil carried to the site and flowers planted out almost in bloom, whose lawns seem to have been produced by alchemists' magic. It was not only the studied elegance that he found admirable – the gilding, the costly carving in the style known as Pompadour, the sumptuous materials – for any tradesman might have ordered and obtained these by the mere expenditure of an ocean of gold. Much more marvellous were the works of art, of a kind that only princes have the discrimination and the ability to choose, find, pay for, and give away: two paintings by Greuze and two by Watteau, two heads by Van Dyck, two landscapes by Ruysdael, two by Le Guaspre, a Rembrandt, a Holbein, a Murillo, and a Titian, two Teniers and two Metzus, a van Huysum and an Abraham Mignon – in sum, two hundred thousand francs' worth of pictures, superbly mounted. The frames were worth almost as much as the canvases.

'Ah! You understand now, old boy?' said Josépha.

She had come on tiptoe through a noiseless door, over Persian carpets, and surprised her adorer in one of those moments of stupefaction when through the ringing in one's ears one can hear only the tolling of disaster.

The use of the expression *old boy*, addressed to such a high official as the Baron, admirably illustrates the audacity with which these creatures pull down the greatest to their own level. The Baron was left paralysed. Josépha, all in white and yellow, was adorned for this festivity so beautifully that even in this magnificently luxurious setting she could still shine, like the rarest jewel of all.

'Isn't it splendid?' she went on. 'The Duke spent on it all the money he made on a company he floated, when he sold the shares on a rise. He's no fool, my little Duke, eh? There's no one like the great lords of the old families for knowing how to change pit coal into gold. The notary brought me the title-deeds to sign before dinner, with the receipted bills. They're all like lords here: d'Escrignon, Rastignac, Maxime, Lenoncourt, Verneuil, Laginski, Rochefide, La Palférine; or bankers, like Nucingen and du Tillet; and Antonia, and Malaga, and Carabine, and Schontz are here as well; and they're all so sorry for you in your hard luck. Yes, old dear, you're invited to join them, but only on condition that you drink the equal of two bottles of Hungarian wine, champagne and *Cap*, straight off, to catch up with them. We're all too tight here, my pet, to do anything but put off the performance. My director is as drunk as a cornet – he's reached the *couac-couac* stage.'

'Oh, Josépha!' cried the Baron.

'Explanations are so stupid!' she interrupted him, smiling. 'Can't you see? Have you got anything like the six hundred thousand francs that this house and the furniture cost? Can you give me the papers for a thirty-thousand-franc annuity in a white paper bag full of sugared almonds, like the Duke did? Such a nice idea!'

'It's iniquitous!' said the Councillor of State, who in that moment of fury would have bartered his wife's diamonds for the chance to borrow the Duc d'Hérouville's shoes for twenty-four hours.

'Iniquity is my business!' she retorted. 'Ah, just look how seriously you take the thing! Why couldn't you have thought up some nice speculation like that? Goodness knows, my poor dyed tom-cat, you ought to be thankful to me. I'm leaving you just when if I stayed I might easily be helping you to squander your wife's future, and your daughter's dowry, and ... oh, you're crying! The Empire is passing! I salute the Empire!'

She struck a tragic pose, and declaimed:

'"Hulot, they call you, sir! I know you now no more!"'

And she returned to the dining-room.

The door, as she opened it, let out, in a sudden explosion, a burst of light, a roar from the revel reaching its climax, and the odours of a first-class banquet.

The singer turned to look back through the half-open door, and finding Hulot standing like a bronze statue where she had left him, she took a step forward and reappeared.

'Monsieur,' she said, 'I handed the cast-offs from the rue Chauchat on to Bixiou's little Héloïse Brisetout; but if you want to collect your cotton night-cap and your bootjack from her, and your stays and your whisker-wax, I told her that you were to have them.'

The effect of this horrible jeer was to make the Baron flee as Lot must have fled Gomorrah, but without, like Lot's wife, looking back.

Hulot walked home, striding like a madman and talking to himself, and found his family placidly playing whist for two-sou stakes, just as he had left them. When she saw her husband, poor Adeline thought that some terrible disaster had happened, some disgrace. She gave her cards to Hortense, and drew Hector into the same little room in which, five hours before, Crevel had prophesied that she was destined to suffer the most humiliating miseries of poverty.

'What is the matter?' she asked, in alarm.

'Oh, forgive me, but I must tell you about these outrages!' And for ten minutes he poured out his fury.

'But my dear,' his poor wife answered heroically, 'creatures like that don't know what love is, the pure devoted love that is what you deserve. How could you, a man of such intelligence, dream of attempting to be a millionaire's rival?'

'Dearest Adeline!' exclaimed the Baron, putting his arms

86

round his wife and pressing her to his heart. The Baroness had poured balm on his vanity's bleeding wounds.

'It's true enough that if the Duc d'Hérouville's fortune were taken away, between the two of us *she* would not hesitate!' he said.

'My dear,' Adeline went on, making a supreme effort, 'if you absolutely must have mistresses, why do you not follow Crevel's example, and take women who do not expect much, from a class content for a long time with the expenditure of a little money? We should all gain by it. I can believe in your need, but I don't understand what empty pride – '

'Oh! what a dear and wonderful wife you are!' he interrupted. 'I am an old fool; I don't deserve to have an angel like you as my partner.'

'I am just a Josephine to my Napoleon,' she answered, with a touch of sadness.

'Josephine could not compare with you,' he said. 'Come, I'll play a game of whist with my brother and the children. I'll have to apply myself to my duties as a family man, find a husband for Hortense, and bury the libertine. . . .'

His resignation and kindness touched poor Adeline so deeply that she was impelled to say:

'That creature has very poor taste to prefer anyone in the world to my Hector. Ah! I would not give you up for all the money in the world. How can a woman leave you, who has the happiness to be loved by you!'

The look with which the Baron rewarded his wife's fanatical devotion confirmed her in her belief that gentleness and submissiveness were a woman's most powerful weapons. She was mistaken in this. Noble sentiments pushed to extremes produce results very like those of the worst vices. Bonaparte became Emperor by turning cannon on the crowd, only two paces away from the spot where Louis XVI lost his kingdom and his head because he would not allow the blood of a certain Monsieur Sauce to be shed. . . .

Next day, Hortense, who had put Wenceslas's seal under her pillow, not to be separated from it while she slept, was up early and sent a message to her father asking him to come to the garden when he was dressed.

At about half past nine her father, willing to indulge his daughter in her wish, gave her his arm, and they walked together along the quays, by the pont Royal, and reached the place du Carrousel.

'Look as if we are idly sauntering, Papa,' said Hortense, as they came through the entrance to cross that great square.

'Idly sauntering, here?' her father teased her.

'We are supposed to be going to the museum, and over there,' she said, pointing to the stalls backing on the walls of the houses that stand at right angles to the rue du Doyenné. 'Look, there are antique shops, pictures ...'

'Your cousin lives down there.'

'I know she does, but she mustn't see us. ...'

'And what do you want to do?' asked the Baron, finding himself only thirty yards or so from the window at which he had seen Madame Marneffe, of whom he was suddenly reminded.

Hortense had led her father to one of the shops on the corner of the block of houses that run the length of the galleries of the old Louvre, facing the Hôtel de Nantes. She went into the shop. Her father remained outside, staring at the windows of the lovely little lady who, the day before, had left her image in the old beau's heart as if to console him for the wound that he was shortly to receive, and he could not resist the thought of putting his wife's advice into effect.

'Let's fall back upon the bourgeoisie,' he said to himself, as he recalled Madame Marneffe's adorable perfections. 'That little woman will soon make me forget Josépha and her greed.'

This is what now happened simultaneously, inside the shop and outside it.

As he scrutinized his new flame's windows, the Baron caught sight of the husband, who, as he brushed his greatcoat with his own hands, was evidently on the watch for someone coming into view on the square. Afraid that he might be noticed and later recognized, the amorous Baron turned his back on the rue du Doyenné, but not squarely, leaving himself in a position to glance down it from time to time. As he turned, he was brought almost face to face with Madame

Marneffe who, coming from the embankment, was turning the corner on her way home. Valérie experienced a slight shock on encountering the Baron's astonished gaze, and met it with a primly rebuking glance.

'Pretty creature!' cried the Baron. 'A man could easily lose his head over you!'

'Ah, Monsieur!' she answered, turning as if in spite of herself, against her better judgement. 'You are Monsieur le Baron Hulot, are you not?'

The Baron, more and more taken aback, made a gesture of assent.

'Well, since chance has twice brought us face to face, and I have been fortunate enough to arouse your curiosity or interest, I will tell you that instead of losing your head you ought to see that justice is done. My husband's fate depends on you.'

'In what way?' the Baron asked gallantly.

'He's employed in your department at the War Office, Monsieur Lebrun's section, Monsieur Coquet's office,' she answered, smiling.

'I feel myself in a state of mind, Madame ... Madame ...?'

'Madame Marneffe.'

'My little Madame Marneffe, to do injustice for your fair sake. ... In your house lives a cousin of mine. I will go to see her one of these days, as soon as possible. Come and make your request to me there.'

'Forgive my boldness, Monsieur le Baron. You will understand how I could venture to speak to you like this when I tell you that I have no one to look after my interests.'

'Aha!'

'Oh, Monsieur! You misunderstand me,' she said, lowering her eyes. To the Baron it seemed as if the sun had suddenly gone in.

'I am in desperate straits, but I am a respectable woman,' she continued. 'Six months ago I lost my only guardian, Marshal Montcornet.'

'Ah! You are his daughter?'

'Yes, Monsieur, but he never acknowledged me.'

'So that he could leave you some share in his fortune?'

'He left me nothing, Monsieur, for no will was ever found.'

'Oh, poor little woman! The Marshal was struck down suddenly, by apoplexy. Well, you must look to the future, Madame: something is due to the daughter of a man who was a Chevalier Bayard of the Empire.'

Madame Marneffe bowed graciously in farewell, as proud of her success as the Baron was of his.

'Where the devil can she be coming from so early in the morning?' he speculated, contemplating the graceful movement of her dress, to which she lent a perhaps exaggerated swing. 'She looks too tired to be returning from the bath, and her husband is waiting for her. It's very strange, and makes one wonder.'

Once Madame Marneffe had gone into the house, it occurred to the Baron to investigate what his daughter was doing in the shop. As he went in, with his eyes still fixed on Madame Marneffe's windows, he nearly collided with a pale young man with sparkling grey eyes, dressed in a light coat of black merino, coarse drill trousers, high-cut boots of yellow leather, who shot from the shop like a madman; and he watched him run towards Madame Marneffe's house and enter it.

As she slipped into the shop, Hortense had immediately noticed the famous group well displayed on a table in the centre, in full view as one entered. Quite apart from the circumstances in which she had learned of it, the work would certainly have struck the girl's attention by that quality, which one can only call *brio*, possessed by great works of art. In Italy, the girl herself might indeed have posed as a model for a personification of Brio.

Not all the works of men of genius possess to the same degree that brilliant quality, that splendour which every eye can see, even the eyes of the ignorant. There are certain paintings by Raphael – for instance the famous *Transfiguration*, the *Madonna of Foligno,* the frescoes of the *Stations* in the Vatican – that do not instantly command admiration like the *Violin Player* in the Sciarra Gallery, the portraits of the *Doni*, and the *Vision of Ezekiel* in the Pitti Gallery, the *Christ Carrying the Cross* at the Borghese, and the *Marriage of the Virgin* in the Brera, in Milan. The *St John the Baptist* of the Tribune, *St Luke Painting the Virgin* in the Academy at Rome, have not the charm of the portrait of *Leo X,* and the Dresden *Virgin.* The paintings, nevertheless, are of equal excellence. One may indeed go further: the *Stations,* the *Transfiguration,* the monochromes, and the three easel pictures in the Vatican are in the highest degree sublime and perfect. But these masterpieces demand from even the most expert critic a certain effort of concentrated attention and close study, if they are to be fully grasped; while the *Violinist,* the *Marriage of the Virgin,* the *Vision of Ezekiel,* enter our hearts spontaneously through our eyes' double gateway and make their own place there. We are enchanted to receive them so, without effort – it is not art's highest achievement that they have revealed to us, it is art's sweet pleasure. The distinction proves that in the creation of works of art the same chance is at work as in the creation of children. Some children are born with a silver spoon in their mouths; are talented, beautiful, and born without pain to their mothers; the world smiles on them, and success crowns all they do. There are, we may say, the flowers of genius that are like the flowers sprung from love.

This *brio,* an untranslatable Italian word which we are beginning to use, is characteristic of an artist's youthful works. It is the product of the vitality, mettle, and ardour of young talent; and although its spirit may return again in certain happy hours, *brio,* later, no longer bursts from the artist's heart. Instead of actively projecting it into his works like a volcano hurling forth its fires, he is acted upon, he is affected by influences from outside, he owes his *brio* to circumstances: to love, to rivalry, often to hatred, more often still to the need to live up to his reputation.

Wenceslas's group was to his future works what Raphael's *Marriage of the Virgin* was to his completed life's work, the first steps of talent, taken with inimitable grace, with the zest of childhood, and revealing childhood's charming plenitude, its vigour belied by the pink and white plumpness whose dimples seem to be echoes of a mother's laughter. Prince Eugène, they say, paid four hundred thousand francs for

Raphael's painting, worth a million in a country poor in Raphaels; and one would not give the same sum for the finest of his frescoes, even though, judged by the standards of supreme art, their value is much greater.

Hortense restrained her admiration as she reflected on the amount of her saved pocket-money, and assumed a casually indifferent air to ask the dealer: 'How much is that?'

'Fifteen hundred francs,' he replied, glancing towards a young man sitting on a stool in a corner.

The young man stared, bemused, as he looked on the living masterpiece that Baron Hulot had created. Hortense, enlightened by the dealer's look, then recognized him as the artist by the colour that flowed into a face pale with suffering. She saw a sparkle in a pair of grey eyes, lit there by her question; she looked at the thin fine-drawn face, like the face of a monk worn by ascetic discipline; she dwelt with delight upon a red well-chiselled mouth, a delicate chin, and chestnut hair of the fine silky texture characteristic of the Slav.

'If it were twelve hundred francs,' she said, 'I would ask you to have it sent to me.'

'It is antique, Mademoiselle,' the dealer pointed out, thinking, like all his fellows, that he had said everything with this *ne plus ultra,* supreme accolade of the bric-à-brac trade.

'Excuse me, Monsieur, it was made this year,' she answered gently, 'and that is precisely why I am here, to ask you – if you will agree to that price – to send the artist to us, for we may be able to obtain quite important commissions for him.'

'If he gets twelve hundred francs, what do I get out of it? I am a dealer,' the man said, good-humouredly enough.

'Ah, that's true,' the girl replied, not hiding her scorn.

'Oh, Mademoiselle, take it! I'll settle things with the dealer,' exclaimed the Livonian, unable to restrain himself.

Fascinated by Hortense's noble beauty and by her evident love of the arts, he added: 'I am the sculptor of the group. For the past ten days I've been coming three times a day to see if someone would realize its value and make an offer for it. You are the first to admire it. Take it!'

'Come an hour from now, with the dealer, Monsieur – here is my father's card,' Hortense said in reply.

Then, as she saw the dealer go into another room to wrap the group in cloths, she added in a whisper, to the artist's amazement, for he thought he must be dreaming: 'In the interests of your career, Monsieur Wenceslas, don't show the card or mention the name of your purchaser to Mademoiselle Fischer. She is our cousin.'

The words 'our cousin' made the artist's eyes dazzle; he caught a glimpse of paradise, at sight of one of the Eves fallen from there. He had been dreaming of the beautiful cousin of whom Lisbeth had spoken, just as Hortense had dreamed of her cousin's sweetheart, and when she had entered the shop he had thought: 'Ah! if only she could be like that!'

One may imagine the look the two lovers exchanged – it was a flame; for virtuous people in love have not the least hypocrisy.

'Well, what in the world are you doing in here?' Hortense's father demanded.

'I have spent my savings, twelve hundred francs. Come home and see.'

She put her arm through her father's again, as he repeated: 'Twelve hundred francs?'

'Thirteen hundred, actually! ... but you will lend me the difference.'

'And what could you possibly find there to spend so much money on?'

'Ah, that's the question!' the girl replied gaily. 'If I have found a husband, it won't be wasted money.'

'A husband, child, in that shop?'

'Listen, darling Papa, would you forbid me to marry a great artist?'

'No, child. A great artist nowadays is an untitled prince; he has fame and fortune, the two highest social advantages ... after virtue,' he added, a little sanctimoniously.

'Of course,' answered Hortense. 'And what do you think of sculpture?'

'It's a very unrewarding profession,' said Hulot, shaking his head. 'One needs powerful patrons, as well as great talent, for the Government is the only purchaser. It's an art without a market nowadays, when there are no longer people who live splendidly; and there are no great fortunes now, no hereditary mansions, nor entailed estates. We have only house-room for small pictures, small statues; and *smallness*, the petty, is a menace to the arts.'

'But suppose he were a great artist who could find a market?' persisted Hortense.

'That would solve the problem.'

'And with influence?'

'Better still!'

'And titled?'

'Come, come!'

'A Count?'

'And a sculptor!'

'He has no money.'

'And he is counting on Mademoiselle Hortense Hulot's?' said the Baron banteringly, with a keen searching look into his daughter's eyes.

'This great artist, a Count and a sculptor, has just seen your daughter for the first time in his life, and for a period of five minutes, Monsieur le Baron,' Hortense answered her father, serenely. 'Yesterday, do you hear, my dear sweet good Papa, while you were at the Chamber, Mama fainted. That faint, which she said was just an attack of nerves, was the result of some distress caused by negotiations for my marriage having been broken off, for she told me that, in order to get me off your hands –'

'She is too fond of you to have used an expression –'

'Which is rather unparliamentary,' finished Hortense, laughing. 'No, she didn't use those words; but I know that a marriageable daughter who doesn't get married is a very heavy cross for proper parents to bear. Well, Mama thinks that if a resolute talented man presented himself, who would be satisfied with a thirty thousand franc dowry, we should all be pleased! The fact is that she thought it right to prepare me for the modesty of my future lot in life, and prevent me from indulging in any too grand castles in the air. And that means that my marriage has been called off and there is no dowry.'

'Your mother is an exceedingly good, noble, and wise

woman,' her father said, deeply humiliated, in spite of considerable relief at this confidence.

'Yesterday, she told me that you would allow her to sell her diamonds to provide for my marriage; but I would rather she kept her diamonds and that I found a husband for myself. I think I have found the man, the suitor who answers to Mama's specifications.'

'There! In the place du Carrousel! In one morning?'

'Oh, Papa, there's more behind this than you know,' she said, teasingly.

'Well, come now, dear child, just tell your old father the whole story,' he coaxed her, concealing his uneasiness.

Under promise of absolute secrecy, Hortense related the substance of her conversations with Cousin Bette. Then, when they had reached home, she showed her father the famous seal to prove how well-founded her conjectures were. The father marvelled, in his heart, at the profound insight and the address of young girls acting on instinct, and admired the simplicity of the plan which an ideal love had suggested, in the course of one night, to this innocent girl.

'You'll see the masterpiece that I have just bought. They're going to bring it, and dear Wenceslas is coming with the dealer. The man who created a group like that is bound to make his fortune; but you must use your influence to get him a commission for a statue, and then rooms at the Institut. . . .'

'How you do run on!' exclaimed her father. 'If you were given your head you would be a wife as soon as it was legally possible, in eleven days. . . .'

'Does one have to wait eleven days?' she said, laughing. 'It took me only five minutes to fall in love with him, just as you did with Mama, at first sight! And he loves me, as if we had known each other for two years. Yes,' she affirmed, as her father shook his head doubtfully, 'I have read ten volumes of love written in his eyes. And you and Mama are surely bound to accept him as my future husband when you have been shown that he is a man of genius? Sculpture is the highest art of all!' she cried, clapping her hands and skipping. 'Listen, I'll tell you everything. . . .'

'So there's more to tell?' her father asked, with a smile.

The transparent innocence of her eager chatter had completely reassured the Baron.

'A declaration of the utmost importance,' she replied. 'I loved him before I knew him, but I am madly in love since I saw him an hour ago.'

'Rather too madly,' observed the Baron, who was delighted and amused by the spectacle of this artless passion.

'Don't make me suffer for confiding in you,' she begged him. 'It is so sweet to cry to one's father's heart "I love, I am so happy to be in love!" You will soon see my Wenceslas ... his brow, shadowed with melancholy! Grey eyes shining in the sun of genius! ... And he looks so distinguished! Is Livonia a beautiful country, do you think? My Cousin Bette marry that young man? Why, she's old enough to be his mother ... it would be a crime! How jealous I feel of what she must have done for him! It seems to me that she will not be very pleased to see me marry him.'

'Come, my angel, we must not keep anything from your mother,' the Baron said.

'But I would have to show her the seal, and I promised not to give my cousin away – she says she's afraid of Mama's making fun of her,' replied Hortense.

'You show some scruples about the seal, but steal your Cousin Bette's sweetheart!'

'I promised about the seal, but made no promises about the man who made it.'

This romantic plan of Hortense's, of a patriarchal simplicity, fitted in remarkably well with the family's secret straits. The Baron, however, when he had commended his daughter for confiding in him, told her that from now on she must rely altogether on her parents' discretion.

'You understand, my dear child, that it is not for you to make sure that your cousin's sweetheart *is* a Count, and has his papers in order, and that his behaviour warrants our trust. As for your cousin, she refused five offers of marriage when she was twenty years younger; she won't stand in your way, I'll answer for that.'

'Listen, Papa. If you want to see me married, don't speak to my cousin about this sweetheart until you come to sign my marriage contract. I've been questioning her about the matter for the last six months! ... Well, there's something unaccountable about her. . . .'

'What, exactly?' said her father, surprised and interested.

'Well, there's no good-will in the way she looks at me when I go too far, even in fun, about her friend. Make your inquiries, but let me steer my own ship. I know what I'm doing, and that should reassure you!'

'Jesus said, "Suffer the little children to come unto me!" You are one of those who go their own way,' the Baron remarked, with a hint of irony.

After lunch the dealer, the artist, and the group were announced. The sudden colour in her daughter's face made the Baroness first uneasy and then watchful, and Hortense's confusion, the ardour in her eyes, soon betrayed the secret so ill-concealed in her young heart.

Count Steinbock, dressed in black, struck the Baron as a very distinguished young man.

'Would you undertake a large bronze figure?' he asked him, with the group in his hand.

Having admired it, with some confidence in his own judgement, he handed the group to his wife, who did not know much about sculpture.

'Don't you think it's lovely, Mama?' Hortense whispered in her mother's ear.

'To make a statue, Monsieur le Baron, is not so difficult as to model a clock like this one, which the dealer has kindly brought,' the artist replied to the Baron's question.

The dealer, at the dining-room sideboard, was busy unwrapping the wax model of the twelve Hours pursued in their flight by Cupids.

'Leave the clock with me,' the Baron said, astonished at the beauty of the piece. 'I want to show it to the Minister of Home Affairs and the Minister of Commerce.'

'Who is this young man that you are so interested in?' the Baroness asked her daughter.

'An artist rich enough to exploit this model might make a hundred thousand francs from it,' said the antique-dealer, looking knowing and mysterious, as he noticed the sympathy between the artist and the girl that shone in their eyes. 'He would only have to sell twenty casts at eight thousand francs, for each cast would cost about a thousand francs to make; and if he numbered the casts and destroyed the model it would be easy enough to find twenty patrons of art pleased to be among the few to possess the work.'

'A hundred thousand francs!' exclaimed Steinbock, looking first at the dealer, and then in turn at Hortense, the Baron, and the Baroness.

'Yes, a hundred thousand francs!' the dealer repeated, 'and if I had the money I would give you twenty thousand for it myself. With the power to destroy the model, I should be making a good investment. But one of the Princes would certainly pay thirty or forty thousand for this fine piece, to adorn his drawing-room. There has never yet been a clock made, in the history of the arts, able to please both the man in the street and the connoisseur, and this one, Monsieur, solves the problem.'

'This is for yourself,' Hortense said, giving the dealer six gold coins, and he left.

'Say nothing to anyone about this visit,' the artist said to the dealer, following him to the door. 'If you are asked where we have taken the group, mention the Duc d'Hérouville's name – you know, the well-known collector who lives in the rue de Varennes.'

The dealer nodded.

'Your name is ...?' the Baron asked the artist when he returned.

'Count Steinbock.'

'Have you papers to prove your identity?'

'Yes, Monsieur le Baron, papers in Russian and German, but not legally authenticated.'

'Do you feel that you are capable of undertaking a nine-foot statue?'

'Yes, Monsieur.'

'Well, if the persons that I am going to consult are pleased with these examples of your work, I can obtain a commission for you – a statue of Marshal Montcornet, which is to be erected at Père-Lachaise over his grave. The Minister of War and his old officers of the Imperial Guard are subscribing a considerable sum, so that we should have a deciding voice in choosing the artist.'

'Oh, that would make my fortune, Monsieur!' said Steinbock, who was dazed by so much good luck descending upon him all at once.

'Set your mind at rest,' the Baron replied graciously. 'If the two Ministers to whom I shall show your group and this model admire the pieces, you are well on the road to success.'

Hortense squeezed her father's arm hard enough to make him wince.

'Bring me your papers, and say nothing of your hopes to anyone, not even to our old Cousin Bette.'

'Lisbeth?' exclaimed Madame Hulot, at last understanding the connexion, although unable to guess the point of contact.

'I could give you some proof of my talent by making a bust of Madame,' Wenceslas added. Struck by Madame Hulot's beauty, the artist had been standing for the last moment or two comparing mother and daughter.

'Well, Monsieur, life promises well for you,' the Baron said, completely won over by Count Steinbock's fine and distinguished appearance. 'You will soon discover that talent does not go unrecognized for long in Paris, and that hard work always brings its reward here.'

Hortense, blushing, handed the young man a pretty Algerian purse containing sixty gold pieces. The artist's colour rose in response, with a reaction – easy enough to interpret – of shocked pride, of insulted patrician dignity.

'Is this, by any chance, the first money you have received for your work?' the Baroness asked.

'Yes, Madame, for my art, though not for my labour, for I have been a workman.'

'Well, we may hope that my daughter's money brings you good luck!' said Monsieur Hulot.

'And have no hesitation in accepting it,' the Baron added, seeing that Wenceslas was still holding the purse in his hand, and making no move to pocket it. 'We shall get back that sum from some nobleman, or perhaps one of the Princes, who may be glad to repay it with interest in order to possess this fine work.'

'Oh, I like it too much, Papa, to give it to anyone, even the Prince Royal, the Duc d'Orléans!'

'I could make another group, prettier than this, for Mademoiselle. ...'

'It would not be this one,' she answered. And, as if ashamed at having said too much, she walked out into the garden.

'Well, I shall break the mould and the model when I get home,' said Steinbock.

'Bring me your papers, then, and you shall hear from me shortly if I find what my impression of you leads me to expect, Monsieur.'

Thus dismissed, the artist was obliged to take his leave. He bowed to Madame Hulot and to Hortense, who had come in from the garden again expressly to receive that bow; then he went to wander in the Tuileries, unable, not daring, to return to his attic, where the tyrant who ruled his days would wear him out with questions and wrest his secret from him.

Hortense's lover designed in his mind groups and single figures by the hundred; he felt strong enough to hew the marble with his own hand – like Canova, a man of frail physique too, who all but killed himself in so doing. He was transfigured by Hortense, who was now for him a living, visible inspiration.

'Now then!' said the Baroness to her daughter. 'What does all this mean?'

'Well, dear Mama, you have just seen Cousin Bette's sweetheart, who, I hope, is now mine. ... But shut your eyes, pretend to know nothing about it. Oh, dear! I meant to keep it all from you, and here I am telling you everything. ...'

'Good-bye, children,' broke in the Baron, kissing his daughter and wife. 'I'll go, perhaps, to see our Nanny. I may find out a good deal about the young man from her.'

'Be careful, Papa,' Hortense said again.

'Oh, my child!' the Baroness exclaimed, when Hortense had finished reciting her poem, the last canto of which was that morning's adventure. 'My dear little girl! The deepest guile on earth is the guile of innocence!'

Genuine passions have an instinct of their own. Set a dish of fruit before an epicure: he will unerringly, without even looking, pick out the best. In the same way, if well-bred young girls are left absolutely free to choose their own husbands, when they are in a position to have those they naturally select they will rarely make a mistake. Natural instincts are infallible; and nature's action in such cases is called 'love at first sight'. Love at first sight is quite simply *second sight*.

The Baroness's happiness, though veiled by maternal dignity, was as great as her daughter's; for of the three ways in which Hortense might be married of which Crevel had spoken, the best, the one most to her taste, seemed likely to be achieved. She saw in this turn of events an answer from Providence to her fervent prayers.

It occurred to Mademoiselle Fischer's prisoner, obliged in the end to return to his lodging, to disguise his lover's joy as the joy of the artist, delighted at his first success.

'Victory! My group has been sold to the Duc d'Hérouville, and he is going to commission some work from me,' he said, throwing twelve hundred francs in gold on the table before the old maid.

As one may imagine, he had hidden Hortense's purse; he wore it next his heart.

'Well,' answered Lisbeth, 'that's a good thing, for I have been wearing myself out working. You see, my boy, that money comes in very slowly in the trade you've chosen, for this is the first you have received, and here you've been grinding away for nearly five years. This money is barely enough to repay what you have cost me since I got that IOU in return for my savings. But don't worry,' she added, when she had counted it, 'this money will all be spent on you. We have enough here to last for a year. After that, in a year from now you'll be able to pay off your debts and have a good sum for yourself too, if you keep on at this rate.'

When he saw that his ruse was successful, Wenceslas embroidered his tale about the Duc d'Hérouville.

'I want to get you fashionable black clothes and buy you

some new linen, for you must be well dressed when you go to see your patrons,' was Bette's response. 'And then you'll have to have larger and more suitable rooms than your horrible attic, and furnish them comfortably. How gay you are! You've changed somehow,' she added, scrutinizing Wenceslas.

'They say my group's a masterpiece!'

'Well, so much the better. Make more!' replied the unsympathetic old maid, matter-of-fact to the last degree and quite incapable of understanding the joy of triumph or of apprehending beauty in the arts. 'Don't go on thinking of what has been sold; make something new to sell. You have spent two hundred silver francs, to say nothing of your labour and time, on that wretched *Samson*. Your clock will cost you more than two thousand francs to cast and have completed. Come, if you take my advice you'll finish those two little boys crowning a little girl with cornflowers – that will take the Parisians' fancy! I shall call on Monsieur Graff, the tailor, on my way to Monsieur Crevel. Now go up to your own room, and let me get dressed.'

Next day the Baron, now quite taken in Madame Marneffe's toils, went to see Cousin Bette, who was much surprised to find him on the threshold when she opened the door for he had never paid her a visit before. And the thought crossed her mind: 'Can Hortense be after my sweetheart?' She had heard the evening before, from Monsieur Crevel, that marriage discussions with the Councillor of the Supreme Court had been broken off.

'What, Cousin! You here? This is the first time in your life that you have come to see me, so it certainly can't be for love of my beautiful eyes!'

'Beautiful indeed! That's true,' replied the Baron. 'You have the most beautiful eyes I have ever seen. . . .'

'What have you come for? I'm really quite ashamed to receive you in such a miserable place.'

The first of Cousin Bette's two rooms served as drawing-room, dining-room, kitchen, and workroom. The furniture was that of a prosperous working-class home, with straw-bottomed walnut chairs, a small walnut dining-table, a work-table. There were colour prints framed in dark stained wood, short muslin curtains at the windows, a large walnut cupboard. The floor was well rubbed up, shining with cleanliness and polish, and there was not a speck of dust anywhere in the room. But the whole scene was very cold in general effect: a perfect Terborch picture complete in every detail, even to the grey tone produced by a wallpaper, once bluish, but now faded to the colour of linen. As for the bedroom, no one had ever set foot inside that.

The Baron, glancing about him, took it all in; saw the stamp of indifferent taste and indifferent circumstances on every piece, from the cast-iron stove to the kitchen utensils, and felt a sickened repulsion as he reflected: 'So this is virtue!'

'Why have I come?' he said aloud. 'You are much too sharp-witted not to guess in the end, so I had better tell you.' He sat down as he spoke, and, pulling the pleated muslin curtains apart a little way, looked across the court. 'In this house there is a very pretty woman ...'

'Madame Marneffe! Oh, now I see!' she said, in complete comprehension. 'And what about Josépha?'

'Alas, Cousin, there's an end of Josépha. I've been dismissed like a lackey.'

'And you want ...?' the cousin asked, regarding the Baron with the dignity of a prude taking offence a quarter of an hour before she need.

'As Madame Marneffe is a lady, an official's wife, and you can visit her without compromising yourself, I would like to see you on neighbourly good terms with her. Oh! don't be afraid; she will have the greatest respect for the Director's cousin.'

At that moment the rustle of a dress was heard on the stair, and the light pad of a woman's feet wearing fine soft ankle-boots. The footsteps came to a stop on the landing. There was a double tap on the door, and Madame Marneffe appeared.

'Forgive me, Mademoiselle, for this intrusion; but I did not find you in yesterday when I came to call on you. We are neighbours, and if I had known that you were the Councillor of State's cousin, I should long ago have asked you to speak to him on my behalf. I saw Monsieur le Directeur go in, and so I ventured to come; because my husband, Monsieur le Baron, has talked to me about a report on the Ministry personnel that is to be submitted to the Minister tomorrow.'

She appeared to be agitated, fluttering with emotion. She had in fact simply run upstairs.

'You have no need to ask favours, fair lady,' the Baron replied. 'It is for me to ask the favour of an interview with you.'

'Very well, if Mademoiselle does not mind, please come!' said Madame Marneffe.

'Yes, go, Cousin. I'll see you presently,' said Cousin Bette discreetly.

The Parisienne was banking so heavily on Monsieur le Directeur's visit and helpful understanding, that she had not only made a toilet suitable for such an interview herself, but had adorned her apartment too. Since early morning, flowers– bought on credit – had decorated it. Marneffe had helped his wife to clean the furniture, polishing up the smallest objects to reflect the light, using soap, brushes, dusters in all directions. Valérie was anxious to be seen in fresh bright surroundings, in order to appear attractive to Monsieur le Directeur, attractive enough to have the right to be cruel, to play hard to get, with all the art of modern tactics; as if she were holding a sweetmeat out of reach to tantalize a child. She had taken Hulot's measure. Give a hard-pressed Parisian woman twenty-four hours to work, and she can bring down a government.

A man of the Empire, accustomed to Empire manners, could know nothing at all of the conventions of modern love, the new fashionable scruples, the different mode of conversation invented since 1830, in which the poor weak woman succeeds in being accepted as the victim of her lover's desires, a kind of sister of charity binding up wounds, a self-sacrificing angel. This new art of love uses an enormous number of evangelical phrases in the devil's work. Passion, for example, is a martyrdom. One aspires towards the ideal, the infinite. Both parties desire to be refined through love. All these fine phrases are a pretext for heaping fuel on the flames, adding more ardour to the act, more frenzy to the fall, than in the past. This hypocrisy, characteristic of our times, has corrupted gallantry. A pair of lovers profess to be two angels, and behave like two demons if they have a chance. Love had no time to analyse itself like this between two campaigns, and in 1809 its victories were achieved as swiftly as the Empire's victories. During the Restoration, the handsome Hulot, now a ladies' man again, had begun by consoling some former partners who had fallen, at that time, like extinguished stars from the political firmament; and gone on, as an old man, to let himself be captured by the Jenny Cadines and Joséphas.

Madame Marneffe had placed her guns in position according to what she had learned of the Director's background, which her husband had filled in for her in detail after making some inquiries at the office. The comedy of modern sentiment might have the charm of novelty for the Baron, so Valérie's plans were laid, and it may be said at once that the trial of its effectiveness that she made that morning answered all her hopes.

Thanks to these romantic, sentimental, novelettish manoeuvres, Valérie, without having promised anything, obtained for her husband the position of deputy head clerk of his office and the Cross of the Legion of Honour.

This campaign was naturally not conducted without dinners at the Rocher de Cancale, visits to the theatre, numerous presents of mantillas, scarves, dresses, and jewellery. The apartment in the rue du Doyenné was not satisfactory; the Baron meditated a scheme for furnishing one in magnificent style in the rue Vanneau, in a charming modern house.

Monsieur Marneffe obtained a fortnight's leave of absence, to be taken in a month's time, in order to attend to some affairs in the country; and a bonus as well. He promised himself a little trip to Switzerland, to study female form there.

Although Baron Hulot was busy in the interests of the lady, he did not forget the young man whose patron he also was. The Minister of Commerce, Count Popinot, was a lover of the arts; he gave two thousand francs for a replica of the Samson group on condition that the mould was broken, so that his Samson and Mademoiselle Hulot's should be the only two in existence. This group excited the admiration of a Prince. He was shown the model of the clock, ordered it on condition that no replica should be made, and offered thirty thousand francs for it. The artists consulted, among them Stidmann, were satisfied that the man who had designed these two works could undertake a statue. Marshal le Prince de Wissembourg, Minister of War and President of the Committee in charge of the fund for Marshal Montcornet's memorial statue, at once called a meeting, which agreed to entrust the commission for the work to Steinbock. Comte de Rastignac, at that time Under-Secretary of State, wanted an example of the work of the artist, whose fellow-competitors for the commission for the statue acclaimed his success, and who was becoming increasingly celebrated. He bought from Steinbock the delightful group of two little boys crowning a little girl, and promised him a studio at the government marble depot, which is situated, as everyone knows, at Le Gros-Caillou.

This was success, but success of the Parisian kind, which means that it was overwhelming, calculated to crush shoulders and loins not strong enough to bear it – a consequence, be it said, which often follows its achievement. Count Wenceslas Steinbock was spoken of in journals and reviews, without his or Mademoiselle Fischer's having any idea of it. Every day, as soon as Mademoiselle Fischer had gone out to dinner, Wenceslas went to call on the Baroness and spent an hour or two in the house, except on the day when Bette dined with the Hulots. This state of affairs lasted for some days.

The Baron, reassured about Count Steinbock's titles and social standing, the Baroness, happy about his character and moral principles, Hortense, proud of her love-affair and the approval given it, and of her suitor's fame, no longer hesitated to speak of the projected marriage. The artist's cup, in fact, was full, when an indiscretion on Madame Marneffe's part imperilled everything. It happened in this way.

Baron Hulot was anxious that Lisbeth should be on friendly terms with Madame Marneffe in order to have a spying eye in her household, and the spinster had already dined with Valérie. Valérie, who on her side wanted to have a listening ear among the Hulot family, made much of the old maid. So the idea naturally occurred to Valérie to invite Mademoiselle Fischer to the house-warming of the new apartment, into which she was shortly moving. The old maid, pleased to find another house to dine in and beguiled by Madame Marneffe, was becoming really fond of her. Of all the persons with whom she was connected, none had ever taken so much trouble on her account. As a matter of fact, Madame Marneffe, full of solicitous little attentions to Mademoiselle Fischer, stood in much the same relation to her as Cousin Bette did to the Baroness, Monsieur Rivet, Crevel – all those persons, indeed, who invited her to dinner. The Marneffes had won Cousin Bette's particular sympathy by letting her see their distressing poverty, painting it, as is customary, in the most flattering colours: as due to friends who had been helped and had proved ungrateful, illnesses, a mother – Madame Fortin – whose poverty had been kept from her, and who had died believing herself to be still in affluent circumstances, thanks to superhuman sacrifices on Valérie's part, and so on.

'That poor young couple!' as Bette said to her Cousin Hulot. 'You are certainly doing the right thing in taking an interest in them; they are the most deserving creatures; they are so brave, so good! They can barely exist on the thousand crowns a year a deputy head clerk earns, for they got into debt after Marshal Montcornet's death. It is barbarous of the Government to expect an official with a wife and family to live, in Paris, on a salary of two thousand four hundred francs a year!'

A young woman who showed her so much friendship, who confided in her about everything, consulted her, flattered her, and apparently wished to be guided by her, quite naturally in a very short time became dearer to the eccentric Cousin Bette than any of her own relations.

The Baron, for his part, admiring a decorum in Madame Marneffe, a standard of education and behaviour that neither Jenny Cadine, nor Josépha, nor any of their friends had possessed, had become infatuated with her in a month, with an old man's passion, a foolishly unconsidered passion, which seemed to him quite sensible. For, certainly, in her there was no sight of the derision, the debauchery, the wild extravagance, the moral depravity, the contempt for social proprieties, the complete independence, which, in the actress and the singer, had been the cause of all his sufferings. Then, too, he had no reason to apprehend that courtesan rapacity, unquenchable as the desert sand.

Madame Marneffe, now his friend and confidante, made an enormous fuss about accepting the slightest thing from him.

'Promotion, bonuses, anything you can obtain from the Government for us, are all very well; but don't begin our friendship by bringing discredit upon the woman you say you love,' Valérie always said, 'or I shall not believe you. And I like believing you,' she would add, with a fetching glance at him, looking rather like St Theresa experiencing a fore-taste of heaven.

To give her a present was like storming a fortress, meant doing violence to a conscience. The poor Baron had to use all kinds of artful devices in order to present her with some trifle, a pretty costly trifle, of course, congratulating himself as he did so on having at last met virtue, on having found the realization of his dreams. In this unsophisticated household (so he said to himself) the Baron was as much a god as in his own home. Monsieur Marneffe appeared to be a thousand leagues from thinking that his Ministry's Jupiter meditated descending upon his wife in a shower of gold, and adopted the attitude of respectful servant of his august chief.

How could Madame Marneffe, twenty-three years of age, a virtuous and easily alarmed middle-class wife, a flower hidden in the rue du Doyenné, possibly know anything of courtesans' depravity and corruption, which nowadays filled the Baron's soul with disgust? He had never before known the delights of a resisting virtue, and the timorous Valérie made him taste them, as the song says, 'all along the river'.

This being the situation between Hulot and Valérie, no one will be surprised to learn that Valérie had heard through Hulot the secret of Hortense's approaching marriage with the celebrated artist, Steinbock. Between a lover who has no rights and a woman who does not easily make up her mind to become a mistress, verbal and moral duels take place in which the word often betrays the thought behind it, as a foil in a fencing bout takes on the purpose of a duelling sword. The most cautious of men, in this situation, may behave like Monsieur de Turenne. And so it happened that the Baron dropped a hint of the complete liberty of action that his daughter's marriage would give him, by way of riposte to the loving Valérie, who had exclaimed on more than one occasion:

'I cannot understand how any woman could give herself to a man who was not entirely hers!'

The Baron had already sworn a thousand times that for the past twenty-five years everything had been over between Madame Hulot and himself.

'They say she is so beautiful!' Madame Marneffe replied. 'I must have proofs.'

'You shall have them,' said the Baron, delighted that in expressing this desire his Valérie was compromising herself.

'How can I? You would have to be by my side always,' Valérie had answered.

Hector had then been forced to reveal his plans and the project he was putting into execution in the rue Vanneau, in order to demonstrate to his Valérie that he was thinking of devoting to her that half of his life which belongs to a legitimate spouse, granted that day and night divide equally the lives of civilized people. He spoke of leaving his wife, with all propriety, to live without him once his daughter was marr'ed. The Baroness would then spend all her time with Hortense and the young Hulots. He was sure of his wife's obeying his wishes.

'From that time, my little angel, my true life – my real home – will be in the rue Vanneau.'

'Heavens! how you dispose of me!' said Madame Marneffe then. 'And what about my husband?'

'That bag of bones!'

'I must admit, compared with you, that's what he is . . .' she replied, laughing.

Madame Marneffe ardently wished to see young Count Steinbock, after hearing his story; perhaps she wanted to obtain some piece of jewellery from him while she still lived under the same roof. This curiosity was so displeasing to the

Baron that Valérie swore never to look at Wenceslas. But, when she had been rewarded for abandoning this fancy with a little tea service of old soft-paste Sèvres, she stored away her wish in the recesses of her heart, written down there as an item on the agenda. And so, one day, when she had asked *her* Cousin Bette to take coffee with her in her room, she introduced the subject of her sweetheart, in order to find out if she might be able to see him without danger.

'My dear,' she said, for they were on *my dear* terms with each other, 'why have you not introduced your sweetheart to me yet? You know that he has become famous overnight?'

'Famous?'

'Why, everyone's talking about him!'

'Ah, bah!' exclaimed Lisbeth.

'He's to make my father's statue, and I could be very useful to him for the likeness, for Madame Montcornet can't lend him a miniature by Sain and I can; a beautiful piece of work, painted in 1809 before the Wagram campaign and given to my poor mother, and so it's a picture of a young, handsome Montcornet. . . .'

Sain and Augustin were recognized as the supreme miniature painters under the Empire.

'You say he's going to make a statue, my dear?' repeated Lisbeth.

'Nine feet high, commissioned by the Minister of War. Really! Where have you been, that I can tell you this as a piece of news? The Government is going to give Count Steinbock a studio and rooms at Le Gros-Caillou, at the marble depot. Your Pole will perhaps be in charge there, a post worth two thousand francs a year, a feather in his cap.'

'How do you come to know all this, when I know nothing about it?' said Lisbeth at last, emerging from her state of stunned bewilderment.

'Listen, my dear little Cousin Bette,' said Madame Marneffe graciously. 'Are you capable of a devoted friendship, proof against anything? Would you like us to be like two sisters? Will you swear to me to have no secrets from me, if I'll keep none from you, to be my secret eye if I'll be yours? Will you swear above all that you'll never give me away to my husband or Monsieur Hulot, and that you'll never say that it was I who told you. . . .'

Madame Marneffe broke off this picador's attack, for Cousin Bette frightened her. The peasant-woman's countenance had grown terrible. Her black piercing eyes had the fixed stare of a tiger's. Her face was like the face of a pythoness, as we imagine it. Her teeth were clenched to prevent them from chattering, and her body was shaken convulsively and horribly. She had pushed the rigid half-closed fingers of one hand under her bonnet to grasp handfuls of her hair and support her suddenly heavy head; she was on fire! The smoke of the conflagration that ravaged her seemed to issue from the wrinkles of her face, as if they were fissures opened by volcanic eruption. It was an unearthly spectacle.

'Well, why do you stop?' she said hollowly. 'I will be for you all that I was for him. Oh! I would have given my life-blood for him!'

'You love him, then?'

'As if he were my child!'

'Well,' Madame Marneffe went on, breathing more easily, 'if you only love him like that, you are going to be very well pleased, for you want him to be happy, don't you?'

Lisbeth replied by nodding her head rapidly and repeatedly, like a madwoman.

'In a month he's going to marry your second cousin.'

'Hortense!' cried the old maid, striking her forehead and rising to her feet.

'Well, now! So you are in love with this young man?' asked Madame Marneffe.

'My dear, we are now sworn friends,' said Mademoiselle Fischer. 'Yes, if you have attachments, I will regard them as sacred. Your very vices shall be virtues to me, for indeed I have need of your vices!'

'So you were living with him?' Valérie exclaimed.

'No, I wanted to be his mother. . . .'

'Ah! I can't make head or tail of it,' returned Valérie; 'for if that's so, then you haven't been deceived or made a fool of, and you ought to be very glad to see him make a good marriage; because now he has got a start in life. Besides, it's all over for you, in any case. Our artist goes every day to Madame Hulot's, as soon as you have gone out to dinner.'

'Adeline!' said Lisbeth to herself. 'Oh, Adeline, you shall atone for this. I will see to it that you grow uglier than I!'

'Why, you're as pale as death!' exclaimed Valérie. 'So there is something behind it? Oh! how silly of me! The mother and daughter must suspect that you might put obstacles in the way of this love-affair, since they are hiding it from you. But if you were not living with the young man,' cried Madame Marneffe, 'all this, my dear, is harder to get to the bottom of than my husband's heart. . . .'

'Oh, but you don't know, how could you know?' returned Lisbeth. 'You don't know how they've intrigued against me! It's the last blow that kills! And how many blows have bruised my spirit? You don't know how, since I've been old enough to be conscious of it, I have been sacrificed to Adeline! They slapped me, and caressed her. I went dressed like a drudge, and she like a lady. I dug the garden, peeled the vegetables, and she never lifted a finger except to arrange her ribbons! She married the Baron and went to shine at the Emperor's Court, and I stayed until 1809 in my village, waiting for a suitable husband, for four years. They took me away from there, but only to make me a work-woman, and propose working-class matches for me – petty officials, captains who looked like porters! For twenty-six years I have had their leavings. . . . And now it's like in the Old Testament, the poor man had one lamb that was his only treasure, and the rich man who owned flocks coveted the poor man's lamb and stole it from him . . . without telling him, without asking him for it. Adeline is robbing me of my happiness! Adeline! Adeline! I will see you in the dust, fallen lower than I am! Hortense, whom I loved, has betrayed me. The Baron – No, it is not possible. See here, tell me again anything in this story that may be true.'

'Keep calm, my dear. . . .'

'Valérie, dear angel, I will keep calm,' this strange woman answered, sitting down. 'There's only one thing can restore my sanity: give me proof!'

'Well, your Cousin Hortense owns the Samson group; here

is a lithograph of it published in a review. She paid for it with her own savings; and it's the Baron who is backing him, since he's his future son-in-law, and getting all these commissions.'

'Water! ... water!' cried Lisbeth, when she had looked at the print and read the words below it: 'Group in the possession of Mademoiselle Hulot d'Ervy'. 'Water! My head's on fire! I'm going mad!'

Madame Marneffe brought water: the spinster removed her bonnet, shook down her black hair, and dipped her head in the basin held by her new friend. She plunged her forehead into the water several times, and arrested the spreading inflammation. After this immersion she regained complete self-control.

'Not a word,' she said to Madame Marneffe as she dried her face and head; 'don't breathe a word of all this. ... You see! ... I am quite easy in my mind now, and it's all forgotten; I have very different things to think of!'

'She'll be in Charenton tomorrow, that's sure,' Madame Marneffe said to herself as she watched the peasant from Lorraine.

'What's to be done?' Lisbeth went on. 'Do you see, my angel? I must hold my tongue, bow my head, and go to the grave as water flows to the river. What could I attempt to do? I would like to grind them all: Adeline, her daughter, and the Baron, into the dust! But what can a poor relation do against a whole rich family? It would be the story of the clay pot against the iron pot.'

'Yes, you are right,' replied Valérie. 'All one can do is to snatch as much hay as one can from the hayrack. That's what life amounts to in Paris.'

'And,' said Lisbeth, 'I'll die very soon, you know, if I lose this child, whose mother I thought I should always be, with whom I counted on living all my life. ...'

She had tears in her eyes as she came to a stop. So much feeling in this woman of fire and brimstone made Madame Marneffe's flesh creep.

'At least, I've found you,' she went on, taking Valérie's hand. 'That's one consolation in this dreadful trouble. We shall be dear friends; and why should we ever leave each other? I will never poach on your preserves. No one will ever fall in love with me! All the men who presented themselves wanted to marry me only for the sake of having my cousin's backing. To have enough vital force to scale the walls of paradise, and to have to spend it earning bread and water, some rags to wear, and a garret: ah, that, my dear, is torture! Under that I have withered.'

She stopped abruptly, and into Madame Marneffe's blue eyes plunged a dark look that pierced that pretty woman's soul, like the blade of a dagger transfixing her heart.

'But what's the use of talking?' she exclaimed, in self-reproach. 'I have never said so much about this before! Treachery, like chickens, will come home to roost,' she added after a pause, in a nursery phrase. 'As you so wisely say – let's sharpen our teeth and snatch as much hay as we can from the hayrack.'

'You're quite right,' said Madame Marneffe, who was frightened out of her wits by all this emotion and did not remember having suggested this principle of conduct. 'I think you have quite the right idea, my dear. It's true, life doesn't last so long; we must get as much out of it as we can and use other people for our own advantage. I have come to see that now, even at my age! I was brought up as a spoilt child. Then my father made an ambitious marriage and practically forgot me, after making me his idol and bringing me up like a queen's daughter! My poor mother, who cherished such fond hopes for me, died of grief when she saw me married to a petty official with a salary of twelve hundred francs, a cold-blooded libertine worn-out at thirty-nine, as corrupt as a convict hulk, who saw in me no more than they saw in you, a means of getting on! Well, in the end, I have found that this contemptible man is the best kind of husband. By preferring the filthy drabs from the street-corner to me, he leaves me free. If he spends his whole salary on himself, he never asks me where my money comes from –'

In her turn, she stopped short, as if she felt herself being carried away by the torrent of her confidences, and, suddenly struck by the close attention that Lisbeth was giving to her, judged it prudent to be sure of her before disclosing her most intimate secrets.

'You see, my dear, how much I trust you!' Madame Marneffe went on, and Lisbeth responded with a gesture of absolute reassurance.

More solemn oaths are often sworn by a look and a movement of the head than are heard in law-courts.

'I keep up all the appearances of respectability,' Madame Marneffe went on, laying her hand on Lisbeth's hand as if in acceptance of her good faith. 'I am a married woman and I am my own mistress: so much so that if Marneffe takes it into his head to say good-bye to me before he leaves for the Ministry in the morning and he finds the door of my room locked, off he goes quite serenely. He cares less for his own child than I care for one of the marble children playing at the feet of the statues of the Rivers in the Tuileries. If I don't come home to dinner, he dines very happily with the maid, for the maid is quite devoted to Monsieur; and every evening after dinner he goes out, and doesn't come back until midnight or one o'clock. Unfortunately, for the past year I have had no maid of my own, which means that for a year I have been a widow. ... I have only been in love once, had one piece of happiness – he was a rich Brazilian, who has been gone a year – my only infidelity! He went to sell his property, realize all he owns, in order to be able to settle in France. What will he find of his Valérie? A dunghill. Bah! it will be his fault, not mine, for why does he stay so long away? I suppose he may have been shipwrecked too, like my virtue.'

'Good-bye, my dear,' said Lisbeth abruptly. 'We will always stick together from now on. I love you and admire you; I am on your side! My cousin has been plaguing me to go and live in your new house in the rue Vanneau. I did not want to, for I could easily guess the reason for his sudden kindness.'

'Yes, you were to be there to keep an eye on me; that's clear enough,' said Madame Marneffe.

'It's certainly the reason for his generosity,' replied Lisbeth. 'In Paris most kindnesses are just investments, and most ingratitude is a plain act of revenge! A poor relation is someone to be treated like the rats, enticed with a scrap of bacon. I will accept the Baron's offer, for this house has become hateful to me. I fancy that we are both sharp enough to know how to keep quiet about things that would damage us, and say what has to be said; so, still tongues, and friendship between us.'

'Come what may!' cried Madame Marneffe joyfully, delighted to have a chaperon, a confidante, a kind of respectable aunt. 'Do you know? The Baron is doing things in style in the rue Vanneau. ...'

'I should just think he is,' Lisbeth answered. 'He's footing a bill for thirty thousand francs for it. Indeed I don't know where he has found the money, for Josépha, the singer, bled him white. Oh! you are in luck,' she added. 'The Baron would commit a robbery for the woman who holds his heart between two soft, white, little hands like yours.'

'Well, my dear,' Madame Marneffe went on, with the confident unconcern of such women, who are generous because they really do not care, 'you may as well take anything from these rooms that might suit you for your new apartment – that chest of drawers, the wardrobe with the mirror, this carpet, the curtains ...'

Lisbeth's eyes dilated with incredulous pleasure; she could not believe that she was being given such a present.

'You do more for me in a moment than my rich relations have done in thirty years!' she exclaimed. 'It has never crossed their minds to wonder whether I had furniture! The first time the Baron visited me, a few weeks ago, he pulled a rich man's face at the sight of my poor things. ... Well, thank you, my dear. I will repay you for this. You shall see later how!'

Valérie saw *her* Cousin Bette out, as far as the landing, where the two women kissed.

'She stinks of hard work!' the pretty woman said to herself when she was alone. 'I won't kiss her often, that cousin of mine! But I had better walk warily; I must handle her carefully. She will be very useful; she will help me make my fortune!'

Like a true Parisian creole, Madame Marneffe detested having to exert herself. She had the cool indifference of cats, who run and pounce only when obliged to by necessity. She required life to be all pleasure, and pleasure to be all calm plain sailing. She loved flowers, provided someone sent them to her. A visit to the theatre could not be considered unless she had a good box of her own, and a carriage to take her there. These courtesan tastes Valérie derived from her mother, who had had everything lavished upon her by General Montcornet during his visits to Paris, and who for twenty years had seen the world at her feet; who, a spendthrift by nature, had frittered away all her wealth, squandered everything, in luxurious living of a kind whose programme has been lost since Napoleon's fall. The great men and women of the Empire, in their follies, rivalled the great aristocrats of the old régime. Under the Restoration the aristocracy has always remembered having been persecuted and robbed, and so, with few exceptions, become economical, careful, and provident: in fact bourgeois and inglorious. Now, 1830 has completed the work of 1793. In France, from now on, there will be great names but no more great houses, unless there are political changes, difficult to foresee. Everything bears the stamp of personal interest. The wisest buy annuities with their money. The family has been destroyed.

The constricting pressure of poverty which was galling Valérie intolerably on that day when, to use Marneffe's expression, she had *made* Hulot, had decided that young woman to use her beauty as a means to fortune. For some time she had felt a need to have a devoted friend at hand, someone rather like a mother, the kind of person to whom may be confided what must be concealed from a maid, who can act, come and go, think on our behalf – a tool in the hand, in fact, resigned to an unequal share of life's spoils. She had guessed, just as easily as Lisbeth, what the Baron's motives were in wishing her to make friends with Cousin Bette. To guide her, she had the formidable knowledge of a Parisian creole who spends her hours lying on a sofa, turning the lantern of her observation on all the dark corners of human souls, studying emotions and investigating intrigues; and she had devised the plan of making an accomplice of the spy. Her wild indiscretion was probably premeditated. She had recognized the true nature of the fiery-spirited spinster whose passionate impulses were being expended in a void, and was anxious to attach her to herself. The conversation she had held with Lisbeth was like the stone a mountaineer casts into a chasm in order to sound its depth; and Madame Marneffe had recoiled in dismay when she found both an Iago and a Richard III in this woman, who to all appearances was so harmless, so humble, and so little to be feared.

In an instant, Cousin Bette had become her true self again. In an instant, this savage, Corsican, nature, having broken the fragile bonds which restrained it, had sprung back to its menacing height, like a branch whipping from the hands of a child who has bent it down in order to steal its unripe fruit.

To any observer of society, it is always astonishing to see how rapidly virgin natures can conceive ideas, and with what abundance and perfection.

Virginity, like all abnormal states, has its characteristic qualities, its fascinating greatness. Life, whose forces have been kept unspent, takes on in the virgin individual an incalculable power of resistance and endurance. The brain has been enriched by the sum of all its untapped faculties. When celibate persons make demands on their bodies or their minds, need to resort to physical action or thought, they find steel stiffening their muscles or knowledge infused into their minds, a diabolical strength or the black magic of the Will.

In this respect, the Virgin Mary, regarding her for the moment only as a symbol, towers in her greatness above all the Indian, Egyptian, and Greek types of deity. Virginity, the source and mother of everything that is great, *magna parens rerum*, holds in her beautiful white hands the key of the higher worlds. Truly this grandiose and awe-inspiring exception to the normal rule of humanity is worthy of all the honours which the Catholic Church regards as rightly hers.

So, in a moment, Cousin Bette became the Mohican whose snares are inescapable, whose thoughts are impenetrably dissembled, whose swift decisions are reached on the evidence brought by senses developed to perfect keenness. She was hate and vengeance uncompromising, as they are known in Italy, Spain, and the East, for those two passions, the reverse side of friendship and love pushed to extremes, are known absolutely only in countries bathed by the sun. But Lisbeth was essentially a daughter of Lorraine, which means that she was determined to play a deep game.

She did not easily undertake the second part of her role; indeed, she made a strange move, which was a result of her profound ignorance. She pictured prison as all children imagine it, confusing imprisonment with solitary confinement. Solitary confinement is the harshest form of imprisonment, and to order it is the prerogative of criminal justice.

On leaving Madame Marneffe, Lisbeth hurried off to see Monsieur Rivet, and found him in his office.

'Well, my dear Monsieur Rivet,' she said, after first bolting the office door, 'you were quite right. Poles, indeed! Low scoundrels! They're all lawless, faithless, men!'

'Men who want to set Europe on fire,' said the pacific Rivet, 'to ruin trade and businessmen, for the sake of a country which, they say, is nothing but bog, full of frightful Jews, not to mention Cossacks and peasants, kinds of ferocious animals not really to be classed as belonging to the human race at all. These Poles don't realize what times we live in. We're not barbarians any more! War is out-of-date, my dear lady; it went out with the kings. Our times have seen the triumph of trade, hard work, and middle-class good sense: the kind of virtues which made Holland what it is. Yes,' he said, warming to his theme, 'we live in an era when the nations must obtain everything by means of the legitimate development of their liberties and *peaceful* functioning of constitutional institutions; that's what the Poles have no idea of, and I hope – You were saying, my dear?' he added, breaking off as he perceived by his forewoman's expression that high politics were beyond her range.

'Here are the papers,' replied Bette; 'and if I am not to lose my three thousand two hundred and ten francs, this scoundrel must be put in prison.'

'Ah! I told you so!' exclaimed the oracle of the Quartier Saint-Denis.

The firm of Rivet, successor to Pons Brothers, was still established in the rue des Mauvaises-Paroles, in the former

Langeais mansion, built by that illustrious family at the time when noble families lived in the neighbourhood of the Louvre.

'Indeed I have been calling down blessings on you, on my way here!' answered Lisbeth.

'If it so happens that he suspects nothing, he will be locked up by four in the morning,' said the magistrate, consulting his calendar to verify the hour of sunrise; 'but not tomorrow, the day after, for he can't be imprisoned without a notification that he is to be arrested by means of an order with a warrant. So ...'

'What a stupid law,' said Cousin Bette, 'for the debtor can make off.'

'He has a good right to,' replied the magistrate, with a smile. 'So this is how –'

'Oh, for that matter, I can take the paper,' Bette interrupted him. 'I'll take it to him and tell him that I have been obliged to raise money, and that the lender required this formality. I know my Pole, he will not even unfold the paper, he'll light his pipe with it.'

'Ah! not bad, not bad, Mademoiselle Fischer! Well, set your mind at rest, we'll get this affair fixed up. But wait a minute! It's not enough just to lock up a man; people only indulge in that luxury of the law for the sake of getting their money back. Who will pay you?'

'The people who give him money.'

'Ah, yes! I was forgetting that the Minister of War has given him the commission for the monument of one of our clients. Ah! this firm has supplied many a uniform for General Montcornet. It didn't take him long to blacken them in cannon smoke, that soldier! A brave man! And he paid on the nail!'

A Marshal of France may have saved the Emperor or his country, but 'He paid on the nail' will always be the finest encomium a tradesman can pronounce on him.

'Well then, I'll see you on Saturday, Monsieur Rivet. You shall have your tassels then. By the way, I am leaving the rue du Doyenné and going to live in the rue Vanneau.'

'I am glad to hear it. I didn't like to see you living in that hole, which I must say, in spite of my aversion to anything that smacks of Opposition views, disgraces, yes, is a disgrace to the Louvre and the place du Carrousel! I worship Louis-Philippe. He is my idol, he is the august and perfect representative of the class on which he has founded his throne, and I'll never forget what he has done for the trimming trade by re-establishing the National Guard. . . .'

'When I hear you talking like this,' said Lisbeth, 'I wonder why you aren't a Deputy.'

'They're afraid of my attachment to the royal house,' replied Rivet. 'My political enemies are the King's. Ah! his is a noble character, an admirable family. In a word,' he went on, returning to his theme, 'he is our ideal – in principles, direction of the country's economy, everything! But the completion of the Louvre was one of the conditions on which we gave him the crown, and the civil list, to which no limit was set; and we're left, I must say, with the heart of Paris in a deplorable state. It's because I am a moderate, strictly middle-of-the-road man, that I would like to see the middle of Paris in a different state. Your district makes one shudder. You would have had your throat cut there sooner or later. . . . Well, I see that your Monsieur Crevel has been nominated Major of his Legion. I hope that we are to have the making of his big epaulettes for him.'

'I am dining there today. I'll send him to see you.'

Lisbeth's belief was that she would have her Livonian to herself, because she assumed that she would be cutting all his means of communication with the outer world. When he was no longer doing any work, the artist would be forgotten, and be like a man buried alive in a vault, where she would be the only one to go to see him. So she had two days of happiness, for she hoped to inflict a mortal blow on the Baroness and her daughter.

To reach Monsieur Crevel's house, which was in the rue des Saussayes, she went by the pont du Carrousel, the quai Voltaire, the quai d'Orsay, the rue Bellechasse, the rue de l'Université, the pont de la Concorde, and the avenue de Marigny. This illogical route was traced by the logic of passion, which is always excessively hard on the legs. While she was walking along the quays, Cousin Bette watched the the right bank of the Seine, loitering and going very slowly. Her reasoning proved correct. She had left Wenceslas getting dressed; she thought that as soon as she was out of the way the lover would go to call on the Baroness by the shortest route. And, in fact, while she was lingering by the parapet of the quai Voltaire, gazing across the river and walking in spirit on the other side, she caught sight of the artist coming from the Tuileries, making for the pont Royal. Her route joined her faithless friend's there, and she was able to follow him without being seen, for lovers rarely look back. She accompanied him as far as Madame Hulot's house, and saw him go in with the air of a habitual visitor.

At this final proof, confirming Madame Marneffe's confidences, Lisbeth was beside herself.

She arrived at the house of the newly-elected Major in the state of mind in which murders are committed, and found old Crevel in his drawing-room, waiting for his children, the young Monsieur and Madame Hulot.

But Célestin Crevel is such a naïve and perfect specimen of the Parisian climber that it is difficult to enter the house of this fortunate successor to César Birotteau without due ceremony. Célestin Crevel is a whole world in himself. And, besides, much more than Rivet he deserves the honour of having his portrait painted, because of the importance of the part he plays in this domestic drama.

Have you observed how readily, in childhood or at the beginning of our social life, we set up a model for ourselves, spontaneously and often unawares? So a bank clerk dreams, as he enters his manager's drawing-room, of possessing one just like it. If he makes his way, twenty years later it will not be the luxury then in fashion that he will want to display in his house, but the out-of-date luxury that fascinated him long before. No one knows how much obvious bad taste this retrospective envy accounts for; and we cannot tell how many wildly foolish actions are due to the secret rivalries that drive men to mirror the type that they have set up as ideal, to consume their energies in making themselves a moonshine reflection of someone else. Crevel was Deputy Mayor because his employer had been a Deputy Mayor; he was a major because he had coveted César Birotteau's epaulettes. And in the same way, because he had been impressed by the marvels created by the architect Grindot at the time when his employer had been carried to the top of fortune's wheel, Crevel, as he said himself, had 'never thought twice about it' when it came to decorating his apartment. He had betaken himself, with his purse open and his eyes shut, to Grindot, an architect by then quite forgotten. Who can tell how long extinct glory may survive, sustained by such post-dated admiration?

So Grindot had created his white and gold drawing-room hung with red damask, for the thousandth time, there. The rosewood furniture decorated with the usual carving, mediocre in design and execution, had been a product of Parisian workmanship to be proud of, in the provinces, at the time of the Paris Industrial Exhibition. The candlesticks, the sconces, the fender, the chandelier, the clock, were highly ornamented, in pseudo-rococo style. The round table, immovable in the middle of the room, displayed a marble top inlaid with samples of all the antique and Italian marbles in Rome, where this kind of mineralogical map, rather like a tailor's display card of patterns, is manufactured. It was a centre of attraction for all the parties of bourgeois visitors that Crevel received at regular intervals. Portraits of the late Madame Crevel, Crevel himself, and his daughter and son-in-law from the brush of Pierre Grassou – a painter, popular in middle-class circles, to whom Crevel was indebted for his ridiculous Byronic pose – adorned the walls, painted and hung as a matching series. The frames, which had cost a thousand francs apiece, were in keeping with all this café splendour, which would certainly have made a true artist shrug his shoulders.

Money never misses the slightest occasion to demonstrate its stupidity. Paris would by now contain ten times the treasures of Venice if our retired businessmen had had the instinct for fine things that distinguishes the Italians. Even in our own times, it is possible for a Milanese merchant to leave five hundred thousand francs to the Duomo for the gilding of the colossal Virgin that surmounts its cupola. Canova in his will instructed his brother to build a church costing four millions, and the brother added something from his own pocket. Would a bourgeois citizen of Paris (and they all, like Rivet, have a warm spot for their Paris in their hearts) ever dream of building the spires missing from the towers of Notre-Dame? And yet, consider the sums of money that have reverted to the state from property left without heirs. The whole of Paris might have been made beautiful with the money spent on idiotic follies of moulded stucco, gilded plaster, pretentious sculpture, during the past fifteen years, by persons of Crevel's kind.

At the far end of this drawing-room there was a magnificent study, furnished with imitation Boule tables and cabinets. The bedroom, all hung and covered with chintz, also led into the drawing-room. The dining-room was overpoweringly filled with mahogany, in all its handsome weight, and had richly framed views of Switzerland set in the panelling. Old Crevel, whose dream it was to travel in Switzerland, enjoyed possessing that country in paintings until the day when he should see it in reality.

Crevel, former Deputy Mayor, officer of the National Guard, wearing the ribbon of the Legion of Honour, had, as we see, faithfully reproduced all the grandeur, even the very furniture, of his unfortunate predecessor. Where under the Restoration the one had fallen, the other, quite overlooked, had risen not by any singular stroke of fortune but simply by the force of events. In revolutions as in storms at sea solid worth goes to the bottom, while the current brings light trash floating to the surface. César Birotteau, a royalist and in favour, was an object of envy, and became a target for bourgeois hostility, while the bourgeoisie triumphant saw its own face mirrored in Crevel.

This apartment, rented for one thousand crowns per annum, stuffed with all the vulgarly fine things that money could buy, occupied the first floor of an old mansion, set between a court and a garden. Everything was in a state of preservation here, like beetles in an entomologist's cabinet, for Crevel lived here very little.

These sumptuous premises constituted the official domicile of the ambitious bourgeois. He was waited upon here by a cook and a valet, and hired two servants to help them, and had a grand dinner brought in from Chevet when he entertained political friends, people whom he desired to impress, or his family.

The seat of Crevel's real existence, formerly in the rue Notre-Dame de Lorette, where Mademoiselle Héloïse Brisetout used to live, had been transferred, as we have seen, to the rue Chauchat. Every morning, the retired merchant (all ex-shopkeepers call themselves 'retired merchants') spent a couple of hours in the rue des Saussayes, attending to his affairs, and gave the rest of his time to Zaïre,* much to Zaïre's annoyance. Zaïre's Orosmane (alias Crevel) had a fixed arrangement with Mademoiselle Héloïse: she owed him five hundred francs' worth of happiness every month, with nothing carried over. Crevel paid for his dinner, and all the extras as well. This contract, with bonuses – for he gave many presents – seemed economical to the ex-lover of the famous singer. On this subject, he was in the habit of saying to widowed merchants who were devoted to their daughters that it was a better bargain to rent horses by the month than to keep your own stable. If one remembers what the porter of the establishment in the rue Chauchat confided to the Baron, however, it seems that Crevel was not spared the expense of either coachman or groom.

Crevel, as we see, had turned his great affection for his daughter to account, as an advantage in seeking his pleasures. The immorality of his situation was justified on highly moral grounds. In addition, the ex-perfumer acquired from this way of life (doing the done thing, living a free life, being Regency, Pompadour, Maréchal de Richelieu, etc.) a gloss of superiority. Crevel saw himself as a broad-minded man, a gentleman who lived like a minor lord, an open-handed man with no narrowness in his views, and all for the expenditure of some twelve to fifteen hundred francs a month. This attitude was the effect, not of political hypocrisy, but of middle-class vanity, but the result was the same. At the Bourse, Crevel was regarded as a man who saw further than most, and above all, as a

Zaïre is a tragedy by Voltaire, inspired by *Othello*. Orosmane is one of its chief characters, a type of passionate jealousy.

gay dog, a convivial soul. In this respect, Crevel considered that he had outdistanced his pace-maker, Birotteau, by about a hundred and fifty yards.

'Well,' exclaimed Crevel, flying into a rage at the sight of Cousin Bette, 'so it's you who are marrying off Mademoiselle Hulot to some young Count that you have been rearing for her by hand?'

'Anyone would suppose that that doesn't please you!' retorted Lisbeth, turning a penetrating eye upon him. 'Why are you interested in preventing my cousin from marrying? I hear that you spoiled her chances of marrying Monsieur Lebas's son. . . .'

'You are a sensible woman, and know how to keep your mouth shut,' the worthy Crevel replied. 'Well, do you imagine that I can ever forgive *Monsieur* Hulot for the crime he committed in stealing Josépha from me? Especially when by it he turned an honest creature, whom I would have married in the end, in my old age, into a worthless baggage, a play-actress, an opera-singer? Oh, no, never in this life!'

'He's a good fellow, Baron Hulot, all the same,' said Cousin Bette.

'A good fellow, very likeable, too likeable!' agreed Crevel. 'I don't wish him any harm; but I want my revenge, and I intend to have it. It's a notion I've got into my head!'

'Has this notion of yours something to do with the fact that you don't come to visit Madame Hulot any more?'

'That may be. . . .'

'Ah! So you were courting my cousin?' said Lisbeth, smiling. 'I thought as much.'

'And she has treated me like a dog! Worse than that, like a lackey! I'll go further still, like a political prisoner! But I'll have my way!' he said, striking his brow with his clenched fist.

'Poor man, it would be too dreadful for him to find his wife deceiving him, after being cast off by his mistress!'

'Josépha!' cried Crevel. 'Josépha has left him, sent him packing, thrown him out? Bravo, Josépha! Josépha, you have avenged me! I will send you two pearls for your ears, my ex-love! This is all news to me, for since I saw you, the day

126

after the fair Adeline last begged me not to darken her door again, I have been at Corbeil, staying with the Lebas, and have only just got back. Héloïse moved heaven and earth to induce me to go to the country, and I have just found out what her little game was: she wanted to have a house-warming party without me, at the rue Chauchat, with artists, barnstormers, literary fellows, I don't know who all. . . . She made a fool of me! But I'll forgive her, for Héloïse makes me laugh. She's a sort of Déjazet, in a new version. The girl's a comedian! Just listen to the note I had from her yesterday:

Dear old chap, I have pitched my tent in the rue Chauchat. I took the precaution of letting some friends dry the plaster out properly first. All goes well. Come when you like, Monsieur. Hagar awaits her Abraham.

Héloïse will tell me all about it, for she has all the bohemian gossip tripping off her tongue.'

'But my cousin has taken this unpleasantness very well,' observed Lisbeth.

'That's not possible!' said Crevel, stopping short in his pacing to and fro like the pendulum of a clock.

'Monsieur Hulot has reached a certain age,' Lisbeth pointed out, with malice.

'I know,' returned Crevel; 'but we are like one another in one respect; Hulot cannot do without an attachment. He is capable of returning to his wife,' he said reflectively. 'That would be a change for him; but farewell my revenge! You smile, Mademoiselle Fischer. . . . Ah! you know something? . . .'

'I'm laughing at your ideas,' Lisbeth replied. 'Yes, my cousin is still beautiful enough to inspire passion. I should fall in love with her myself, if I were a man.'

'The man who has tasted pleasure once will go to the well again,' exclaimed Crevel. 'You're making fun of me! The Baron must have found some consolation.'

Lisbeth nodded.

'Well, he's very lucky to be able to replace Josépha overnight!' Crevel went on. 'But I'm not really surprised. He told me once, over supper, that when he was a young man he always had three mistresses so that he should never be caught unprovided for: one that he was on the verge of leaving, the reigning queen, and one that he was courting for the future. He must have kept some gay little shop-girl in reserve in his fish-pond! In his deer-park! He is very Louis XV, the rascal! Oh, what a lucky man he is to be so handsome! All the same, he's not getting younger, he's showing signs ... he must have taken up with some little working girl.'

'Oh, no!' answered Lisbeth.

'Ah!' said Crevel. 'What would I not give to prevent him from hanging his hat up! I could never hope to cut him out with Josépha. Women like her don't return to their first love. Besides, as they say, a return is never the same thing. But, Cousin Bette, I would certainly give – that is I would willingly spend – fifty thousand francs to take that big handsome fellow's mistress away from him and let him see that a fat old papa with a Major's corporation and the panache of a future Mayor of Paris doesn't let his girl be snaffled from him without getting even.'

'In the position I am in,' replied Bette, 'I have to hear everything and know nothing. You can talk to me freely; I never repeat a word of the things people care to tell me in confidence. What reason should I have to break this rule I follow? If I did, no one would ever trust me again.'

'Yes, I know,' answered Crevel. 'You are a pearl among spinsters. ... Only, there are exceptions, hang it! See here, they have never made up an income for you, in the family. ...'

'But I have my pride. I don't want to be beholden to anyone,' said Bette.

'Ah! if you were willing to help me to have my revenge,' the retired shopkeeper continued, 'I could set aside a life interest in ten thousand francs for you. Tell me, fair cousin, only tell me who Josépha's successor is, and you shall have the wherewithal to pay your rent and buy your breakfast in the morning, your morning coffee, the good coffee you like so much, pure Mocha you will be able to treat yourself to ... how about that? Oh! just think how delicious the best Mocha is!'

'I don't care so much for a ten-thousand-franc annuity, which would mean nearly five hundred francs a year, as I do for keeping my own counsel absolutely,' said Lisbeth;

'because you know, my good Monsieur Crevel, the Baron is very kind to me, he is going to pay my rent. . . .'

'Oh, yes, and for how long? You think you can count on that!' cried Crevel. 'Where will the Baron find the money?'

'Ah, that I don't know. But he's spending more than thirty thousand francs on the apartment he's preparing for the little lady.'

'She's a lady, is she? What! a society woman? The rascal, doesn't he land on his feet! He has all the luck!'

'A married woman, a real lady,' Cousin Bette went on.

'You don't say?' exclaimed Crevel, opening envious eyes set burning by the magic words 'a real lady'.

'Yes,' answered Bette, 'talented, musical, twenty-three years old, with a pretty innocent face, a dazzlingly fair skin, teeth like a puppy's, eyes like stars, a superb brow . . . and tiny feet; I've never seen anything like them, they're no bigger than her bodice front.'

'What about her ears?' demanded Crevel, deeply stirred by this recital of charms.

'Ears you would like to take a cast of,' she replied.

'Little hands?'

'I tell you, in a word, she's a jewel of a woman, and with such perfect good manners, such reserve, such refinement! . . . with a lovely nature, an angel, distinguished in every way, for her father was a Marshal of France.'

'A Marshal of France!' Crevel exclaimed, with a prodigious start of excitement. 'Good Lord! Bless my soul! Confound it! Blast it and bother it! Ah! the scoundrel! Excuse me, Cousin, it drives me mad! I would give a hundred thousand francs, I believe . . .'

'Yes, indeed! I can tell you she's a respectable woman, a virtuous wife. And the Baron has done things handsomely for her.'

'He hasn't got a sou, I tell you.'

'There's a husband that he has pushed . . .'

'Pushed where?' said Crevel with a sardonic laugh.

'He's already been appointed deputy head clerk, this husband, and he'll no doubt prove accommodating . . . and nominated for the Cross of the Legion of Honour.'

'The Government ought to be careful and respect the persons it has decorated, and not go scattering Crosses broadcast,' said Crevel, with the air of a man piqued on political grounds. 'But what has that confounded sly old dog of a Baron got?' he went on. 'It seems to me I'm just as good as he is,' he added, turning to look at himself in a glass, and striking his pose. 'Héloïse has often told me, at a moment when women tell the truth, that I am astonishing.'

'Oh!' replied Cousin Bette, 'women love fat men, they are nearly all kind-hearted; and if I had to choose between you and the Baron, I would choose you. Monsieur Hulot is clever, a handsome man, he cuts a fine figure; but you, you're solid, and then, you see . . . you strike one as being even more of a scamp than he is!'

'It's incredible how all the women, even the pious ones, fall for men who have that look!' exclaimed Crevel, advancing upon Bette and taking her by the waist in his exhilaration.

'That's not where the difficulty lies,' continued Bette. 'You understand that a woman who is doing so well for herself will not be unfaithful to her protector for a mere trifle, and *that* would cost at least a hundred thousand francs, because the little lady looks forward to seeing her husband head clerk of a department within two years from now. It is poverty that's driving this poor little angel astray . . .'

Crevel strode up and down his drawing-room frantically.

'He must think a lot of this woman?' he asked, after a pause during which his desire, spurred on by Bette, rose to a kind of frenzy.

'It's not hard to guess!' replied Lisbeth. 'I don't believe he's had *that* from her!' she added, clicking her thumb-nail against one of her huge white teeth, 'and he's already spent about ten thousand francs in presents for her.'

'Oh, what a joke,' cried Crevel, 'if I got in before him!'

'Heavens, it's very wrong of me to pass on this tittle-tattle,' said Lisbeth, appearing to experience some feeling of remorse.

'No. I'm going to put your family to shame. Tomorrow I'll set aside a sum of money in five per cents, enough to give you six hundred francs a year, but you must tell me everything:

the name of this Dulcinea, and where she lives. I may as well tell you, I've never had a real lady, and the greatest of my ambitions is to have one as my mistress. Mohammed's houris are nothing in comparison with society women as I imagine them. In short, they are my ideal, my passion, to such a degree that, believe me or not, Baroness Hulot will never be fifty years old in my eyes,' he said, echoing unawares one of the finest wits of the past century. 'Listen, my good Lisbeth. I've made up my mind to sacrifice a hundred, two hundred ... Hush! here come my young folk, I see them crossing the court. I have never heard a whisper of this from you, I give you my word; for I don't want to lose the Baron's trust – on the contrary. ... He must be pretty deeply in love with this woman, my old crony!'

'Oh, he's mad about her!' said Cousin Bette. 'He couldn't find forty thousand francs for his daughter's dowry, and he has managed to dig them up for this new flame.'

'And do you think she cares for him?' asked Crevel.

'What! At his age?' the old maid answered.

'Oh, what a fool I am!' exclaimed Crevel. 'Of course I put up with Héloïse's artist, just like Henri IV letting Gabrielle have Bellegarde. Oh! old age, old age! How are you, Célestine, how are you, my pet? And where is the youngster? Ah! here he is! Upon my word, he's beginning to look like me. How d'ye do, Hulot, my boy, how are you? ... So we are soon to have another wedding in the family?'

Célestine and her husband looked at Lisbeth, and then exchanged a look with Crevel; and the girl coolly answered her father:

'A marriage? Whose?'

Crevel looked slyly at her, as if to reassure her that he would cover up his indiscretion, and said: 'Hortense's marriage; but it's not settled yet, of course. I've been staying with the Lebas, and they were talking of Mademoiselle Popinot for our young Councillor. He is very anxious to become president of a provincial court. ... Come, let's have dinner.'

By seven o'clock Lisbeth was already on an omnibus on her way home, for she could not wait to see Wenceslas again, whose dupe she had been for the past three weeks. She was bringing him her work-basket piled high with fruit by Crevel himself; for Crevel had become twice as solicitously attentive to *his* Cousin Bette.

She climbed to the attic in breathless haste, and found the artist busy completing the decoration of a box which he intended to give to his dear Hortense. The lid was ornamented with a border of hydrangeas – *hydrangea hortensis* – among whose flower-heads Cupids played. To raise money for the malachite box, the penniless lover had made two candelabra, fine pieces of work, for Florent and Chanor, selling them the copyright.

'You have been working too hard, lately, my dear boy,' said Lisbeth wiping the sweat from his forehead and kissing him. 'So much exertion in the month of August seems dangerous to me. Really, you might damage your health by it. Look, here are some peaches and plums from Monsieur Crevel. There is no need to worry so much. I have borrowed two thousand francs, and all being well we can pay it back if you sell your clock! I have some doubts about the lender, all the same, for he has just sent this document.'

She placed the writ of arrest for debt under a sketch of Marshal Montcornet.

'For whom are you making these lovely things?' she asked, lifting the red wax clusters of hydrangea flowers that Wenceslas had laid down in order to eat the fruit.

'A jeweller.'

'Which jeweller?'

'I don't know. Stidmann asked me to twist the thing together for him because he's very busy.'

'But these are hortensias,' she said in a hollow voice. 'Why is it that you have never modelled anything in wax for me? Was it so difficult to design a dagger, or a little box, or some little thing as a keepsake!' she said, flashing a terrifying look at the artist, whose eyes, fortunately, were lowered. 'And you say that you love me!'

'Can you have any doubt about that ... Mademoiselle?'

'Oh, that's a nice cordial "Mademoiselle".... You know, you have been my only thought since I saw you dying there. When I saved you, you gave yourself to me. I have never spoken to you of that pledge, but I pledged myself too, in my own mind. I said to myself: "Since this boy gives himself into my hands, I will make him happy and rich!" Well, now I have succeeded in making your fortune!'

'How?' asked the poor artist, brim-full of happiness, and too naïve to suspect a trap.

'In this way,' the Lorraine peasant continued. Lisbeth could not deny herself the agonizing pleasure of watching Wenceslas, who was looking at her with a son's affection, made more intense by the overflow of his love for Hortense; and the spinster was misled. When she saw for the first time in her life the fires of passion in a man's eyes she believed she had lighted them there.

'Monsieur Crevel is ready to advance us a hundred thousand francs to start a business, if, so he says, you wish to marry me. He has odd notions, that fat man. ... What do you think of it?' she asked.

The artist, grown deathly pale, looked at his benefactress with a dulled eye which revealed all his thought. He stood there dumbfounded and dazed.

'No one has ever told me so plainly before,' she said with a bitter laugh, 'that I am hideously ugly!'

'Mademoiselle,' replied Steinbock, 'my benefactress will never be ugly to me. I have a very deep affection for you, but I am not yet thirty years old, and ...'

'And I am forty-three!' said Bette. 'My cousin, Baroness Hulot, who is forty-eight, still inspires desperate passion; but then she is beautiful!'

'Fifteen years between us, Mademoiselle! What kind of marriage would that be? For our own sakes I think we should reflect very seriously. My gratitude to you will certainly not fall short of your great goodness to me. And your money, what's more, will be returned in a few days!'

'My money!' she exclaimed. 'Oh! you treat me as if I were a heartless usurer!'

'I beg your pardon,' replied Wenceslas, 'but you have talked so often about it. ... Well, it is you who have made me, do not destroy me.'

'You want to leave me, I see,' she said, shaking her head.

'Who can have given you the power to be ungrateful, you who are like a man made of papier mâché? Do you not trust me – me, your good angel? I have so often spent the night working for you, have handed over to you the savings of my whole life-time; for four years I have shared my bread with you, a poor working-woman's bread; have lent you everything I had, even to my courage!'

'Mademoiselle, stop! stop!' he said, throwing himself on his knees and holding out his hands to her. 'Don't say anything more! In three days' time I will explain, I will tell you everything. Let me ...' he went on, and kissed her hand, 'let me be happy. I love someone and I am loved in return.'

'Very well, be happy, my child,' she said, as she drew him to his feet. Then she kissed his forehead and hair, with the desperation a condemned man must feel as he lives his last morning on earth.

'Ah! you are the noblest and best of human beings; you are the peer of the woman I love,' said the poor artist.

'I love you dearly enough to tremble for your future,' she said sombrely. 'Judas hanged himself! All ingrates come to a terrible end. You are leaving me, and you will never do work worth while again. Consider: we need not marry – I am an old maid, I know. I do not want to stifle the flower of your youth, your poetry as you call it, in my arms that are like vine-stocks, but, without marrying, can we not stay together? Listen. I have a head for business. I can gather a fortune for you in ten years' work, for my name is Thrift; whereas with a young wife, who will bring only expenses, you will throw everything away, you will only work to make her happy. Happiness creates nothing but memories. When I think of you, I stay for hours with my hands idle. ... Well, Wenceslas, stay with me. ... You know, I understand everything. You shall have mistresses, pretty women like that little Marneffe who wants to meet you, who will give you the kind of happiness you could not find with me. Then you shall get married when I have saved thirty thousand francs a year for you.'

'You are an angel, Mademoiselle, and I shall never forget this moment,' Wenceslas answered, wiping away tears.

'I see you now as I want you to be, my child,' she said, gazing at him in ecstasy.

So strong is vanity in us, that Lisbeth believed that she had triumphed. She had made such a great concession in offering Madame Marneffe! She experienced the keenest emotion of her life. For the first time she felt joy flood her heart. For such another hour she would have sold her soul to the devil.

'My word is pledged,' he answered, 'and I love a woman against whom no other can prevail. But you are and you will always be the mother I have lost.'

These words fell like an avalanche of snow upon that blazing crater. Lisbeth sat down and sombrely contemplated the youthfulness and distinguished good looks before her: the artist's brow, the mane of silky hair, everything that called to her repressed instincts as a woman; and a few tears, instantly dried, dimmed her eyes for a moment. She looked like one of the frail, meagre, figures carved by medieval sculptors above tombs.

'I place no curse upon you,' she said, rising abruptly. 'You are only a child. May God protect you!'

She went away, and shut herself in her room.

'She's in love with me,' Wenceslas said to himself, 'poor soul. What a torrent of burning eloquence! She's out of her mind.'

The supreme effort of that stiff, matter-of-fact nature to hold the image of beauty and poetry in its keeping can only be compared, in its vehemence, to a shipwrecked sailor's wild striving as he makes his last attempt to reach the shore.

Two days later, at half past four in the morning, when Count Steinbock was wrapped in deep sleep, he was awakened by knocking at his garret door. He went to open it, and two shabbily dressed men walked in, accompanied by a third who looked like a wretched process-server.

'You are Monsieur Wenceslas, Count Steinbock?' this third man said.

'Yes.'

'My name is Grasset, Monsieur, successor to Louchard, sheriff's officer.'

'Yes. Well?'

'You are under arrest, Monsieur. You must come with us to the Clichy prison. Please get dressed. We have done this as courteously as possible, as you see. I have not brought police, and there's a cab waiting downstairs.'

'You are properly caught,' added one of the bailiff's men, 'and we count on your coming quietly.'

Steinbock dressed and walked downstairs with a bailiff's man gripping each arm. When he had been put in the cab, the driver set off without being directed, like a man who knows where to go. Within half an hour, the poor foreigner found himself well and truly locked up, and had lodged no protest, so completely had he been surprised.

At ten o'clock he was called to the prison office, and there found Lisbeth, who, bathed in tears, gave him money to pay for additional food and a room large enough to work in.

'My child,' she said, 'speak of your arrest to no one; don't write to a living soul. It would be the ruin of your career. This stigma must be kept concealed. I'll soon have you out of this. I'll get the money together ... never fear. Write down what I should bring for your work. I'll die or you'll soon be free.'

'Oh! I'll owe you my life again!' he exclaimed. 'For I should lose more than life if my reputation were lost.'

Lisbeth left, with joy in her heart. She was hoping, with the artist under lock and key, to wreck his marriage with Hortense by saying that he was a married man, had been pardoned through his wife's efforts on his behalf, and had left for Russia. And so, in order to carry out this plan, she betook herself about three o'clock to visit the Baroness, although it was not the day when she usually dined there. She was anxious to savour the tortures her young cousin would suffer at the time when Wenceslas generally arrived.

'You are staying to dinner, Bette?' the Baroness asked, concealing her disappointment.

'Oh, yes.'

'Good!' answered Hortense. 'I'll go and tell them to be punctual, since you don't like being late.'

Hortense nodded reassuringly to her mother, for she intended to tell the man-servant to send Monsieur Steinbock away when he presented himself; but as the man had gone out, Hortense was obliged to give her message to the parlour maid, and the parlour maid went upstairs to fetch her needle-work before taking up her post in the anteroom.

'And what about my sweetheart?' Cousin Bette said to Hortense, when she returned. 'You never ask me about him nowadays.'

'Now that I think of it, what's he doing?' said Hortense. 'For he's famous now. You must be pleased,' she added, whispering in her cousin's ear. 'Everyone's talking of Monsieur Wenceslas Steinbock.'

'He's talked about far too much for his own good,' Lisbeth answered. 'It unsettles Monsieur. If it was only a matter of my charms carrying the day against the pleasures of Paris, I know my own power, but they say that the Czar Nicholas is anxious to attach an artist of such talent to his own Court, and is going to pardon him. . . .'

'Nonsense,' said the Baroness.

'How do you know that?' Hortense asked, with a sudden pang.

'Well,' the fiendish Bette went on, 'a person to whom he is bound by the most sacred ties, his wife, wrote to tell him so, yesterday. And he wants to go. Ah! he would be very foolish to leave France for Russia. . . .'

Hortense looked towards her mother, as her head drooped sideways. The Baroness had just time to catch her daughter as she fell fainting, as white as the lace of her fichu.

'Lisbeth! You have killed my girl!' exclaimed the Baroness. 'You were born to bring misfortune upon us.'

'Why, how am I to blame for this, Adeline?' the peasant-woman demanded, rising to her feet menacingly. But, in her anxiety, the Baroness did not notice her.

'I was wrong,' answered Adeline, supporting Hortense in her arms. 'Ring the bell!'

At that moment the door opened. The two women simul-taneously turned their heads and saw Wenceslas Steinbock, who had been admitted by the cook during the parlour maid's absence.

'Hortense!' cried the artist, springing towards the three women. And he kissed his love on her forehead before her mother's eyes, but so reverently that the Baroness could not be angry. For a fainting fit it was a better restorative than smelling-salts. Hortense opened her eyes, saw Wenceslas, and colour returned to her cheeks. In a few moments she had quite recovered.

'So this is what you have been hiding from me?' said Cousin Bette, smiling at Wenceslas, and appearing to guess the truth from the confusion of her two cousins. 'How did you contrive to steal my sweetheart?' she said to Hortense, leading her into the garden.

Hortense artlessly told her cousin the story of her love. Her mother and father, she said, convinced that Bette would never marry, had permitted Count Steinbock's visits. Not like a naïve girl, however, but with maturity's complex motives, she attributed to chance the purchase of the group, and the arrival of the artist, who, according to her, had wanted to know the name of his first patron.

Steinbock came quickly to join the two cousins, to thank the old maid with the utmost warmth for his swift deliverance from prison. To his thanks Lisbeth jesuitically replied that as the creditor had made only vague promises to her, she had not expected to obtain his release until the following day, and that this money-lender must have been ashamed of his petty persecution, and so had no doubt taken the initiative himself. The old maid, moreover, appeared to be pleased, and congratulated Wenceslas upon his good fortune.

'Wicked boy!' she said, before Hortense and her mother. 'If you had confessed, two days ago, that you loved my cousin Hortense and were loved by her in return, you would have spared me many tears. I thought that you were deserting your old friend, your governess, while, on the contrary, you are going to be my cousin. From now on you will be part of my family. The link is slender, it is true; but strong enough to justify my affection for you.'

And she kissed Wenceslas on the forehead. Hortense threw herself into her cousin's arms, and burst into tears.

'I owe my happiness to you,' she said. 'I will never forget it.'

'Cousin Bette,' the Baroness added, kissing Lisbeth in the

exhilaration of seeing everything turn out so well, 'the Baron and I owe you a debt, and we will pay it. Come, let us talk these matters over in the garden.' And she led the way there.

So Lisbeth was, to all appearances, the family's good angel. She had everyone at her feet: Crevel, Hulot, Adeline, and Hortense.

'We don't want you to work any longer,' said the Baroness. 'I suppose that you may earn forty sous a day, not counting Sundays: that makes six hundred francs a year. Well, how much have you put away in savings?'

'Four thousand five hundred francs.'

'Poor Cousin!' said the Baroness.

She raised her eyes to heaven, she was so moved to think of all the hardships and privations that that sum of money, gathered together through thirty years, represented. Lisbeth misunderstood the nature of the Baroness's exclamation, saw in it a successful woman's contempt, and her hatred acquired a new intensity of bitterness, at the very moment when her cousin was abandoning all her mistrust of the tyrant of her childhood.

'We will add ten thousand five hundred francs to that,' Adeline continued, 'placed in trust, the interest to go to you, the principal to revert to Hortense; so that you will have an income of six hundred francs a year.'

Lisbeth's cup was full, or so it seemed. When she returned to the drawing-room, her handkerchief to her eyes, wiping away happy tears, Hortense told her of all the commissions and favours pouring in on Wenceslas, the darling of the whole family.

When the Baron came in, therefore, he found his family complete, for the Baroness had formally greeted Count Steinbock by the name of son and fixed the date of the marriage, subject to her husband's approval, at a fortnight from that day. As soon as he appeared in the drawing-room, the Councillor of State was taken possession of by his wife and daughter, who ran to meet him, one anxious to have a word with him in private, the other to throw her arms round him.

'You have gone too far in promising my consent like this, Madame,' the Baron said severely. 'This marriage is not made,' he added, casting a look at Steinbock, whom he saw turn pale.

The unhappy artist said to himself, 'He knows of my arrest.'

'Come, children,' the father said, leading his daughter and proposed son-in-law into the garden; and he took them to sit on one of the moss-grown benches of the summer-house.

'Monsieur le Comte, do you love my daughter as dearly as I loved her mother?' the Baron asked Wenceslas.

'More dearly, Monsieur,' said the artist.

'Her mother was the daughter of a peasant, and had no fortune, not a farthing.'

'Give me Mademoiselle Hortense, just as she is, without even a trousseau. ...'

'That would be a fine thing!' said the Baron, smiling. 'Hortense is the daughter of Baron Hulot d'Ervy, Councillor of State, a Director of the War Office, Grand Officer of the Legion of Honour, brother of Count Hulot, whose glory is immortal and who is shortly to be a Marshal of France. And ... she has a dowry ...'

'It is true,' said the lover, 'that I must appear to be ambitious; but if my dear Hortense were a labourer's daughter I would marry her.'

'That is what I wanted to hear you say,' replied the Baron. 'Run away, Hortense, and let me talk to Monsieur le Comte. You can see that he really loves you.'

'Oh, Father, I knew very well that you were joking,' answered the happy girl.

'My dear Steinbock,' said the Baron, with the greatest sweetness and charm, when he was alone with the artist, 'I made a marriage settlement of two hundred thousand francs on my son, of which the poor boy has not received two farthings: he will never see a penny of it. My daughter's dowry will be two hundred thousand francs, for which you will give me a receipt.'

'Yes, Monsieur le Baron.'

'Not so fast,' said the Councillor of State. 'Will you listen to me, boy? One cannot ask of a son-in-law the self-sacrifice that one expects of a son. My son knew all that I could and

140

would do for his career. He will be a Minister; he will easily find his two hundred thousand francs. As for you, young man, your case is different. You will receive sixty thousand francs invested in five per cent Government stock, in your wife's name. This sum will be charged with a small annuity to be made to Lisbeth, but she is not likely to live long, she has a weak chest, I know. Don't mention this to anyone, I'm speaking in confidence; let the poor woman die in peace. My daughter will have a trousseau worth twenty thousand francs, to which her mother will add six thousand francs' worth of diamonds of her own.'

'Monsieur, you overwhelm me,' said Steinbock, at a loss for words.

'As for the remaining hundred and twenty thousand francs . . .'

'Don't say anything further, Monsieur,' said the artist. 'All I want is my dear Hortense.'

'Can you restrain your ardour, and let me speak, young man? As for the hundred and twenty thousand francs, I haven't got the money; but you will receive it.'

'Monsieur!'

'You will receive it from the Government in the form of commissions that I shall obtain for you, I give you my word. You know that you are going to be given a studio at the Marble Depository. Exhibit some good statues, and I will get you elected to the Institut. There's a certain amount of good-will in high places towards my brother and me, so I may hope to be successful in obtaining sculpture commissions for you at Versailles worth a quarter of the sum. Then you will get some commissions from the City of Paris, others from the House of Peers. You will have so many, in fact, my dear boy, that you will have to employ assistants. In this way I shall fulfil my obligation to you. Decide whether such a payment of the dowry suits you. Consider whether you are equal to the work. . . .'

'I feel equal to making a fortune for my wife single-handed, without help!' said the unworldly artist.

'That's the spirit I love!' exclaimed the Baron. 'Glorious youth, confident of itself, and ready to fight the world! I would have routed armies for a wife, myself! Well,' he went on, shaking the young sculptor's hand, 'you have my consent The civil contract next Sunday, and the following Saturday to the altar with you – it's my wife's birthday!'

'All is well,' said the Baroness to her daughter, who was glued to the window. 'Your future husband and your father are embracing each other.'

When Wenceslas returned home that evening, the mystery of his release was explained. He found, left with the porter, a large sealed package, containing the file of documents relating to his debt, together with the official discharge, recorded at the bottom of the writ, and the following letter:

My dear Wenceslas,

I came to see you this morning, at ten o'clock, in order to arrange your introduction to a Royal Highness who wishes to meet you. Here I learned that the English had carried you off to one of their little islands, whose capital is Clichy's Castle.

I at once went to see Léon de Lora, and told him as a joke that you were unable to leave your present territory for want of four thousand francs, and that your future would be compromised if you failed to present yourself to your royal patron. Bridau, a man of genius who has known poverty himself and is aware of your story, luckily happened to be there. Between them, my boy, they raised the money, and I shall pay off the barbarian who committed the crime of contempt of genius in locking you up. As I have to be at the Tuileries at twelve, I shall not be able to wait to see you breathing free air. I know you to be an honourable man. I have answered for you to my two friends; but go to see them tomorrow.

Léon and Bridau will not want money from you. They will both ask you for a group, and they will be well-advised to do so. That is the opinion of one who would like to be able to call himself your rival, but is just your sincere friend,

STIDMANN

P.S. I told the Prince that you would not be returning from your travels until tomorrow, and he said, 'Very well, tomorrow!'

Count Wenceslas went to sleep in the purple sheets that Popular Acclaim spreads for us, without one crumpled rose-leaf. That limping goddess walks even more hesitantly towards men of genius than Justice or Fortune, because by Jupiter's decree she wears no bandage on her eyes. She is easily taken in by charlatans; and their eye-catching display, bright costumes, and blaring trumpets induce her to waste on *them* the time and money that should be spent on seeking out men of merit, in their obscurity.

At this point it must be explained how Monsieur le Baron Hulot had managed to raise the money for Hortense's dowry, and meet the frightening expenses of the delightful flat in which Madame Marneffe was to be installed. The talent shown in his financial manipulations was of the kind that always guides spendthrifts and passion-driven men among the quagmires, where so many perils await them. The devil looks after his own, and to his powers are due those *tours de force* sometimes achieved by ambitious men, sensualists, and all the other subjects of his kingdom.

*

On the previous morning, the old man Johann Fischer, unable to pay back the sum of thirty thousand francs which had been raised in his name for his nephew, found himself faced with the prospect of filing his petition in bankruptcy if the Baron did not repay the money.

This worthy white-haired old man, seventy years of age, reposed such blind confidence in Hulot, who for this Bonapartist was a ray of Napoleon's sun, that he was tranquilly passing the time with the bank messenger in the back room of the little ground-floor premises, rented for eight hundred francs a year, from which he carried on his various enterprises in connexion with the supply of grain and forage.

'Marguerite has gone to get the money, not far away,' he told him.

The other man, in grey and silver-braided livery, was so well aware of the old Alsatian's probity that he was ready to leave the bills for thirty thousand francs with him; but the old man made him stay, pointing out that it had not yet struck eight o'clock.

A cab stopped outside. The old man hurried into the street and held out his hand with sublime confidence to the Baron, who gave him thirty thousand-franc notes.

'Go a few doors further on. I'll explain why later,' said

old Fischer. 'Here you are, young man,' said the old man, returning to count out the money to the bank representative and see him to the door.

When the bank messenger was out of sight, Fischer beckoned to the cab where his eminent nephew, Napoleon's right hand, was waiting, and said as they went into the house:

'You don't want it to be known at the Bank of France that you have paid thirty thousand francs on bills endorsed by you. It's too bad as it is that they have the signature of a man like you on them!'

'Let's go to the end of your garden, Uncle Fischer,' said the high official. 'Your health is sound?' he began, sitting down in a vine arbour and scrutinizing the old man as a dealer in human beings might scrutinize some substitute to be hired for army service.

'Sound enough to place your money on,' the thin, seasoned, wiry, bright-eyed little man replied gaily.

'Does a hot climate upset you?'

'On the contrary.'

'What do you think of Africa?'

'A fine country! The French were there with the Little Corporal.'

'It may be necessary, for the sake of us all, for you to go to Algeria.'

'What about my business?'

'A War Office official who is retiring and has not enough to live on will buy your business.'

'And what's to be done in Algeria?'

'I want you to raise Army supplies, grain and forage. I have your commission signed. You will be able to purchase your supplies in the country at seventy per cent less than the price you will return on your accounts to us.'

'The supplies will come from what sources?'

'Raids ... levies ... from the caliphate. Very little is known about Algeria, although we have been there for the past eight years, but there are vast quantities of grain and forage in the country. When this is in Arab hands, we take it from them under a variety of pretexts; then when we have it, the Arabs do everything in their power to get it from us. There's a great deal of competition for grain; but it's never known exactly how much has been stolen, one way or the other. There's no time in the open country to weigh out wheat by the hectolitre as it's done in the Paris corn market, or hay as they do it in the rue d'Enfer. The Arab chiefs, like our own Spahis, prefer hard cash, and sell their produce very cheaply for it. The Army, on the other hand, has its fixed requirements; so purchases made at exorbitant prices are passed, allowing for the difficulty of procuring supplies and the risks of transport. That's Algeria from the Army Supply point of view. It's chaos, made bearable by the underground transactions of all infant administrations. As officials, we shall not be able to see clearly what's going on there for a dozen years yet, but private individuals have good eyes in their heads; so I am sending you out there to make a fortune. I am placing you there, as Napoleon used to place a poor Marshal in charge of a kingdom where a traffic in smuggled goods could be secretly protected. I am ruined, my dear Fischer. I need a hundred thousand francs within a year.'

'I see no harm in getting it from the Arabs,' the Alsatian replied tranquilly. 'That was done under the Empire. . . .'

'The purchaser of your business will be coming to see you this morning, and will give you ten thousand francs,' Baron Hulot went on. 'That's all you need, isn't it, to get to Africa?'

The old man nodded.

'As for funds out there, you need not worry,' continued the Baron. 'I shall keep the balance of the payment for your business. I need it.'

'It's all yours. My life too,' the old man said.

'Oh! fear nothing,' answered the Baron, crediting his uncle with greater perspicacity than he possessed; 'as far as our collecting of levies is concerned, your honour will not be questioned. Everything depends on the central authority, and I myself made the appointments, so I am sure of it. This, Uncle Fischer, is a life-or-death secret. I can trust you: I have spoken to you frankly, without mincing matters.'

'That journey is decided upon,' said the old man. 'But for how long?'

'Two years! You will make a hundred thousand francs on

your own account, and live happily ever after in the Vosges!'

'It shall be just as you wish. My honour is yours,' the little old man said, serenely.

'That's the spirit I like in men. However, you must not go until you have seen your great-niece happily married. She is to be a Countess.'

Making levies, raiding the raiders, and selling the Fischer business could not immediately raise sixty thousand francs for Hortense's dowry, and about five thousand francs for her trousseau, in addition to the forty thousand francs already spent or about to be spent on Madame Marneffe. And how had the Baron found the thirty thousand francs which he had brought with him? In this way.

A few days before, Hulot had insured his life for a hundred and fifty thousand francs, for three years, with two different insurance companies. Armed with the policies, with the premiums paid, he had spoken as follows to Monsieur le Baron de Nucingen, Peer of France, on the way home to dinner with him, after a sitting of the House of Peers:

'Baron, I need seventy thousand francs, and I am asking you to lend it to me. If you will appoint some man of straw, I can assign my salary to you under cover, or at least such part of it as money can be raised on. It amounts to twenty-five thousand francs a year, that's seventy-five thousand in three years. You will say, "What if you die?"'

'The Baron nodded.

'Here are insurance policies for one hundred and fifty thousand francs, which you can hold as security until eighty thousand francs have been paid off,' the Baron continued, drawing papers from his pocket.

'And subbose you are tismissed?' said the German-Jewish millionaire Baron, with a laugh.

The other Baron, the reverse of a millionaire, knitted his brow.

'Ton't worry. I only raised the opjection to show you that it's rather goot of me do gif you the money. You musd pe hart bressed, for the Pank has your signadure?'

'I'm marrying my daughter,' said Baron Hulot, 'and I have no money, like everyone else who has gone on serving the

Government of the country in this ungrateful age, for it will be a long time before five hundred bourgeois representatives sitting on benches know how to reward devoted service in the grand manner, as the Emperor did.'

'Gome now, you had Chosépha!' returned the Peer of France. 'And that egsblains eferything. Bedween ourselves, the Tuke of Héroufille did you ein goot durn when he bulled that ploodsucker off your burse. "I haf known like mischance, and can mingle my tears,"' he added, in the belief that he was quoting a line of French verse. 'Dake a frient's atvice: shud ub shob, or you will gome to grief. . . .'

This dubious piece of business was arranged through the intermediary of a little money-lender named Vauvinet, one of those agents that hang about large banking-houses, rather like the little fish that seems to attend the shark. This apprentice predator promised Monsieur le Baron Hulot – so anxious was he to win the favour of an eminent man – to raise thirty thousand francs in bills at ninety days, renewable four times, pledging himself not to put them into circulation.

Fischer's successor was to give forty thousand francs for the business, with the promise of a contract to supply forage in a Department near Paris.

Such was the frightening labyrinth into which his venery was leading a man until then of unimpeachable integrity, one of the ablest administrators of the Napoleonic régime: peculation, in order to repay money borrowed for the sake of his passions, whose indulgence had forced him to borrow to marry his daughter. This ingeniously organized expenditure of money and effort, all this endeavour, were for the sake of impressing Madame Marneffe, to play Jupiter to this bourgeoise Danaë. The energy, intelligence, and enterprise the Baron employed in order to dive head first into a hornet's nest might have made an honest fortune. He attended to the affairs of his department, urged on the decorators, superintended the workmen, minutely checked every detail of the establishment in the rue Vanneau. Although all his thoughts and plans were for Madame Marneffe, he attended the sittings of the Chamber. He was everywhere at once; and neither his family nor anyone else noticed his preoccupation.

Adeline, amazed to learn that her uncle had been repaid, to see a dowry figuring in the marriage contract, felt a certain uneasiness, in spite of the happiness with which she saw Hortense's marriage arranged on such honourable terms. But on the eve of her daughter's wedding, planned by the Baron to coincide with the day when Madame Marneffe was to take possession of her apartment in the rue Vanneau, Hector ended his wife's surprise with this magisterial pronouncement.

'Adeline, our daughter's future is now provided for, and all our anxieties on her account are at an end. It is now time for us to withdraw from social life, for in another three years I shall reach retiring age and take my pension. Why should we go on bearing expense not necessary now? Our rent is six thousand francs a year, we keep four servants, we run through thirty thousand francs per annum. If you want me to fulfil my obligations, since I have signed away my salary for three years in exchange for the sums needed for Hortense's establishment, and to meet your uncle's bills . . .'

'Ah! you did well, my dear,' she interrupted, and kissed her husband's hands.

This confession allayed Adeline's fears.

'I have some small sacrifices to ask of you,' he went on, disengaging his hands and placing a kiss on his wife's forehead. 'I have been told of a very good apartment in the rue Plumet, on the first floor. It's a handsome place with very fine wood panelling, very suitable, and costs only fifteen hundred francs. You would need only one maid there, and I could make do with a boy.'

'Yes, dear.'

'To run the house simply, and at the same time keep up appearances, you'll need to spend barely six thousand francs a year, apart from my personal expenses, which I'll take care of myself . . .'

This generous wife threw her arms round her husband's neck, in complete content.

'What joy to be able to show you once more how much I love you! And what a resourceful man you are!' she exclaimed.

'We will have our family to dinner once a week, and I rarely dine at home, as you know. .... You can very well go out to dinner twice a week with Victorin, and twice with Hortense; and as I think I'll be able to make it up with Crevel, we'll dine once a week with him. These five dinners and our own will fill the week, allowing for some invitations outside the family.'

'I'll save money for you,' said Adeline.

'Ah!' he exclaimed. 'You are a pearl among women!'

'My dear wonderful Hector! I'll bless you to my dying day,' she replied, 'for having made such a good marriage for our darling Hortense.'

So was the beautiful Baroness Hulot's household diminished, and she herself, it must be said, deserted, in accordance with the solemn promise made to Madame Marneffe.

Little Monsieur Crevel, portly and self-important, who was naturally invited to the ceremony of signing the marriage contract, behaved as if the scene with which this story opened had never taken place, as if he had no grudge against Baron Hulot. Célestin Crevel was genial; he was, as always, a little too much the ex-perfumer, but he was beginning to acquire an air of majestic patronage in keeping with his new dignity as Major. He talked of dancing at the wedding.

'Fair lady,' he said graciously to Baroness Hulot, 'people like ourselves know how to forget. Do not banish me from your home, and deign to adorn my house sometimes by accompanying your children there. Do not fear, I will never speak to you of what lies hidden in my heart. I acted like a fool, for I should lose too much if I never saw you again ...'

'Monsieur, a self-respecting woman doesn't listen to speeches like those you are referring to; and if you keep your promise, you may be sure that I shall be very glad to see the end of a difference between us, always a sad thing in one's family. ...'

'Well, my sulky friend,' said Baron Hulot, carrying Crevel off to the garden; 'you keep out of my way wherever you are, even in my own house. Is it right that two old amateurs of the fair sex like us should quarrel over a petticoat? Really, upon my word, it's too vulgar.'

'Monsieur, I'm not such a handsome man as you, and my

slight powers of attraction prevent me from making good my losses as easily as you do.'

'Ah, sarcasm!' replied the Baron.

'It is permissible against victors by the vanquished.'

The conversation begun on this note ended in complete reconciliation; but Crevel was careful to state and reserve his right to have his revenge.

Madame Marneffe wanted to be invited to Mademoiselle Hulot's wedding. In order to see his future mistress in his own drawing-room the Councillor of State was obliged to invite all the underlings of his department as far down in grade as to include the deputy head clerks, so that it became necessary to give a large ball. As an economical housekeeper, the Baroness calculated that an evening party would cost less than a dinner, and would allow more people to be received. Hortense's wedding, therefore, made a great stir.

Marshal Prince de Wissembourg and Baron de Nucingen were the witnesses on behalf of the bride, and Counts de Rastignac and Popinot for Steinbock. Since Count Steinbock had become well known, the most distinguished members of the colony of *émigré* Poles had taken him up, and the artist thought that he was bound to invite them. The Council of State, the Baron's own department, and the Army, in compliment to the Comte de Forzheim, were to be represented at the highest level. It was estimated that there were two hundred indispensable invitations. Small wonder, then, that little Madame Marneffe should be eager to appear in all her finery among such an assembly!

A month before, the Baroness had sold her diamonds, keeping back the finest stones for the trousseau, and had devoted the money to furnishing her daughter's house. The sum realized was fifteen thousand francs, of which five thousand was spent on Hortense's trousseau. And how far does ten thousand francs go towards furnishing a flat for a young couple, with all the requirements of modern luxury? But young Monsieur and Madame Hulot and old Crevel and the Comte de Forzheim gave valuable presents; for Hortense's old uncle had kept a sum of money in reserve to buy silver plate. Thanks to many contributions, the most exigent woman in

Paris would have been satisfied with the way in which the new young couple were set up in the apartment they had chosen in the rue Saint-Dominique, near the Invalides. It made a harmonious setting for their love, so whole-hearted, so transparent and sincere on both sides.

At last the great day arrived, for this was to be a great day for Hortense's father as well as for Hortense and Wenceslas. Madame Marneffe had decided to have a house-warming on the day after she had burned her boats, and the wedding day of the two lovers.

Everyone has attended a wedding ball at least once in his life, and can hardly fail to smile as he recalls all those wedding guests in their Sunday best with expressions to match. Of all ceremonial social occasions, this is the one that most effectively demonstrates the influence of atmosphere, afflicting even habitually well-dressed people with the self-consciousness of those dressed up for a red-letter day in their lives. Then one thinks of the unfestive guests: the old men so indifferent to all the fuss that they have not changed their everyday black suits, and the men, many years married, whose faces proclaim their sad experience of the life that the young are just beginning. Do you remember the effervescing gaiety, like the bubbles in the champagne, and the envious girls, and the women with their minds preoccupied with the success of their toilettes, and the poor relations in their skimped finery, and the smart people *in fiocchi* – in their smartest – and the greedy thinking only of supper, and the gamblers only of the game? There they all are, as one remembers them, rich and poor, envious and envied, the cynics and the dazzled dreamers, all clustered like the flowers in a bouquet around one rare flower, the bride. A wedding ball is a miniature world.

When the excitement was at its height, Crevel took the Baron by the arm, and said in his ear, in the most natural manner possible:

'Bless me, what a pretty woman that is, there, in pink, aiming killing glances at you!'

'Which one do you mean?'

'The wife of that deputy head clerk that you're pushing on, God knows how! Madame Marneffe!'

'How do you come to know that?'

'Look here, Hulot, you have done me some damage, but I will try to forgive you if you will introduce me to her, and in return I will invite you to meet Héloïse. Everyone is asking who that charming creature is. Are you sure that no one in your department will tumble to the circumstances in which her husband's nomination was signed? Oh, you lucky rascal, she's worth more than a department! Ah! I would gladly work in her department. . . . Come now. "Let us be friends, Cinna"!'

'The best of friends, never better!' said the Baron to the perfumer. 'And I'll show you what a real friend I am. I'll ask you to dinner before a month is out, with that little angel. . . . For we're dealing with angels now, old man. Take my advice, do like me and give up the devils.'

Cousin Bette, now installed in the rue Vanneau in a pretty little set of rooms on the third floor, left the ball at ten o'clock in order to go home and look at her bonds, representing an income of twelve hundred francs, one in the name of Countess Steinbock, and the other in that of the younger Madame Hulot. Monsieur Crevel, by what means we now guess, had been able to speak to his friend Hulot with full knowledge of something no one knew; for, with Monsieur Marneffe away, only Cousin Bette, the Baron, and Valérie were in the secret.

The Baron had been so unwise as to give Madame Marneffe a dress much too expensive for a deputy chief clerk's wife. The other wives were jealous both of Valérie's toilette and of her beauty. There were whisperings behind fans, for the Marneffes' money troubles had been common gossip in the department. The clerk had been applying for an advance of salary at the very moment when the Baron had become enamoured of his wife. Besides, Hulot was quite unable to hide his intoxication while he watched Valérie's success as, demure but conspicuous and envied, she underwent that careful scrutiny so dreaded by many women when they enter a new social world for the first time.

When he had seen his wife, daughter, and son-in-law to their carriage, the Baron managed to slip away unnoticed, leaving the duty of playing host and hostess to his son and daughter-in-law. He got into Madame Marneffe's carriage to escort her home; but he found her silent and pensive, to the point of melancholy.

'My happiness makes you very sad, Valérie,' he said, drawing her to him in the darkness of the cab.

'My dear, would you not expect a poor woman to be a little thoughtful when she first falls from virtue, even when her husband's ill-treatment sets her free? Do you think I have no soul, no beliefs, no religion? The way you showed your joy this evening was most indiscreet, and you have made me horribly conspicuous. Really, a schoolboy would have been less youthfully triumphant. And all those women have been tearing me to pieces, with any amount of knowing glances and spiteful remarks! What woman does not value her reputation? You have done for mine. Ah! I am certainly all yours now, and if I'm to justify my lapse I'll have to be faithful to you. Oh! you're a monster!' she said, laughing and letting him kiss her. 'You knew very well what you were doing. Madame Coquet, the wife of our chief clerk, came and sat down beside me and admired my lace. "It's English lace," she remarked. "Is that very expensive, Madame?" "I haven't the least idea," I answered her. "It was my mother's. I can't afford to buy anything like that!"'

Clearly, Madame Marneffe had succeeded in fascinating the old Empire beau so completely that he believed that he was persuading her to be unfaithful for the first time and that he had inspired her with a passion strong enough to make her forget all her vows. She told him that the odious Marneffe had completely neglected her after three days of marriage, and for the vilest of motives. Since then she had been living a quiet virtuous life like a well-behaved child, and been glad to do so, for marriage seemed horrible to her. That was the reason for her present sadness.

'Suppose love should be like marriage!' she said, in tears.

These coy fairy-tales, invented by nearly all women in Valérie's situation, raised the Baron to a rose-strewn seventh heaven. So Valérie coquettishly delayed her surrender, while the love-sick artist and Hortense were waiting, perhaps impatiently, until the Baroness should have given her last blessing and her final kiss to the girl.

At seven in the morning, the Baron, full of bliss – for he had found a girl's innocence and the most consummate devilry in his Valérie – returned to relieve his son and daughter-in-law at their post of duty. Those dancers, almost strangers to the house, who at all weddings soon take possession of the floor, were still engaged in the final interminable figure-dances called cotillions, the bouillotte players were intent on their tables, old Crevel was in process of winning six thousand francs.

The morning papers being distributed by the newsvendors carried the following short notice among the social news of Paris:

The marriage of Monsieur le Comte Steinbock and Mademoiselle Hortense Hulot, daughter of Baron Hulot d'Ervy, Councillor of State and a Director of the Ministry of War, niece of the illustrious Comte de Forzheim, was solemnized this morning at the Church of Saint-Thomas d'Aquin. The ceremony was attended by a large gathering. Among those present were a number of our best-known artistic celebrities: Léon de Lora, Joseph Bridau, Stidmann, Bixiou; eminent representatives of the Ministry of War and the Council of State; and several Members of both the Upper and Lower Chambers; as well as distinguished members of the Polish colony, Count Paz, Count Laginski, and others.

Monsieur le Comte Wenceslas Steinbock is the grand-nephew of the famous general who served under King Charles XII of Sweden. The young Count took part in the Polish rising, and has found political refuge in France, where his high reputation as a sculptor has made it possible for him to obtain naturalization papers.

And so, in spite of Baron Hulot's desperate financial straits, his daughter's wedding lacked nothing that public opinion requires, not even newspaper publicity, and was in all respects similar to the celebration of his son's marriage with Mademoiselle Crevel. This occasion did something to kill the rumours that were being spread about the Director's financial position; and the dowry given to his daughter, too, explained his need to borrow money.

Here ends what may be called the introduction to this story. This account is to the drama that completes it, as the premises to a syllogism, or the exposition to a classical tragedy.

*

In Paris, when a woman has made up her mind to use her beauty as her livelihood and merchandise, it does not necessarily follow that she will make her fortune. Lovely spirited creatures are to be met with in that city in desperately poor circumstances, ending in squalor a life that began in pleasure. The reason is this. It is not enough simply to take the decision to adopt a courtesan's shameful profession and reap its fruits, while still preserving the appearances of a respectable middleclass wife. Vice does not achieve its triumphs easily. It is like genius in this respect: that both require a conjunction of favouring circumstances, so that they may use both fortune and talent to the best effect.

If the strange events of the Revolution had never taken place, the Emperor would not have existed either; he would have been no more than a second Fabert. Venal beauty, with no admirers, with no celebrity, without the Cross of Dishonour awarded by squandered fortunes, is like a Correggio in a lumber-room; it is genius dying in a garret.

A Laïs in Paris, then, must first of all find a rich man sufficiently enamoured of her to pay her price. She must, most important of all, maintain a high standard of elegance, for that is her hallmark of quality; be sufficiently cultured and polished to flatter men's self-esteem; possess the sparkle of a Sophie Arnould, with her power to stimulate the indifferent rich man's interest. Finally, she must make libertines desire her by appearing to be faithful to one, whose good fortune then becomes envied by the rest.

The conditions she needs, which women of that kind call *luck*, are quite hard to realize in Paris, for all that the city is full of millionaires, idlers, the bored and the sophisticated. For Providence seems to have set a strong wall about the homes of clerks and the lower middle class, whose wives find their difficulties at least doubled by the social environment in which they move. There are enough Madame Marneffes in Paris, however, for Valérie to represent a type in this record of manners.

Of such women, some yield to a combination of true passion and financial necessity, like Madame Colleville, who was for so long attached to one of the most distinguished orators of the Left, the banker Keller; and others are impelled by vanity, like Madame de la Baudraye, whose reputation remained almost unblemished, in spite of her elopement with Lousteau. Some are led astray by their love of fine clothes, and some by the impossibility of making ends meet on a salary obviously inadequate to the running of a household. The parsimony of the state, or of the Chambers, if you like, is the cause of a great deal of unhappiness, the source of much corruption. A considerable amount of sympathy is expressed at the present time with the hard lot of the working classes: they are represented as the manufacturers' sweated victims. But the state is a hundred times harder than the most grasping industrialist – in the matter of salaries it carries economy to absurd extremes. If you work hard, Industry rewards you in proportion to your effort; but what does the state do for its hosts of obscure and devoted toilers?

To stray from the path of virtue is for the married woman an inexcusable fault; but there are degrees of guilt. Some women, far from becoming depraved, conceal their frailty, and remain apparently worthy of respect, like the two whose stories have just been recalled; while certain others add to their disgrace the shame of deliberate investment in their dishonour. Madame Marneffe may be considered a type of the ambitious married courtesan who from the start accepts moral depravity and all that it implies, resolving to make her fortune and enjoy herself too, with no scruples about the means. Like Madame Marneffe, such women almost always have their husbands as their agents and accomplices.

Machiavellis in petticoats such as these are the most dangerous and the worst among all the evil kinds of women in Paris. A true courtesan – like Josépha, Madame Schontz, Malaga, Jenny Cadine, and the rest – conveys in the unmistakable nature of her situation a warning as brightly shining as prostitution's red lamp or the blazing lights of gambling dens. A man knows that he risks ruin in such company. But the sweetly prim respectability, the outer semblance of virtue, the hypocritical ways of a married woman who never spends anything, apparently, but the day-to-day housekeeping expenses, who demurs at any show of extravagance, lead men to unsignposted, unspectacular ruin, ruin all the stranger because the victim finds excuses, and cannot find a cause for his disaster. It is inglorious household bills that consume fortunes, not gay dissipation. The father of a family beggars himself ignominiously, and does not even have, in his ruin, the major consolation of gratified vanity.

This cap will fit in many a household: this little sermon should fly like an arrow home to many a heart. Madame Marneffes are to be seen at every level in society, even at Court; for Valérie is a sad reality of existence, modelled from life, correct in every particular. Unfortunately, painting her portrait will cure no one of an addiction to loving sweetly smiling angels with a dreamy air, an innocent face, and a strong-box for a heart.

About three years after Hortense's marriage, in 1841, everyone thought that Baron Hulot d'Ervy had settled down – 'laid by his horses', to use the expression of Louis XV's first surgeon – and yet he was spending more than twice as much on Madame Marneffe as he had ever done on Josépha. But Valérie, although always charmingly dressed, affected the simplicity suitable in the wife of a junior official. She kept luxury for private occasions, for her dress when she was at home, and in this way offered up her Parisian vanities as a sacrifice to her dear Hector. All the same, when she went to the theatre, she always appeared wearing a pretty hat and a very smart, fashionable dress. The Baron escorted her there in a carriage, to one of the best boxes.

The apartment in the rue Vanneau, which occupied the whole of the second floor of a modern house standing between a court and a garden, exhaled respectability. Its luxury consisted in nothing more than chintz hangings and handsome comfortable furniture, except in the bedroom, which displayed the extravagant profusion of a Jenny Cadine or a Schontz. It was all lace curtains, cashmere draperies, brocade door-hangings; with a set of chimneypiece ornaments designed by Stidmann and a little cabinet of knick-knacks crammed with treasures. Hulot had not wished to see his Valérie in a nest in any way inferior in magnificence to a

Josépha's gold-and-pearl-bedecked den of wickedness. Of the two principal rooms, the drawing-room was furnished in red damask, and the dining-room with carved oak. And, led on by the wish to have everything in keeping, the Baron, by the end of six months, had added more solid luxury to the knick-knacks, and given some very valuable household possessions: silver plate, for instance, worth more than twenty-four thousand francs.

Madame Marneffe's house within two years had acquired the reputation of being a very pleasant place to visit. People went there to play cards. Valérie herself quickly became known as an agreeable and amusing woman. In order to explain the change in her circumstances, the story was put about of a huge legacy left to her by her natural father, Marshal Mont-cornet, in trust. With some thought for the future, Valérie had added religious hypocrisy to her social kind. She was a regular attender at church services on Sunday, and was given due credit for her piety. She collected for the church, became a member of a women's charitable organization, contributed the consecrated bread, and did some good work among the poor in the neighbourhood, all at Hector's expense. Every-thing in her household, indeed, bore the mark of respect-ability. Many people affirmed that her relations with the Baron were quite innocent, pointing out the age of the Councillor of State, and believing that he had a platonic taste for Madame Marneffe's pleasing wit, charming manners, and lively conversation, rather like the late Louis XVIII's pleasure in a neatly turned love-letter.

The Baron always left the house with everyone else, about midnight, and returned a quarter of an hour later. The secret of the profound secrecy of this secret was as follows:

The doorkeepers of the house were Monsieur and Madame Olivier, and it was through the Baron's influence, as a friend of the landlord, who was looking for a caretaker, that they had left their obscure and ill-paid place in the rue du Doyenné for the lucrative and splendid position in the rue Vanneau house. Now, Madame Olivier, a former linen-maid in Charles X's household who had fallen from that estate like the occupant of the throne, had three children. The eldest, already junior clerk to a lawyer, was adored by his parents. This Benjamin, with the threat of six years of military service hanging over his head, had seen his brilliant career about to be broken off, when Madame Marneffe managed to secure his exemption on account of one of those physical defects that examining boards can always find when a word is spoken in their ear by some power in the War Office. Olivier, a former groom in Charles X's stables, and his wife would therefore have put Christ on the cross again for Baron Hulot and Madame Marneffe.

What could the world say, to whom the earlier episode of the Brazilian, Monsieur Montès de Montejanos, was quite unknown? Nothing at all. The world, besides, looks with an indulgent eye on the mistress of a house where it finds good entertainment. In addition to all her pleasant attractions Madame Marneffe had the much prized advantage of under-cover power. For this reason Claude Vignon, who had become secretary to Marshal Prince de Wissembourg and who dreamed of being a member of the Council of State as Master of Requests, frequented her drawing-room, to which also came several Deputies who were convivial fellows and liked a flutter. Madame Marneffe's set was built up by careful slow degrees; a coterie was formed exclusively of men of similar tastes and outlook, with an eye open to their own interest and a voice to proclaim the infinite merits of the mistress of the house. Complicity in vice, remember this, is the real Holy Alliance in Paris. Men pursuing some financial interest in the end break away from one other; those with a vice have always a common interest.

Within three months of moving to the rue Vanneau, Madame Marneffe was entertaining Monsieur Crevel, who quite soon afterwards became Mayor of his borough and Officer of the Legion of Honour. Crevel had hesitated for a time before taking that step: it meant laying aside the famous uniform of the National Guard in which he was accustomed to peacock at the Tuileries, thinking himself as much a soldier as the Emperor himself. But ambition, with Madame Marneffe's advice to back it, proved stronger than vanity. The Mayor had deemed his liaison with Mademoiselle Héloïse

Brisetout to be quite incompatible with his political status. For some time before his accession to the bourgeois throne of the Mayoralty, his gallantries had been wrapped in complete mystery. But Crevel, it may be guessed, had paid for the right to take, as often as he could, his revenge for Josépha's carrying off, by a settlement worth six thousand francs a year in the name of Valérie Fortin, a wife holding property independently of her husband. Valérie, perhaps inheriting from her mother the kept woman's sharpness of eye, had understood in the flicker of an eyelid the character of that grotesque admirer. Crevel's exclamation to Lisbeth 'I have never had a real lady!' reported by Lisbeth to her dear Valérie, had greatly strengthened Valérie's hand in the transaction to which she owed her six thousand francs a year in five per cents. From that time she had never allowed her prestige to suffer diminution in the eyes of César Birotteau's former traveller.

Crevel had married money in the person of the daughter of a miller of Brie, an only child whose inheritance made up three-quarters of his fortune; for shopkeepers grow rich, as a rule, not so much from their business as by the alliance of the shop with rural interests. A large number of the farmers, millers, stock-breeders, market-gardeners round Paris dream of the glories of shopkeeping for their daughters, and in a retailer, a jeweller, a moneylender, see a son-in-law much more to their taste than a solicitor or an attorney would be; for the lawyers' social status makes them uneasy; they are afraid of later being despised by persons so influential in the bourgeois world.

Madame Crevel, a rather plain woman, very vulgar and stupid, had died early and unregretted, having given her husband no pleasures but those of paternity. At the beginning of his career in trade, then, this libertine, restrained by the duties of his position, his passions curbed by lack of means, had experienced the thirst of Tantalus. In touch, to use his own expression, with the most elegant women in Paris, he used to bow them to the door with a shopkeeper's effusive politeness, admiring as he did so their grace, their way of wearing their fashionable clothes, and all the indefinable marks of what is called 'good breeding'. To raise himself to the height of one of these presiding geniuses of the *salon* had been an aspiration conceived in his youth and held repressed in his heart. To win Madame Marneffe's 'favours' therefore, meant the realization of his castle in Spain; as well as involving his injured pride, striking a necessary blow on behalf of vanity and self-respect, as we have seen. His ambition grew with success. His swelling sense of his own importance gave him enormous pleasure; and when the imagination is captivated, the heart responds, and happiness increases tenfold. Madame Marneffe, besides, gave Crevel a refinement of pleasure that he had never before thought possible, for neither Josépha nor Héloïse had loved him, while Madame Marneffe deemed it necessary to pull the wool thoroughly over the eyes of this man, whom she saw as a perennially available cash-box.

The illusions of pretended love are more beguiling than the real thing. True love admits of sparrows' bickering quarrels, in which one may be pierced to the heart; but a quarrel which is only make-believe, on the contrary, is a caress to a dupe's vanity. Also, the rarity of his opportunities with Valérie maintained Crevel's passion at white heat. He was for ever coming up against Valérie's obdurate virtue, for she feigned remorse and talked of what her father must be thinking of her in his heaven of the brave. He had to overcome a kind of coldness, over which the wily lady made him think he won a victory, as she appeared to yield before this shopkeeper's consuming passion; but she clothed herself again, as if she were ashamed, in her respectable woman's pride and airs of virtue, like nobody so much as an Englishwoman, and always crushed her Crevel with the heavy weight of her dignity; for Crevel had swallowed her virtuous pose whole from the beginning. Finally, Valérie possessed special accomplishments in tenderness that made her indispensable to both Crevel and the Baron. When the world was present she displayed an enchanting combination of dreamy, modest innocence, impeccable propriety, and native wit, enhanced by charm, grace, and easy creole manners. But in a private conversation she outdid the courtesans, she was droll, amusing, fertile in invention. A contrast of this sort is enormously pleasing to a man of Crevel's kind: he is flattered to be the unique inspirer of such a comedy; he believes that it is played for his benefit exclusively, and laughs at the delicious hypocrisy, while admiring the actress.

Of Baron Hulot Valérie had taken complete possession, and she performed wonders in adapting him to suit herself. She had persuaded him to let himself grow old, using a kind of subtle flattery that serves well enough to show the diabolical cleverness of women of her sort. To even a privileged human constitution, as to a besieged fortress that has stood long apparently impregnable, there comes a moment when the true state of affairs declares itself. Foreseeing the approaching collapse of the Empire beau, Valérie thought it necessary to hasten it.

'Why do you bother, my own old soldier?' she said to him, six months after their clandestine and doubly adulterous union. 'Have you aspirations elsewhere, I wonder? Do you want to be unfaithful to me? I should like you so much better if you stopped using make-up. Sacrifice artificial charms for my sake. Surely you don't think that the things I love you for are the two sous' worth of polish on your boots, your rubber belt, your tight waistcoat, the dye on your hair? Besides, the older you look, the less afraid I shall be of seeing my Hulot carried off by some rival!'

And so, believing that Madame Marneffe loved him and was a divine friend too, and meaning to end his days with her, the Councillor of State followed her private counsel and gave up dyeing his whiskers and hair. The imposing, handsome Hector, one fine day, after Valérie had made this touching declaration, appeared white-haired. Madame Marneffe easily convinced her dear Hector that she had, dozens of times, noticed the white line made by the growing hair.

'White hair suits your face admirably,' she said, when she saw him. 'The effect is softening. You look infinitely nicer; you are charming.'

And by degrees the Baron, once started off in that direction, left off wearing his leather waistcoat and his stays; he got rid of all his harness. His stomach sagged; obesity was obvious. The oak tree became a tower. The Baron's heaviness of movement was the more ominous because he had greatly aged in the role of Louis XII. His eyebrows were still black, and vaguely recalled the Hulot of his handsome days, as on bare medieval walls some dim detail of carving may remain to suggest the bygone glories of the castle. The incongruity made his eyes, which were still alert and young, seem all the stranger in his weathered face. There, where Rubens's ruddy flesh-tones had bloomed for so long, one could see, in certain ravages and tense taut lines, the struggling of a passion in rebellion against nature. Hulot, during this period, was one of those fine human ruins whose virility asserts itself in a kind of bushy growth of hair from ears and nose and fingers, like the moss springing up on the almost indestructible monuments of the Roman Empire.

How had Valérie managed to keep Crevel and Hulot together at her side, when the Major was yearning for revenge, and all agog to score an open triumph over Hulot? Leaving this question unanswered for the moment to be resolved in the unfolding of the drama, we may note that Lisbeth and Valérie between them had concocted a wonderful plot, which worked very effectively to help her.

Marneffe, seeing his wife in her glory at the centre of the circle of admirers over whom she ruled as queen, like the sun of a solar system, seemed, in the eyes of the world, to have felt his passion for her spring to life again – he was now obviously quite mad about her. If this jealousy made Marneffe, the lord and master, something of a spoil-sport, it added enormously to the value of Valérie's favours. At the same time, Marneffe manifested a trust in his Director that degenerated into a compliant good nature verging on the ridiculous. The only person to arouse fierce resentment in him was Crevel!

Marneffe, destroyed by the debaucheries characteristic of great cities, described by the Roman poets, but for which our modern squeamishness has no name, had grown hideous as a wax anatomical figure, but this walking disease was clothed in fine cloth, walked on its hop-pole legs in an elegant pair of trousers. The emaciated chest was dressed in scented white linen, and musk overlaid the fetid odours of human corruption. Crevel was intimidated by this personification of the hideousness of vice: dying, yet sporting red-heeled shoes – for Valérie had seen to it that Marneffe's dress was in keeping with his situation, his promotion, and his Cross – and he could not easily meet the deputy head clerk's pale-eyed gaze. Marneffe was the Mayor's nightmare. As he became aware of the singular power that Lisbeth and his wife had conferred upon him, the malicious scamp diverted himself by using it, by playing upon it as if it were an instrument; and, drawing-room games of cards being the last resource of a mind as worn-out as his body, he fleeced Crevel, who thought himself obliged to 'go easy' with the respectable official 'whom he was deceiving'.

Seeing Crevel as a child in the hands of that vile and hideous mummy, whose depravity was a sealed book to the Mayor, and more important, seeing him so completely despised by Valérie, who laughed at Crevel as if he had been created for her entertainment, the Baron believed, apparently, that he had little to fear from any rivalry in that quarter, and often invited Crevel to dinner.

Valérie, protected by these two passions standing sentinel on either side, and by a jealous husband, was the cynosure of all eyes, excited everyone's desires, in the sphere in which she shone. Thus, while keeping up appearances, in about three years she had attained the difficult success that courtesans seek by means of scandal, their audacity, and the glitter of their life in the sun, and that they so rarely achieve. Like a well-cut diamond exquisitely set by Chanor, Valérie's beauty, once buried in the gloomy depths of the rue du Doyenné, was worth more than its intrinsic value. She broke men's hearts! Claude Vignon secretly loved Valérie.

This retrospective account, very necessary when people are met again after a three years' interval, shows Valérie's balance-sheet. Now that of her associate, Lisbeth, must be considered.

*

In the Marneffe household, Cousin Bette held the position of a relation acting as both companion and housekeeper; but she had none of the humiliations to endure which are most often the lot of poor creatures so unlucky as to be obliged to take those ambiguous situations. Lisbeth and Valérie presented the touching spectacle of a bosom friendship, one of those friendships so close and so unlikely between women that Parisians, always too clever by half, are quick to call scandalous. The contrast between the masculine stiff temperament of the peasant from Lorraine and Valérie's warm creole indolence gave colour to the calumny. Madame Marneffe, moreover, had unthinkingly lent weight to the gossiping tales by the trouble she took over her friend's appearance, with an eye to a certain marriage, which was, as we shall see, to complete Lisbeth's vengeance. A revolutionary change had taken place in Cousin Bette, and Valérie, anxious to reform her way of dressing, had turned it to the best possible account. This strange woman, now properly corseted, cut a figure of slender elegance; she used bandoline lotion on her smooth well-brushed hair, wore her dresses without protest as the dressmaker made them, and fine little boots, and grey silk stockings. Their cost was added, of course, to Valérie's accounts, and paid for by whoever had the privilege of settling these.

Thus groomed, Bette, still wearing the yellow cashmere shawl, at the end of three years was improved out of all recognition. This other different diamond, a black diamond, the most rare of all, cut by an expert hand and mounted in the setting that suited it, was appreciated at its full value by several ambitious clerks. To see Bette for the first time was to thrill involuntarily at the savage poetic beauty which Valérie's skill had thrown into relief, by her use of dress to dramatize the appearance of this bitter nun, by the art with which she framed the sharp olive face with its glittering black eyes in heavy bands of jet-black hair and called attention to the stiff narrow-waisted figure. Bette, like one of Cranach's Virgins, or Van Eyck's, or a Byzantine Virgin, stepping from the frame, maintained the inflexibility, the erect hieratic carriage of those mysterious figures, which are cousins-german of Isis and the sheath-swathed divinities of the Egyptian sculptors. She was walking granite, basalt, porphyry.

Secure from want for the rest of her days, Bette was in a

charming mood; she brought gaiety with her wherever she went to dine. To add to her satisfaction, the Baron paid the rent of her little apartment, furnished, as we know, from the discarded contents of her friend Valérie's boudoir and sitting-room.

'After starting life as a hungry nanny, I am ending it now like a lioness,' she used to say.

She continued to sew the most difficult pieces of _passementerie_ work for Monsieur Rivet, but only, so she said, in order not to have to sit with her hands idle. And yet her life, as we shall see, was exceedingly busy. But it is ingrained in the nature of people come up from the country to be very chary of giving up their means of earning a living; they resemble the Jews in this.

Every morning, very early, Cousin Bette went herself to the central market with the cook. In Bette's design, the household bills, by which the Baron was being ruined, were to enrich her dear Valérie, and did in fact effectively enrich her.

What mistress of a house has not, since 1838, experienced the disastrous consequences of anti-social doctrines spread among the lower classes by inflammatory writers? The leakage of money through servants is the most serious of all the unnecessary drains upon the family purse. With only very few exceptions, deserving the Montyon prize, chefs and women cooks are domestic robbers, and brazen salaried robbers at that; and the Government complaisantly make themselves receivers of the booty, thus encouraging the tendency to steal, which in cooks is practically given official approval by the ancient jest about 'waggling the market-basket handle', or making sure of one's cut. Where these women once looked for forty sous to buy their lottery ticket, they now appropriate fifty francs to put in the savings-bank. And yet the cold puritans who amuse themselves by making philanthropic experiments in France imagine that they have raised the moral standards of the common people! Between the market-place and the master's table the servants have set up their secret toll-bar, and the City of Paris is much less efficient at collecting its import duty than they are at levying their tax upon everything. In addition to charging all foodstuffs with a fifty-per-cent toll, they demand handsome presents from the shopkeepers. The most solidly established tradesmen tremble before their underground power; they all pay up without a word: carriage-builders, jewellers, tailors, and everyone else. If any attempt is made to control them, the servants retaliate with insolence or the costly accidents of deliberate clumsiness. They make inquiries about employers' characters now, as formerly employers inquired about theirs.

The evil has indeed gone beyond all bounds, and the law-courts are at last beginning to deal with it severely, though ineffectively. Only a law compelling wage-earning servants to hold a workman's testimonial-book will eradicate it. That would end it as if by magic. If servants were obliged to produce their book, and masters to enter the reasons for dismissal, corruption would undoubtedly receive a powerful check. The heads of government, absorbed in the high politics of the moment, have no idea of the extreme dishonesty of the lower classes in Paris: it is equalled only by their consuming greed. No statistics are available to reveal the alarming number of twenty-year-old working men who marry cooks of forty or fifty, enriched by theft. One trembles at the thought of the consequences of such unions, considering the possible effects in increase of crime, degeneracy of the race, and unhappy family life. As for the economic consequences of the merely financial loss caused by domestic thieving, they are enormous. The cost of living, doubled in this way, deprives many households of a margin for luxury. Luxury! It is responsible for half the trade of a nation, as well as for life's elegance. Books and flowers are as necessary as bread to a very great many people.

Lisbeth, who knew all about this shocking imposition on Paris households, had had management of Valérie's housekeeping in mind when she had promised her support during that terrible scene in the course of which they had sworn to be like sisters. She had therefore brought from the depths of the Vosges to Paris a relative on her mother's side, a former cook to the Bishop of Nancy, a pious spinster of the strictest honesty. Because she was afraid, nevertheless, of the dangers of her inexperience in Paris, above all the danger of evil counsels, which destroy so many necessarily fragile loyalties,

Lisbeth accompanied Mathurine to the central market, and tried to train her in the art of buying.

She taught her to know the proper price of goods in order to command the salesmen's respect, to include luxuries, fish for example, in the menu when they were least expensive, to watch prices and be able to forecast a rise in order to buy before it occurred. In Paris such housewifely thrift is most necessary for the domestic economy. As Mathurine was paid good wages and given generous presents, she was sufficiently attached to the household to delight in making bargains on its behalf. For some time now her judgement had been almost equal to Lisbeth's, and Lisbeth thought her sufficiently well-trained, sufficiently dependable, to do the marketing alone, except on the days when Valérie was entertaining guests – which, by the way, were frequent, and for this reason:

The Baron had at first observed unimpeachable propriety; but his passion for Madame Marneffe was, within a very short time, so ardent, so all-absorbing, that he became anxious to spend as little time away from her as possible. He began by dining with her four times a week, and soon found it delightful to dine there every day. Six months after his daughter's marriage, he was paying an allowance of two thousand francs a month for his board. Madame Marneffe invited to her table any friends that the dear Baron wished to entertain. Dinner, then, was always prepared for six, for the Baron might bring in three guests without warning. Lisbeth, by her good management, solved the difficult problem of keeping a lavish table for an expenditure of one thousand francs, so handing over a thousand francs a month to Madame Marneffe. As Valérie's wardrobe was amply paid for by both Crevel and the Baron, the two friends made another thousand francs a month on that.

In this way, the candid, transparently open creature had already amassed about a hundred and fifty thousand francs. She had saved her yearly allowance and monthly benefits, used them as capital to invest, and increased them by vast profits gained through Crevel's generosity in making the capital of his 'little duchess' share in the successes of his own financial speculation. Crevel had initiated Valérie into the jargon and procedure of the Bourse; and, like all Parisian women, she had rapidly become more adept than her master. Lisbeth, who never spent a sou of her twelve hundred francs, whose rent and clothes were paid for, who did not need to put her hand into her pocket for anything, also possessed a little capital of five or six thousand francs, which Crevel, in a fatherly way, made the most of for her.

The Baron's love and Crevel's were, all the same, a heavy burden for Valérie. On the day on which this drama is taken up again, Valérie, irritated by one of those crisis-provoking incidents that are rather like the bell whose clamour induces swarming bees to settle, had gone upstairs to Lisbeth. She wanted to indulge in the soothingly long-drawn lamentations, the equivalent of sociably smoked cigarettes, with which women alleviate the minor miseries of their lives.

'Lisbeth, my love, two hours of Crevel this morning! What a frightful bore! Oh, how I wish I could send you in my place!'

'That can't be done, unfortunately,' said Lisbeth, with a smile. 'I'm an old maid for life.'

'Belonging to those two old men! There are times when I'm ashamed of myself! Ah, if my poor mother could only see me!'

'No need to talk to me as if I were Crevel,' replied Lisbeth.

'Tell me, my own little Bette, you don't despise me, do you?'

'Ah! if I had been pretty ... such adventures I would have had!' exclaimed Lisbeth. 'That's how I excuse you.'

'But you would only have listened to your heart,' said Madame Marneffe, sighing.

'Bah!' replied Lisbeth. 'Marneffe is a corpse that they've forgotten to bury, the Baron is practically your husband, Crevel is your admirer. As I see it, you're like any other married woman, perfectly in order.'

'No, that's not the point, my sweet, my trouble's different. But you don't choose to understand me. ...'

'Oh, yes, I understand you all right!' said the peasant from Lorraine. 'For what you are hinting at is part of my revenge. But what do you want me to do? I'm doing my best.'

'Loving Wenceslas to the pitch of pining away for him!'

169

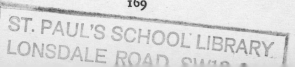
ST. PAUL'S SCHOOL LIBRARY
LONSDALE ROAD SW13

cried Valérie, flinging her arms wide, 'and not being able to contrive to see him – how can I bear it? Hulot suggests that he should come to dinner here, and my artist declines! He doesn't know how he's idolized, that monster of a man. What has his wife got? A good figure, that's all! She's beautiful, there's no denying; but I am a good deal more than that, I should think!'

'Set your mind at rest, my child; he shall come,' said Lisbeth, in the tone of voice nurses use to impatient children. 'I'll see to that.'

'But when?'

'Perhaps this week.'

'Here's a kiss for you.'

As may be seen, these two women were in complete accord. All Valérie's actions, even the most apparently wilful, her pleasures, her fits of the sulks, were decided upon only after mature deliberation on the part of the two women.

Lisbeth, who found this courtesan existence strangely exciting, advised Valérie in everything, and pursued the course of her vengeance with relentless logic. She adored Valérie, moreover; she had made a daughter of her, a friend, someone to love. She found in her a creole docility, a voluptuary's yielding temper. She chatted with her all morning, with much more pleasure than she had taken in talking to Wenceslas. They could laugh together over the mischief they were plotting and the stupidity of men; and count up in company the accumulating interest of their respective treasure hoards. In both her new plot and her new friendship, Lisbeth had indeed found an outlet for her energy much more rewarding than her insensate love for Wenceslas. The delights of gratified hatred are among the fiercest and most ardent that the heart can feel. Love is the gold, but hate is the iron of that mine of the emotions that lies within us. And then Lisbeth saw beauty in Valérie, in all its splendour, the beauty that she worshipped as we adore what can never be our own, embodied in a person much more sympathetic than Wenceslas, who towards her had always been cold and unresponsive.

By the end of nearly three years Lisbeth was beginning to see some progress in the undermining tunnel, in the driving of which her whole existence was consumed and the energies of her mind absorbed. Lisbeth plotted; Madame Marneffe acted. Madame Marneffe was the axe, Lisbeth the hand that wielded it; and the hand was striking blow upon rapid blow to demolish that family which from day to day became ever more hateful to her; for hatred continually grows, just as love every day increases, when we love. Love and hatred are passions that feed on their own fuel; but of the two, hatred is the more enduring. Love is limited by our human limits; its strength derives from life and giving. Hate is like death and avarice, a denial, a negation, although active, above human beings and human concerns. Lisbeth, having entered upon the life that was congenial to her nature, was devoting to it the strength of all her faculties. She was to be reckoned with, like the Jesuits, as an underground force. Her physical regeneration, too, was complete. Her countenance shone. And Lisbeth dreamed of becoming the wife of Marshal Hulot.

This scene, in which the two friends bluntly told each other all that was in their minds, without the least reserve, took place on Lisbeth's return from the market, where she had gone to buy the materials for a choice dinner. Marneffe, who coveted Monsieur Coquet's position, had invited him and the staid, respectable Madame Coquet, and Valérie was hoping to have the subject of the head clerk's resignation discussed by Hulot that same evening. Lisbeth was dressing for a visit to the Baroness, with whom she was going to dine.

'You will be back in time to pour out tea, Bette dear?' asked Valérie.

'I hope so. . . .'

'What do you mean, you hope so? Have you reached the point of staying the night with Adeline, to gloat over her tears while she sleeps?'

'If only I could!' replied Lisbeth, with a laugh. 'I would not refuse. She is paying for the days of her good fortune now, and that suits me, for I remember my childhood. Turn about is fair play. It's her turn to bite the dust, and I shall be Countess de Forzheim!'

*

Lisbeth went off to the rue Plumet, where she now usually

went in the mood of a person visiting the theatre, to indulge in an emotional feast.

The apartment that Hulot had chosen for his wife comprised a large high-ceilinged hall, a drawing-room, and a bedroom with a dressing-room. The dining-room lay beyond the drawing-room and opened into it. Two servants' rooms and a kitchen, on the third floor, completed the suite, which was not unworthy of a Councillor of State and Director at the War Office. The house, the courtyard, and the staircase were of imposing proportions. The Baroness, as she had to furnish her drawing-room, bedroom, and dining-room with the relics of her days of splendour, had taken the best of the worn-out furniture from her home in the rue de l'Université. The poor woman was fond of these silent witnesses to her happiness: for her they spoke with an eloquence which was almost consoling. In these remembrances of happier days she caught glimpses of flowers, just as she could see on the carpets the patterned roses barely visible to others.

Entering the vast hall, where a dozen chairs, a barometer, a huge stove, and long white calico curtains bordered with red suggested the comfortless waiting-rooms in government buildings, one felt one's heart contract; one had an oppressive sense of the solitude in which this woman lived. Sorrow, like pleasure, creates its own atmosphere. A first glance into any home tells one whether love reigns there, or despair.

Adeline was to be found in an enormous bedroom, surrounded by the fine furniture created by Jacob Desmalters, in speckled mahogany, with that Empire ornament of ormolu that contrives to look colder even than Louis XVI bronzes. And it was a chilling sight to see this woman, seated on a Roman chair before her work-table decorated with sphinxes, her colour gone, affecting a show of gaiety, preserving her proud Imperial air, as she had so carefully preserved the blue velvet dress that she wore in the house. Her proud spirit sustained her body and maintained her beauty. The Baroness, by the end of the first year of her exile in this place, had taken the full measure of the extent of her misfortune.

'He may banish me here, but my Hector has still given me a better life than a simple peasant woman has any right to expect,' she said to herself. 'This is the decision he has made: his will be done! I am Baroness Hulot, sister-in-law of a Marshal of France. I have done nothing that I can reproach myself with. My two children are established in life. I am able to wait for death, wrapped in the immaculate veils of a virtuous wife, in the crape of my vanished happiness.'

A portrait of Hulot in the uniform of a Commissary general of the Imperial Guard, painted by Robert Lefebvre in 1810, hung above the worktable. When a visitor was announced, Adeline would put away in a drawer of the table a copy of the *Imitation of Christ* which was her constant study. This blameless Magdalen in her retreat heard the voice of the Holy Spirit.

'Mariette, my girl,' said Lisbeth to the cook, who opened the door to her, 'how is my dear Adeline?'

'Oh, well enough, she *seems*, Mademoiselle. But, between ourselves, if she goes on with her notions, they'll be the end of her,' said Mariette, in a whisper. 'Indeed, you really ought to make her promise to eat more. Yesterday, Madame told me to give her only two sous' worth of milk and one little roll in the morning, and for dinner either a herring or a little cold veal, and to cook a pound of veal to last the week, with her dining here alone, of course. She won't spend more than ten sous a day on her food. It's not right. If I said a word about this pinching and scrimping to Monsieur le Maréchal, he could easily have a quarrel with Monsieur le Baron about it and cut him out of his will; instead of which, you are so good and clever, perhaps you'll be able to fix things up. . . .'

'But why don't you speak to Monsieur le Baron?' inquired Lisbeth.

'Ah, my dear Miss, it's quite twenty or twenty-five days since he was here; well, the length of the time since we last saw you! Besides, Madame said I'm not ever to ask Monsieur for money. She says she'll send me away if I do. But talk about trouble . . . ah! what poor Madame has had to bear! It's the first time Monsieur has forgotten her for so long . . . Every time there was a ring at the door, she used to fly to the window . . . but for the past five days she hasn't stirred from her chair. She goes on reading! Every time she goes to see Madame la Comtesse, she says to me "Mariette," she says, "if

Monsieur comes, tell him that I'm at home, and send the porter for me; he'll be well paid for his trouble!"'

'Poor Cousin!' said Bette. 'It breaks my heart to hear it. I speak to Monsieur le Baron about her every day, but what use is it? He says, "You are right, Bette, I'm a wretch. My wife is an angel and I am a monster! I'll go tomorrow...." And he stays with Madame Marneffe. That woman is ruining him and he adores her; he can't bear to let her out of his sight. I do what I can! If I were not there, and if I hadn't Mathurine with me, the Baron would have spent twice as much; and as he has hardly anything left, he might easily have blown his brains out before this. And you know, Mariette, Adeline would not go on living after her husband's death, I'm sure of that. At least I can try to make ends meet there, and stop my cousin from throwing too much money away....'

'Ah, that's just what the poor mistress says herself. She knows well enough how much she owes you,' replied Mariette. 'She says that for a long time she misjudged you.'

'Ah!' said Lisbeth. 'She didn't say anything else?'

'No, Mademoiselle. If you want to please her, talk about Monsieur. She thinks you're lucky to see him every day.'

'Is she alone?'

'I'm sorry, Miss, the Marshal is here. Oh! he comes every day; and she always tells him that she has seen Monsieur that morning, that he comes in very late at night.'

'And is there a good dinner today?' asked Bette.

Mariette hesitated, and lowered her eyes. Just then the drawing-room door opened, and Marshal Hulot came out in such a hurry that he bowed to Bette without looking at her, and dropped a paper. Bette picked it up and ran to the stairs, for it was no use calling after a deaf man; but she managed not to overtake the Marshal, and returned, surreptitiously reading the following note, written in pencil:

My dear brother,

My husband has given me my allowance for this quarter; but my daughter Hortense needed it so badly that I have lent her the entire sum, which is barely enough to tide her over her difficulty. Can you lend me a few hundred francs? Because I do not want to ask Hector for money again; I should be too miserable if he reproached me.

'Ah!' thought Lisbeth, 'if she can bend her pride to this, she must be in desperate straits!'

Lisbeth went in, taking Adeline by surprise, and, finding her in tears, threw her arms round her neck.

'Adeline, my poor dear, I know everything!' she said. 'Look, the Marshal let this paper fall; he seemed so distressed, he was dashing away like a greyhound. When did that dreadful Hector last give you any money?'

'He gives me my allowance regularly,' replied the Baroness; 'but Hortense needed some money, and ...'

'And you had nothing to pay for our dinner,' Bette interrupted her. 'Now I understand why Mariette looked so embarrassed, when I said something to her about the soup. You're behaving childishly, Adeline! Let me give you what I have saved.'

'Thank you, my kind Bette,' Adeline answered, wiping away a tear. 'This little difficulty is only temporary, and I have made arrangements for the future. I shall not have to spend more than two thousand four hundred francs a year, in future, including rent, and I shall have enough. But, whatever you do, Bette, don't say a word to Hector. How is he?'

'Oh! as solid as the pont Neuf! He's as blithe as a lark; he has no thought for anything but his bewitching Valérie.'

Madame Hulot was looking at a tall silver fir, in the field of her vision from the window, and Lisbeth could read nothing of what her eyes might express.

'Did you remind him that this is the day when everyone dines here?'

'Yes; but bah! Madame Marneffe is giving a big dinner; she is hoping to get Monsieur Coquet to resign! And that takes precedence of everything! Listen, Adeline, you know how fiercely determined I have always been to live an independent life. Your husband, my dear, is certainly going to ruin you. I thought that I could be helpful to you all by staying with that woman, but the depravity of the creature goes beyond all bounds; she will extract so much from your husband that in the end he will bring disgrace upon you all.'

Adeline recoiled as if she had been struck by a dagger, thrust through her heart.

'Indeed, my dear Adeline, I'm sure of it. It's my duty to try to open your eyes. Well, now we must think of the future! The Marshal is old, but he will live a long time yet; in his circumstances he is likely to wear well. His widow, when he died, would have a pension of six thousand francs. With that amount I could undertake to look after you all! Use your influence with the old man to persuade him to marry me. It's not that I want to be Madame la Maréchale – that sort of nonsense means nothing to me, or as little as Madame Marneffe's conscience; but then you would all be assured of your daily bread. I can see that Hortense is in want of hers, since she has to borrow yours.'

The Marshal appeared. The old soldier had gone home and returned with all possible speed, and was mopping his forehead with his silk handkerchief.

'I have given two thousand francs to Mariette,' he whispered in his sister-in-law's ear.

Adeline blushed to the roots of her hair. Tears hung on her lashes, which were still as long as ever, and she silently pressed the old man's hand; while his face expressed a favoured lover's contentment.

'I meant to use this money to give you a present, Adeline,' he went on. 'Don't repay it. Instead you shall choose for yourself the present you would like best.'

He came forward to take the hand that Lisbeth held out to him, and in his pleasure he kissed it absentmindedly.

'That's promising,' Adeline told Lisbeth, smiling as well as she could.

Victorin Hulot and his wife arrived as she was speaking.

'Is my brother dining with us?' the Marshal inquired sharply.

Adeline took a pencil and wrote on a slip of paper:

I expect him; he promised me this morning that he would dine here. But if he doesn't come it will be because the Marshal has kept him, because he's terribly busy.

And she handed him the note. She had contrived this method of conversation with the Marshal, and a supply of little slips of paper and a pencil were laid ready on her work table.

'I know,' the Marshal replied, 'that he is overwhelmed with work because of events in Algeria.'

Hortense and Wenceslas came in at this moment, and with her family about her the Baroness turned again to the Marshal with an expression whose significance only Lisbeth understood.

The artist, now happily married, adored by his wife and flattered by society, had considerably improved in looks.

His face had become almost full. The breeding of a true aristocrat was seen to advantage in his elegant figure. His early success, his eminence, the deluding praises tossed by the social world to artists as carelessly as one might say 'good morning' or speak of the weather, had given him the kind of consciousness of his own merits which may degenerate into fatuity when talent goes. The Cross of the Legion of Honour seemed to him to add the final touch to the great man that he believed himself to be.

After three years of marriage, Hortense's attitude to her husband was like a dog's to his master. She followed his every movement with an apparently questioning gaze; her eyes never left him, as if she were a miser watching hoarded treasure. Her admiring self-effacement was touching to see. One could perceive in her the temper of her mother, and her mother's upbringing. Her beauty, as great as ever, was changed, given a tinge of poetry, by the soft shadows of a hidden melancholy.

As she watched her cousin come in, it occurred to Lisbeth that complaint, long repressed, was on the point of breaking the frail envelope of discretion. It had been Lisbeth's view from the first days of the honeymoon that the young couple possessed an income much too small to sustain so great a passion.

Hortense as she kissed her mother whispered a few heartfelt words to her, whose sense was clear to Lisbeth as they both shook their heads.

'Adeline will come, like me, to work for her living,' thought Cousin Bette. 'I must see that she tells me what she is going to do. Those pretty fingers will know at last, like mine, what it is to be forced to work, by necessity.'

At six o'clock the family went into the dining-room. Hector's place was laid.

'Leave it,' the Baroness said to Mariette. 'Monsieur sometimes comes late.'

'Oh, yes, my father will certainly be here,' said young Hulot to his mother. 'He promised me so in the Chamber, when we were leaving.'

Lisbeth, like a spider in the centre of her web, watched every face. She had known Hortense and Victorin since they were born, and their faces were as glass through which she read their young souls. Now, as Victorin kept glancing furtively at his mother, she realized that some misfortune was about to break upon Adeline, and that Victorin was reluctant to give her the bad news. The eminent young lawyer had some sad preoccupation. His profound regard for his mother was strikingly evident in the unhappiness with which he gazed at her. Hortense, too, was obviously preoccupied with troubles of her own. For the past fortnight Lisbeth had known that she was experiencing for the first time the cares that lack of money brings to honest people, to young wives on whom life has always until now turned a smiling face, who try to dissemble the dismay they feel. Cousin Bette had known at a glance, moreover, that the mother had given nothing to her daughter; so that, unable in her sensitive feeling for her husband to tell the truth, Adeline had stooped to the deceit necessity suggests to borrowers.

Hortense's preoccupation and her brother's, and the Baroness's profound dejection, combined to make this a dull dinner-party, chilled too, as one may imagine, by the old Marshal's deafness. Three people did something to enliven the occasion: Lisbeth, Célestine, and Wenceslas. Hortense's love had stimulated the artist's Polish animation. Vaunting vivacity, like a Gascon's, attractive high spirits, are qualities characteristic of Poles, those Frenchmen of the north. Wenceslas's untroubled assurance, his expression, left no doubt of his belief in himself, and made it clear that poor Hortense, faithful to her mother's counsel, hid all her domestic worries from him.

'You must be very relieved,' said Lisbeth to her young

cousin, as they left the dining-room, 'that your mother was able to help you out with her own money.'

'Mama?' answered Hortense, in astonishment. 'Oh, poor Mama! Her money for me! I only wish I could make some for her! You have no idea, Lisbeth, but I have a horrible feeling that she is working in secret.'

They were crossing the great dark unlighted drawing-room, following Mariette, who was carrying the lamp from the dining-room into Adeline's bedroom, and just then Victorin touched Lisbeth and Hortense on the arm. They understood, and, letting Wenceslas, Célestine, the Marshal, and the Baroness go on into the bedroom, stopped in a window recess.

'What's wrong, Victorin?' asked Lisbeth. 'I could hazard a guess that your father has caused some disaster.'

'Yes, unfortunately,' Victorin replied. 'A moneylender called Vauvinet holds bills of my father's amounting to sixty thousand francs, and means to have them protested! I wanted to talk to my father about this deplorable business in the Chamber, but he refused to understand me, he practically avoided me. Do you think we ought to warn Mother?'

'No, no,' said Lisbeth. 'She has too many troubles already; it would be a death blow. We must spare her all we can. You do not know what straits she is reduced to. If it hadn't been for your uncle, you would have had no dinner here tonight.'

'Ah, good heavens, Victorin, what monsters we are!' Hortense said to her brother. 'Lisbeth has to tell us what we ought to have guessed. My dinner chokes me!'

Hortense stopped short, put her handkerchief to her mouth to stifle a sob, and burst into tears.

'I have told this Vauvinet to come and see me tomorrow,' Victorin went on. 'But will he be satisfied with my warranty? I doubt it. People like him always want ready money in order to put it out at exorbitant interest.'

'We could sell our capital!' Lisbeth said to Hortense.

'What would that amount to? Fifteen or sixteen thousand francs,' replied Victorin; 'and we need sixty thousand!'

'Dear Cousin!' exclaimed Hortense, kissing Lisbeth with all the fervour of an innocent heart.

'No, Lisbeth, keep your little income,' said Victorin, with a warm pressure of the peasant-woman's hand. 'I'll see tomorrow what this man intends to do. If my wife agrees, I may be able to prevent, or at least delay, the proceedings; for how can I possibly see my father's good name attacked? It's unthinkable! What would the Minister of War say? My father's salary has been pledged for the past three years, and will not become available until December, so it can't be offered as security. This Vauvinet has renewed the bills eleven times, so just imagine what my father must have paid in interest! We must cover this bottomless pit.'

'If only Madame Marneffe would leave him. . . .' said Hortense bitterly.

'Oh, heaven forbid!' said Victorin. 'Father would perhaps go elsewhere; and with her the most costly expenses have already been incurred.'

What a change in children once so respectful, in whom their mother had instilled for so long an absolute veneration of their father! They had now passed judgement upon him for themselves.

'If it were not for me,' Lisbeth went on, 'your father would be even more completely ruined than he is.'

'Let's go in,' said Hortense. 'Mama is quick: she will suspect something, and as our kind Lisbeth says, we must hide all we can from her. We must be cheerful!'

'Victorin, you don't know what ruin your father will bring on you, with his passion for women,' said Lisbeth. 'Think of the future, and try to make sure of some resources by marrying me to the Marshal. You should speak to him about it this evening. I'll leave early, on purpose.'

Victorin went on into his mother's room.

'Well, my poor little girl,' said Lisbeth in a whisper to her young cousin, 'what about you? What are you going to do?'

'Come to dinner with us tomorrow, and we can talk,' replied Hortense. 'I don't know which way to turn. You know how to deal with the difficulties of life; you will advise me.'

While the whole family in concert was preaching marriage to the Marshal and Lisbeth was on her way back to the rue Vanneau, one of those incidents occurred which give new impetus to the evil in women like Madame Marneffe, by compelling them to have recourse to vice, to make use of all the help it can give them. We may at least acknowledge an unquestionable fact: in Paris life is lived in a whirl too giddy for vicious people to seek occasion for wickedness. They use vice as a defensive weapon, that is all.

*

Madame Marneffe, with a drawing-room full of her faithful admirers, had set the usual games of whist going, when the footman, an old soldier that the Baron had taken into his service, announced:

'Monsieur le Baron Montès de Montejanos.'

Valérie experienced a violent shock, but she flew to the door, exclaiming, 'My cousin!'

And as she met the Brazilian, she whispered to him:

'You are a relative of mine, or everything is over between us! Well, Henri,' she went on aloud, leading the Brazilian to the fire: 'so you weren't shipwrecked after all, as I was told? I've been mourning you for three years. ...'

'How are you, my dear fellow?' said Monsieur Marneffe, holding out his hand to the Brazilian, who looked exactly like a millionaire from Brazil as one imagines him.

Monsieur le Baron Henri Montès de Montejanos, the product of an equatorial climate, had the physique and complexion that we all associate with Othello. At first sight he intimidated by his glowering looks, but this was a purely plastic effect, for his character was extremely gentle and affectionate, and predestined him to the kind of exploitation that weak women practise on strong men. The disdain expressed in his face, the muscular strength of his body, his obvious aggressive powers, were offensive only to men; to women homage from such a man was flattering, and flattering in a way that goes powerfully to women's heads. All men are conscious of women's susceptibility to pugnacious masculinity; and one may see a man, giving his arm to his mistress, assume a swashbuckling swagger that is very amusing. With his superb figure set off by a blue coat with buttons of solid gold, and black trousers, wearing well-polished boots of fine leather, conventionally gloved, the Baron had nothing Brazilian about his dress but a huge diamond, worth about a hundred thousand francs, that glittered like a star on a sumptuous blue silk cravat. A white waistcoat revealed a glimpse of shirt of fabulously fine material. His forehead, projecting like a satyr's, a sign of obstinate tenacity in passion, was surmounted by a jet-black head of springing hair like a virgin forest, below which a pair of clear eyes glittered, so tawny and untamed as to make it seem credible that his mother when carrying him had been frightened by a jaguar.

This magnificent specimen of Portuguese Brazilian manhood took up his stand, back to the fireplace, in an attitude which showed Parisian habits; and, his hat in one hand, resting an arm against the velvet-draped mantelpiece, he bent over Madame Marneffe to talk in a low voice to her, concerning himself very little about all the frightful bourgeois people who seemed to him to be very inopportunely cluttering up the room.

This dramatic entry upon the scene, and the Brazilian's bearing and air, provoked an identical reaction of curiosity mixed with apprehension in Crevel and the Baron. The same expression appeared on both faces, revealing the same foreboding. And the sudden, simultaneous, emotion of these two genuinely passion-possessed men was so comical that those of the company who were sufficiently observant to perceive that a secret had been disclosed could not but smile. Crevel, unalterably a middle-class shopkeeper, Mayor of Paris or no, unfortunately remained frozen in his attitude longer than his fellow-victim, so that the Baron caught a fleeting glimpse of Crevel's involuntary self-revelation. It was an additional blow to the heart of the elderly lover, who made up his mind to have the matter out with Valérie.

'This evening,' Crevel, too, was saying to himself as he arranged his cards, 'we'll have an end put to this. . . .'

'*You have a heart!*' cried Marneffe, 'and you have just revoked!'

'Ah! excuse me,' said Crevel, putting out his hand to take back his card. 'That Baron strikes me as being a bit too much,' he continued in his interior monologue. 'If Valérie lives with my own Baron, that's my revenge, and I know how to get rid of him, but that cousin! . . . that's a Baron too many. I don't intend to be made a fool of. I should like to know in exactly what way he is related to her!'

That evening, by one of those happy chances that occur only to pretty women, Valérie was looking charming. Her bosom gleamed dazzlingly white, framed in lace whose russet tint set off the matt satin of her beautiful shoulders. All Parisian women, by what means no one knows, manage to possess lovely contours and yet remain slender. Her dress, of black velvet, seemed about at any moment to slip from her shoulders; and she wore a lace cap trimmed with clusters of flowers. Her arms, at once slender and rounded, emerged from puff sleeves frilled with lace. She was like those luscious fruits, arranged enticingly on a fine plate, which make the very metal of the knife-blade ache to bite into them.

'Valérie,' the Brazilian was saying in the young woman's ear, 'I have come back still faithful to you. My uncle is dead, and I am twice as rich as I was when I went away. I want to live and die in Paris, for your sake and with you!'

'Hush, Henri, for heaven's sake!'

'Ah bah! Even if I have to throw all this mob out of the window first, I mean to speak to you this evening, especially as I've wasted two days trying to find you. You'll let me stay after the others, won't you?'

Valérie smiled at her so-called cousin, and said:

'Remember that you are the son of a sister of my mother's, who married your father during Junot's campaign in Portugal.'

'I, Montès de Montejanos, great-grandson of one of the conquerors of Brazil, tell a lie!'

'Not so loud, or we'll never see each other again. . . .'

'And why not?'

'Because of Marneffe. He's like all dying men – they set their minds on a last passion, and he's taken a fancy for me.'

'That worm?' said the Brazilian, who knew his Marneffe. 'I'll settle him. . . .'

'You're dreadfully violent!'

'I say, where did you get all these fine things?' said the

Brazilian, at last taking note of the splendours of the drawing-room.

She began to laugh.

'What bad manners, Henri!' she said.

She had just caught two pairs of eyes fixed on her, full oi such blazing jealousy that she could not help but look at the two souls in pain. Crevel was playing against the Baron and Monsieur Coquet, and had Marneffe for partner. The pairs were equally matched, because Crevel and the Baron were equally distracted, and were piling mistake upon mistake. The two old men had both, in the same instant, declared the passion that Valérie had succeeded in making them conceal for three years; but Valérie herself had not known how to hide the joy in her eyes, her happiness at seeing again the first man to make her heart beat faster, her first love. The rights of these fortunate mortals endure for the whole life-time of the woman over whom they have acquired them.

In the centre of these three absolute passions, sustained in one man by the insolent pride of money, in another by right of possession, and in the third by youth, strength, fortune and priority, Madame Marneffe remained as calm and self-possessed as Bonaparte besieging Mantua, when he had to hold off two armies in order to continue his blockade of the city.

The jealousy distorting Hulot's face made him as terrible to look upon as the late Marshal Montcornet leading a cavalry charge against a Russian square. As a handsome man, the Councillor of State had never before known jealousy, just as Murat never experienced fear. He had always been confident of triumph. His setback with Josépha, the first of his life, he had attributed to her greed for money. He told himself that he had been supplanted by a million and not by an abortion, meaning the Duc d'Hérouville. The poisons and dizzy potions which that insane emotion secretes in quantity had poured into his heart, in that instant. Throwing down his cards, he turned violently from the whist-table towards the fireplace with an eloquent gesture, reminiscent of Mirabeau; and fixed the Brazilian and Valérie with a challenging stare. The company felt the mixed alarm and curiosity excited by the spectacle of violence threatening momently to erupt. The so-called cousin looked at the Councillor of State as if he were examining some globular Chinese pot. The situation could not continue without leading to a shattering scene. Marneffe was just as much afraid of what Baron Hulot might do as Crevel was of Marneffe, for he did not care for the idea of dying a deputy head clerk. Dying men have their minds fixed on life as convicts have on liberty. This man was determined to be head clerk, come what might. Alarmed, with good reason, by the pantomime being enacted by Crevel and the Councillor of State, he got up and said a word in his wife's ear; and to the great surprise of the company, Valérie went into her bedroom with the Brazilian and her husband.

'Has Madame Marneffe ever mentioned this cousin to you?' Crevel demanded of Baron Hulot.

'Never!' replied the Baron, rising to his feet. 'That's enough for this evening,' he added. 'I've lost two louis; here they are.'

He tossed two gold coins down on the table, and went to sit on the divan with an expression on his face that everyone interpreted as a hint to be gone. Monsieur and Madame Coquet exchanged a few remarks and left the room, and Claude Vignon, in despair, followed their example. These two departures gave a lead to the more unperceptive guests, who now realized that they were in the way. The Baron and Crevel were left alone, neither of them saying a word. Hulot, who had reached the point of not even noticing that Crevel was there, went on tiptoe to listen at the bedroom door, only to recoil with a hasty leap backwards as Marneffe opened the door and appeared, looking quite calm, and evidently astonished to find only two people in the room.

'What about tea?' he said.

'Where is Valérie?' returned the Baron furiously.

'My wife?' said Marneffe. 'Oh, she's gone up to your cousin, Mademoiselle Lisbeth. She'll come back.'

'And why has she given us the slip for the sake of that stupid nanny?'

'Oh, but Mademoiselle Lisbeth,' said Marneffe, 'came back from visiting Madame la Baronne, your wife, with some kind of indigestion, and Mathurine asked Valérie for tea, and she has just gone to see what's the matter with Mademoiselle Lisbeth.'

'What about the cousin?'

'He's gone!'

'And you believe that?'

'I saw him to his carriage!' replied Marneffe, with a leer.

Wheels were heard rolling down the rue Vanneau. The Baron, accounting Marneffe's word as not worth a fig, left the room and climbed the stairs to Lisbeth's apartment. One thought filled his mind, kindled by a spark from the blazing fires of jealousy in his heart. He was so well aware of Marneffe's baseness that he suspected a shameful complicity between wife and husband.

'What's become of everyone?' asked Marneffe, finding himself left alone with Crevel.

'When the sun goes to bed, so does the poultry-yard,' replied Crevel. 'Madame Marneffe has disappeared, her adorers have left. What about a game of piquet?' Crevel added, for he intended to stay.

He too believed that the Brazilian was in the house. The Mayor was as wily as the Baron: he could remain where he was indefinitely, playing with the husband, who, since the suppression of public gambling, had had to content himself with the restricted penny-counting game played socially. Monsieur Marneffe agreed to his suggestion.

Baron Hulot hurried upstairs to his Cousin Bette's room; but he found the door shut, and the conventional inquiries through the door gave sufficient time for alert and guileful women to stage the spectacle of a sufferer from indigestion being well plied with tea. Lisbeth was evidently in such pain that Valérie felt the most serious concern, and so paid practically no attention to the Baron's furious entrance. Illness is women's most useful storm-screen against a quarrel's tempests. Hulot looked covertly about him into every corner of Cousin Bette's bedroom, but found no spot suitable for hiding a Brazilian in.

'Your indigestion, Bette, does credit to my wife's dinner,' he said, scrutinizing the old maid, who felt extremely well and was doing her best to simulate an attack of hiccups as she drank her tea.

'You see how fortunate it is that our dear Bette lives in my house! If I hadn't been here the poor girl would have died. . . .' said Madame Marneffe.

'You look as if you don't believe me,' Lisbeth added, to the Baron. 'And that would be scandalous. . . .'

'Why?' the Baron asked peremptorily. 'So you know the reason for my visit, do you?'

And he eyed the door of a dressing-room, from which the key had been removed.

'Are you talking Greek?' said Madame Marneffe in reply, with a heart-rending expression on her face, of misunderstood love and fidelity.

'And it's all on your account, my dear cousin; yes, it's your fault that I'm in such a state,' said Lisbeth, with some emphasis.

This accusation distracted the Baron's attention, and he stared at the old maid in complete surprise.

'You have reason to know my devotion to you,' Lisbeth went on. 'I am here – I need say no more than that. I wear out my strength and spend what's left of my life, here, watching over your interests by looking after our dear Valérie's. Her housekeeping costs only a tenth of what it would in any other household, run as well as hers. If it were not for me, Cousin, instead of two thousand francs a month, you would be paying out three or four thousand.'

'I know all that,' replied the Baron impatiently. 'You shelter and guard us in all sorts of ways,' he added, walking over to Madame Marneffe and taking her by the throat. 'Doesn't she, my dear little beauty?'

'Upon my word,' screamed Valérie, 'I think you're mad!'

'Well, you can't doubt my attachment,' said Lisbeth; 'but I also love my Cousin Adeline, and I found her in tears. She hasn't seen you for a month! No, that's not right. You leave poor Adeline without any money. Your daughter Hortense nearly broke her heart when she heard that it was only thanks to your brother that we had a dinner to eat! There wasn't a crust of bread in your house today! Adeline has made up her mind like a heroine to do what she can for herself. She said to me, "I shall do as you have done!" That lay so heavy on my

187

heart, after dinner, that, thinking of what my cousin was in 1811, and what she is now, thirty years later in 1841, I could not digest my food. I did my best to fight off the attack; but when I got home, I thought I should die. . . .'

'You see, Valérie,' said the Baron, 'what my adoration for you has driven me to! . . . to crimes against my family. . . .'

'Oh, how right I was to remain a spinster!' Lisbeth exclaimed with savage joy. 'You are a good and fine man; Adeline is an angel – and look at the reward of blind devotion!'

'An old angel!' said Madame Marneffe softly, casting a half-tender half-laughing look at her Hector, who was contemplating her like an examining magistrate considering the accused.

'Poor woman!' said the Baron. 'It's more than nine months since I had any money to give her, and I always find money for you, Valérie, and at such a cost! You will never be loved by anyone as I love you, and what unhappiness you give me in return!'

'Unhappiness?' she said. 'What do you call happiness then?'

'I don't yet know what your relations have been with that alleged cousin, whom you never mentioned to me before,' the Baron went on, paying no attention to Valérie's exclamation; 'but when he came in, it was like a knife-stab in my heart. I may be hoodwinked, but I am not blind. I read your eyes and his. Sparks flew from that gorilla's eyes, and you, your look . . . Oh! you have never looked at me like that, no, never! As for this mystery, Valérie, it must be cleared up. You are the only woman who has ever made me know jealousy, so you need not be surprised that I speak to you like this. . . . But there's another mystery, another cat has jumped out of the bag, and it seems disgraceful to me.'

'Well, well,' said Valérie.

'And it is that Crevel, the great gross idiotic lump, loves you, and you receive his gallantries so kindly that the fool displays his passion to the whole world.'

'So that makes three! You can't find any more?' inquired Madame Marneffe.

'There may be more!' said the Baron.

'If Monsieur Crevel loves me, he's within his rights as a man. If I looked kindly on his passion, it would be the act of a coquette, or of a woman who had many shortcomings to forgive you. ... Very well, love me as I am, or leave me. If you let me go, neither you nor Monsieur Crevel shall ever return here. I will take my cousin; since you accuse me of such charming habits I must do something to deserve my reputation. Good-bye, Monsieur le Baron Hulot.'

And she rose, but the Councillor of State seized her arm and forced her to sit down. The old man could never again replace Valérie; she had become more imperatively necessary to him than the necessaries of life, and he would rather remain in uncertainty than be given the faintest shadow of proof of Valérie's infidelity.

'My dear Valérie,' he said, 'do you not see how I am suffering? I am only asking you to tell me why ... Give me some explanation ...'

'Well, go downstairs and wait for me there, for you don't want to stay and watch the treatment I have to give your cousin, I suppose.'

Hulot walked slowly to the door.

'Old debauchee!' cried Cousin Bette. 'You don't even ask for news of your children! What are you going to do about Adeline? What I'll do, for a start, is take her my savings to-morrow.'

'A man owes his wife at least wheaten bread,' said Madame Marneffe, with a smile.

The Baron took no offence at Lisbeth's aggressive tone, although she was sending him about his business as roughly as Josépha had done, and slipped away like a man glad to evade an inconvenient question.

Once the door was bolted, the Brazilian appeared from the dressing-room where he had been waiting, his eyes full of tears, in a pitiable state. Montès had clearly overheard everything.

'You don't love me any more, Henri, I can see,' said Madame Marneffe, hiding her face in her handkerchief and dissolving in tears.

189

It was a cry of real love. A woman's outburst of despair melts a lover's heart, and the forgiveness that he is secretly eager to give her is easily yielded, especially when the woman is young, beautiful, and wearing a dress so low cut that she could rise from the top of it in the costume of Eve.

'But if you love me, why don't you leave everything for me?' the Brazilian demanded.

This son of America, logical like all children of nature, immediately took up the conversation at the point where he had left it, and seized possession again of Valérie's waist.

'Why?' she said, raising her head and looking at Henri, her gaze so full of love that he was silent. 'Because, my darling, I am married; because we're in Paris and not in the savannahs, or the pampas, or the wide, open spaces of America! Henri, my sweet, my first and only love, you must listen to me. This husband of mine, an ordinary under clerk at the War Office, is determined to be head clerk and an Officer of the Legion of Honour. Can I help his being ambitious? And so, for the same reason that he used to leave us entirely free (nearly four years ago, do you remember, wretch? ...), Marneffe forces Baron Hulot on me now. I can't get rid of that frightful chief of his, who puffs like a grampus and has whiskers in his nostrils, and is sixty-three years old, and has aged ten in the last three years in his attempt to keep young. I detest him so much that when the day dawns that sees Marneffe head clerk and an Officer of the Legion of Honour ...'

'How much more will your husband be paid then?'

'A thousand crowns.'

'I will pay him that, as an annuity,' said Montès. 'Let's leave Paris and go ...'

'Where?' said Valérie, pulling one of those charming pouting faces with which women challenge men of whom they are sure. 'You know we could only be happy in Paris. I care too much for your love to want to watch it fade away when we found ourselves alone in a desert. Listen, Henri; you are the only man in the whole universe who means anything to me. Get that into your tiger's skull!'

Women always persuade men that they are lions, with a will of iron, when they are making sheep of them.

'Now, listen to me! Marneffe has not five years to live. There is disease in the very marrow of his bones. Of the twelve months of the year, he spends seven drinking medicine and herb infusions; he lives wrapped in flannel. In fact, as the doctor says, he's ripe for the scythe at any moment. An illness that would be trifling to a healthy man will be mortal to him. His blood is infected, his life attacked at its source. In the past five years I have not let him kiss me once, for the man is pestilence! One day, and the day is not far distant, I shall be a widow. Well then, I declare to you – and I have already had a proposal from a man with sixty thousand francs a year, and I hold him in the hollow of my hand like this lump of sugar – I swear that if you were as poor as Hulot, as leprous as Marneffe, and beat me as well, you are the man I would choose for my husband; you are the only man I love, whose name I want to bear. And I am ready to give you any pledge of love you ask.'

'Well then, tonight . . .'

'But, dear child of Rio, my handsome jaguar come from the virgin forests of Brazil in search of me,' she said, taking his hand, kissing it, and caressing it, 'have a little mercy on the creature you want to make your wife. . . . Shall I be your wife, Henri?'

'Yes,' said the Brazilian, overwhelmed by her frank declaration of passion. And he fell on his knees.

'Listen, Henri,' said Valérie, taking both his hands and looking steadily into the depths of his eyes; 'do you swear to me here, in the presence of Lisbeth, my best and only friend, my sister, to take me for your wife at the end of my year of widowhood?'

'I swear it.'

'That's not enough! Swear by your mother's ashes and her eternal salvation; swear it by the Virgin and your hopes as a Catholic!'

Valérie knew that the Brazilian would keep that oath, no matter into what social mire she should have fallen. The Brazilian took the solemn oath, his face almost touching Valérie's white bosom, and his eyes held fascinated. He was as intoxicated as a man may be, seeing the woman he loves, once more, after a four-months' voyage!

'Well, now you can be quite calm and happy. You must treat Madame Marneffe with the respect that's due to the future Baroness de Montejanos! Don't spend a farthing on me, I forbid you to. Wait here, in this room; you can rest on the sofa. I'll come myself and tell you when you can leave. Tomorrow we'll have lunch together, and you can depart about one o'clock, as if you had come to pay me a visit at twelve. Don't worry about anything; the porters are as devoted to me as if I were their daughter. And now I must go down to my own apartment to serve tea.'

She beckoned to Lisbeth, who went with her as far as the landing. There Valérie whispered in the old maid's ear:

'This blackamoor has come back a little too soon! I'll die if I can't help you to your revenge on Hortense!'

'Don't worry, my dear kind little demon,' said the old maid, kissing her on the forehead. 'Love and vengeance, hunting together, will always strike down their prey. Hortense expects me tomorrow; she is in distress. Wenceslas needs a thousand francs and is ready to give you a thousand kisses for them.'

When he left Valérie, Hulot had gone down to the porters' lodge, taking Madame Olivier by surprise.

'Madame Olivier!'

At this imperious call, noting the beckoning gesture with which the Baron emphasized it, Madame Olivier left her lodge and followed the Baron to the court.

'You know that if anyone can help your son to acquire a practice some day, I can. It's thanks to me that he is now third clerk in a solicitor's office and reading for the law.'

'Yes, Monsieur le Baron. And Monsieur le Baron can count on our gratitude. There's not a day passes but what I don't pray to God for Monsieur le Baron's happiness.'

'Not so many words, my good woman,' said Hulot. 'Deeds!'

'What I am to do?' asked Madame Olivier.

'A man came here tonight in a carriage. Do you know him?'

Madame Olivier had of course recognized Montès. How should she have forgotten him? In the rue du Doyenné house, Montès had always slipped a five-franc piece into her hand whenever he left a little too early in the morning. If the Baron had addressed himself to Monsieur Olivier, he might perhaps have learned the whole story. But Olivier was asleep. Among the lower classes, a man's wife is not only superior to the man, she is usually the dominant partner as well. Madame Olivier had long before made up her mind which side she should support if her two benefactors should come into collision; and she regarded Madame Marneffe as the stronger power.

'Do I know him?' she replied. 'No, indeed. No, I've never seen him before!'

'What! Madame Marneffe's cousin never came to see her when she lived in the rue du Doyenné?'

'Ah! Was that her cousin?' exclaimed Madame Olivier. 'He did come perhaps, but I didn't recognize him. The very next time he comes, Monsieur, I'll take a good look at him.'

'He'll be coming down,' said Hulot sharply, cutting her short.

'But he has gone,' replied Madame Olivier, understanding the situation now. 'His carriage has left. . . .'

'Did you see him go?'

'As plain as I see you. He said to his man "To the Embassy!" he said.'

Her tone of conviction, the assurance she gave, drew a sigh of relief from the Baron. He took Madame Olivier's hand and pressed it.

'Thank you, my dear Madame Olivier; but there's another thing. . . . What about Monsieur Crevel?'

'Monsieur Crevel? What do you mean? I don't understand,' said Madame Olivier.

'Listen to me! He's in love with Madame Marneffe. . . .'

'That's not possible, Monsieur le Baron! Not possible at all!' she said, clasping her hands.

'He's in love with Madame Marneffe!' repeated the Baron emphatically. 'What's going on, I don't know; but I mean to know, and you must find out. If you can help me unravel this intrigue, your son shall be a solicitor.'

'Monsieur le Baron, don't you fret and worry yourself like this,' said Madame Olivier. 'Madame loves you and nobody else; and well enough her maid knows it. We say to each other sometimes, just like that, that you're surely the luckiest man alive, because you know what Madame is ... Ah! just perfection. ... She gets up at ten o'clock every day; and then she has lunch; well. Then there's an hour it takes her to get dressed, and all that brings her to two o'clock. And then she goes to walk about in the Tuileries, in sight and nod of everyone, and is always back at four o'clock for when you come. Oh! she's that regular, she's like a clock. She has no secrets from her maid, and Reine has none from me. Well, naturally not. Reine couldn't have on account of my son, that she's a fancy for. ... So you see very well if Madame had anything to do with Monsieur Crevel we couldn't not know about it.'

The Baron climbed the stairs again to Madame Marneffe's apartment with a radiant face, convinced that he was the man, the only man, loved by that shameless courtesan, as treacherous, but also as beautiful and enchanting, as a siren.

Crevel and Marneffe were beginning their second piquet. Crevel was losing, as a man cannot help losing when his mind is not on the game. Marneffe, who was well aware of the cause of the Mayor's distraction, had no scruples about taking full advantage of it. He was looking at the cards to be drawn, and discarding accordingly; then, knowing his opponent's hand, he played with confidence. Playing for twenty-sou stakes, he had already rooked the Mayor of thirty francs when the Baron came in again.

'Well, well,' said the Councillor of State, surprised to find all the guests gone; 'so you're all alone! Where is everyone?'

'Your charming display of temper frightened them all away,' answered Crevel.

'No, it was my wife's cousin arriving,' said Marneffe. 'The visitors thought that Valérie and Henri must have something to say to each other after three years, so they showed their tact by going away. If I had been here I would have made them stay; but as it happens I should have been doing the wrong thing, because Lisbeth always serves tea at half past ten, and her indisposition has put everything at sixes and sevens.'

'Is Lisbeth really not well?' asked Crevel angrily.

'So they told me,' replied Marneffe with the amoral unconcern of a man for whom women have ceased to exist.

The Mayor looked at the clock. By his reckoning the Baron had spent forty minutes in Lisbeth's room. Hulot's joyful expression cast the gravest suspicion upon Hector, Valérie, and Lisbeth.

'I have just seen her. She's in dreadful pain, poor thing,' said the Baron.

'Other people's pain is your pleasure, then, is it?' returned Crevel acidly. 'Because you've come back to us, my dear friend, with a face positively beaming with jubilation! Can it be that Lisbeth is in serious danger? Your daughter is her heir, I think. You look like a different person: you went off with a face like the Moor of Venice, and come back looking like Saint-Preux! I would very much like to see Madame Marneffe's face. ...'

'Just what do you mean by that?' demanded Marneffe, gathering his cards together and slapping them down in front of him.

The dull eyes of this worn-out man, decrepit at forty-seven, kindled; faint colour suffused his cold and flabby cheeks; he opened his denuded mouth with its discoloured lips, to which rose a white chalky foam. The rage of this impotent man, whose life hung on a thread, who in a duel would be risking nothing, while Crevel would have everything to lose, inspired the Mayor with fear.

'I say,' Crevel replied, 'that I would like to see Madame Marneffe's face, and I have all the more reason, because yours at this moment is a very unpleasant sight. Upon my word, you are as ugly as sin, my dear Marneffe.'

'Do you know that you are not very polite?'

'A man who wins thirty francs from me in forty-five minutes never looks very handsome to me.'

'Ah! if you had only seen me,' the deputy head clerk said, 'seventeen years ago. ...'

'You were captivating?' inquired Crevel.

'That's what's been my ruin. Now if I had been like you, I should be a Mayor and a Peer too.'

'Yes,' said Crevel, with a smile, 'you have gone to the

wars too often. There are two different metals to be won by cultivating the god of commerce, and you've got the baser – dross, dregs, drugs!' And Crevel burst into a roar of laughter.

Although Marneffe might take offence when his honour was imperilled, he always took such coarse and vulgar pleasantries well. They were the ordinary small change of conversation between Crevel and himself.

'Eve has cost me dear, that's true enough; but, faith – short and sweet is my motto.'

'A better one, to my mind, is happy ever after,' said Crevel.

Madame Marneffe, coming in, saw her husband and Crevel playing cards, and the Baron: the three remaining occupants of the drawing-room. One glance at the Mayor's face told her all the agitating thoughts that had passed through that dignitary's mind, and her line of action was at once determined.

'Marneffe, my pet,' she said, going to lean on her husband's shoulder, and drawing her pretty fingers through his uninviting grey hair in an unsuccessful attempt to cover his scalp, 'it is very late for you; you ought to go to bed. You know that tomorrow you have to take a dose; the doctor said so, and Reine is to give you some herb tea at seven. If you want to go on living, that's enough piquet. . . .'

'Shall we do five more?' Marneffe asked Crevel.

'All right . . . I have two already,' replied Crevel.

'How long will that take?' Valérie asked.

'Ten minutes,' replied Marneffe.

'It's eleven o'clock,' said Valérie. 'Really, Monsieur Crevel, anyone would think that you wanted to kill my husband. Well, at least, don't be too long about it.'

This ambiguous command made both Crevel and Hulot smile, and even Marneffe himself. Valérie went over to speak to her Hector.

'Leave now, my dear,' she whispered in Hector's ear. 'Go for a little walk in the rue Vanneau, and come back when you see Crevel leave.'

'I would rather leave the apartment, and then come back to your room by the dressing-room door. You could tell Reine to open it for me.'

'Reine is upstairs, looking after Lisbeth.'

'Well, suppose I went up to Lisbeth's room?'

Danger awaited Valérie on all sides. Knowing that there would be a scene with Crevel, she did not want Hulot in her room, where he might overhear everything. ... And the Brazilian was waiting in Lisbeth's apartment.

'Really, you men,' she said to Hulot, 'when you get an idea into your heads, you would burn down the house to force your way in. In Lisbeth's present state she's not fit to receive you. Are you afraid of catching cold in the street? Off you go ... or good night to you!'

'Good night, gentlemen,' said the Baron, aloud.

Once piqued in his old man's vanity, Hulot was set on proving that he could play the young man and wait for the lovers' hour in the street, and he departed.

Marneffe said good night to his wife, and took her hands with a show of affection. Valérie pressed her husband's hand significantly, meaning 'Get rid of Crevel for me'.

'Good night, Crevel,' said Marneffe. 'I hope you don't intend to stay long with Valérie. I'm a jealous man. Ah! jealousy's caught me a bit late in life, but it has fairly got me in its clutches. ... And I'll come back to see if you have gone.'

'We have business to discuss, but I won't stay long,' said Crevel.

'Speak softly!' said Valérie under her breath, and then aloud, 'Well, what is it?' And she looked Crevel up and down with a mixture of arrogance and contempt.

When he met her haughty stare, Crevel, who had rendered great services to Valérie, and had been counting on making the most of the fact, subsided into humility and submission.

'That Brazilian ...'

Quailing before Valérie's fixed contemptuous stare, Crevel broke off.

'What of him?' she said.

'That cousin ...'

'He's not my cousin,' she said flatly. 'He's my cousin to the world, and to Monsieur Marneffe. If he were my lover, you would have no right to say a word. A tradesman who buys a woman in order to have his revenge, in my opinion, is lower than the man who buys her for love. You did not fall in love with me. You saw only Monsieur Hulot's mistress in me, and you bought me like a man buying a pistol to do his enemy to death. I needed money to buy my bread, and I agreed!'

'And you haven't kept your part of the bargain,' replied Crevel, the shopkeeper coming uppermost in him again.

'Ah! you want Baron Hulot to know that you have robbed him of his mistress, to have your revenge for his carrying Josépha off? Could anything prove more clearly how despicable you are? You say you love a woman, call her a duchess, and then you want to bring dishonour upon her! Well, perhaps, my dear, you are right. This woman that you have bought is not to be compared with Josépha. That young lady stands up bravely in her shame, while I'm just a hypocrite who deserves to be publicly whipped. Josépha, of course, is protected by her talent and her wealth. The only protection I possess is my reputation. I am still a respectable middle-class wife of good repute; but if you create a scandal, what shall I be? If I had a lot of money, it wouldn't matter so much; but all I have, as you know very well, is fifteen thousand francs a year at most.'

'Oh, much more,' said Crevel; 'I have doubled your savings during the last couple of months, in Paris–Orléans Railway shares.'

'Well, no one counts for anything in Paris who has less than fifty thousand francs a year; you needn't try to tell me in francs the value of the reputation I shall lose! And all I am asking is to see Marneffe made a head clerk. Then his salary would be six thousand francs. He has twenty-seven years' service, so that in three more years I should be entitled to a pension of fifteen hundred francs when he dies. And yet you, on whom I have lavished kindness, whom I have gorged with happiness, you can't wait. And that's what you call love!' she exclaimed.

'If I began with a selfish motive,' said Crevel, 'I have become your own *bow-wow* since. You trample all over my feelings, crush me and humiliate me, and I love you as I have never loved anyone before. Valérie, I love you as much as I love Célestine! I would do anything for you. . . . Listen! Instead of coming twice a week to the rue Dauphin, come three times.'

'Is that all? You are growing young again, my dear. . . .'

'Let me send Hulot packing, take him down a peg, get rid of him for you,' said Crevel, disregarding her insolence. 'Don't see that Brazilian again; be all mine and you will not regret it. To begin with, I'll set apart shares for you worth eight thousand francs a year, but just for the interest at first; I'll give you the capital only when you have been faithful to me for five years.'

'There's no end to these bargains! Shopkeepers will never learn to give! Do you want to set up relays of love for yourself throughout life with your transfers of shares? . . . Ah! shopkeeper, hair-oil seller that you are, you put a price-ticket on everything! Hector told me that the Duc d'Hérouville brought Joséjpha bonds worth thirty thousand francs a year in a cornet of sugared almonds! And I'm worth six Joséphas! Ah! to be loved!' she sighed, twisting her ringlets round her fingers and going to look at herself in the glass. 'Henri loves me. He would kill you like a fly at a flicker of my eyelids! Hulot loves me – he leaves his wife destitute! Go away and be a good family man, my dear. Why, you have three hundred thousand francs just to play about with, over and above your fortune – a stack of money, in fact, and all you think of is how to make more. . . .'

'For you, Valérie, for I offer you half of it!' he said, falling on his knees.

'Well, so you're still here!' cried the hideous Marneffe, appearing in his dressing-gown. 'What are you doing?'

'He's begging my pardon, my love, for an insulting proposal that he's just made to me. As he couldn't get anything from me, it occurred to Monsieur that he might buy me. . . .'

Crevel would have liked to sink through the floor to the cellar, vanish through a trapdoor, as the trick is worked on the stage.

'Get up, my dear Crevel,' said Marneffe, grinning. 'You look quite ridiculous. I can see from Valérie's expression that I'm in no danger.'

'Go to bed, and sleep well,' said Madame Marneffe.

'How quick-witted she is!' thought Crevel. 'She is adorable! She has saved my life!'

When Marneffe had gone back to his room, the Mayor took Valérie's hands in his and kissed them, leaving traces of tears there as he raised his head.

'Everything in your own name!' he said.

'That is the way to love,' she murmured in his ear. 'Well, love for love. Hulot is below, in the street. The poor old fellow is waiting, hoping to come up when I place a candle at one of my bedroom windows. I give you permission to tell him that you are the only man I love. He will never dream of believing you, so take him to the rue du Dauphin, give him proofs, sink him without trace. I allow you – no, I command you to do it. That great walrus bores me, bores me to extinction. Keep your man close in the rue du Dauphin for the whole night, roast him over a slow fire, take your revenge for Josépha's carrying off. It will perhaps be the death of Hulot, but we shall be saving his wife and children from utter ruin. You know that Madame Hulot is working for her living? ...'

'Oh, poor lady! Upon my word, that's dreadful!' exclaimed Crevel, his native good nature reviving.

'If you love me, Célestin,' she said in a whisper, lightly touching Crevel's ear with her lips as she spoke, 'keep him away, or I am lost. Marneffe is suspicious, and Hector has the key of the carriage entrance door and means to come back!'

Crevel clasped Madame Marneffe in his arms, and left, walking on air. Valérie accompanied him fondly as far as the landing, and then like a woman magnetically attracted, unable to break free, followed him to the first floor, and on to the foot of the staircase.

'My own Valérie, go upstairs again! Don't compromise yourself in the porters' eyes. ... Go back, my life and my wealth, everything is for you. ... Go back, my duchess!'

'Madame Olivier!' called Valérie softly when the door had closed behind him.

'Why, Madame! You here?' said Madame Olivier, in surprise.

'Bolt the big door top and bottom, and don't open it again.'

'Very well, Madame.'

When the door was bolted, Madame Olivier told the story of how the high official had stooped to trying to bribe her.

'You have behaved angelically, dear Olivier; but we'll talk about that tomorrow.'

Valérie sped like an arrow to the third floor, tapped three times lightly on Lisbeth's door, and returned to her own apartment, where she gave her instructions to Mademoiselle Reine; for a woman must do her best to seize her opportunities when a Montès comes back from Brazil.

*

'No, upon my soul, only a society lady could love like that!' Crevel said to himself. 'How she came down the stairs, a light beaming from her eyes, following me! I was drawing her after me! Why, Josépha never ... Josépha! She's only a common piece. ...' exclaimed the retired commercial traveller. 'What did I say? *a common piece*. ... Good God! I might come out with that one day at the Tuileries. ... No, if Valérie doesn't see to my education I can never amount to much – and I want so much to be a real gentleman. ... Ah! what a woman! She upsets me just like a colic when she looks at me coldly. What grace! What spirit! I never had such emotions about Josépha. And then such hidden perfections! Ah, here's my man.'

He saw in the shadows of the rue de Babylon Hulot's tall figure, a little stooped, skulking by the scaffolding of a half-built house, and he went straight up to him.

'Good-morning, Baron, for it's past midnight, old man! What the devil are you doing here? ... You're taking your walk on a nice fine drizzly evening. At our age that's not a wise thing to do. Would you like me to give you a piece of good advice? Let's both go home; for between ourselves, you will see no light in the window tonight.'

On hearing Crevel's last remark, the Baron was suddenly aware that he was sixty-three years old, and that his coat was damp.

'Who can have told you?' he said.

'Valérie, of course! *Our* Valérie, who wants to be only *my* Valérie. We are game and game, Baron; we'll play the final match whenever you like. You needn't be angry, you know quite well that I always said that I was entitled to have my revenge. It took you three months to rob me of Josépha. I carried off Valérie in ... well, never mind that. Now I want to have her all to myself. But we can remain good friends all the same.'

'Crevel, don't make jokes,' the Baron said, in a voice choking with rage. 'This is a matter of life and death.'

'Goodness, how seriously you take it! ... Baron, don't you remember what you said to me on Hortense's wedding day? "Why should two old beaux like us quarrel over a petticoat? It's common, it's ill-bred ..." And we, we are agreed, are Regency, blue jerkins, Pompadour, eighteenth-century, everything that is most Maréchal de Richelieu, rococo, and I may go so far as to say, *Liaisons dangereuses*! ...'

Crevel might have gone on adding to his literary allusions for much longer; the Baron was listening to him as deaf men listen when deafness first comes upon them. But seeing, by the street gas-lamp, his enemy's face grown pale, the victor stopped. It was a thunder-clap for the Baron, after Madame Olivier's assurances, after Valérie's parting look.

'God! There were so many other women in Paris! ...' he exclaimed at last.

'That's what I said to you when you took Josépha from me,' rejoined Crevel.

'Look here, Crevel, it's not possible. ... Give me proof! Have you got a key, like me, to let yourself in?'

And the Baron, now reaching the house, pushed a key into the lock; but he found the door immovable, and tried in vain to shake it.

'Don't make such a row here at night,' said Crevel calmly. 'Believe it or not, Baron, I have far better keys than yours.'

'Prove it! Prove it!' the Baron reiterated, almost frantic with misery.

'Come with me; I'm going to give you proof,' replied Crevel.

And in obedience to Valérie's instructions, he led the Baron away towards the quay, along the rue Hillerin-Bertin. The unfortunate Councillor of State walked along like a business-man who next day must file his petition to the Bankruptcy Court. He lost himself in conjectures about the causes of the depravity hidden in Valérie's heart, and dreamed that he must be the victim of some hoax. Crossing the pont Royal, he saw his existence as so empty, so completely ended, so en-tangled in financial snarls, that he all but yielded to a strong impulse to push Crevel into the river and throw himself in after.

When they reached the rue du Dauphin, which at that time had not yet been widened, Crevel stopped before a door in the wall. This door opened on a long passage paved with black and white tiles, forming an entrance hall, at the end of which were a flight of steps and a porter's lodge lighted by an inner court-yard, a lay-out common enough in Paris. This court, shared with the neighbouring house, was unusual in its unequal division. Crevel's little house – for he was the owner – had an annexe with a glass roof, built on the adjoining land. The structure, which was restricted by order to its present height, was completely hidden from view by the lodge and the cor-belling of the steps.

This place had for a long time served as store-room, back premises, and kitchen for one of the two shops facing the street. Crevel had separated these three ground-floor rooms from the space let to the shop, and Grindot had transformed them into a snug little house. There were two entrances: through a furniture-dealer's shop, let cheaply and by the month so that Crevel could easily get rid of the shopkeeper if he talked indiscreetly, and by a door set so inconspicuously in the passage wall as to be almost invisible. This little dwelling, consisting of a dining-room, a drawing-room, and a bedroom, lighted from above, standing partly on Crevel's ground and partly on his neighbour's, was therefore almost impossible to find. With the exception of the furniture-dealer, none of the tenants knew of the existence of this little paradise. The porter's wife, who was paid to keep her mouth shut, was an excellent cook. Monsieur le Maire, then, could enter his neat little house and leave it at any hour of the night without fear of being spied upon. By day, a woman dressed as a Parisian dresses to do her shopping, and provided with a key, risked nothing by visiting Crevel. She could stop to consider a piece of second-hand furniture, haggle a little over prices, enter the shop or leave it, without arousing the slightest suspicion if anyone chanced to meet her.

When Crevel had lit the candles in the boudoir, the Baron was quite astonished at the charming effect produced by an intelligent use of money. The retired perfumer had given Grindot a free hand, and the old architect had distinguished himself by the creation of an interior in Pompadour style, which, as a matter of fact, had cost sixty thousand francs.

'I want,' Crevel had said to Grindot, 'a duchess coming in here to be impressed. . . .'

He had wanted a most lovely Parisian Eden in which to enjoy his Eve, his society lady, his Valérie, his duchess.

'There are two beds,' Crevel told Hulot, pointing to a divan from which a bed could be drawn out, like a drawer from a chest of drawers. 'There's one; the other is in the bedroom. So we can both stay the night here.'

'Proof!' said the Baron.

Crevel took a candlestick and led his friend into the bedroom, and there, on a sofa, Hulot saw a luxurious dressing-gown of Valérie's, which she had worn at home in the rue Vanneau to show it off before bringing it to Crevel's little house. The Mayor pulled out the secret drawer of a pretty little inlaid writing table, of the kind called *bonheur-du-jour*, rummaged in it, and found a letter which he handed to the Baron.

'Here; read this.'

The Councillor of State read the little pencilled note:

I have waited for you in vain, wretched man! Women like me never wait for retired perfumers. No dinner had been ordered, and there were no cigarettes. I'll make you pay for this!

'Do you recognize her writing?'

'God!' said Hulot, sitting down, helplessly. 'All these

things are hers. I know her caps, her slippers. But, heavens above, tell me when ... since when?'

Crevel nodded understandingly and picked up a bundle of bills from the little inlaid desk.

'Look, old chap! I paid the contractors in December 1838. This lovely little house was used for the first time in October, two months before.'

The Councillor of State bowed his head.

'How the devil do you manage it? I know how her time is spent, every hour of it.'

'What about her walk in the Tuileries?' said Crevel, rubbing his hands exultantly.

'What about it?' Hulot said, in bewilderment.

'Your so-called mistress goes to the Tuileries; she's supposed to be walking there from one o'clock to four. But hey presto! she's here in a flash. You know your Molière? Well, Baron, there's nothing imaginary about the title that applies to you.'*

Hulot, not able to doubt any longer that it was all true, remained ominously silent. Catastrophes incline all strong and intelligent minds to philosophy; but the Baron was, in spirit, like a man trying to find his way through a forest at night. His dull silence, the change that had come over his drawn features, disturbed Crevel, for he did not want to cause his old fellow-sinner's death.

'As I was saying, old man, we are game-all now; let's play off the deciding game. You want to finish the rubber, don't you? May the wiliest man win!'

'Why is it,' said Hulot, as if to himself, 'that out of ten beautiful women, at least seven are utterly bad?'

The Baron was too upset to find an answer to the question. The power of beauty is the most compelling of all human powers; and power – with nothing to balance it, unchecked by any absolute control – leads to abuse, to mad excess. Despotism is power run mad; and for women gratifying their whims may involve a kind of despotism.

'You have no need to be sorry for youself, my dear

*The reference is to Molière's *Le malade imaginaire*. Crevel is suggesting that Hulot is a cuckold.

fellow. You have a very beautiful wife, and she is virtuous.'

'I deserve my fate,' Hulot said, in a low voice. 'I have not appreciated my wife as I ought; I have made her suffer, and she's an angel! Oh, my poor Adeline, truly you have been avenged! She is suffering in silence, alone; she deserves to be adored, she deserves my love. I should ... for indeed she is still beautiful, so pale and innocent, so almost virginal again ... But has ever a woman been seen more unspeakable, more shameless, more utterly wicked than that Valérie?'

'She's a bad lot,' said Crevel, 'a hussy who deserves to be whipped on the place du Châtelet. But, my dear Canillac,* though we may be blue jerkins, Maréchal de Richelieu, glasses of fashion, Pompadour, du Barry, rakes, profligates, and as eighteenth century as it is possible to be, we have no Lieutenant of Police any more.'

'What does one do to make a woman love one?' Hulot asked himself, paying no heed to Crevel.

'It's just a piece of silliness for us, for men like you and me, to want to be loved, old man,' said Crevel. 'We can't be more than tolerated. And Madame Marneffe is a hundred times more of a wanton than Josépha. ...'

'And so grasping! She has cost me a hundred and ninety-two thousand francs!' exclaimed Hulot.

'And how many centimes?' asked Crevel, with the insolence of a man of capital, thinking the sum trifling.

'It's easy to see that you don't love her,' said the Baron, in a melancholy tone.

'I've had enough,' replied Crevel. 'She's had more than three hundred thousand francs from me. ...'

'Where is that money? Where does it all go?' said the Baron, holding his head in his hands.

'If we had made an arrangement between ourselves, like those hard-up young fellows who club together to keep a penny-farthing prostitute, she would have cost us less.'

'That's an idea!' replied the Baron. 'But she would still have deceived us; for what, my stout friend, do you make of that Brazilian?'

*Philippe de Montbrison de Beaufort, marquis de Canillac (1669–74), soldier, wit, voluptuary, and friend of the Duke of Orleans.

'Ah, indeed, old boy, you're right! We've been spoofed like . . . like shareholders!' said Crevel. 'All women of her sort are limited liability companies!'

'It was really she, was it,' said the Baron, 'who told you about the light in the window?'

'My dear fellow,' exclaimed Crevel, striking his pose, 'we've been diddled! Valérie is a . . . She told me to keep you here . . . I see the whole thing now . . . She has her Brazilian there. Ah! I give her up, for if you held her hands, she would find some way of cheating you with her feet! She's unspeakable! A real strumpet!'

'She's worse than the prostitutes,' said the Baron. 'Josépha, Jenny Cadine, had the right to deceive us. Their charms are their profession, after all!'

'And she pretends to be a saint, a prude!' said Crevel. 'Look here, Hulot, go back to your wife. Your affairs are in none too good a state: people are beginning to talk about certain IOUs, held by a little money-lender called Vauvinet who specializes in lending to women of easy virtue. As for me, I'm cured of real ladies. Besides, at our age, what do we want of these hussies, who, to be quite candid, can hardly fail to deceive us? Your hair is white, Baron, and your teeth are false; and I look like Silenus. I'm going to devote my energies to making money. There's no deception about money. The Treasury may be open to everyone every six months, but at least it gives you interest on what you lend, and doesn't spend it, like that woman. . . . With you, dear friend Gubetta, my old partner in sin, I might have accepted a situation *chocnoso* . . . unseemly? . . . no, I mean arranged philosophically; but a Baron who, it may be, brings dubious colonial goods from his country. . . .'

'Woman,' said Hulot, 'is an inexplicable creature!'

'I can explain her,' said Crevel. 'We are old, the Brazilian is young and handsome. . . .'

'Yes, that's true,' said Hulot. 'I must admit that we are not getting younger. But how, my friend, is a man to give up seeing these lovely creatures undressing, twisting up their hair, peeping at us through their fingers with a little smile as they roll their curl-papers in, practising all their little arts, telling their fibs, saying that we don't love them when they see us preoccupied with business worries, and distracting us from our troubles in spite of everything?'

'Yes, upon my word, it's the only pleasure in life! ...' exclaimed Crevel. 'Ah! when a little puss smiles at you, and you hear her say: "My darling pet, if you only knew how nice you are! I suppose other women are different. I just don't understand how they can go mad about youths with billy-goat tufts on their chins, silly brats who smoke and have manners like footmen, because being so young they think they can be as impudent as they please! And then they're here today and gone tomorrow. ... You think I am a flirt, but really I would much rather have men of fifty than those little whipper-snappers: they stay with us longer. They're devoted: they know that women are not so easily found, and they appreciate us. That's why I love you, you old rascal!" And while they are confiding these thoughts to you they are petting and caressing you, and smiling. ... Ah! it's all as false as the promises on election posters. ...'

'Falsehood is often better than the truth,' said Hulot, recalling some charming scenes evoked by Crevel's mimicry of Valérie. 'They have to decorate their act, sew spangles on their stage costumes. ...'

'And then, after all, we have them, these lying little cheats!' said Crevel brutally.

'Valérie is a witch,' said the Baron, with conviction. 'She can change an old man into a young one.'

'Ah, yes, she really is,' Crevel joined in. 'She's a snake that slips between your fingers, but the prettiest of snakes ... so white, and as sweet as sugar! As funny as Arnal, and so full of devilish inventions! Ah!'

'Oh, yes, she is a lively spirit!' enthusiastically agreed the Baron, no longer thinking of his wife.

The two comrades went to bed the best friends in the world, recalling Valérie's perfections to each other, one by one, the inflections of her voice, her malicious remarks, her ges-tures, the comic things she did, her flashes of wit, the warm impulses of her heart; for that artist in love had admirable moments when she surpassed herself, as tenors may sing a part better one day than the next. And they both fell asleep rocked by these tender and diabolical reminiscences, lit by the fires of hell.

Next day, at nine o'clock, Hulot spoke of going to the Ministry; Crevel had business in the country. They left the house together, and Crevel held out his hand to the Baron, saying:

'There's no ill-feeling between us, is there? For after all, we've no further interest in Madame Marneffe, either of us.'

'Oh, we're finished with her!' replied Hulot, with something approaching horror.

At half past ten, Crevel was climbing Madame Marneffe's stairs, four at a time. He found the shameless creature, the adorable enchantress, in the most charming boudoir wrap imaginable, eating a choice little luncheon in the company of Baron Henri Montès de Montejanos and Lisbeth. In spite of the painful shock of seeing the Brazilian there, Crevel begged Madame Marneffe to give him two minutes in private, and Valérie passed into the drawing-room with him.

'Valérie, my angel,' said the amorous Crevel, 'Monsieur Marneffe has not long to live. If you will be faithful to me, when he dies we can be married. Think it over. I have got rid of Hulot for you. . . . So just consider whether that Brazilian is worth a Mayor of Paris, a man who would be ambitious to attain the highest dignities for your sake, and who, at this very moment, possesses eighty-odd thousand francs a year.'

'I'll think about it,' she said. 'I'll be at the rue du Dauphin at two o'clock, and we can talk about it. But be careful! And don't forget the transfer of shares you promised me yesterday.'

She returned to the dining-room, followed by Crevel, who was delighted to think that he had found the way to have Valérie to himself; but the first person he saw was Baron Hulot, who, during this short interview, had come in with the same object in mind. The Councillor of State, like Crevel, asked for a moment in private. Madame Marneffe rose to return to the drawing-room, smiling at the Brazilian as she did so, as if to say: 'They're mad! Can't they see you here?'

'Valérie,' said the Councillor of State, 'my child, that cousin of yours is a cousin from the blue. . . .'

'Oh, that's enough!' she interrupted the Baron, with some emphasis. 'Marneffe has never been, shall never be, and never can be my husband. The first and only man that I have ever loved has just returned, quite unexpectedly. . . . That's not my fault! But just take a look at Henri, and then look at yourself. And ask yourself how any woman, especially a woman in love, could hesitate. My dear, I am not a kept woman. From today, I don't intend to be any longer like Susannah between the two Elders. If you care for me, you can be, you and Crevel, our friends; but everything else is at an end between us, for I am twenty-six years old, and in the future I mean to be a saint, a woman worthy of respect and admiration . . . like your wife.'

'So that's the way of it?' said Hulot. 'Is that how you welcome me, when I was coming, like a Pope, with my hands full of indulgences? Well, your husband will never be a head clerk nor an Officer of the Legion of Honour. . . .'

'We'll see about that!' said Madame Marneffe, looking at Hulot in no uncertain fashion.

'Don't let's quarrel,' said Hulot in despair. 'I'll come back this evening and we can talk things over.'

'In Lisbeth's room, then. Very well!'

'Well, then,' said the love-sick old man; 'in Lisbeth's room!'

Hulot and Crevel went downstairs together to the street without a word. But on the pavement, they looked at each other and began to laugh ruefully.

'We are two old fools!' said Crevel.

'I have got rid of them,' Madame Marneffe told Lisbeth, sitting down again at the table. 'I have never loved, do not now love, and never shall love anyone but my jaguar,' she added, smiling at Henri Montès. 'Lisbeth, my dear, do you know that Henri has forgiven me all the dreadful things that my need for money forced me to do?'

'It's my fault,' the Brazilian said. 'I ought to have sent you a hundred thousand francs. . . .'

'Poor dear!' exclaimed Valérie. 'I ought to have worked for

my living, but my fingers weren't made for that ... ask Lisbeth if they were.'

The Brazilian went away the happiest man in Paris.

About noon, Valérie and Lisbeth were talking in the luxurious bedroom where this formidable Parisian was adding those finishing touches to her toilette that no woman cares to entrust to a maid. Behind locked doors and drawn curtains, Valérie related all the happenings of the previous evening, the night, and that morning, in the most minute detail.

'Are you pleased, my sweet?' she asked Lisbeth when she had finished. 'Which should I choose to be, Madame Crevel or Madame Montès? What do you say?'

'Crevel won't last more than ten years, he's such a libertine,' said Lisbeth, 'and Montès is young. Crevel will leave you about thirty thousand francs a year. Let Montès wait; he'll be happy enough to be the Benjamin. And then, at about thirty-three, my dear child, if you take good care of your looks, you can marry your Brazilian and cut a fine figure in society with sixty thousand francs a year of your own – under the wing of a Marshal's wife!'

'Yes, but Montès is a Brazilian – he'll never get anywhere,' observed Valérie.

'We live in an age of railway construction,' said Lisbeth; 'and foreigners now may reach high positions in France.'

'We shall see,' answered Valérie, 'when Marneffe is dead, and he has not a long time left now to suffer.'

'These attacks of illness which keep returning,' said Lisbeth, 'seem like his body's penitence. ... Well, I must go to visit Hortense.'

'Yes, do go, my angel,' Valérie answered, 'and bring me my artist! In three years, it's unbelievable, I have not gained an inch of ground! That's no credit to either of us. Wenceslas and Henri – those are my two only passions. One is love, and the other my fancy!'

'How lovely you look this morning!' said Lisbeth, coming over to put her arm round Valérie's waist and kiss her forehead. 'I share in the enjoyment of all your pleasures, your good fortune, your dresses ... I didn't know what it was to live until the day when we became sisters.'

'Wait a moment, my tigress!' said Valérie, laughing. 'Your shawl is crooked. ... After three years you still don't know how to wear a shawl, in spite of all my lessons – and you aspire to be Madame la Maréchale Hulot!'

*

Lisbeth, wearing prunella ankle boots and grey silk stockings and equipped for battle in a dress of beautiful Levantine silk, her hair braided and coiled round her head under a very pretty black velvet bonnet lined with yellow satin, set off for the rue Saint-Dominique, going by way of the boulevard des Invalides; and as she walked along she wondered whether Hortense's despondency might at last give that strong spirit into her hand, and whether Slavonic instability, worked upon at a time when the course such natures as his may take is unpredictable, might make Wenceslas's devotion falter.

Hortense and Wenceslas occupied the ground floor of a house at the corner of the rue Saint-Dominique and the esplanade des Invalides. This apartment, originally suitable for a honeymoon, now had a rather wilted freshness that might be called the furnishings' autumn of the year. Young couples are extravagantly wasteful and destructive of their belongings without meaning to be, without even realizing that they are – their love is subject to the same misuse. They are wrapped up in themselves and little concerned about the future, which is later to become the preoccupation of the mother of a family.

Lisbeth found her Cousin Hortense just as she had finished dressing a little Wenceslas, who had been put out in the garden.

'Good afternoon, Bette,' said Hortense, who had opened the door to her cousin herself.

The cook had gone to market. The maid, who was also the nurse, was doing some washing.

'Good afternoon, dear child,' said Bette, and kissed her; and then, in a whisper, she added, 'Is Wenceslas at his studio?'

'No, he's in the drawing-room, talking to Stidmann and Chanor.'

'Where can we have a moment alone together?'

'Come into my bedroom.'

The floral chintz with which this room was hung, of pink flowers and green leaves on a white ground, and the carpet, left unshaded from the sun, had faded. The curtains had not been laundered for some time. The smell of cigar smoke hung about, for Wenceslas, an aristocrat by birth and now an eminent artist, scattered tobacco ash on the arms of chairs and over the prettiest pieces of furniture in a lordly fashion, like a spoilt darling who is forgiven anything and a rich man above bourgeois carefulness.

'Well, now, let's talk about your affairs,' commanded Lisbeth, seeing her lovely cousin sit silent in the big chair into which she had thrown herself. 'But what's the matter? I think you look a little pale, my dear.'

'There have been two more articles, slating poor Wenceslas mercilessly. I've read them, but I'm hiding them from him, because he would be utterly discouraged. They consider the statue of Marshal Montcornet a poor piece of work. They allow some merit to the bas-reliefs and praise Wenceslas's talent for ornament, but it's only out of a mean kind of treachery, to give more weight to the opinion that serious *art* is beyond him! I begged Stidmann to tell me the truth, and he utterly shattered me by confessing that privately he concurs with the opinion of the other artists, the critics, and the public. "If Wenceslas does not exhibit something really good before the end of the year," he said to me there in the garden before lunch, "he will have to give up large-scale sculpture and concentrate on romantic groups, small figures, jewellery and high-class goldsmith's work!" I felt dreadful when I heard him say this, because I know Wenceslas will never agree; he knows his own talent; he has so many brilliant ideas.'

'Ideas don't pay the tradesmen,' Lisbeth observed, 'I used to wear myself out telling him that. It's money that pays them, and you will only get money for finished work that ordinary people like well enough to buy. When it comes to earning a living, it's better for the artist to have a model for a candlestick, a fender or a table on his work-bench, than a group or a statue; because everyone needs those things, but the buyer of a group and his money have to be waited for, maybe for months.'

'You are absolutely right, dear Lisbeth! I wish you would tell him that – I haven't got the courage. Besides, as he said to Stidmann, if he goes back to decorative work and small-scale sculpture, it means giving up the Institut, and large works, and then we shall not get the three hundred thousand francs commission that the Ministry has promised us for work at Versailles and for the City of Paris. You see how those dreadful articles are damaging us! They're inspired by rivals who would like to fall heir to our commissions.'

'And you dreamed of things turning out quite differently, poor little puss!' Bette said, giving Hortense a kiss on the forehead. 'You wanted an aristocrat ruling the world of art, a leading sculptor dominating the rest. ... But that's just romantic dreaming, you know. You need fifty thousand francs a year to realize a dream like that, and you have only two thousand four hundred so long as I'm alive, three thousand after my death.'

Tears rose to Hortense's eyes, and Bette watched them with greedy absorption, like a cat lapping milk.

Here follows the brief history of that honeymoon. The tale will perhaps not be lost on artists.

The work of the mind, tracking down a quarry in the high regions of the intellect, is one of the most strenuous kinds of human endeavour. To achieve fame in art – and in *art* must be included all the mind's creations – courage, above all, is needed, courage of a kind that the ordinary man has no idea of, which is perhaps described for the first time here.

Driven by the relentless pressure of poverty, kept to his path by Bette like a horse blinkered to prevent its looking to right or left, whipped on by that harsh old maid, an embodiment of Necessity, a kind of underling of Fate, Wenceslas, born a poet and a dreamer, had passed from conception to execution, leaping over the abysses that separate those two hemispheres of art without noticing their depth.

To think, to dream, to conceive fine works, is a delightful occupation. It is dreaming cigar-smoke dreams, or living a courtesan's self-indulgent life. The work of art to be created is envisaged in the exhilaration of conception, with its infant grace, and the scented colour of its flower and the bursting juices of its fruit. These are the pleasures in the imagination of a work of art's conception.

The man who can formulate his design in words is held to be out of the common run of men. This faculty all artists and writers possess; but execution needs more than this. It means creating, bringing to birth, laboriously rearing the child, putting it to bed every evening gorged with milk, kissing it every morning with a mother's never spent affection, licking it clean, clothing it over and over again in the prettiest garments, which it spoils again and again. It means never being disheartened by the upheavals of a frenetic life, but making of the growing work of art a living masterpiece, which in sculpture speaks to all eyes, in literature to all minds, in painting to all memories, in music to every heart. This is the travail of execution. The hand must constantly progress, in constant obedience to the mind. And the ability to create is no more to be commanded at will than love is: both powers are intermittent.

The habit of creation, the unwearying cherishing love which makes a mother (that masterpiece of nature so well apprehended by Raphael!), the intellectual maternal power, in short, which is so difficult to acquire, is exceedingly easily lost. Inspiration is the opportunity that genius may seize; and is not even balanced on a razor's edge, but instantly in the air and flying off with the quick alarm of crows. Inspiration has no scarf by which the poet may grasp her. Her hair is a flame. She is gone like those rose-coloured and white beautiful flamingos that are the despair of sportsmen. And work is a fatiguing struggle, dreaded as well as passionately loved by the fine and powerful natures that are often broken by it. A great poet of our own times, speaking of this appalling toil, has said, 'I begin it with despair, and leave it with grief'.

Let the ignorant take note! If the artist does not throw himself into his work like Curtius into the gulf, like a soldier against a fortress, without counting the cost; and if, once within the breach, he does not labour like a miner buried under a fallen roof; if, in short, he contemplates the difficulties instead of conquering them, one by one, like those lovers in the fairy-tales who, to win their princesses, fought ever-renewed enchantments; then the work remains unfinished, it perishes, is lost within the workshop, where production becomes impossible, and the artist is a looker-on at his talent's suicide. Rossini, Raphael's brother genius, is a striking example to artists in the battle fought from indigent youth to the success of his maturity. It is for these reasons that the same laurel wreath is bestowed on great poets and great generals: a similar reward is accorded to a similar triumph.

Wenceslas, a dreamer by nature, had spent so much energy in producing work, in teaching himself, and working under Lisbeth's despotic rule, that love and happiness brought a reaction. His true character reasserted itself. Indolence and lethargy, the yielding softness of the Slav, returned to find the ready haven in his soul from which the school-mistress's rod had driven them. The artist, during the first months, was in love with his wife. Hortense and Wenceslas gave themselves up to the charming youthful pleasures of unlimited, happy, married, passion. Hortense was the first, at this time, to excuse Wenceslas from all work, proud of being able to triumph over her rival – his sculpture. A woman's caresses make the muse languid, and melt the fierce, the brutal, resolution of the worker. Six or seven months went by. The sculptor's fingers forgot how to hold the chisel. When it became urgently necessary to work, when Prince de Wissembourg, president of the committee representing the subscribers, asked to see the statue, Wenceslas gave the idler's usual answer, 'I'm just starting work on it!' And he deluded his dear Hortense with self-deceiving words, with the splendid creations an artist can make from tobacco smoke.

Hortense was twice as deeply in love with her poet. She pictured a sublime statue of Marshal Montcornet. Montcornet was to be valiance personified, the type of the cavalry officer, courage itself, in Murat's style. This statue would make it easy to understand how the Emperor had won all his victories! And how finely it would be executed! The facile pencil was accommodating: it confirmed the artist's words.

The only statue produced was a ravishing little Wenceslas.

Whenever Wenceslas was about to go to the studio at Gros-Caillou to complete the clay model, the Prince's clock was likely to require his presence at the studio of Florent and Chanor, where the figures were being finished; or the sky would be overcast and grey. On one occasion there might be business to attend to, and a family dinner on the day after. Then there were the days, hardly worth mentioning, when the artist was not in the mood, or did not feel well; besides those spent in dalliance with an adored wife. Marshal Prince de Wissembourg had actually to show anger, and say that he would go back on his decision to give the commission to Wenceslas, before he could succeed in seeing the model. It was only after innumerable complaints and many heated words that the subscribers' committee were allowed to see the plaster cast. Steinbock came home visibly fatigued at the end of each day he spent at work, complaining of having to labour like a mason, and of his own lack of robustness.

During the first year this household was comfortably off. Countess Steinbock, madly in love with her husband, in the flush of requited passion, inveighed against the War Minister. She went to see him, and told him that great works could not be manufactured like cannon, and that the state should take orders from genius, as Louis XIV, Francis I, and Pope Leo X had done. Poor Hortense believed that she held a Phidias in her arms, and treated her Wenceslas with fond weakness, like an idolized son.

'Don't hurry,' she told her husband. 'Our whole future is in this statue. Take your time. Create a masterpiece.'

She used to go to the studio. Steinbock, in love, would waste five hours out of seven with his wife, describing his statue to her instead of working on it. And so he took eighteen months to complete this work, of such cardinal importance for him.

When the plaster was cast, and the model was actually in existence, poor Hortense thought the piece admirable. She had witnessed the tremendous effort her husband had made, and seen his health suffer from the extreme fatigue to which the muscles, arms, and hands of sculptors are subject. Her father, who knew nothing about sculpture, and the Baroness, equally ignorant, acclaimed it as a masterpiece. The War Minister then came, brought by them to admire it, and, infected by their enthusiasm, he was pleased with this model, placed by itself before a green cloth, shown in the best light and to the best possible advantage.

Alas! at the 1841 Exhibition, unanimous condemnation in the mouths of people antagonized by the speed with which Steinbock had become an idol raised upon a pedestal degenerated into shouts of mockery and derision. Stidmann tried to tell his friend the truth; he was accused of jealousy. The newspaper articles, to Hortense, were so many shrieks of envy. Stidmann, a loyal friend, had articles written, challenging the critics, and pointing out that sculptors modify their works greatly in transposing them from the plaster model to the finished marble, and that it was the marble they were judged by. 'Between the plaster and the marble a masterpiece may be ruined, or a great work created from a poor model,' so wrote Claude Vignon. 'The plaster is the manuscript; the marble is the book.'

In two and a half years Steinbock produced a statue and a child. The child was of exquisite beauty; the statue execrable.

The Prince's clock and the statue paid the young couple's debts. Steinbock had by that time formed the habit of going into society, to the theatre, to the Italian Opera. He could talk admirably about art. He maintained his reputation as a great artist, in the eyes of the social world, by his conversation, his critical disquisitions. There are talented men in Paris who spend their lives *talking* their life-work, and are satisfied with a kind of drawing-room fame. Steinbock, following the usual course of such charming eunuchs, developed an aversion to work that grew from day to day. In the very moment of feeling the impulse to begin his work, he became conscious of all the difficulties of the task, and was so discouraged that his will to tackle them collapsed. Inspiration, the frenzy that leads to intellectual procreation, took flight with a flip of her wings at sight of this sick lover.

Sculpture is like Drama; at once more difficult and easier than all the other arts. One can copy a model and the work is done; but to impart a soul to it, in the representing of a man

218

or woman to create a type, is to snatch fire from heaven like Prometheus. Sculptors who have succeeded in this are rare and glorious landmarks in human history, like poets. Michelangelo, Michel Colomb, Jean Goujon, Phidias, Praxiteles, Polyclitus, Puget, Canova, Albrecht Dürer, are brothers of Milton, Virgil, Dante, Shakespeare, Tasso, Homer, and Molière. Their work is so impressive that one statue is enough to make a man immortal, just as it took only Figaro, Lovelace, and Manon Lescaut to immortalize Beaumarchais, Richardson, and the Abbé Prévost.

Superficial minds (and there are too many of them among sculptors) have said that sculpture of the nude is the only viable sculpture, that the art died with the Greeks, and is made impossible by modern dress. But, for one thing, there were sublime statues fully draped in the ancient world, the *Polyhymnia*, the *Julia*, for example; and not more than one tenth of the sculpture of antiquity survives today to furnish examples. True lovers of art, besides, need only go to see Michelangelo's *Thinker* in Florence, and, in Mainz Cathedral, to see Albrecht Dürer's ebony *Virgin*, a living woman in her triple robes, with rippling hair as airy in texture and vital as ever maid combed. Let the ignorant go at once to see them, and they will all acknowledge that genius may inform drapery, armour, a gown, with thought and feeling about the substance of a body, just as convincingly as a man impresses his nature and the habits of his life upon his envelope. Sculpture is the constant creation of reality in a way that, in painting, was achieved once and uniquely by Raphael!

The solution of the sculptor's tremendous problem is only to be found in untiring unremitting labour, for the material difficulties must be so completely mastered, the hand must be so disciplined, so ready and obedient, as to enable the sculptor to struggle, in a combat of spirit with spirit, with that inapprehensible moral element that he must transfigure and embody. If Paganini, who made the strings of his violin tell his whole soul, had let three days pass without practising, he would have lost, together with his power of expression, what he called the *register* of his instrument, by which he meant the close union existing between the wood, bow, strings, and himself. If this accord were broken, he would at once become no more than an ordinary violinist. Constant labour is the law of art as well as the law of life, for art is the creative activity of the mind. And so great artists, true poets, do not wait for either commissions or clients; they create today, tomorrow, ceaselessly. And there results a habit of toil, a perpetual consciousness of the difficulties, that keeps them in a state of marriage with the Muse, and her creative forces. Canova lived in his studio, and Voltaire in his study. Homer and Phidias must have so lived, too.

Wenceslas Steinbock had had his feet set on the hard road trodden by those great men, leading to the heights, when Lisbeth had kept him on the chain in his garret. Happiness, in the person of Hortense, had delivered the poet over to idleness, a state quite natural to all artists, for their kind of idleness is an occupation in itself. They enjoy the pleasure of the pasha in his seraglio: they toy with ideas, intoxicating themselves at the fountains of the mind. Certain gifted artists who, like Steinbock, have wasted themselves in reverie, have been rightly termed dreamers. Such opium-eaters all fall into penury, although if they had been driven by harsh necessity they would have risen to greatness. These demi-artists are, for the most part, charming people. The world delights in them, and turns their heads with adulation. They appear superior to real artists, who are taxed with aloofness, unsociability, rebellion against the conventions and civilized living; because great men belong to their creations. The entire detachment from all worldly concerns of true artists, and their devotion to their work, stamp them as egoists in the eyes of fools, who think that such men ought to go dressed like men about town performing the gyration that they call 'their social duties'. People would like to see the lions of Atlas combed and scented like a marchioness's lapdogs. Such men, who have few peers and rarely meet them, grow accustomed to shutting out the world, in their habit of solitude. They become incomprehensible to the majority, which, as we know, is composed of blockheads, the envious, ignoramuses, and skaters upon the surface of life.

Do you now understand the part a wife must play in the life of these impressive exceptional beings? A wife must be what Lisbeth had been for five years, and in addition give love, a humble and tactful love, ever ready, ever smiling.

Hortense, her eyes opened by her sufferings as a mother, beset by dire necessity, realized too late the mistakes that she had made in her excessively indulgent love; but she was a true daughter of her mother, and the thought of nagging Wenceslas broke her heart. She loved her dear poet too much to be his scourge, though she saw the day approaching when she, her son, and her husband would be destitute.

'Now, now, my dear,' said Bette, seeing tears gather in her cousin's beautiful eyes, 'you mustn't give way to despair. A whole cupful of tears wouldn't pay for one plate of soup! How much do you need?'

'Between five and six thousand francs.'

'I have only three thousand, or barely that,' said Lisbeth. 'What is Wenceslas doing at present?'

'He's been asked to make a dessert service for the Duc d'Hérouville, in collaboration with Stidmann, for six thousand francs. If he does, Monsieur Chanor will advance four thousand francs that we owe to Monsieur Léon de Lora and Monsieur Brideau – a debt of honour.'

'Do you mean to tell me that you have been paid for the statue and the bas-reliefs of Marshal Montcornet's monument, and that you haven't settled that debt?'

'But,' said Hortense, 'for the past three years we have been spending twelve thousand francs a year, on an income of two thousand francs. The Marshal's monument, when all the expenses were paid, did not give us more than sixteen thousand francs. In plain fact, if Wenceslas does not work, I don't know what is going to become of us. Ah! if only I could learn to make statues, how I would make the clay fly!' she said, throwing wide her lovely arms.

In the mature woman, the young girl's promise was fulfilled. Hortense's eyes sparkled. In her veins the impetuous blood ran red. She lamented that her energy should be only partly used in looking after her baby.

'Ah, my dear innocent child, a sensible girl marries an

artist after he has made his fortune, not when it is still to make.'

Just then they heard footsteps and the voices of Stidmann and Wenceslas, who came in after showing Chanor to the door. Stidmann, an artist popular in the world of journalists, prominent actresses, and socially well known courtesans, was a distinguished young man whom Valérie was anxious to have in her own circle, and whom Claude Vignon had already introduced to her. Stidmann's liaison with the celebrated Madame Schontz had recently been broken off. She had married some months before and gone to live in the country. Valérie and Lisbeth, who had learned of the break through Claude Vignon, thought it good policy to attract this friend of Wenceslas's to the rue Vanneau. Stidmann, through a feeling of delicacy, visited the Steinbocks infrequently, and Lisbeth had not been present when Claude Vignon had introduced him, so she was meeting him for the first time. As she watched the artist, she several times surprised him glancing in Hortense's direction, and this suggested to her the possibility of giving him by way of consolation to Countess Steinbock, if Wenceslas should be unfaithful. The thought had occurred to Stidmann, as a matter of fact, that, if Wenceslas were not his friend, the wonderfully lovely young Countess, Hortense, would be an adorable mistress; but he had honourably repressed the thought and kept away from the house. Lisbeth took note of his revealing embarrassment, as of a man in the presence of a woman with whom he refuses to allow himself to flirt.

'He's a very good-looking young man,' she whispered to Hortense.

'Oh, do you think so?' she replied. 'I have never noticed him. . . .'

'Stidmann, my boy,' said Wenceslas in a low voice to his friend. 'You know we don't stand on ceremony with each other. Well, we've some business to discuss with this old girl.'

Stidmann took his leave of the two cousins, and departed.

'That's arranged,' said Wenceslas, returning after seeing Stidmann out. 'But the work will take six months, and we have to live meantime.'

'I have my diamonds!' cried young Countess Steinbock, with the superb impulsive generosity of a woman in love.

Wenceslas suddenly had tears in his eyes.

'Oh, but I'm going to work,' he said, sitting down beside his wife and drawing her to his knee. 'I'll do knick-knacks, wedding presents for bridegrooms, bronze groups ...'

'Well, my dear children,' said Lisbeth, '– for you are my heirs, you know, and believe me I'll have a nice little pocketful to leave you some day, especially if you help me to marry the Marshal; if we could manage to fix that up quickly, I would have you all to live with me, you and Adeline. Ah, we could live very happily together! But meantime listen to what long experience has taught me. Don't borrow money on the security of your possessions: that spells ruin for the borrower. I have seen it happen time and again that when the interest had to be paid there was no money to pay it, and so the borrowers lost everything. I can get someone to lend you the money at five per cent, on your note of hand.'

'Ah, that would save us!' said Hortense.

'Well, child, Wenceslas should come with me to see the person who will help him if I ask her. It is Madame Marneffe. If you flatter her, for she's very vain like all newly rich climbers, she'll be quite ready to help you out. Come and see her too, my dear Hortense.'

Hortense gazed at Wenceslas, looking like a condemned prisoner mounting the scaffold.

'Claude Vignon took Stidmann there,' said Wenceslas. 'It's a very pleasant house.'

Hortense bowed her head. One word only is adequate to describe what she felt: it was not a mere agonizing pang, it was death.

'But, my dear Hortense, you must learn what life is like!' exclaimed Lisbeth, rightly interpreting Hortense's eloquent gesture. 'If you don't face it, you'll be like your mother – relegated to a deserted lodging to weep like Calypso after the departure of Ulysses, and at an age when there's no hope of a Telemachus!' she went on, repeating one of Madame Marneffe's witticisms. 'You must look on people in the social world as tools to be made use of, taken up or laid down as serves one's purpose. Make use of Madame Marneffe, my dear children, and drop her later. Are you afraid of Wenceslas, who adores you, being overwhelmed with passion for a woman four or five years older than you, and as withered as a bundle of lucerne hay, and ...'

'I would rather pawn my diamonds,' said Hortense. 'Oh, don't ever go there, Wenceslas! It's hell itself!'

'Hortense is quite right!' said Wenceslas, kissing his wife.

'Thank you, dear,' the young wife said, her cup full. 'You see, Lisbeth, what an angel my husband is. He doesn't gamble, we go everywhere together, and if he could only settle down to work ... no, that would be just too much joy. Why should we publicly call on our father's mistress, a woman who is ruining him, and who is the cause of the troubles which are killing our heroic Mama?'

'That's not what ruined your father, child. It was his opera-singer that ruined him, and then your marriage!' returned Cousin Bette. 'Heavens! Madame Marneffe is very useful to him, if you only knew! But I mustn't say anything. ...'

'Dear Bette, you stand up for everyone.'

Screams from her baby called Hortense to the garden, and Lisbeth was alone with Wenceslas.

'You have an angel for a wife, Wenceslas!' said Cousin Bette. 'Love her well; never give her cause for sorrow.'

'Yes, I love her so much that I'm hiding our situation from her,' Wenceslas answered; 'but I can talk to you, Lisbeth. Well, if we did pawn my wife's diamonds, we should be no better off.'

'Borrow from Madame Marneffe, then,' said Lisbeth. 'Persuade Hortense to let you go there, Wenceslas; or, goodness me, go without her knowing!'

'I thought of that,' said Wenceslas, 'when I said I would not go, in order to spare Hortense's feelings.'

'Listen, Wenceslas. I love you both too much not to warn you of the danger. If you go there you must hold fast to your heart, for that woman is a demon. Everyone who sees her, adores her; she is so wicked, and so enticing! She fascinates men like a work of art. Borrow her money, but don't leave your heart as a pledge. I should never forgive myself if you were unfaithful to my cousin. ... Here she comes! Say nothing more. I will arrange things for you.

'Give Lisbeth a kiss, darling,' Wenceslas said to his wife. 'She's going to help us out of this difficulty by lending us her savings.'

And he glanced meaningly at Lisbeth.

'I hope that you are really going to set to work now, my cherub?' said Hortense.

'Yes, indeed!' assented the artist. 'Tomorrow.'

'The word *tomorrow* is our ruin!' said Hortense, smiling at him.

'Well, dear child, don't you know that there has been one thing after another getting in my way, business to be done and other hindrances, every single day?'

'Yes, you're right, dear.'

'In here,' Steinbock went on, tapping his forehead, 'I have such wonderful ideas! Oh, I'm going to astonish all my enemies. I'll make a dinner service in the sixteenth-century German style, the fantastic style, with convoluted foliage full of insects, and children laid sleeping among the leaves, and new inventions of real chimeras, live fantasies never seen before, the stuff of our dreams embodied! I have them in my mind! The work will be intricate in detail, but airy, in spite of all its rich ornament. When Chanor left me, he was filled with admiration. ... I needed some encouragement, I can tell you, for that last article about Montcornet's monument really had me down.'

When Lisbeth and Wenceslas were alone for a moment, later in the day, the artist arranged with the spinster to go to see Madame Marneffe next day, for either his wife would have agreed to his going, or he would go without telling her.

Valérie, informed of this triumph the same evening, dispatched Baron Hulot to invite Stidmann, Claude Vignon, and Steinbock to dinner; for she was beginning to send him on errands, be the domestic tyrant that women of her kind usually become to old men, who are sent trotting here and there round the town, carrying invitations to anyone whose presence is necessary to the interests or vanity of their exacting mistresses.

Next day, Valérie prepared for battle by making such a toilet as Parisians can confection when they intend to make use of all their natural weapons. She studied her appearance to this end, much as a man about to fight a duel works at his lunges and recoils. There was not a blemish, not a wrinkle anywhere! Valérie was in her finest bloom: white, soft, and delicate. As a crowning touch, her beauty 'patches' insensibly drew the eye. People imagine that artifices to heighten beauty, such as eighteenth-century patches, have disappeared, been discarded as out of date, but they are quite mistaken. Women today are cleverer than they ever were in the use of daring devices to provoke quizzing opera-glasses. One woman may invent the knot of ribbons with a diamond set in the centre, and for a whole evening all eyes turn in her direction. Another revives the net veiling cap, or twists a dagger-like pin in her hair in a way that somehow reminds you of her garter. Someone else ties black velvet ribbon round her wrists; and a rival appears with feather plumes. The results of this high endeavour, achievements in coquetry or love comparable with Austerlitz, then become fashionable in lower spheres, while their happy creators are looking round for new inspirations.

For that evening, when Valérie intended to be a brilliant success, she applied the equivalent of three patches. First, she had her hair washed with a rinse which for a few days turned her fair hair to ashen fairness. Madame Steinbock was a golden blonde, and she did not want to resemble her at all. This change of colour gave something piquant and strange to Valérie's appearance, which disturbed the minds of her faithful adorers to the point of making Montès say 'What's come over you this evening?' Next, she tied a rather wide black velvet ribbon round her neck, throwing the whiteness of her bosom into relief. The third provocative patch was what our grandmothers used to call 'the man-slayer'. Valérie set a darling little rosebud in the stiffened top of her bodice, just in the centre, in the sweetest hollow. It was calculated to draw the eyes of all men under thirty downwards.

'I look delicious, good enough to eat!' she said to herself, practising her poses before the glass, exactly like a dancer doing her *pliés*.

Lisbeth had gone to market, and the dinner was to be a choice repast, such as Mathurine used to cook for her bishop when he entertained the prelate of the neighbouring diocese.

Stidmann, Claude Vignon, and Count Steinbock arrived almost together, about six o'clock. Any ordinary woman, or a natural one if you like, would have hurried down when the name of the person so ardently desired was announced; but Valérie, who since five o'clock had been waiting in her room, left her three guests together, certain of being the subject of their conversation or of their secret thoughts. With her own hands, when she was directing the arrangement of her drawing-room, she had placed her trinkets where they would catch the eye, a collection of those delightful toys that Paris produces, and that no other city could, which evoke a woman and, as it were, declare her presence: keepsakes bound in enamel and set with pearls, goblets filled with pretty rings, pieces of Sèvres or Dresden china mounted with exquisite taste by Florent and Chanor, statuettes, albums – all the madly expensive baubles that passion commissions from the makers in its first delirium, or to celebrate its latest reconciliation.

Success, moreover, had gone to Valérie's head. She had promised Crevel to marry him, if Marneffe died; and the amorous Crevel had arranged the transfer of shares worth ten thousand francs a year to the account of Valérie Fortin. This sum was the amount of his profit on his investments in railways for the past three years, the yield of a hundred thousand crowns once offered to Baroness Hulot. So Valérie was the possessor of an income of thirty-two thousand francs. Crevel had just blurted out a promise even more substantial than the gift of his profits. In the paroxysm of passion into which 'his duchess' had thrown him between two o'clock and four (he gave Madame *de* Marneffe that title to make his illusion complete), for Valérie had surpassed herself that day in the rue du Dauphin, he felt himself compelled to encourage her promised fidelity by holding out the prospect of a pretty little house that a rash speculator had built for himself in the rue Barbette, and now wanted to sell. Valérie saw a vision of herself in this charming house, set in its court and garden, with her own carriage!

'What respectable life could give all this so quickly and with so little trouble?' she had asked Lisbeth, as she put the finishing touches to her toilet.

Lisbeth was dining with Valérie on this occasion, in order to be able to say those things about her to Steinbock that a person cannot say about herself. Madame Marneffe, her face radiant with pleasure, made her entrance with modest grace, followed into the drawing-room by Bette, who, dressed in black and yellow, served as her foil, to use a studio term.

'Good evening, Claude,' she said, giving her hand to the distinguished former critic.

Claude Vignon, like so many others, had become a 'politician' – a word newly invented to denote an ambitious man in the first stages of his career. The 'politician' of 1840 more or less fills the place of the eighteenth-century 'abbé'. No *salon* would be complete without its 'politician'.

'My dear, this is my cousin, Count Steinbock,' said Lisbeth, introducing Wenceslas, whom Valérie apparently had not noticed.

'Yes, I recognized Monsieur le Comte,' replied Valérie with a gracious little inclination of the head to the artist. 'I often used to see you in the rue du Doyenné. I had the pleasure of being present at your wedding. My dear,' she turned to Lisbeth, 'it would be difficult to forget your foster-child, even if one had only seen him once. . . . Monsieur Stidmann, how very good of you,' she went on, bowing to the sculptor, 'to have accepted my invitation at such short notice! You know, necessity is above the law! I knew that you were a friend of these two gentlemen, and as nothing is more chilling, more tedious, than a dinner at which the guests are strangers to one another, I begged your company for their sakes; but you will come on another occasion for mine, won't you? Do say yes!'

And she turned aside for a few moments with Stidmann, her attention apparently wholly preoccupied with him.

In succession, Crevel, Baron Hulot, and a Deputy named Beauvisage were announced. This personage, a provincial Crevel, one of those people born to be one of a crowd, voted under the banner of Giraud, the Councillor of State, and

Victorin Hulot. Those two politicians were anxious to create a nucleus of progressives in the solid mass of the Conservative party. Giraud was in the habit of coming occasionally in the evening to the rue Vanneau, and Madame Marneffe had hopes of also capturing Victorin Hulot; but the strait-laced barrister had so far found pretexts for refusing his father and father-in-law. To be seen in the house of the woman who was the cause of his mother's tears would, it seemed to him, be a crime. Among the puritanical element in politics, Victorin Hulot held the same place as a pious woman among the devout.

Beauvisage, a former hosier of Arcis, was anxious to 'pick up the Parisian style'. This out-of-touch back-bencher was at the rue Vanneau to acquire sophistication under the tutelage of the delicious, the ravishing, Madame Marneffe, and there he had been fascinated by Crevel, and had adopted him, under Valérie's guidance as model and master. He consulted him in everything, asked for the address of his tailor, imitated him, tried to strike poses like him; in short, Crevel was his great man.

Valérie, surrounded by these personages and the three artists, well seconded by Lisbeth, impressed Wenceslas as a woman of no common kind, all the more so because Claude Vignon sang Madame Marneffe's praises to him, like a man in love.

'She is Madame de Maintenon in Ninon's skirts!' said the critic. 'To please her, one need only be on one's wittiest form for an evening; but to be loved by her, ah, there's a triumph to satisfy a man's pride, and fill his life!'

Valérie, by her apparent coldness and indifference to her former neighbour, insulted his vanity, quite unwittingly, as she knew nothing of the Polish temperament.

All Slavs have a childish side, as have all primitive races that have rather made incursion among the civilized nations than become properly civilized themselves. The primitive races have spread like a flood and cover an immense area of the globe, inhabiting desert wastes, in whose vast empty spaces they feel at home, untroubled by the European jostling of neighbour against neighbour; and civilization is impossible without the constant rubbing upon one another of minds and the rivalry of material interests. The inhabitants of the

Ukraine, Russia, the plains of the Danube, in short, the Slav peoples, are a link between Europe and Asia, between civilization and barbarism. And the Pole, who belongs to the richest of the Slav nations, has in his character the childishness and instability of immature peoples. He possesses courage, quick intelligence and vigour; but since he lacks consistency of purpose, his courage, vigour and keen wits are not controlled, have no intellectual direction; and the Pole is as unstable as the wind that sweeps over his vast plains broken by swamps. He may havé the irresistible impetus of avalanches telescoping houses and carrying them away, but like those formidable snow masses of the mountain heights he ends by losing himself in the first pool reached, dissolved in water.

Men always assimilate something from the regions where they live. In their ceaseless struggle against the Turks, the Poles have acquired the Oriental taste for magnificence. They often sacrifice the necessaries of life in order to make a show; they have a feminine love of dress. And yet, the climate has given them the Arabs' tough constitution.

In his sublime endurance of suffering, the Pole has exhausted his oppressors' power to strike, and has shown the world again, in the nineteenth century, the same victory that was won by the early Christian martyrs. Add ten per cent of English guile to the Polish nature, which is so frank and open, and the noble white eagle would be reigning today in all those regions where the two-headed eagle has stealthily glided in. A little Machiavellism would have prevented Poland from going to the aid of Austria, who has partitioned her; from borrowing from Prussia, the usurer who has undermined her; from splitting into factions at the time of the first partition. At Poland's christening, a Fairy Carabosse, forgotten by the spirits who endowed this captivating nation with the most brilliant qualities, must have turned up to say, 'Keep all the gifts that my sisters have bestowed upon you, but you shall never know what you want!' If in her heroic duel with Russia, Poland had triumphed, the Poles would be fighting one another today, as they formerly fought in their Diets, to prevent one another from being king. On the day when this nation, uniquely constituted of beings of full-blooded courage, has the good sense to seek out a Louis XI in her midst, to accept a tyranny and a dynasty, she will be saved.

What is true of Poland in politics, is true of most Poles in their private lives, especially in time of disaster. And so Wenceslas Steinbock, who had adored his wife for three years, and knew that to her he was a god, was so nettled at seeing himself barely remarked by Madame Marneffe that it became a point of honour with him to obtain some notice from her. Comparing her with his wife, he thought Valérie superior. Hortense was lovely in form and flesh, as Valérie had observed to Lisbeth; but Madame Marneffe had mettle in every inch of her body, and the piquancy of vice. Hortense's devotion was a grace that a husband takes for granted as his due. The consciousness of the enormous value of an absolute love is soon lost, by the same process that makes a debtor imagine after a lapse of time that the money he has borrowed is his own. Sublime loyalty becomes the equivalent of daily bread to the soul, and infidelity attracts like a delicacy. A disdainful woman, above all a dangerous woman, stimulates curious interest as spice seasons good food. Moreover, disdain, so cleverly feigned by Valérie, was a novelty for Wenceslas, after three years of easily-won pleasures. Hortense was a wife, but Valérie was a mistress.

Many men desire to have these two editions of the same work, although it is proof of deep inferiority in a man if he cannot make his wife his mistress. Seeking variety is a sign of impotence. Constancy will always be the guardian spirit of love, evidence of immense creative vigour, the vigour that makes a poet! A man must be able to find all women in his wife, as the disreputable poets of the seventeenth century made Irises and Chloes of their Manons!

'Well,' Lisbeth asked Wenceslas when she saw that he was fascinated, 'what do you think of Valérie?'

'Only too charming!' he replied.

'You wouldn't listen to me,' said Cousin Bette, driving the point home. 'Ah, my dear boy, if you and I had only stayed together, you would have been that siren's lover; you could have married her when she becomes a widow, and had her forty thousand francs a year!'

'Do you really think so?'

'Certainly,' replied Lisbeth. 'Now, take care. I warned you of the danger. Don't get singed in the candle-flame! Give me your arm, for dinner is served.'

Nothing she might have said could have been more demoralizing, for a Pole has only to be shown a precipice to cast himself instantly over it. In the people of this race the cavalryman's temperament is predominant; they are confident of their ability to ride down all obstacles and come through victorious. The spur which Lisbeth had applied to her cousin's vanity pricked more sharply at sight of the dining-room, shining with splendid silver. There Steinbock took note of all the refinement and elegance of Parisian luxury.

'I should have done better,' he said to himself, 'to marry Célimène.'*

Hulot was in his best form during dinner. He was pleased to see his son-in-law there, and still happier because he felt certain of a reconciliation with Valérie, who, so he assured himself, would be faithful to him in return for the promise of Coquet's post for her husband. Stidmann responded to the Baron's geniality with his artist's verve and fireworks of Parisian wit. Steinbock could not let himself be eclipsed by his friend; he set himself to shine, had gay inspirations, made an impression, and felt pleased with himself. Madame Marneffe several times smiled at him in token of her good understanding and sympathetic feeling. The good food, the heady wines, also had their effect, and Wenceslas was submerged in what can only be called the slough of pleasure. After dinner, a little excited with wine, he stretched himself on a divan, filled with a sense of physical and mental well-being that Madame Marneffe sharpened and completed by coming to perch beside him, light, scented, lovely enough to damn the angels. She bent over Wenceslas, she almost brushed his ear to whisper to him privately:

'We can't talk business this evening, unless you would like to stay after everyone has gone? Between us, you, Lisbeth, and I should be able to arrange things to suit you. . . .'

'Ah, you are an angel, Madame!' said Wenceslas, whispering

*The worldly and coquettish heroine of Molière's *Le Misanthrope*.

in the same intimate fashion. 'I was a fool not to listen to Lisbeth.'

'Why, what did she say?'

'She maintained, in the rue du Doyenné, that you were in love with me!'

Madame Marneffe looked at Wenceslas, seemed embarrassed, and got up abruptly. A young and pretty woman never without consequences awakens in a man the idea of immediate success. Her gesture, as of a virtuous woman repressing a passion kept secret in the depths of her heart, was a thousand times more eloquent than the most passionate declaration. And Wenceslas's desire was so effectively stimulated that he redoubled his attention to Valérie. A woman in the limelight is a woman coveted! Hence derives the formidable power of actresses. Madame Marneffe, aware that she was under scrutiny, comported herself like an idol of the popular stage. She was charming, and her triumph was complete.

'I'm not surprised at my father-in-law's follies now,' said Wenceslas to Lisbeth.

'If you're going to talk like this, Wenceslas,' replied his cousin, 'I'll regret to my dying day getting the loan of those ten thousand francs for you. Are you going to be like all the others,' she added, indicating the guests, 'doting on that creature? Just consider – that would make you your father-in-law's rival. And think of all the unhappiness you would cause Hortense.'

'That's true,' said Wenceslas. 'Hortense is an angel. I should be a monster!'

'One in the family is quite enough,' replied Lisbeth.

'Artists ought never to marry!' Steinbock exclaimed.

'Ah! that's what I used to tell you when we lived in the rue du Doyenné. Your children, your real children, are your groups, your statues, the things you make.'

'What's that you're discussing?' asked Valérie, coming over and joining Lisbeth. 'Pour out the tea, Cousin.'

Steinbock, out of Polish swagger, wanted to show himself as on familiar terms with the presiding genius of the *salon*. With an insolent glance at Stidmann, Claude Vignon, and

Crevel, he took Valérie's hand and obliged her to sit down beside him on the divan.

'You lord it over us rather too much, Count Steinbock!' she said, resisting a little.

And she began to laugh as she was pulled down beside him, and toyed, not unnoticed, with the little rosebud displayed on her bodice.

'Alas! If I could lord it, I should not come here to borrow money,' he said.

'Poor boy! I remember your nights of toil at the rue du Doyenné. You were rather a noodle. You snatched at marriage like a starving man snatching bread. You haven't an idea what Paris is like! And now just see where you've been landed! But you wouldn't listen to Bette. You cared as little for her and her devotion as you did for the love of a Parisian woman who knows her Paris by heart.'

'Don't say another word,' Steinbock begged. 'I bow my head.'

'You shall have your ten thousand francs, my dear Wenceslas; but on one condition,' she said, running her fingers through his fine wavy hair.

'What condition?'

'Well, I don't want interest.'

'Madame!'

'Oh, don't be angry; you shall repay me with a bronze group. You began the story of Samson; go on and finish it. . . . Show Delilah cutting off the hair of her Jewish Hercules! Oh, but I hope you really know your subject – you'll be a great artist if you listen to me! It's the woman's power that you must show. Samson is nothing now. He's the strength that has been destroyed – a dead body. Delilah is the passion that brings down everything to destruction. That replica – is that the correct term?' she went on, less intimately, as she saw Claude Vignon and Stidmann coming towards them, to join in what sounded like talk about sculpture, ' – the replica showing Hercules at the feet of Omphale, has a far finer subject than the Greek myth! Did the Greeks copy the Jews, or was it the Jews who took that symbol from the Greeks?'

'Ah! you raise an important question there, Madame – the

question of the dates when the different books of the Bible were composed. The great and immortal Spinoza, so idiotically classed as an atheist, who worked out mathematical proofs of the existence of God, declared that Genesis and the political parts – if one may so call them – of the Bible date from the time of Moses, and he deduced the various interpolations by philological considerations. And for that he was stabbed three times at the door of the synagogue.'

'I had no idea I was so learned,' said Valérie, rather piqued at this interruption of her *tête à tête*.

'Women know everything by instinct,' replied Claude Vignon.

'Well, do you promise me?' she asked Steinbock, taking his hand with the shy hesitation of a young girl in love.

'You're a lucky man, my dear fellow,' exclaimed Stidmann, 'if Madame Marneffe has asked you to do something for her.'

'What is it?' asked Claude Vignon.

'A little bronze group,' Steinbock replied. 'Delilah cutting off Samson's hair.'

'A difficult subject,' observed Claude Vignon, 'because of the bed.'

'Not at all; it's perfectly simple,' Valérie said, smiling.

'Ah! Do some sculpture for us!' said Stidmann.

'But Madame is sculpture's subject!' objected Claude Vignon, with a languishing look at Valérie.

'Well,' she went on, 'this is how I see the composition. Samson has awakened with no hair, like plenty of dandies who wear false fronts. The hero sits on the bed, so you have only to indicate it as a base concealed by sheets and drapery. He is sitting there like Marius on the ruins of Carthage, his arms crossed, his head shaved: Napoleon on Saint Helena, if you like! Delilah is on her knees, rather like Canova's *Magdalen*. A woman adores the man she has destroyed. As I see it, the Jewess feared Samson when he was terrible in his strength, but she must have loved him when he was brought low and was like a little boy again. So Delilah is weeping for her sin, she wishes she could restore his locks to her lover, she hardly dares look at him, and yet she is looking at him, smiling, because in Samson's weakness she sees her forgiveness. With a group like that, and another of the ferocious Judith, you would have shown the whole truth about woman. Virtue cuts off the head. Vice only cuts off the hair. Look out for your toupées, gentlemen!'

And she left the two artists – beaten on their own ground and the critic to sing her praises.

'No one could be more delightful!' exclaimed Stidmann.

'Oh, she's a very intelligent woman,' said Claude Vignon, 'the cleverest as well as the most attractive that I have ever met. It is so rare to have wit as well as beauty!'

'And you had the honour of knowing Camille Maupin well! If you think so highly of her, you may guess what we think!'

'If you make Delilah a portrait of Valérie, my dear Count,' said Crevel, who had left the card-table for a moment and overheard the conversation, 'I will stump up a thousand crowns for the group. Yes, a thousand crowns, damn me! I'll fork that out!'

'*Fork that out*? What does that mean?' Beauvisage asked Claude Vignon.

'Madame would perhaps do me the honour of sitting,' Steinbock said to Crevel, with a glance at Valérie. 'Ask her.'

At that moment Valérie brought Steinbock a cup of tea. It was more than an attention; it was a favour. There is a whole language in the way this office is performed, and women are very well aware of it. It is a rewarding study to watch their movements, gestures, looks, the intonation and varying emphasis of their voices, when they proffer this apparently simple courtesy. From the inquiry 'Do you drink tea?' 'Will you have some tea?' 'A cup of tea?' coldly made, with the order to the nymph at the tea-urn to bring it, to the dramatic poem of the odalisque walking from the tea-table, cup in hand, approaching her heart's pasha and presenting it to him as an act of submission, with a caressing voice and a look of voluptuous promise, the physiologist may observe the entire gamut of feminine emotions, from aversion, through indifference, to Phèdre's declaration to Hippolyte. A woman can make this act of politeness, as she chooses, disdainful to the point of insult, or humble to a degree of Oriental servility. And Valérie was not only a woman; she was the serpent in woman's form. She completed her devil's work, walking towards Steinbock with a cup of tea in her hand.

'I will take as many cups of tea as you offer me,' whispered the artist in Valérie's ear, rising and touching her fingers with his own, 'just to see them brought to me like this!'

'What were you saying about posing?' she asked, with no sign that this explosion of feeling, awaited with such passionate expectation, had gone straight to her triumphant heart.

'Papa Crevel wants to buy a cast of your group for a thousand crowns.'

'A thousand crowns, from Crevel, for a piece of sculpture?'

'Yes, if you will sit for Delilah,' said Steinbock.

'He won't be present, I hope,' she rejoined; 'the group would be worth more than his entire fortune, for Delilah's dress must be a trifle scanty.'

Just like Crevel, striking his favourite attitude, all women have an all-conquering mannerism, a studied pose, in which they are irresistible and know that they must be admired. One may see them, in a drawing-room, pass hours of their lives gazing down at the lace on their bodice, or pulling the shoulders of their dress into place, or making play with the brilliance of their eyes by raising them to the cornices. Madame Marneffe's prize card was not played face to face, as most other women play theirs. She turned away abruptly to go to Lisbeth at the tea-table, swinging her skirts in the dancer's movement that had captivated Hulot. Steinbock was enchanted.

'Your vengeance is complete now,' Valérie whispered to Lisbeth. 'Hortense shall weep all the tears she's got, and curse the day when she took Wenceslas from you.'

'Until I am Madame la Maréchale, nothing is complete,' replied the peasant woman. 'But *they* are all beginning to wish for it. . . . This morning I saw Victorin – I forgot to tell you. The young Hulots have bought back the Baron's bills from Vauvinet, and tomorrow they are going to sign a bond for seventy-two thousand francs, at five per cent interest repayable in three years, with a mortgage on their house as security. So there are the young Hulots, in straitened circumstances for three years, and they won't be able to raise any more money on that property. Victorin is terribly depressed: he knows now just what his father is like. And then Crevel is quite capable of refusing to see them again, he will be so enraged at their throwing their money away.'

'The Baron can have nothing at all left now?' Valérie said softly to Lisbeth, while she smiled at Hulot.

'Nothing, so far as I can see; but he will be able to draw his salary again in September.'

'And he has his insurance policies; he had them renewed! Well it's high time he made Marneffe head clerk. I'll deal with him this evening.'

'Cousin,' said Lisbeth, walking over to Wenceslas, 'do please go home now. You are making a fool of yourself. You will compromise Valérie, looking at her like that, and her husband is a wildly jealous man. Don't imitate your father-in-law's conduct. Go home; I'm sure Hortense is waiting up for you. . . .'

'Madame Marneffe told me stay until the others had gone, so that the three of us could arrange our little piece of business,' Wenceslas replied.

'No,' said Lisbeth. 'I'll get the ten thousand francs for you, for her husband has his eye on you and it would not be wise for you to stay. Bring your note of hand tomorrow, at eleven o'clock. That Turk, Marneffe, is at his office by that time, and Valérie is not worried about him. . . . Did you really ask her to pose for you for a group? . . . Come up to my apartment first. . . . Ah! I always knew,' she went on, as she caught the look with which Steinbock said good-bye to Valérie, 'that you were a promising young rake. Valérie is very lovely, but try not to hurt Hortense!'

Nothing is more irritating to a married man than to meet his wife at every turn, standing in the way of a desire, however fleeting.

*

Wenceslas returned home about one in the morning. Hortense had been expecting him since nine thirty. Between half past nine and ten, she listened for the sound of carriage wheels, telling herself that Wenceslas had never stayed so late before when he had dined without her with Chanor and Florent. She was sewing as she sat by her son's cradle, for she had begun to save a sewing-woman's wages by doing some of the mending herself. Between ten and ten thirty, a certain suspicion entered her mind. She said to herself:

'Has he really gone to dinner with Chanor and Florent, as he told me? When he was dressing he picked out his best cravat and his finest tie-pin. He spent as long over his toilet as any woman trying to look her most attractive.... Oh, I'm crazy! He loves me. And here he comes.'

But instead of stopping, the carriage that the young wife had heard went past. Between eleven and midnight, nightmare terrors assailed Hortense, inspired by the loneliness of their quarter.

'If he returned on foot,' she said to herself, 'some accident may have happened! People have been killed stumbling over a kerb or an unexpected hole in the road. Artists are so absent-minded! He may have been held up by thieves! This is the first time he has ever left me alone like this, for six and a half hours. ... Why do I torment myself? He loves me, and he loves only me.'

Men have a moral obligation to be faithful to the women who love them, if only because of the perpetual miracles that true love can create in the supernatural regions that we call the world of the spirit. In her knowledge of the man she loves, a woman in love is like a hypnotist's subject to whom the hypnotist has given the unhappy power of remembering what she has seen in her trance. Passion heightens a woman's nervous tension to the point of inducing an ecstatic state, in which presentiment has an acute awareness like clairvoyant vision. A woman knows when she is betrayed, although her love will not allow her to acknowledge or heed the voice of her sibylline power. This sharpened vision of love is worthy of religious veneration. In noble minds, wonder at this divine phenomenon will always be a barrier in the way of infidelity. How can a man fail to adore a beautiful, divinely gifted being, whose soul attains the power of such revelations?

... By one o'clock in the morning, Hortense's torturing anxiety had reached such a pitch that she rushed to the door when she recognized Wenceslas's ring, threw her arms round him, and clung to him as if he were her child.

'Here you are, at last!' she said, when she had recovered the power of speech. 'Dearest, in future wherever you go I shall go too, for I could not bear the torture of waiting for you like this again. . . . I was sure you must have had a fall, stumbling over a kerb, and broken your head, or been killed by thieves! No, if that ever happened again, I know I should go mad. . . . Were you having a good time? Without me? How could you?'

'What could I do, my darling little good angel? Bixiou was there, and he had some new commissions for us; and Léon de Lora, overflowing with wit, as usual; and Claude Vignon, who wrote the only article I had that gave me any encouragement about Marshal Montcornet's monument – I feel I owe him something. Then there were . . .'

'There were no women?' asked Hortense quickly.

'The worthy Madame Florent.'

'You told me that it was at the Rocher de Cancale . . . but it was at their house, was it?'

'Yes, at their house. I was mistaken.'

'You did not take a cab home?'

'No.'

'You walked all the way from the rue des Tournelles?'

'Stidmann and Bixiou walked back with me along the boulevards as far as the Madeleine, as we were talking.'

'It must be quite dry on the boulevards and the place de la Concorde and the rue de Bourgogne – not a sign of mud,' said Hortense, examining her husband's shining boots.

It had been raining; but Wenceslas had had no occasion to get his boots dirty between the rue Vanneau and the rue Saint-Dominique.

'Look, here's five thousand francs that Chanor has generously lent me,' said Wenceslas, in an attempt to cut this quasi-judicial inquiry short.

He had divided his ten thousand-franc notes into two packets, one for Hortense and one for himself, for he had debts for five thousand francs that Hortense knew nothing about. He owed money to his rough-hewer and his workmen.

'Now you've nothing more to worry about, dear,' he said, kissing his wife. 'Tomorrow I'm really going to set to in earnest! Oh, I'll clear out at half past eight tomorrow, and be off to the studio. I'll go to bed at once so as to be able to get up early. You don't mind, my sweet?'

The suspicion that had crossed Hortense's mind vanished; she was a thousand leagues from the truth! Madame Marneffe? The thought of her never entered her head. What she was afraid of for her Wenceslas was the company of courtesans. The names of Bixiou and Léon de Lora, two artists known for their wild lives, had made her uneasy.

Next day, as she saw Wenceslas off at nine o'clock, she felt entirely reassured.

'Now he has set to work,' she thought to herself, as she dressed her baby. 'Oh, I can see he's in the right frame of mind! Well, if we can't have Michelangelo's glory, we shall have Benvenuto Cellini's!'

Deluding herself with her own hopes, Hortense believed that the future was bright; and she was talking to her little boy, twenty months old, in the happy onomatopoeic language that makes children laugh, when at about eleven o'clock, the cook, who had not seen Wenceslas go out, showed Stidmann into the room.

'I'm sorry to disturb you, Madame,' the artist said. 'Has Wenceslas gone out already?'

'He is at his studio.'

'I came to discuss some work we are doing together.'

'I'll send for him,' said Hortense, offering him a chair.

The young woman, inwardly thanking heaven for this chance, wanted to keep Stidmann, in order to hear some details about the party the evening before. Stidmann bowed in acknowledgement of the Countess's kindness. Madame Steinbock rang, the cook appeared and was told to go to the studio to fetch her master.

'Did you have an enjoyable evening yesterday?' said Hortense. 'Wenceslas didn't come in until after one in the morning.'

'Enjoyable? . . . not really,' replied the artist, who had been anxious to *make* Madame Marneffe the evening before. 'To find society enjoyable you have to have some special interest there. That little Madame Marneffe is certainly very clever, but she's a flirt.'

'And what did Wenceslas think of her?' asked poor Hortense, endeavouring to remain calm. 'He said nothing to me.'

'I'll tell you only one thing about her,' replied Stidmann, 'and that is that I think she's a very dangerous woman.'

Hortense grew as pale as a woman in childbirth.

'So it was really . . . at Madame Marneffe's . . . and not at the Chanors' that you dined . . .' she said, 'yesterday . . . with Wenceslas, and he . . .'

Stidmann, while not knowing what unlucky blunder he had made, saw that he had made one. The Countess could not finish her sentence, and fainted away. The artist rang the bell and the maid came.

When Louise tried to help Countess Steinbock to her room, she was seized with the hysterical convulsions of a severe nervous attack. Stidmann, like everyone whose unwitting indiscretion destroys the flimsy edifice of a husband's lie to his family, could not believe that what he had said could have caused such damage. He thought that the Countess must be in a delicate state of health in which it was dangerous to vex her in any way. The cook returned and said, in a loud voice, unfortunately, that Monsieur was not in his studio. Half-fainting as she was, the Countess heard this announcement, and hysterics began again.

'Fetch Madame's mother!' said Louise to the cook. 'Hurry!'

'If I knew where to find Wenceslas, I would go and tell him,' said Stidmann, in desperation.

'He's with that woman!' cried poor Hortense. 'He's dressed very differently from the way he dresses when he goes to his studio.'

Stidmann hurried to the rue Vanneau, realizing that with passion's second sight Hortense had divined the truth. At that moment Valérie was posing as Delilah.

Too wary to ask for Madame Marneffe, Stidmann walked

straight past the porters' lodge and rapidly upstairs to the second floor, reasoning thus to himself: 'If I ask for Madame Marneffe, she will be not at home. If I ask for Steinbock, like a fool, they will laugh in my face. . . . Better take the bull by the horns!'

Reine answered his ring.

'Tell Count Steinbock to come at once. His wife is dying!'

Reine, as wide awake as Stidmann, stared at him in stupid incomprehension. 'But, Monsieur, I don't understand. What do you . . .'

'I tell you, my friend Steinbock is here, and his wife is dying. The matter is serious enough to be worth disturbing your mistress for.'

And Stidmann turned away.

'Oh, he's there all right!' he said to himself. He loitered for a few minutes in the street, and as he expected, saw Wenceslas emerge, and beckoned to him to come quickly. Stidmann told him of the tragic scene at the house in the rue Saint-Dominique, and then reproached Steinbock for not having warned him to keep quiet about the dinner the evening before.

'I'm done for,' replied Wenceslas; 'but it's not your fault. I completely forgot our appointment for this morning, and I stupidly omitted to tell you that we were supposed to have dined with Florent. That's how things happen! That Valérie drove everything out of my mind. But you know my dear fellow, she's a prize as much worth having as fame, she's worth unlucky accidents like this. . . . Ah! she's . . . My God! I'm in a terrible fix. Advise me. What am I to say? What excuses can I make?'

'Advise you? I don't know how to,' said Stidmann. 'But your wife loves you, doesn't she? Well then, she'll believe anything. At least you can tell her that you were on your way to see me while I was calling on you, and that will keep this morning's sitting dark. Good-bye!'

At the corner of the rue Hillerin-Bertin they were joined by Lisbeth, who, warned by Reine, had hurried after Steinbock, for she did not want to be compromised, and was afraid of what in his Polish naïveté he might say. She spoke a few words to Wenceslas, who in his relief hugged her in the open street. She had no doubt thrown him a floating spar to help him to cross these conjugal narrows.

On seeing her mother, who had come in all haste, Hortense had shed floods of tears, and her state of nervous tension was to some extent relieved.

'Wenceslas has deceived me, Mama!' she said. 'After giving me his word not to visit Madame Marneffe, he dined there yesterday, and he didn't come home until a quarter past one in the morning! If you only knew how we had talked to each other the day before, not having a quarrel but making our feelings clear. I had said such touching things to him; that I was jealous by nature and an infidelity would kill me; I was quick to feel suspicion, but that he ought to respect my weaknesses since they came from my love for him; in my veins I had as much of my father's blood as of yours; at the first discovery of an infidelity I should be beside myself and capable of anything, taking my revenge, dishonouring us all, him and his son and myself – truly I might kill him and then myself; and a great deal more. And yet he went there, and he's there now! That woman has made up her mind to destroy us all! Yesterday my brother and Célestine made themselves responsible for redeeming bills for seventy-two thousand francs drawn for the benefit of that abominable woman – Yes, Mama, they were going to sue my father and send him to prison. Is that horrible creature not content with my father, and with your tears? Must she take Wenceslas too? I'll go to her house and stab her!'

Madame Hulot, stricken to the heart by the heart-rending secret that Hortense had unthinkingly blurted out in her fury, controlled her feelings by such a heroic effort as truly great mothers are capable of. She drew her daughter's head to her breast and kissed her tenderly.

'Wait till Wenceslas comes, child, and he will explain everything. Things are probably not so bad as you think! I have been deceived too, my dear Hortense. You think me beautiful, and I have been faithful, and yet for the last twenty-three years I have been deserted for Jenny Cadines, and Joséphas, and Marneffes! Did you know?'

'You, Mama, you! You have endured that for twenty- ....'
She stopped, aghast at her own thoughts.

'Follow my example, child,' her mother went on. 'Be gentle
and kind, and your conscience will be at peace. On his death-
bed a man may say "My wife has never caused me the smallest
pain!" And God hears those last sighs, and counts them as
blessings. If I had given way to rages, like you, what would
have happened? Your father would have grown bitter; perhaps he might have left me, and he would not have been
restrained by the fear of hurting me. Our ruin, which is
complete now, would have been so ten years ago, and we
should have presented the spectacle to the world of a husband and wife living selfishly apart – a dreadful and heart-
breaking scandal, because it means the death of the Family.
Neither your brother nor you would have been able to get a
start in life. ... I sacrificed myself, and did so with sufficient
spirit to make the world go on believing, until this latest
liaison of your father's, that I was happy. The bold front I
cheerfully maintained has protected Hector until now; he is
still respected; only this passion of his old age carries him too
far, I see. I dread that his folly may break down the screen I
placed between us and the world. ... But I have held it there
for twenty-three years, a curtain behind which I have wept,
without a mother or a friend to confide in, with no support
but that given by religion, and I have procured twenty-three
years of honourable life for the family.'

Hortense listened to her mother with her eyes held fixed.
The calm voice and the resignation of that supreme suffering
made her no longer feel the sting of a young wife's first wound.
Tears overcame her, flowing in torrents. On an impulse of
daughterly devotion, overwhelmed by her mother's sublime
nobility, she knelt at her feet, seized the hem of her dress and
kissed it, as pious Catholics kiss the holy relics of a martyr.

'Come, don't kneel, my Hortense,' said the Baroness; 'such
a testimony of my daughter's love wipes out some very bitter
memories. Let me put my arms round you and hold you to
my heart, a heart that is full only of your grief. Your happiness was my only joy, my poor little girl, and your despair

has broken the seal placed on my lips, that should have remained as silent as the grave. Indeed it was my wish to take my sorrows with me to the tomb, wrapped secretly round me like a second shroud. In order to quiet your frenzy I have spoken. . . . God will forgive me. Oh, if you were to live the life that I have lived, I do not know what I should do! Men, society, the chances of life, the nature of human beings, God himself, I feel, grant us love at a cost of the most cruel suffering. I shall have paid with twenty-four years of despair, unending sorrow, and bitterness, for ten years of happiness. . . .'

'You had ten years, dear Mama; I've had only three!' observed Hortense, with the egoism of her own love.

'Nothing is lost yet, child. Wait until Wenceslas comes.'

'Mother,' she said, 'he has lied! He has deceived me. He said to me "I shall not go", and he went. And that before his child's cradle!'

'For the sake of their pleasure, men are capable of the utmost wickedness, my angel, the most shameful and dastardly acts. It is part of their nature, so it seems. We wives are destined sacrifices. I believed the tale of my miseries to be complete, and they are just beginning; I did not expect to suffer in the same way again through my daughter. But we must suffer with courage and in silence! ... My Hortense, swear to me never to speak of your sorrows to anyone but me, to let no hint of them be seen by any third person. ... Oh! be as proud as your mother!'

At this moment Hortense started, for she heard her husband's step.

'It appears,' said Wenceslas, coming in, 'that Stidmann came here, looking for me, while I was at his house.'

'Is that so?' exclaimed poor Hortense, with the bitter sarcasm of an injured woman using words as a weapon.

'Yes, indeed; we have just met,' replied Wenceslas, feigning surprise.

'What about yesterday?' Hortense went on.

'Well, I deceived you there, my dearest love, and your mother shall judge ...'

Such candour was a relief to Hortense's spirit. All really noble women prefer the truth to a soothing lie. They hate to see their idol with feet of clay, it is true; they want to be able to be proud of the man whose domination over them they accept. Russians have something of the same feeling with regard to their Czar.

'Listen, dear Mother,' said Wenceslas. 'I love my sweet good Hortense so much that I kept the full extent of our difficulties from her. What else could I do? She was still nursing our baby, and worries would have done her a lot of harm. You know what risks a woman runs at such a time – her beauty and bloom and her health may be damaged. Was I wrong? She thinks that we owe only five thousand francs, but I owe five thousand more than that. The day before yesterday we were in despair! No one in the world wants to lend an artist money. People believe in our talent about as readily as they believe in the fantastic creations we imagine. I knocked in vain on every door. Lisbeth offered us her savings.'

'Poor soul!' said Hortense.

'Poor soul!' the Baroness repeated.

'But Lisbeth's two thousand francs, what did that amount to? Her all to her, but a drop in the ocean to us. Then our cousin spoke to us, you remember, Hortense, about Madame Marneffe, who, as a matter of self-respect, owing so much as she does to the Baron, would not take any interest at all. . . . Hortense wanted to pawn her diamonds. We should have had a few thousand francs, and we needed ten thousand. Those ten thousand francs were there for the taking, without interest, for a year! I said to myself, "Hortense doesn't have to know about it. I'll go and take them." That woman sent me an invitation, through my father-in-law, to dinner yesterday, giving me to understand that Lisbeth had spoken to her and that I should have the money. Between seeing Hortense in despair and going to that dinner, I did not hesitate. That's all. How Hortense could imagine, at twenty-four years of age, fresh, pure, and faithful as she is, she who is my whole happiness and my pride, with whom I have spent all my days since we were married, how could she imagine that I could prefer to her, what? . . . a woman jaded, faded, *raddled*! . . .' he said, using vulgar studio slang to demonstrate his utter contempt, by the kind of exaggeration that pleases women.

'Ah! if your father had only spoken to me like that!' exclaimed the Baroness.

Hortense, as an act of grace and forgiveness, put her arms round her husband's neck.

'Yes, that's what I would have done,' said Adeline. 'Wenceslas, my boy, your wife was at death's door,' she went on, gravely. 'You see how much she loves you. She is yours, alas!' And she sighed deeply.

'He has the power to make a martyr of her, or a happy woman,' she said to herself, with the thoughts all mothers have when their daughters marry. 'It seems to me,' she added aloud, 'that I suffer sufficiently myself to be allowed to see my children happy.'

'Set your mind at rest, dear Mama,' said Wenceslas, overjoyed to see this tempest happily ended. 'Within two months I shall have repaid the money to that horrible woman. Life is like that!' he went on, repeating the typically Polish phrase with Polish grace. 'There are times when a man would borrow from the devil. After all, the money belongs to the family. And, since she had invited me, should I have had the money that has cost us so dear if I had answered a polite gesture with rudeness?'

'Oh, Mama, what a lot of harm Papa does us!' Hortense exclaimed.

The Baroness put her finger to her lips, and Hortense regretted her complaint, the first words of blame that she had ever spoken of a father so heroically protected by a sublime silence.

'Good-bye, my children,' said Madame Hulot. 'Here is fine weather come now. But don't quarrel with one another again.'

When Wenceslas and his wife returned to their room, after seeing the Baroness out, Hortense said:

'Tell me about your evening!'

And she studied her husband's face as he told his story, which she interrupted with the questions that spring naturally to a wife's lips in such circumstances. His account made Hortense thoughtful. She grasped some idea of the diabolical entertainment that artists must find in such vicious company.

'Tell me the whole truth, Wenceslas! Stidmann was there, and Claude Vignon, Vernisset, and who else? In fact, you had a good time!'

'I? Oh, I was only thinking of our ten thousand francs, and I was saying to myself, "My Hortense will be spared anxiety!"'

The Livonian found this questioning desperately tiresome, and in a change of mood he said lightly,

'And what would you have done, my angel, if your artist had been found guilty?'

'Oh, I would have taken Stidmann as my lover,' Hortense said, with an air of decision; 'but without any love for him, of course!'

'Hortense!' cried Steinbock, with a theatrical gesture, springing to his feet. 'You should not have had time. I would have killed you first!'

Hortense threw herself into her husband's arms, and clung to him stiflingly, covering him with kisses, and said:

'Ah! you do love me, Wenceslas! Now I'm not afraid of anything! But no more Marneffe. Don't ever touch such pitch again.'

'I swear to you, dearest Hortense, that I'll never go back there, except to redeem my note of hand.'

She pouted, but only as loving wives pout when they want to be petted out of their sulky fit. Wenceslas, tired out by such a morning, left his wife to sulk, and went off to his studio to make the clay model for the Samson and Delilah group, the sketch for which was in his pocket. And then Hortense, repenting the sullen temper she had shown, and thinking that Wenceslas was angry, followed him to the studio, which she reached just as her husband was finishing the fashioning of his clay, working on it with the fierce passion of artists under the sway of the creative impulse. When he saw his wife, he hastily threw a damp cloth over the roughly worked out model, and put his arms round Hortense, saying:

'We're not cross, are we, my puss?'

Hortense had seen the group, and the cloth thrown over it. She said nothing, but before leaving the studio she turned back, pulled away the rag and looked at the model.

'What's this?' she asked.

'A group I have an idea for.'

'And why did you hide it from me?'

'I didn't want you to see it till it was finished.'

'The woman is very pretty!' said Hortense. And a thousand suspicions sprang up in her heart, like the jungle vegetation that, in India, springs tall and luxuriant between one day and the next.

*

By the end of about three weeks Madame Marneffe was feeling thoroughly exasperated with Hortense. Women of her kind have their pride. To please them, obeisance must be made to the devil, and they never forgive virtue that does not fear their power, or that fights against them. Now, in that time, Wenceslas had not paid a single visit to the rue Vanneau, not even the visit required by courtesy after a woman's posing as Delilah. Whenever Lisbeth had gone to visit the Steinbocks she had found no one at home. Monsieur and Madame lived at the studio. Lisbeth, tracking the two turtle-doves to their nest at Gros-Caillou, found Wenceslas working with zeal and diligence, and was told by the cook that Madame never left Monsieur. Wenceslas had submitted to the tyranny of love. So Valérie had reasons of her own for embracing Lisbeth's hatred of Hortense. Women will not give up lovers for whose possession they have rivals, just as men prize women desired by several empty-headed adorers. Indeed, reflections made here on the subject of Madame Marneffe apply equally well to men of easy love-affairs, who are a kind of male courtesan.

Valérie's whim became an obsession; she must have her group at all costs, and she was planning to go to the studio one morning to see Wenceslas, when one of those serious occurrences intervened that for women of her kind may be called *fructus belli* – the fortunes of war. This is how Valérie broke the news of this quite personal matter, at breakfast with Lisbeth and Monsieur Marneffe.

'Tell me, Marneffe, did you guess that you are about to have another child?'

'Really? You are going to have a child? Oh, allow me to embrace you!'

He rose and walked round the table. His wife turned her face to him in such a way that his kiss fell on her hair.

'By this stroke,' he went on, 'I become head clerk and Officer of the Legion of Honour! But of course, my dear girl, I don't want Stanislas to have his nose put out of joint, poor little man!'

'Poor little man?' exclaimed Lisbeth. 'You haven't set eyes on him for the past seven months. They take me for his mother at the school, because I'm the only one in this house that bothers about him!'

'A little man we have to pay a hundred crowns for every three months!' said Valérie. 'Besides, that one's your child, Marneffe. You certainly ought to pay for his schooling out of your salary. The one that's to come won't cost us any bills for his food. ... On the contrary, he'll keep us out of the poor-house!'

'Valérie,' rejoined Marneffe, striking Crevel's pose, 'I trust that Monsieur le Baron Hulot will take proper care of his son, and not burden a poor civil servant with him. I intend to take a very stern line with Monsieur le Baron. So get hold of your evidence, Madame! Try to have some letters from him, mentioning his felicity, for he's hanging fire a little too long over my promotion.'

And Marneffe left for the Ministry, where, thanks to his Director's invaluable friendship, he did not need to arrive before eleven o'clock. He had little to do there, in any case, in consideration of his notorious incapacity and his aversion to work.

Left alone, Lisbeth and Valérie looked at each other for a moment like a couple of Augurs, then burst simultaneously into a great gust of laughter.

'Look here, Valérie, is this true?' said Lisbeth. 'Or are you only playing a farce?'

'It's a physical fact!' replied Valérie. 'But Hortense *riles* me! And last night I had the brilliant idea of dropping this baby like a bomb into Wenceslas's household.'

Valérie went back to her bedroom, followed by Lisbeth, and she showed Lisbeth the following letter, already concocted:

Wenceslas dear, I still believe that you love me, although it is nearly three weeks since I saw you. Is that because you despise me? Delilah believes that cannot be true. It seems more likely to be due to some exercise of power on the part of a woman whom you told me you could never love again. Wenceslas, you are too great an artist to let yourself be so tyrannized over. Family life is the tomb of glory. ... Ask yourself whether you are the Wenceslas that you were in the rue du Doyenné. In my father's statue you scored a failure; but in you the lover far exceeds the artist – you were more successful with my father's daughter, and you are to be a father, my adored Wenceslas. If you did not come to see me in my present condition, your friends would hold a very low opinion of you; but I love you so madly, I feel in my heart that I should never have the strength to think badly of you. May I call myself, always,

Your VALÉRIE?

'What do you think of my plan to send this letter to the studio at a time when our dear Hortense is alone there?' Valérie asked Lisbeth. 'Stidmann told me, yesterday evening, that Wenceslas is to call for him at eleven to go to Chanor's to discuss some work; so that ninny Hortense will be alone.'

'After a trick like that,' Lisbeth replied, 'I cannot still be your friend openly. I'll have to walk out of your house. I must be thought not to visit you any more, or even speak to you.'

'I suppose so,' said Valérie; 'but ...'

'Oh, don't worry,' Lisbeth interrupted. 'We'll see each other again when I am the Marshal's wife. *They* are all in favour of it now. The Baron is the only one who doesn't know of the plan; but you'll persuade him.'

'But,' returned Valérie, 'it is possible that my relations with the Baron may soon be slightly strained.'

'Madame Olivier is the only person we can trust to let Hortense make her give up the letter,' said Lisbeth. 'We'll have to send her first to the rue Saint-Dominique, on her way to the studio.'

'Oh, our pretty little dear will be at home,' replied Madame Marneffe, ringing for Reine, in order to send her for Madame Olivier.

Ten minutes after the despatch of the fateful letter, Baron

Hulot arrived. Madame Marneffe, with a kittenish spring threw herself upon the old man's neck.

'Hector, you are a father!' she whispered in his ear. 'That's what happens when people quarrel and make it up again. ...'

Perceiving a certain surprise which the Baron was not quick enough to dissemble, Valérie looked coldly in a way that reduced the Councillor of State to despair. She allowed him to draw the most convincing proofs from her, one after another. When persuasion, taken sweetly by the hand by vanity, had entered the old man's mind, she told him of Monsieur Marneffe's rage.

'My own old soldier of the Old Guard,' she said to him, 'it will be really very difficult for you to avoid having your responsible editor, our managing director if you like, appointed head clerk and Officer of the Legion of Honour, for you have dealt the man a cruel blow. He adores his Stanislas, the little *monstrico* who takes after him, whom I can't endure. Unless you would rather give Stanislas an annuity of twelve hundred francs, with possession of the capital, naturally, and the interest in my name.'

'But if I bestow annuities, I prefer it to be for the benefit of my own son, not for the *monstrico*!' said the Baron.

That imprudent remark, from which the words 'my own son' burst like a river in flood, was transformed at the end of an hour's discussion into a formal promise to settle twelve hundred francs a year on the child that was to come. And after that, the promise, on Valérie's lips and in her rapturous face, was like a drum in a small boy's hands; she had to beat on it without stopping for twenty days.

Baron Hulot left the rue Vanneau, as happy as a man a year married who wants an heir. Meanwhile, Madame Olivier had induced Hortense to demand the letter from her that she was to deliver only into Monsieur le Comte's own hands. The young wife paid twenty francs for this letter. The suicide pays for his opium, his pistol, or his charcoal. When Hortense had read the letter, and re-read it, she could see only the white paper barred with black lines; only the paper existed in the universe, everything else was darkness. The glare of the conflagration that was consuming the edifice of her happiness lit up the paper, while utter darkness surrounded her. Her little boy's cries as he played came to her ear as if he were in a deep valley and she were high on a mountain. To be so insulted, at twenty-four years of age, in the full splendour of her beauty, adorned with a pure and devoted love: it was not a mere dagger-thrust, it was death. The first attack she had suffered had been nervous – her body had reacted in the grip of jealousy; but certainty of the truth assailed the soul, and the body was unconscious of pain. Hortense remained for about ten minutes in this stunned state; then her mother's image came before her mind, and produced a sudden violent change. She became collected and cold; she recovered her reason. She rang the bell.

'My dear, get Louise to help you,' she said to the cook. 'You must pack everything here that belongs to me, as quickly as possible, and all my son's things. I give you an hour. When everything is ready, fetch a cab from the square, and let me know. Make no comment! I'm leaving the house, and I shall take Louise with me. You must stay here with Monsieur. Take good care of him. . . .'

She went into her room, sat down at her table and wrote the following letter:

Monsieur le Comte,

The enclosed letter will explain why I have taken the course that I have resolved to follow.

When you read these lines, I shall have left your house and returned to my mother, with our child.

Do not imagine that I shall ever change my mind about this decision. Do not think that I am acting on impulse with youthful hotheadedness, with the vehement reaction of outraged young love: you would be quite mistaken.

I have thought very deeply, during the past fortnight, about life, love, our marriage, and our duty to each other. I have heard the whole story of my mother's devotion – she has told me all her sorrows. She bears her sufferings heroically every day, and has done so for twenty-three years; but I do not feel that I have the strength to follow her example, not because I have loved you less than she loves my father, but for reasons deriving from my nature. Our home could easily become a hell, and I might lose my head to the point of dishonouring you, dishonouring myself, and our child. I have no desire to be a Madame Marneffe, and on that slope a woman of my temperament might perhaps not be able to stop herself. I am, unhappily for me, a Hulot, not a Fischer.

Alone, and away from the sight of your dissipation, I can answer for myself, especially occupied as I shall be with our child, near my strong and sublime mother, whose living example will have its effect on the tumultuous impulses of my heart. There I can be a good mother, bring up our son well, and live. If I stayed with you, the wife would kill the mother, and incessant quarrels would embitter my character.

I could accept death at one stroke; but I cannot bear to suffer for twenty-five years, like my mother. If you have betrayed me after three years of absolute, unwavering, love, for your father-in-law's mistress, what rivals would you not give me later? Ah, Monsieur, you have begun much earlier in life than my father the rake's progress, the vicious way of life, that disgraces the father of a family, loses him his children's respect, and leads in the end to shame and despair.

I am not irreconcilable. Unforgiving resentment does not befit frail human beings who live under the eye of God. If you achieve fame and success by sustained effort, if you give up courtesans, ignoble and defiling courses, in me you will find a wife worthy of you again.

I believe you have too much dignity to have recourse to law-courts. You will respect my wish, Monsieur le Comte, and leave me with my mother; and above all, never present yourself there. I have left you all the money that that vile woman lent you. Good-bye.

HORTENSE HULOT

The letter was written painfully. As she wrote Hortense gave way to tears, to the outcries of slaughtered passion. She laid down her pen, but took it up again to write simply what love usually, in such testamentary letters, declaims in un-measured terms. Her heart poured out its emotion in excla-mations, cries, and tears; but what she wrote was dictated by reason.

The young wife, informed by Louise that all was ready, slowly wandered through the little garden, the bedroom, the drawing-room, looking at everything for the last time. Then to the cook she gave the most earnest injunctions to look after Monsieur well, promising to reward her if she behaved like an honest reliable girl. And at last she got into the cab to go to her mother's, her heart broken, weeping so bitterly that her maid was distressed, covering the baby Wenceslas with kisses, with a feverish joy in him that revealed much love still remaining for his father.

The Baroness had already been told by Lisbeth that Wenceslas's father-in-law was much to blame for his son-in-law's fault. She was not surprised to see her daughter arrive; she approved of the action she had taken, and agreed to keep her with her. Adeline, perceiving that gentleness and devotion had never done anything to check Hector, for whom her regard was beginning to diminish, considered that her daughter was right to take another way. Within three weeks the poor mother had received two blows that had given her greater pain than even the tortures previously endured. Through the Baron, Victorin and his wife had been impoverished; and now, according to Lisbeth, it was his fault that Wenceslas had gone astray, he had corrupted his son-in-law. The veneration in which the head of this family had been held, for so long maintained by means of extravagant sacrifices, was losing its authority. While not bewailing the lost money, the younger Hulots began to feel both mistrust and anxiety with regard to the Baron. This feeling of theirs, which was obvious enough, deeply distressed Adeline; she had a foreboding of the dissolution of the family.

The Baroness gave up her dining-room to her daughter's use, and it was quickly transformed into a bedroom, with the help of the Marshal's money; and the hall became, as it is in many households, the dining-room.

When, on his return home, Wenceslas had read and laid down the two letters, he experienced something like a feeling of joy amidst his sadness. Not allowed to stray, so to speak, out of sight of his wife, he had inwardly rebelled against this new form of the imprisonment that Lisbeth had imposed upon him. He had been gorged with love for three years. He too had had reason to reflect during the past fortnight; and the outcome was that he found family life a tiresome burden to bear. He had just heard himself congratulated by Stidmann on the passion he had aroused in Valérie; for Stidmann, with an ulterior motive easy to guess, deemed it an opportune moment to flatter the vanity of Hortense's husband in the hope of consoling the victim. And so Wenceslas was glad to be able to return to Madame Marneffe. Yet at the same time he could not help remembering the entire and undiluted happiness that he had enjoyed with Hortense, all her perfections, her wisdom, her innocent and uncomplicated love, and he acutely regretted her. He had an impulse to hurry after her to his mother-in-law's and beg forgiveness, but he did as Hulot and Crevel had done, he went to see Madame Marneffe, and he took his wife's letter with him in order to show her what a disaster she had caused and, so to speak, profit by this misfortune to demand favours from his mistress as a recompense.

He found Crevel with Valérie. The Mayor, swollen with pride, was restlessly moving about the drawing-room as if blown before a gusty wind of emotion. He repeatedly struck his pose as if about to burst into speech, and then, not daring, stopped the words on his lips. He looked radiant. Time and again he was drawn to the window to drum with his fingers on the panes. He followed Valérie with his eyes, with a touched and tender expression on his face. Fortunately for Crevel, Lisbeth came in.

'Cousin,' he whispered to her, 'have you heard the news? I am a father! It seems to me that I love my poor Célestine less. Oh! what a wonderful thing it is to have a child by a woman whom one idolizes, to be a father in one's heart as well as by blood! Oh, do tell Valérie what I say. I intend to work for this child, I mean him to be rich! She told me that from certain signs she believes it is to be a boy! If it's a boy I want him to have the name Crevel: I'll see my lawyer about it.'

'I know how much she loves you,' said Lisbeth; 'but for the sake of your own future and hers, control yourself; don't keep rubbing your hands every two minutes.'

While Lisbeth and Crevel were talking aside, Valérie had asked Wenceslas for her letter; and her whisperings soon dispelled his sadness.

'Now that you're free, my dear,' she said, 'do you really think great artists ought to marry? You only live by your imagination and your liberty! Don't worry. I'll love you so

much, my dear poet, that you'll never miss your wife. However, if you want to preserve appearances, as many people do,
I'll undertake to see to it that Hortense returns to you,
without delay. . . .'

'Oh, if only that were possible!'

'I'm sure it is,' said Valérie, rather piqued. 'Your poor
father-in-law is in every way a finished man. Out of vanity
he wants to appear as a man who is loved, he likes people to
think that he has a mistress, and the point means so much to
his pride that I can twist him round my fingers. The Baroness still loves her old Hector so much (I seem to be perpetually
talking about the *Iliad*) that the old people will induce Hortense to make it up with you. Only, if you don't want to
raise storms at home, don't leave your mistress for three weeks
without a visit from you . . . I felt like dying. My sweet, an
aristocrat like you owes a certain respect and consideration
to a woman whom he has compromised to the degree that
you have compromised me, especially when the woman has
to be very careful about what she does, for the sake of her
reputation. Stay to dinner, my angel . . . and remember that
I must treat you with great coldness, all the more so since
you are responsible for my only too apparent fall.'

Baron Montès was announced. Valérie rose and ran to meet
him, and whispered to him for a few moments, and gave him
the same injunctions as to his behaviour and the reserve he
must show as she had just given Wenceslas, for the Brazilian
wore an exalted expression appropriate to the great news
that had raised him to the seventh heaven – he, at least, had
no doubt of his paternity!

Thanks to these tactics, based on the pride and conceit of
man in his capacity as lover, Valérie had four delighted men
round her table, all excited and under her spell, each believing
that he was adored; Marneffe dubbed them in a jocose aside to
Lisbeth, including himself in the band, the five Fathers of the
Church.

Only Baron Hulot, at first, looked care-ridden, and for this
reason. When he was ready to leave his office, he had gone to
see the head of the Personnel Department, a general, his
comrade for thirty years, and had spoken to him about

appointing Marneffe to Coquet's place, for Coquet had agreed to send in his resignation.

'My dear fellow,' the Baron had said, 'I would not ask this favour of the Marshal without discussing the matter first with you, and having your concurrence.'

'My dear fellow,' replied the Director of Personnel, 'allow me to point out to you that for your own sake you ought not to press this nomination. I have already given you my views. It would cause scandalous talk in the Department, where there is already far too much interest in you and Madame Marneffe. This is between ourselves, of course. I do not want to hurt your feelings, or to go against your wishes in any way, and I'll prove it to you. If you are absolutely set on this thing, if you must ask for Coquet's place (and he will be a real loss to the Ministry – he's been here since 1809), I'll take a fortnight's leave and go away to the country to leave you a clear field with the Marshal, who is as fond of you as if you were his son. In this way I'll be neither for nor against, and I'll have done nothing against my conscience as responsible Director.'

'Thank you,' said the Baron. 'I'll think over what you say.'

'I may perhaps be allowed to make these comments, my dear fellow, since the matter affects your personal interests more than it does me, or my position. The Marshal has the last word, after all. And of course, my dear fellow, we are blamed for so many things – what does one more or less matter? We can reckon ourselves hardened to criticism. Under the Restoration men were appointed just to give them a salary, without too much concern about the advantage to the Civil Service. ... We are old comrades. ...'

'Quite so,' said the Baron, 'and it's just because I do not want to do anything that might impair an old and valued friendship that I ...'

'Ah, well,' said the Director of Personnel, seeing embarrassment painted on Hulot's face, 'I'll go off for a short time, my dear fellow. But take care! You have enemies, people who covet your fine salary, and you have only one anchor to hold you. Ah! if you were a Deputy, like me, you would have nothing to fear. So be careful!'

These remarks, so full of friendly feeling, made a strong impression on the Councillor of State.

'But why do you make so much of this, Roger? Is there something behind these mysterious warnings?'

The person addressed as Roger looked at Hulot, took his hand and clasped it.

'We have been friends for too long for me not to give you a piece of advice. If you want to maintain your position you must look after your own interests, make the bed you mean to lie in. In your place, instead of asking the Marshal to give Coquet's place to Marneffe, I would beg him to use his influence to ensure a place for me on the General Council of State, where I could end my days in peace. I should act like the beaver retreating before the hunters, and give up what they're attacking – the Director-generalship.'

'What do you mean? The Marshal would surely never forget ...'

'My friend, the Marshal defended you so hotly in one Council of Ministers that no one now thinks of giving you the sack; but there was some question of it! So don't give them a pretext. I don't want to say more. Just at present you can make what conditions you like, be a Councillor of State and Peer of France. If you wait too long, if you give them a handle to use against you, I don't answer for anything. ... Do you still want me to go off on leave?'

'Wait for a while. I'll see the Marshal,' Hulot answered; 'and I'll send my brother to sound him first and see how matters stand.'

The frame of mind in which the Baron returned to Madame Marneffe's may be imagined; he had almost forgotten that he was to be a father. Roger, in warning him of the realities of his situation, had acted as a true and kind friend. Yet such was Valérie's influence that by the time dinner was half over the Baron was in harmony with the rest, and waxed all the louder in his merriment because he had more worries to silence. The unfortunate man did not suspect that that very evening he was to find himself caught between the prospect of losing his happiness and the danger that the Personnel Director had warned him of, forced to choose between Madame Marneffe and his position.

About eleven o'clock, when the party was at its height and very gay, for the room was full of people, Valérie beckoned Hector to a corner of her sofa.

'My dear old thing,' she said to him, in a lowered voice, 'your daughter is so vexed with Wenceslas for coming here that she has left him. She's a bit too hot-headed is Hortense. Ask Wenceslas to let you see the letter the little fool wrote him. This separation of two lovers, of which I'm made out to be the cause, might do me an enormous amount of harm; for that's the sort of slanderous gossip by which virtuous women assert their superiority. It's a shocking thing that a person should pretend to be injured in order to throw blame on a woman who is guilty of nothing but having a house that people find agreeable. If you love me, you will clear me by sending the two turtle-doves home to their nest. I'm not at all anxious, anyway, to receive your son-in-law; it was you who brought him here, so you take him away again! If you have any authority over your family, it seems to me that you might well make your wife arrange a reconciliation. Tell the good old lady from me that if I am unjustly credited with coming between a young husband and wife, breaking up a family and grabbing both father and son-in-law, then I'll live up to my reputation by harrying them in my own fashion! Haven't I got Lisbeth, here, talking of leaving me? She prefers her family to mine, and I can't very well blame her. She has told me she will stay only if the young people patch up their quarrel. Just see the fix that leaves us in! Expenses in this house will be tripled!'

'Oh, leave that to me,' said the Baron, when he had heard the scandalous story of his daughter's flight. 'I'll soon put that right.'

'Well,' went on Valérie, 'to go on to another thing. What about Coquet's place?'

'That is more difficult,' replied Hector, lowering his eyes, 'not to say impossible!'

'Impossible, my dear Hector?' said Madame Marneffe,

softly and confidentially. 'But you just don't know what lengths Marneffe is prepared to go to. I am in his power. He is quite immoral where his own interests are concerned, like most men; but he is exceedingly vindictive, in the way only petty and physically weak people can be. In the position you have placed me in, I am at his mercy. If I were obliged to smooth him down for a few days, he is capable of never leaving my room again!'

Hulot gave a violent start.

'He was leaving me alone on condition that he should be head clerk. It's an outrage, but it's logical.'

'Valérie, do you love me?'

'To ask me such a question now, my dear, in the condition I'm in, is grossly unjust.'

'Well, if I should try, merely attempt, to ask the Marshal for promotion for Marneffe, I should be done for and Marneffe would be dismissed.'

'But I thought that you and the Prince were intimate friends!'

'Certainly we are, and he has often proved it; but, child, above the Marshal there are others ... there's the whole Council of Ministers, for example. With a little time, if we beat about and manoeuvre, we'll get there. To have what we want, we need to wait for the opportune moment when I'm asked to do some service. Then I can say "One good turn deserves another. ..."'

'If I say that to Marneffe, my poor Hector, he will do us an ill turn. Go and tell him yourself that he'll have to wait, I won't undertake it. Oh! I know what will happen to me; he knows how to punish me; he won't leave my bedroom. ... Don't forget the twelve hundred francs annuity for the little one.'

Hulot, feeling his pleasure threatened, took Marneffe aside; and for the first time he dropped the authoritative tone he had used until then – he was so revolted by the thought of that moribund man in his pretty wife's room.

'Marneffe, my dear fellow,' he said, 'I was talking about you at the Ministry today! But you can't be promoted head clerk just yet. ... We need time.'

'Oh yes I can, Monsieur le Baron,' Marneffe said flatly.

'But, my dear fellow . . .'

'Oh yes I can, Monsieur le Baron,' Marneffe repeated cold-ly, looking from the Baron to Valérie, and then at the Baron again. 'My wife finds it necessary to be reconciled to me, thanks to your behaviour, so I shall keep her; for she is charming, *my dear fellow*,' he added, with scathing irony. 'I am master here, even though you can't say the same at the Ministry.'

The Baron felt a pain at his heart like an agonizing tooth-ache, and it was all he could do to prevent tears appearing in his eyes. During this brief exchange, Valérie was whispering to Henri Montès, telling him of the course Marneffe was determined on, so she said, and so getting rid of Montès for a time.

Of the four faithful adorers, only Crevel, the possessor of his snug little house, was exempted from this treatment; and his face wore an expression of almost insolent beatitude, in spite of the reproofs that Valérie silently addressed to him by frowning and looking at him meaningfully. His radiant pater-nity beamed in every feature. When Valérie went up to him to whisper an urgent reproach, he caught her hand and said:

'Tomorrow, my duchess, you shall have your little house! I shall be signing the conveyance document tomorrow.'

'And what about the furniture?' she asked, smiling.

'I have a thousand shares in the Versailles and South Seine railway bought at a hundred and twenty-five francs, and they'll go to three hundred because the two lines are to be linked – I have had secret information about it. You'll have furniture fit for a queen! But from now on you'll belong only to me, won't you? . . .'

'Yes, my big Mayor,' said that middle-class Madame de Merteuil, with a smile; 'but behave nicely! Respect the future Madame Crevel.'

'My dear Cousin,' Lisbeth was saying to the Baron, 'I'll be with Adeline early tomorrow, for you know I can't in all decency stay here. I'll go and keep house for your brother, the Marshal.'

'I'm going home tonight,' said the Baron.

'Well then, I'll come to lunch tomorrow,' said Lisbeth, with a smile.

She knew how necessary it was that she should be present at the family scene that was bound to take place the following day. Early in the morning, too, she paid a visit to Victorin, and told him that Hortense and Wenceslas had separated.

*

When the Baron returned home about half past ten that evening, Mariette and Louise, who had spent a hard-working day, were just locking the door of the apartment, so that he did not need to ring. This husband, virtuous perforce and very vexed at having to be so, went straight to his wife's room; and through the half-open door saw her kneeling before her crucifix, lost in prayer, in one of those poses that are the inspiration and glory of painters and sculptors endowed with the genius to reproduce them. Adeline, lost in exaltation, was saying aloud:

'Have mercy upon us, O God, and open his eyes to see the light! ...'

So prayed the Baroness for her Hector. This scene, so different from the one he had just left, and these words, prompted by the events of that day, affected the Baron, and he sighed. Adeline turned a face wet with tears towards him. She so instantly believed that her prayer had been answered that she jumped to her feet and embraced her Hector fervently. Adeline's feminine self-regarding instincts were all outworn; grief had drowned even the memory. There was no passion left in her but motherhood, reverence for the family honour, and the purest affection of a Christian wife for a husband who has gone astray, that saintly tenderness that survives all else in a woman's heart. All this was evident.

'Hector,' she said at last, 'have you come back to us? Has God taken pity on our family?'

'Dear Adeline!' replied the Baron, leading his wife to a chair and sitting down beside her. 'You are the saintliest person that I have ever known, and for a long time I have felt myself no longer worthy of you.'

'You would have very little to do, my dear,' she said,

holding Hulot's hand and trembling violently, as if her feeling were physically uncontrollable, 'very little indeed to do to set things right again.'

She dared not go on; she felt that every word would be a reproach, and she did not wish to mar the happiness that filled her heart to overflowing in this meeting with her husband.

'It is Hortense who brings me here,' Hulot began. 'That little girl may do us more harm by her hasty action than my absurd passion for Valérie. But we will talk about all that tomorrow morning. Hortense is asleep, so Mariette tells me, so let's leave her in peace.'

'Yes,' said Madame Hulot, suddenly overwhelmed by profound sadness.

She saw that it was less a desire to see his family that had brought the Baron home to them, than some interest in which they had no share.

'Let's leave her in peace tomorrow too, for the poor child is in a pitiable state; she's been weeping all day,' said the Baroness.

The next morning at nine, the Baron was waiting for his daughter, whom he had sent for, and was walking up and down the vast empty drawing-room, searching his mind for arguments to overcome the most obdurate kind of determination, the obstinacy of an offended young wife, uncompromising like all the blameless young, who cannot envisage the shameful compromises commonly arrived at, because they are untouched by worldly passions and selfish interests.

'Here I am, Papa!' said a trembling voice, and Hortense appeared, pale with unhappiness.

Hulot, sitting down, put his arm round his daughter and made her sit on his knee.

'Well, child,' he said, setting a kiss on her forehead, 'so there's been some upset at home, and we have acted impulsively? That's not behaving like a well-brought-up girl. My Hortense should not have taken a decisive step like leaving her home, deserting her husband, by herself, without consulting her parents. If my dear Hortense had come to see her kind and admirable mother, she would have spared me the acute regret I feel! ... You do not know the world; it is very malicious. People may quite likely say that your husband has sent you back to your parents. Children brought up, like you, by their mother's side, remain children longer than others; they do not know what life is! An innocent and naïve love, like yours for Wenceslas, unhappily considers nothing; it is at the mercy of any impulse that moves it. Our little heart takes the lead, our head follows. We would burn down Paris to have our revenge, without a thought of the police courts! When your old father comes to tell you that you have not acted with propriety, you may believe him; and I say nothing of the deep sorrow I have been feeling. It is very bitter, for you are throwing blame on a woman whose heart you do not know, whose hostility may have terrible consequences. A girl like you, who are so open, so full of innocence and purity, has no conception of how things are in the world, I am sorry to say; it is possible you may be slandered, your name blackened. Besides, my dear little angel, you have taken a joke seriously; and I, personally, can vouch for your husband's innocence. Madame Marneffe . . .'

So far, the Baron, an artist in diplomacy, had admirably modulated the tone of his remonstrances. He had, as we see, skilfully led up to the introduction of that name. But Hortense when she heard it, started, as if cut to the quick.

'Listen to me. I am a man of experience, and I have seen the whole thing,' her father went on, preventing her from speaking. 'That lady treats your husband very coldly. Yes, you've been taken in by some hoax, and I'll give you proofs of it. For example, yesterday Wenceslas was there at dinner. . . .'

'He dined there?' exclaimed the young wife, jumping to her feet and staring at her father with a horror-stricken face. 'Yesterday! After reading my letter? Oh! God! Why did I not enter a convent instead of marrying? My life is not mine to dispose of now, I have a child!' she said, sobbing.

Her tears reached Madame Hulot's heart. She left her room, ran to her daughter, took her in her arms and asked her the futile questions of grief, the first that come to the lips.

'Here's a fine tempest!' said the Baron to himself. 'And it was all going so well! Now what's a man to do with crying women?'

'Listen to your father, child,' the Baroness said to Hortense.
'He loves us, you know. ...'

'Come now, Hortense, my dear little daughter, don't cry,
it spoils your looks,' the Baron said. 'Come now, be reasonable. Go back, like a good girl, to your home, and I promise
you that Wenceslas will never set foot in that house again. I
ask you to make the sacrifice, if you call it a sacrifice to forgive your own husband whom you love, for a trifling fault! I
ask you to do it for the sake of my grey hairs, for the love
you bear your mother. You do not want to fill the days of my
old age with bitterness and grief, do you?'

Hortense flung herself in a frenzy at her father's feet, so
wildly that her loosely-knotted hair came down, and she held
out her hands to him in a gesture that showed her utter
despair.

'Father, you are demanding my life!' she said. 'Take it if
you will, but at least take it pure and blameless, and I will
give it to you gladly indeed. But do not ask me to die dis-
honoured, stained with crime! I am not like my mother! I
will not swallow outrages! If I return to the home I share
with Wenceslas, I may strangle Wenceslas in a fit of jealousy,
or do worse still. Do not exact from me what is beyond my
strength. Do not have to mourn me while I am still alive! For
the least evil thing that may happen to me is to go mad. ... I
feel madness only two steps away! Yesterday, yesterday, he
dined with that woman! After reading my letter! Are other
men made like that? I give you my life, but let death not be
shameful! His fault? trifling! To have a child by that
woman!'

'A child!' said Hulot, recoiling. 'Come! That's certainly a
joke.'

Just at that moment Victorin and Cousin Bette came in,
and stood dumbfounded at the sight that met their eyes – the
daughter prostrate at her father's feet, the Baroness, silent,
torn between her feelings as a mother and as a wife, watching
with an agonized, tear-stained face.

'Lisbeth,' said the Baron, seizing the spinster by the hand
and indicating Hortense, 'you can help me. Poor Hortense is
out of her mind. She thinks Madame Marneffe is her

Wenceslas's mistress, while all Valérie wanted was simply to have a group by him.'

'*Delilah!*' cried the young wife, 'the only piece of work he has done since our marriage that he finished at once, without endless delay. This man was not able to work for my sake, or for his son, but he worked for that abominable woman with such ardour. ... Oh! give me a stroke to finish me, Father, for every word you speak is a stab.'

Turning to the Baroness and Victorin, with a glance at the Baron, unseen by him, Lisbeth shrugged her shoulders pityingly.

'Listen to me, Cousin,' said Lisbeth, 'I did not know what Madame Marneffe was when you begged me to go and live in the flat above her and look after her house, but in three years one learns a lot. That creature is a *harlot*! And so depraved! Only her dreadful hideous husband is comparable to her. You are the dupe, the Milord Pot-au-feu of these people, the contented deceived victim that they are keeping in their pocket, and they will lead you farther than you think! I am forced to speak to you quite plainly, for you have fallen into a pit.'

Hearing her speak in these terms, the Baroness and her daughter gazed at Lisbeth like devout persons thanking the Madonna for preserving their lives.

'She wanted, horrible woman, to disturb your son-in-law's marital happiness. Why? I've no idea. I'm not clever enough to get to the bottom of shady intrigues like this, so perverse and mean and shameful. Your Madame Marneffe does not love your son-in-law, but she wants him on his knees before her as an act of revenge. I have just treated the wretched woman as she deserves. She's a shameless courtesan, and I told her that I was leaving her house, that I did not want to run the risk of contamination in that sink of vice any longer. I belong to my family, first and foremost. I heard that my cousin's child had left Wenceslas, and here I am! Your Valérie, whom you think of as a saint, is the person who has caused this cruel separation. Can I stay with such a woman? Our darling Hortense,' she went on, touching the Baron's arm meaningfully, 'may be the victim of a whim, because women of her sort are capable of sacrificing a whole family in order to possess some trifle of artist's work. I do not think that Wenceslas is guilty, but I think he is weak, and I do not say that he would not yield to such high-powered fascinations. I have made up my mind. That woman is deadly dangerous to you; she will bring you to the gutter. I don't want to seem to be implicated in my family's ruin, especially as I've been staying there for the past three years for the express purpose of preventing it. You are being deceived, Cousin. Say firmly that you will have nothing to do with the promotion of that scoundrelly Monsieur Marneffe and you'll see what will happen! You're in for a beating if you do.'

Lisbeth raised her young cousin to her feet, and kissed her demonstratively.

'My dear Hortense, don't give way,' she whispered.

The Baroness embraced her Cousin Bette with the rapture of a woman who sees herself avenged. Gathered round the father of the family, they spoke no word to him, and he was sensitive enough to know what the silence meant. The clear signs of a formidable anger appeared on his brow and spread over his face: all the veins swelled, his eyes became suffused with blood, his colour grew blotched. Adeline rushed to throw herself on her knees before him, and took his hands.

'My dear, my dear, I beg of you! . . .'

'I am hateful to you!' said the Baron. It was the voice of his conscience crying.

We are all conscious of our own secret wrong-doing; and we nearly always imagine that our victims feel the hatred that the desire to strike back may well inspire in them. And so, in spite of all that hypocrisy can do, our words or our looks give us away when we are faced with some unforeseen ordeal, as once the criminal confessed in the hands of the torturer.

'Our children,' he said, as if in an effort to retract his confession, 'end by becoming our enemies.'

'Father . . .' said Victorin.

'Do you interrupt your father?' thundered the Baron, staring at his son.

'Father, listen,' Victorin said, firmly and flatly, in the tone of a puritan Deputy. 'I know the respect that is due to you too well ever to fail in it, and you will certainly always find in me a most submissive and obedient son.'

Anyone who attends the sittings of the two Chambers will recognize the platitudes of parliamentary debate in these cumbrous phrases employed to soothe irritation and gain time.

'We are far from being your enemies,' Victorin continued. 'I have strained my good relations with my father-in-law, Monsieur Crevel, by paying sixty thousand francs to redeem Vauvinet's bills of exchange; and that money is certainly in Madame Marneffe's hands. Oh! I'm not in the least blaming you, Father,' he added, as the Baron made an impatient gesture. 'All I want to do is to add my voice to Cousin Lisbeth's, and point out to you that although my devotion to you, Father, is blind, and indeed without limit, my dear Father, our financial resources, unfortunately, are limited.'

'Money!' said the furious old man, sinking into a chair, overwhelmed by this answer. 'And this is my son! ... Monsieur, your money shall be returned to you,' he said, rising. He strode to the door.

'Hector!'

The cry made the Baron stop, and he abruptly turned a face down which tears were pouring to his wife, who flung her arms round him with the vehemence of despair.

'Don't go away like this ... don't leave us in anger. I have said nothing!'

At that heartrending cry, the children threw themselves at their father's feet.

'We all love you,' said Hortense.

Lisbeth, motionless as a statue, watched the group, a contemptuous smile on her lips. At that moment Marshal Hulot arrived, and they heard his voice in the hall. The family realized the importance of concealment, and the scene rapidly dissolved. The two young people rose, and they all made an effort to cover their emotion.

Meanwhile at the door an altercation was taking place between Mariette and a soldier, who was so insistent that finally the cook came to the drawing-room.

'Monsieur, a regimental quartermaster, back from Algeria, says he has to speak to you.'

'Tell him to wait.'

'Monsieur,' Mariette added, in a low voice, 'he said to tell you privately that it's something to do with Monsieur Fischer, your uncle.'

The Baron started, for he thought that this must mean the arrival of funds he had secretly asked for, two months before, in order to redeem his bills of exchange. He left his family and hurried to the hall. There he saw an Alsatian face.

'*Am I sheaking to Mennesir the Paron Hilotte? . . .*'

'Yes.'

'Himself?'

'Himself.'

The quartermaster, who had been fumbling in the lining of his cap during this exchange, drew out a letter which the Baron hastily tore open, and read as follows:

Dear Nephew,

Far from being able to send you the hundred thousand francs that you ask me for, I find my position here no longer tenable unless you take vigorous action to save me. We have the Public Prosecutor at our heels, talking morality and babbling about our duty as trustees. Impossible to shut the fellow's mouth – he's a civilian! If the Ministry of War lets the black-coats bite its fingers, I am done for. I can trust the bearer of this. Try to get him promoted, for he has done us good service. Don't leave me to the crows!

The letter was a bombshell. There the Baron saw the earliest signs of the internal strife between civil and military authorities that, today, still bedevils the administration of Algeria. He realized that he must at once endeavour to find some way to deal with the threatening situation that suddenly faced him. He told the soldier to return on the following day; and when he had dismissed him, with handsome assurances of promotion, went back to the drawing-room.

'Good morning and good-bye, Brother!' he said to the Marshal. 'Good-bye, children. Good-bye, my dear Adeline – And what will you do now, Lisbeth?' he asked.

'Oh, I'll go and keep house for the Marshal. I must follow

my appointed course in life, helping one member of the family or another.'

'Don't leave Valérie until I have seen you again,' Hulot whispered to his cousin. 'Good-bye, Hortense, my rebellious little girl. Try to be calm and sensible. Serious matters have come up unexpectedly that I must attend to; we'll take up the question of your reconciliation later. Meantime give some thought to it, my good little pet.' And he kissed her.

He left his wife and children, so manifestly worried that they were filled with the gravest apprehensions.

'Lisbeth,' said the Baroness, 'we must find out what can be worrying Hector. I have never seen him in such a state before. Stay with that woman for two or three more days. He tells her everything, so if you do we may learn what has had such an effect on him, so suddenly. Don't worry: we'll arrange your marriage with the Marshal, for the marriage is certainly necessary.'

'I'll never forget your courage this morning,' said Hortense, kissing Lisbeth.

'You have avenged our poor mother,' said Victorin.

The Marshal watched with some curiosity the demonstrations of affection lavished upon Lisbeth, who went off to describe the scene to Valérie.

This sketch gives innocent souls some faint idea of the various havocs that the Madame Marneffes of this world may wreak in families, and by what means they can strike at poor virtuous wives, apparently so far beyond their reach. If we consider how such evils may affect the highest level of society, that about the throne, we realize the price paid for kings' mistresses, and can estimate the debt of gratitude a nation owes its sovereigns who set an example in moral conduct and proper family life.

*

In Paris, every Ministry is like a small town from which the women have been banished, but with no less gossip, slander, and blackening of reputations than if there were a feminine population. After three years, Monsieur Marneffe's position had been, one may say, exposed, set in the light of day, and in the various offices people were asking, 'Will Monsieur Marneffe succeed Monsieur Coquet?' exactly as they used to ask in the Chamber not so long ago, 'Will the Bill for the Royal Allowance to the Duc de Nemours be passed?' Every move in the Personnel Department was watched. Nothing in Baron Hulot's department escaped scrutiny. The wily Councillor of State had strategically won over the man who would suffer by Marneffe's promotion, an efficient worker, telling him that if he could help in Marneffe's promotion he would certainly succeed him, and pointing out that Marneffe was a dying man. This clerk was now intriguing in Marneffe's interest.

As Hulot walked through his outer office, full of people waiting to see him, he caught sight of Marneffe's pallid face in a corner, and Marneffe was the first man summoned.

'Have you something to ask me, my dear fellow?' said the Baron, concealing his uneasiness.

'Monsieur le Directeur, I'm being made a mock of in the Department, because we've just heard that the personnel chief went on sick leave this morning and he's to be away for a month. Waiting for a month – everyone knows what that's as good as; and it's quite bad enough for me to be a drum beaten on one side, but if you beat me on both sides at once, Monsieur le Directeur, the drum may burst.'

'My dear Marneffe, it takes a great deal of patience to achieve one's ends. You cannot be made head clerk, if you ever are, for at least two months. A time when I'm going to be obliged to consolidate my own position is not a suitable moment to ask for a promotion likely to cause some scandal.'

'If you get the sack, I'll never be head clerk,' said Monsieur Marneffe coldly. 'If you send my name forward, it won't make any difference to you one way or the other.'

'You think I ought to sacrifice myself for you?' inquired the Baron.

'If you do not, I shall be much surprised.'

'You are much too Marneffe altogether, Monsieur Marneffe!' said the Baron, rising and motioning the clerk to the door.

'I wish you good morning, Monsieur le Baron,' Marneffe replied meekly.

'What an impudent blackguard!' the Baron said to himself. 'That's as good as a summons to pay within twenty-four hours under pain of distraint.'

Two hours later, as the Baron was finishing giving instructions to Claude Vignon, whom he was sending to the Ministry of Justice to get information about the judicial authorities in whose jurisdiction Johann Fischer's work lay, Reine opened the door of the Director's office and came in to give him a note, to which she asked for an answer.

'How could she send Reine!' the Baron said to himself. 'Valérie is mad; she's compromising us all, as well as compromising that abominable Marneffe's appointment!'

He dismissed the Minister's private secretary, and read as follows:

Ah, my dear, what a scene I've just had to endure! If you have given me three years of happiness, I've certainly had to pay for it! *He* came in from his office in a state of fury that made my blood run cold. I knew that he was an ugly man, but I've now seen him look a monster. The four teeth that are all that he owns fairly chattered with rage, and he threatened me with his odious company if I continued to receive you. My poor darling, alas! our door will be shut to you from now on. You can see my tears – they're falling all over the paper, it's quite drenched in them! Can you read this, dearest Hector? Oh! not to see you any more, to have to give you up – when I hold a little of your life, as I believe I have always held your heart – it will mean my death! Think of our little Hector, and don't desert me; but don't damage your reputation for Marneffe's sake, don't give way to his threats! Ah! I love you as I have never loved anyone before! I have been counting all the sacrifices you have made for your Valérie – she does not and never will forget them. You are, and you will always be, my only real husband. Don't give another thought to the twelve hundred francs a year that I asked you to give the dear little Hector who is to be born in a few months' time ... I don't want to cost you any more. Indeed, my money will always be yours.

Ah! if you loved me as much as I love you, my Hector, you would retire now; we should both leave our families behind, and our worries, and all the hatred that surrounds us, and we should go away to live, with Lisbeth, in some delightful place, in Brittany or wherever you liked. We would see nobody there, and we should be happy, far away from all these people. Your pension and the little that I have in my own name would be enough for us. You are sometimes jealous now, are you? Well, you would see your Valérie with no one in her mind but her Hector, and you would never have to use your big gruff voice, as you did the other day. There will always be only one child for me – ours; you may be very sure of that, my darling old soldier. No, you really cannot imagine what I feel like, for you don't know how he has treated me, and the scurrilous language he spat out all over your Valérie – the words would stain the paper. A woman like me, Montcornet's daughter, ought never in her whole life to have had to listen to a single one of them. Oh! I would have liked you to be there, so that I could have punished him by letting him see how utterly I adore you! My father would have run his sword through the wretch; but I can only do what a woman can – that is, love you madly! And so indeed, my darling, in my present distressed state, it is impossible for me to give up seeing you. Yes! I must see you, in secret, every day. We women are made like that. I cannot help feeling as my own your resentment against Marneffe. I beg you, if you love me, do not make him head clerk – let him end his days as a deputy head clerk! Just now I'm still beside myself, I can still hear his abuse ringing in my ears. Bette, who wanted to leave me, has taken pity on me; she is to stay for a few days.

My poor dear, I don't know yet what I should do. I can only think of flight. I have always adored the country, Brittany, Languedoc, anywhere you like, provided I can be free to love you there. Poor pet, how I pity you, forced to return to your old Adeline, that urn of tears; because, as he must have told you, the monster, he has made up his mind to watch me day and night. He even spoke of the police! Do not come here! I know that he is capable of anything, now that he is using me as a counter in the basest kind of bargaining. I only wish that I could give you back all I owe to your generosity. Oh, my dearest Hector, I may have flirted, and seemed frivolous to you, but you do not know your Valérie; she loved teasing you, but prizes you above anyone in the world. You can't be prevented from going to see your cousin. I'll plan with her some means by which we can talk. My kind dear, do write a little note to reassure me, since I can't have your dear presence. . . . (Oh! I would give a hand to have you with me on our sofa.) A letter will work a charm for me; write me something with your whole noble soul in it. I shall give you back the letter, for we must be careful. I should not know where to hide it; he rummages everywhere. But do write, to reassure your Valérie, your wife, the mother of your child. Imagine my having to write to you, after seeing you every day! As I say to

Lisbeth, 'I did not know how lucky I was'. A thousand kisses, my
pet. Keep all your love for

Your VALÉRIE

'And tears on it!' said Hector to himself, as he finished
reading this letter. 'Tears blotting her name! – How is she?'
he asked Reine.

'Madame is in bed; she had frightening hysterics,' replied
Reine. 'Her nervous attack twisted Madame up in knots like a
piece of string. It took her after writing. Oh! it was because
of the way she cried. ... We heard Monsieur's voice on the
stairs.'

The Baron in his distress wrote the following letter, on his
official notepaper with its printed heading:

Don't worry, my angel; he shall die a deputy head clerk! Your
idea is excellent; we will go away, and live far from Paris and be
happy with our little Hector. I shall retire, and can find a good
position as director of some Railway Company. Ah, my dear love,
your letter makes me feel young again! Yes, I shall begin life again,
and I'll make a fortune, you'll see, for our little child. Reading
your letter, a thousand times more ardent than the letters of *La
Nouvelle Heloïse*, I saw a miracle happen! I had not imagined that my
love for you could increase. This evening at Lisbeth's you shall see
your

HECTOR (yours for life!)

Reine went off with this reply, the first letter that the
Baron had written to his 'dear love'! Such emotions as these
counterbalanced the heavy news of disaster grumbling like
thunder on the horizon. At this moment, indeed, the Baron,
certain of his ability to ward off the blows aimed at his uncle,
Johann Fischer, was only concerned about the deficit.

One of the peculiar traits of the Bonapartist character is its
belief in the power of the sword, its conviction of the superiority of the military to the civil authority. Hulot did not care a
straw for the Public Prosecutor in Algeria, where the Ministry
of War ruled. A man is conditioned by his past. How could
the officers of the Imperial Guard forget having seen the
Mayors of the fair cities of the Empire, and the Emperor's
Prefects, lesser emperors themselves, come to pay homage to
the Imperial Guard at the frontiers of the Departments it was

passing through, and in fact accord it sovereign honours?

At half past four, the Baron went straight to Madame Marneffe's. His heart was beating like a young man's as he walked upstairs, his brain repeating the questions, 'Shall I see her? Shall I not see her?' How should he remember that morning's scene, and his family in tears, kneeling at his feet? Did not Valérie's letter, placed in a thin note-case to be kept always over his heart, prove that he was more greatly loved than the most attractive of young men? When he had rung, the unlucky Baron heard the dragging slippers and execrable coughing of the invalid Marneffe. Marneffe opened the door, only to strike an attitude, and motion Hulot down the stairs, with a gesture identical with Hulot's own when he had shown Marneffe his office door.

'You are much too Hulot altogether, Monsieur Hulot!' he said.

The Baron attempted to pass him. Marneffe drew a pistol from his pocket, and cocked it.

'Monsieur le Conseiller d'État, when a man is as vile as you think me – for you think me extremely vile, don't you – he would be the most incompetent kind of criminal if he did not collect all the proceeds of his sold honour. You ask for war. You shall have it: war to the hilt, with no quarter given. Don't come back here again, and don't try to pass me. I have given notice to the police of my situation with regard to you.'

And, taking advantage of Hulot's state of stupefaction, he pushed him outside and shut the door.

'What a downright rascal the fellow is!' Hulot said to himself as he climbed the stair to Lisbeth's apartment. 'Oh, I understand her letter now! We'll leave Paris, Valérie and I. Valérie is mine for the rest of my days; she will close my eyes.'

Lisbeth was not at home. Madame Olivier informed Hulot that she had gone to call on Madame la Baronne, expecting to find Monsieur le Baron there.

'Poor woman! I should not have thought her capable of such a grasp of the situation as she showed this morning,' thought the Baron, recalling Lisbeth's behaviour, as he walked from the rue Vanneau to the rue Plumet.

At the corner of the rue Vanneau and the rue de Babylone

he looked back at the Eden from which Conjugal Right was banishing him, armed with the sword of the Law. Valérie, at her window, was watching Hulot on his way. When he looked up she waved her handkerchief; but the miserable Marneffe aimed a cuff at his wife's cap and pulled her violently from the window. Tears rose to the Councillor of State's eyes.

'How can a man bear to be loved as I am loved, see a woman ill-treated, and be nearly seventy years old!' he thought.

Lisbeth had gone to carry the good news to the family. Adeline and Hortense already knew that the Baron, unwilling to dishonour himself in the eyes of the entire Ministry by appointing Marneffe chief clerk, was to be shown the door by the husband, who, now turned Hulotophobe, was violently against him. And so Adeline, rejoicing, had ordered such a dinner as her Hector should find superior to those that Valérie could provide, and the devoted Lisbeth was helping Mariette to achieve this difficult aim. Cousin Bette was the heroine of the hour, almost the idol. Mother and daughter kissed her hands, and they had told her with a touching joy that the Marshal had consented to take her as his housekeeper.

'And from that, my dear, to becoming his wife, there is only one step,' said Adeline.

'In fact, he didn't say no when Victorin spoke to him about it,' added Countess Steinbock.

The Baron was welcomed by his family with such graceful, touching marks of affection, with such overflowing love for him, that he was forced to conceal his anxieties. The Marshal came to dinner. After dinner Hulot stayed at home. Victorin and his wife came in. A rubber of whist was started.

'It's a long time, Hector,' said the Marshal gravely, 'since you have given *us* a pleasant evening like this.'

This speech from the old soldier, who was so indulgent to his brother and who in these words was implicitly rebuking him, made a profound impression. It was realized then that during the past months his heart, in which all the sorrows that he had divined had found an echo, had been deeply hurt. At eight o'clock, when Lisbeth took her departure, the Baron insisted on escorting her home, promising to return.

'Do you know, Lisbeth, *he* ill-treats her!' he said to her, in the street. 'Ah! I have never before felt so deeply in love with her.'

'I should never have believed that Valérie could be so much in love with you,' Lisbeth replied. 'She is volatile and flirtatious, she likes to see herself a centre of attraction, to have the comedy of love played out for her, as she says; but she is really attached only to you.'

'What message did she give you for me?'

'Here it is,' answered Lisbeth. 'You know she has been kind to Crevel. You must not bear her a grudge for that, for it has spared her poverty for the rest of her life. But she detests him, and the affair is practically finished. Well, she has kept the key of some rooms . . .'

'In the rue du Dauphin!' exclaimed the delighted Hulot. 'If it were only for that, I would forgive her Crevel. I have been there; I know.'

'Here is the key,' said Lisbeth. 'Have a duplicate made tomorrow – two if you can.'

'And then?' said Hulot, avidly.

'Well, I will come to dinner with you again tomorrow. You ought to return Valérie's key, for old Crevel may ask for the one he gave her, and you can go and meet her the day after. Then you can make up your minds about what you are going to do. You will be quite safe there, for there are two entrances. If, by any chance, Crevel, who has Regency habits, or so he says, should come in by the passage, you would go out through the shop, and vice versa. Now you see, you rascal, you owe all this to me. What are you going to do for me?'

'Anything you like!'

'Well then, don't oppose my marrying your brother!'

'You, the Maréchale Hulot! The Comtesse de Forzheim!' exclaimed Hulot, in some surprise.

'Adeline is a Baroness, after all!' returned Bette, in an acid and formidable tone. 'See here, my old rake, you know the state your affairs are in! Your family may find itself begging bread, in the gutter. . . .'

'That's what I'm terrified of!' said Hulot, with a sudden shock.

'If your brother should die, who would look after your wife and daughter? The widow of a Marshal of France could get a pension of six thousand francs at least, couldn't she? Well, I only want to marry in order to make sure that your daughter and wife will have bread to eat, you old fool!'

'That didn't occur to me,' said the Baron. 'I will talk to my brother, for we can rely on you. . . . Tell my angel that my life is *hers*!'

And the Baron, after seeing Lisbeth home to the rue Vanneau, returned to play whist, and stayed at home. The Baroness's cup of happiness was full. Her husband apparently had returned to family life; and for nearly a fortnight he left every morning for the Ministry at nine o'clock, came back at six for dinner, and spent the evening with his family. He twice took Adeline and Hortense to the theatre. Mother and daughter had three thanksgiving masses said, and prayed to God to keep safely with them the husband and father he had restored. Victorin Hulot, seeing his father go off to bed one evening, said to his mother:

'Well, we are fortunate my father has come back to us; and my wife and I will not regret our lost capital, if only this lasts. . . .'

'Your father is nearly seventy years old,' answered the Baroness. 'He still thinks of Madame Marneffe, I realize that, but it will not be for long. A passion for women is not like a passion for gambling or speculation or hoarding money; one can see an end to it.'

The beautiful Adeline – and she was still beautiful, at fifty, and in spite of her sorrows – was mistaken in this. Libertines, those men endowed by nature with the precious faculty of loving beyond the usual term of love, rarely appear to be their age. During this virtuous interlude the Baron had gone three times to the rue du Dauphin, and there he had never seemed to be seventy. The new lease of life granted to his passion made him young again, and he would have thrown away his reputation for Valérie, and his family, everything and anyone, without a qualm. But Valérie, now completely changed, never mentioned money to him, nor spoke of the twelve hundred francs a year to be settled on their son. On the contrary, she offered him money, and loved Hulot as a woman of thirty-six might love a handsome law student who is very poor, very romantic, and very much in love. And poor Adeline believed that she had recaptured her dear Hector!

The fourth rendez-vous of the two lovers had been arranged in the last moment of the third, exactly as the next day's play used to be announced in the old days, at the end of a play by the Comédie-Italienne. Nine in the morning was the appointed time. About eight o'clock on the day when this felicity was due, the expectation of which made it possible for the passionately fond old man to accept family life, Reine asked to see the Baron. Hulot, apprehensive of catastrophe, went out to speak to her, as she would not enter the apartment. The faithful maid handed the following letter to the Baron:

Dear Old Soldier,

Don't go to the rue du Dauphin now; our nightmare is ill and I must look after him; but be there this evening at nine o'clock. Crevel is at Corbeil, with Monsieur Lebas, and I am sure that he will not be bringing a princess to his little house. I'll make arrangements to spend the night there; I can be home before Marneffe wakes. Send me an answer to this, for perhaps your long elegy of a wife doesn't let you do as you please, as you used to. They say she is sufficiently beautiful still to make you unfaithful to me, you are such a rake! Burn my letter; I don't trust anything.

In reply, the Baron wrote this little note:

My love,

In twenty-five years, my wife, as I have told you, has never stood in the way of my pleasure. I would sacrifice a hundred Adelines for you! I will be there this evening, at nine o'clock, in Crevel's temple, awaiting my divinity. May the deputy clerk soon expire, and then we need never be separated again! That is the dearest wish of

Your

HECTOR

That evening the Baron told his wife that he had some work to do with the Minister at Saint-Cloud, and would be back between four and five in the morning, and he went to the rue du Dauphin. It was then the end of June.

Few living men have actually experienced the terrible sensation of going to their death, for few return from the scaffold; but there are some who have been vividly conscious of that agony in dreams. They have felt everything, to the very edge of the knife laid against their necks at the moment when dawn woke them up and brought deliverance. ... The Councillor of State's sensations at five in the morning, in Crevel's elegant and stylish bed, were far more horrible than those of a man laid on the fatal block, in the presence of ten thousand spectators, watching him with eyes that seared him with twenty thousand jets of flame.

Valérie was sleeping in a charming pose. She was lovely, with the superb loveliness of women who can even look lovely sleeping – an instance of art invading nature, literally a living picture.

In his horizontal position, the Baron's eyes were three feet from the ground. His eyes, straying vaguely as eyes do when a man wakes and collects his scattered thoughts, fell on the door sprinkled with flowers painted by Jan, an artist who despises fame. Unlike a man being executed, the Baron did not see twenty thousand seeing rays of flame, he saw only one, but that one was more acutely painful than the gaze of ten thousand in the public square. Such a sensation in mid-pleasure, much rarer than the sensations of condemned prisoners, would certainly be paid for highly by a great many Englishmen suffering from spleen.

The Baron lay where he was, still stretched out horizontally, bathed in a cold sweat. He tried to doubt his senses; but that murderous eye was talking. A murmur of voices whispered behind the door.

'Let it be only Crevel, wanting to play a trick on me!' prayed the Baron, no longer able to doubt the presence of some person in the temple.

The door opened. The majesty of the law, which on public notices comes second only to that of the king, manifested itself in the shape of a jolly little police superintendent, accompanied by a long-legged magistrate, both ushered in by the Sieur Marneffe. The police officer, standing solidly in shoes with barbarously knotted laces, and topped at the other end with an almost hairless yellow cranium, looked a ribald sly old fellow, genial in nature, for whom the life of Paris held no more mysteries at all. His eyes, glittering behind spectacles, shot shrewd and satirical glances through the glass. The magistrate, a retired solicitor, long an adorer of the fair sex, felt some envy of the delinquent.

'Kindly excuse us – we are forced to do our duty, Monsieur le Baron!' said the officer. 'We are required to act by a complainant. This gentleman is a magistrate, present to authorize our entrance of a private house. I know your identity, and that of the lady.'

Valérie opened amazed eyes, uttered the piercing scream that is conventional for actresses demonstrating their madness on the stage, and writhed in convulsions on the bed, like a woman possessed of the devil in the Middle Ages, in her sulphur shift, on a bed of faggots.

'Death! ... my dearest Hector! But a police court? Oh! Never!'

She leapt up, swept like a white cloud past the three spectators, and tried to efface herself under the writing-table, hiding her face in her hands.

'Betrayed! Worse than dead!' she shrieked.

'Monsieur,' said Marneffe to Hulot, 'if Madame Marneffe goes mad, you will be more than a debauchee, you'll be a murderer!'

What can a man do, what can he say, when surprised in a bed which is not his, not even on lease, with a woman who is not his either?

'Gentlemen,' said the Baron, with dignity, 'kindly have some care for the unfortunate lady whose reason appears to me to be in danger ... and you can get on with your official business later. The doors are no doubt locked; you need not fear that she or I may escape, in our present state. ...'

The two officials listened to the Councillor of State's injunction respectfully, and drew back.

'Come here, you miserable reptile, and talk to me!' said Hulot under his breath to Marneffe, taking him by the arm and pulling him closer. 'It's not I who will be the murderer, but you! You want to be head clerk and an Officer of the Legion of Honour, do you?'

'Most certainly I do, sir,' answered Marneffe, with a bow.

'You shall be all that. Reassure your wife, and send these gentlemen away.'

'No fear,' replied Marneffe, with spirit. 'These gentlemen have to note the evidence that you were caught in the act, and draw up the report. My case rests on that document; without it where should I be? Everyone knows all the double-dealing that goes on at the top in the Civil Service. You have stolen my wife and haven't made me head clerk, Monsieur le Baron. I give you just two days to arrange the promotion. I have letters here . . .'

'Letters?' the Baron interrupted him sharply.

'Yes, letters which prove that the child my wife is carrying at this very moment is yours. You get the point? You ought by rights to provide an income for my son equal to the amount this bastard does him out of. But I'll not be too hard on you; that's nothing much to do with me. I'm not a besotted parent – paternity doesn't go to *my* head! A hundred louis a year will do. By tomorrow morning I must be Monsieur Coquet's successor, and my name must be on the list of Legion of Honour nominations for the July celebrations, or else . . . the official report will be lodged, with my charge, in court. You'll agree that that's letting you off lightly?'

'Heavens, what a pretty woman!' the magistrate was saying to the police officer. 'A loss to the world if she goes mad!'

'She's not mad,' pronounced the officer authoritatively. The police are always scepticism itself.

'Monsieur le Baron Hulot has walked into a trap,' he added, loud enough for Valérie to hear.

The rage in Valérie's eyes, as she turned to look at him, would have killed him if looks could kill. The officer smiled. He had set his trap too, and the woman had fallen into it. Marneffe invited his wife to return to the bedroom and get decently dressed, for all points had been agreed with the Baron, who took a dressing-gown and went to the other room.

'Gentlemen,' he said to the two officials, 'I don't need to ask you to keep this secret.'

They bowed. The police officer rapped twice on the door. His secretary entered, sat down at the writing-table, and began to write, as the officer dictated in a low voice. Valérie continued to shed copious tears. When she had finished her toilet, Hulot entered the bedroom and dressed. Meanwhile the official report was completed. Then Marneffe was about to take his wife away, but Hulot, believing that he was seeing her for the last time, made a gesture asking to be permitted to speak to her.

'Monsieur, your wife is costing me dear, so I think you may allow me to say good-bye to her ... in the presence of you all, of course.'

Valérie went over to him, and Hulot whispered:

'We can do nothing now but run away; but how can we keep in touch? We have been betrayed. ...'

'By Reine!' she answered. 'But, my dear, after this outrage we ought not to see one another again. I am disgraced. Besides, people will tell you dreadful things about me, and you will believe them. ...'

The Baron shook his head protestingly.

'You will believe them, and I thank heaven for it, for then you will perhaps not regret me.'

'*He shall not die a deputy head clerk!*' said Marneffe, at the Councillor of State's ear, coming back to reclaim his wife, to whom he said roughly:

'That's enough, Madame! I may be weak with you, but I don't intend to be made a fool of by anyone else.'

So Valérie left Crevel's little house, with a parting look at the Baron of such roguish complicity that he was sure she adored him. The magistrate gallantly gave his arm to Madame Marneffe, and escorted her to the cab. The Baron, who had to sign the official report, was left standing there in stunned silence, alone with the superintendent. When the Councillor of State had signed the document, the officer looked at him shrewdly over his spectacles.

'You are very fond of that little lady, Monsieur le Baron?'

'Unfortunately for me, as you see ...'

'But suppose she were not fond of you?' the officer pursued. 'Suppose she were playing you false?'

'I have already heard about that, Monsieur, here in this house Monsieur Crevel and I told each other ...'

'Ah! so you know that this is Monsieur le Maire's little house?'

'Certainly.'

The officer slightly raised his hat from his head in respectful salutation.

'You are unquestionably in love, so I hold my peace,' he said. 'I respect incurable passions, just as doctors do incurable diseases. ... I have seen Monsieur de Nucingen, the banker, stricken with an infatuation of this kind. ...'

'He's one of my friends,' replied the Baron. 'I have often had supper with the lovely Esther. She was worth the two millions she cost him.'

'More than that,' said the officer. 'That fancy of the old banker's cost four persons their lives. Oh, these infatuations are like cholera.'

'What are you trying to tell me?' the Councillor of State demanded, taking this indirect warning very badly.

'Why should I deprive you of your illusions?' replied the officer. 'It is such a rare thing to have any left at your age.'

'Illusions? Open my eyes then!' commanded the Councillor of State.

'The doctor gets cursed later,' the superintendent answered with a grin.

'I ask you, Monsieur le Commissaire ...'

'Well, that woman was in collusion with her husband.'

'Oh ...'

'It happens, Monsieur, in two cases out of ten. Oh, we meet plenty like them.'

'What proof have you of collusion?'

'Oh, the husband, to begin with!' said the shrewd superintendent, with the calm unconcern of a surgeon, to whom probing wounds is all in the day's work. 'It's written in his mean ugly face that he's a scamp. But there's also a certain letter, written by that woman, in which the child is mentioned, that must have some value for you?'

'That letter means so much to me that I always carry it on me,' Baron Hulot replied, fumbling in his breast pocket for the little note-case that he was never parted from.

'Leave the note-case where it is,' said the officer, as if he were pronouncing an indictment; 'here is the letter. I now know all I wanted to know. Madame Marneffe must have known what this note-case contained.'

'She is the only person in the world who did. . . .'

'That's what I thought. Now, here's the proof you were asking for of that little lady's complicity.'

'It's not possible!' said the Baron, still incredulous.

'When we came here, Monsieur le Baron,' the superintendent went on, 'that cur, Marneffe, went in first, and he took the letter, here, from the writing-table, where his wife must have placed it. Obviously, putting it here was pre-arranged between the pair, if she could manage to take it from you while you were asleep; because the letter the lady wrote to you, taken with those you sent to her, is conclusive evidence for the court.'

The police officer showed Hulot the letter that Reine had brought to the Baron's office at the War Office.

'It's a document in the case,' he said. 'Give it back to me, Monsieur.'

'If this is true,' said Hulot, changing countenance, 'the woman is battening on calculated debauchery. I am certain, now, that she has three lovers.'

'It's as clear as day,' said the officer. 'Ah! they're not all walking the streets, women of that sort. When they ply that trade with their carriages, their drawing-rooms, and their fine houses, Monsieur le Baron, it's not a matter of pence and ha'pence. That Mademoiselle Esther whom you mentioned, who poisoned herself, swallowed up millions. If you'll take my advice, you'll settle down, Monsieur le Baron. This little party will cost you dear. That rascally husband has the law behind him. And if I hadn't told you, the little lady would have caught you again!'

'Thank you, Monsieur,' said the Councillor of State, trying to preserve his dignity.

'We are going to close the apartment now, Monsieur; the farce is played out, and you will return the key to Monsieur le Maire.'

Hulot went home in a state of depression verging on collapse, plunged in unutterably sombre thoughts. He woke his noble, pure, and saintly wife, and cast the story of the past three years upon her heart, sobbing like a child deprived of a toy. This confession, from an old man still young in heart, an appalling and heart-rending tale, moved Adeline to pity, but at the same time she experienced a sensation of the keenest joy. She thanked heaven for this final blow, for she saw her husband as now made fast for ever in the bosom of his family.

'Lisbeth was right!' Madame Hulot said gently, avoiding useless reproaches. 'She warned us of this some time ago.'

'Yes. Ah, if only I had listened to her instead of getting angry that day when I wanted poor Hortense to return to her husband, in order not to compromise the reputation of that – Oh, dear Adeline, we must save Wenceslas! He is in this morass up to the chin!'

'My poor dear, you have been no luckier with the middle-class wife than you were with the actresses,' said Adeline, trying to smile.

The Baroness was alarmed at the change in her Hector. When she saw him, unhappy, suffering, bowed under the weight of trouble, she was all tenderness, all compassion, all love. She would have given her life to make Hulot happy.

'Stay with us, dear Hector. Tell me how those women contrive to make themselves so attractive. I will try. ... Why have you not taught me to be what you want? Is it because I am not clever? There are still men who think me beautiful enough to pay court to.'

Many married women, faithful to family duty and their husbands, will at this point probably ask themselves why such strong men, so really good and kind, who are so vulnerable to women like Madame Marneffe, do not find the realization of their dreams and the fulfilment of their passions in their wives, especially when their wives are like Adeline Hulot.

The reason is linked with one of the most fundamental mysteries of human nature. Love, which awakens the mind to joy and delight, the virile, austere pleasure of the most noble faculties of the soul, and sex, the vulgar commodity sold in the market, are two aspects of the same thing. Women capable of satisfying the hunger for both are geniuses in their own kind, and no more numerous than the great writers, artists, and inventors of a nation. Men of all kinds, the distinguished man and the fool, the Hulots as much as the Crevels, desire both an ideal love and pleasure. They are all in quest of that mysterious hermaphrodite, that rare work, which most often turns out to be a work in two volumes. Morally and socially, their search is reprehensible. Obviously, marriage must be accepted as a duty: it is life, with its toil and its bitter sacrifices exacted from both partners. Libertines, those treasure-seekers, are as culpable as other malefactors more severely punished.

Such reflections are no mere sop to conventional morality; they offer an explanation of the causes of many misunderstood social evils. This drama, moreover, has its own moral lessons, of different kinds.

The Baron went without delay to Marshal Prince de Wissembourg, whose high protection was his last resource. As the old warrior's protégé for thirty-five years, he had access to him at all times, and might call on him very early.

'Ah, good morning, my dear Hector!' said that great leader and fine man. 'What's the matter? You look worried. And yet the parliamentary session is over. That's another one finished with! Nowadays I talk about the sittings as I once used to do about our campaigns. Well, I believe the newspapers do refer to parliamentary campaigns.'

'We have had our troubles, indeed, Marshal; but we live in difficult times!' said Hulot. 'We have to put up with the world as we find it. Every age has its own difficulties. Our great trouble in the year 1841 is that neither the King nor his Ministers have the freedom of action that the Emperor had.'

The Marshal cast one of his eagle's looks at Hulot, proud, piercing, acute. It was evident that, in spite of his years, that noble mind was still strong and vigorous.

'You want me to do something for you?' he asked genially.

'I find myself obliged to ask you, as a personal favour, for the promotion of one of my deputy clerks to the grade of head clerk of a department, and his nomination as Officer of the Legion of Honour.'

'What is his name?' the Marshal asked, turning an eye like a lightning flash on the Baron.

'Marneffe.'

'He has a pretty wife. I saw her at your daughter's wedding. ... If Roger ... but Roger isn't here. Hector, my boy, this is a matter of amorous intrigue. What! you are still at it? Ah! you're a credit to the Imperial Guard. That's the result of having been in the Commissariat, you have reserves! Let this affair go, my dear boy. It is too much a matter of gallantry to become an administrative concern.'

'No, Marshal, it's a bad business, for the police are interested in it. You would not like to see me in a police court?'

'Ah! the devil!' exclaimed the Marshal, looking concerned. 'Continue.'

'Well, as things stand, I'm caught like a fox in a trap. You have always been so good to me that I take courage to hope you may come to my rescue in this shocking tight corner.'

And Hulot recounted his misadventure as wittily and as lightly as he could.

'My dear Prince,' he said in conclusion, 'I am sure you could not allow my brother, your dear friend, to die of grief, or one of your Directors, a Councillor of State, to be disgraced. This man Marneffe is a miserable wretch; we can pension him off in two or three years.'

'How you talk, with your two or three years, my dear fellow!' said the Marshal.

'But the Imperial Guard is immortal, Prince.'

'I am now the only Marshal left of the first list,' said the Marshal. 'Listen, Hector. I have more affection for you than you know. You shall see. On the day I leave the Ministry, we shall both go. Ah! you're not a Deputy, my friend. There are many men who covet your place, and if it were not for me, you would not still hold it. Yes, I have broken many a lance in your defence in order to keep you. ... Well, I'll grant your two requests, for it would be much too painful to see you on the stool of repentance, at your age and in your position. But you make too many inroads in your credit. If this promotion gives an opportunity to start trouble, we shall not be in favour. For myself, I don't care, but it will be another thorn under your foot. At the next session you will be pushed out. Your Directorship is a bait held out to five or six different people with influence, and it is only my wily argument that has preserved you so far. I said that on the day when you retired on pension and your place was handed on, we should have made five persons discontented and only pleased one, while by leaving you tottering on your perch for two or three years we should have our six men voting for us. They began to laugh, in the Council Meeting, and it was agreed that the old boy of the Old Guard, as they call me, was getting very clever at parliamentary tactics. ... I tell you all this frankly. You're getting on, besides – you're growing grey. ... You're a fortunate fellow to be able to get into such fixes still! Where are the days when Sub-Lieutenant Cottin had mistresses?'

The Marshal rang.

'We must have that police report torn up!' he added.

'You are treating me like a father, Monseigneur! I did not dare tell you how anxious I was about it.'

'I always need Roger here,' exclaimed the Marshal, seeing Mitouflet, his doorkeeper, come in, 'and I was just going to have him sent for. You go off, Mitouflet. And you go too, my old comrade, go and get this nomination prepared and I will sign it. But that rascally intriguer shall not enjoy the fruit of his crimes for long. We'll have him watched and drummed out at the first slip. Now that you are saved, my dear Hector, take care. Don't wear your friends out. Notice of the appointment will be sent to you this morning, and your man shall be Officer of the Legion of Honour! ... How old are you now?'

'Seventy, in three months' time.'

'What a fellow you are!' said the Marshal, with a smile. 'You're the man who ought to be promoted; but, cannon-balls and bullets! we're not living under Louis XV now!'

Such is the comradeship uniting the glorious survivors of the Napoleonic phalanx that they think of themselves as still fighting their campaigns together, and still bound to defend one another against all comers.

'One more favour like that,' Hulot said to himself as he crossed the court, 'and I am finished.'

The unfortunate civil servant went to Baron de Nucingen, to whom he now owed only an unimportant sum. He succeeded in borrowing forty thousand francs from him, against his salary for two more years; but the Baron stipulated that in the case of Baron Hulot's retirement, the disposable part of his pension should be attached for repayment of the debt and the interest on it. This new transaction, like the first, was made through Vauvinet, to whom the Baron signed bills for twelve thousand francs. On the following day the fatal police evidence, the husband's charge, and the letters were all destroyed. The scandalous promotion of the Sieur Marneffe passed almost unnoticed amid the stir of the July celebrations, and occasioned no newspaper comment.

Lisbeth, now to all appearances estranged from Madame Marneffe, had installed herself in Marshal Hulot's household. Ten days after these events the first banns of marriage were published between the spinster and the illustrious old soldier. Adeline, in order to obtain his consent, had told the story of her Hector's financial catastrophe, begging him never to speak of it to the Baron, who, she said, was despondent, in very low spirits, really quite crushed.

'We can see now that he's no longer a young man, I'm afraid,' she added.

And so Lisbeth triumphed! She was about to attain the goal of her ambition, she was about to see her plan accomplished, her hatred satisfied. She revelled in anticipation in the joy of ruling the family that had despised her for so long. She promised herself that she would patronize her patrons, be the guardian angel supporting the ruined family. She hailed herself as 'Madame la Comtesse' and 'Madame la Maréchale', bowing to her reflection in the looking-glass. Adeline and Hortense should end their days in penury, miserably struggling to keep their heads above water, while their Cousin Bette, received at the Tuileries, was playing the fine lady.

A dreadful event occurred that threw the old maid down from the social height where she was so proudly preparing to take her place.

On the same day that these first banns were published, the Baron received another message from Africa. Another Alsatian presented himself, handed over a letter when he had made sure that it was to Baron Hulot that he was giving it, and, having told the Baron the address of his lodgings, departed, leaving that high official staggered by the first few lines he read:

Dear Nephew,

You will receive this letter, as I calculate, on August 7th. Supposing that it takes you three days to obtain the help we urgently require, and a fortnight more for it to reach us, we should have it before September 1st.

If you can act within that time, you will have saved the honour and the life of your devoted Johann Fischer.

This is what the clerk you gave me as confederate tells me to ask; for I am liable, so it seems, to be brought before a court – either an assize court or a court martial. You know that Johann Fischer will never be brought before any earthly tribunal; he will go by his own act before God's.

Your clerk appears to me to be a young scamp, quite capable of compromising you; but he is a clever rascal. His scheme is that you should make a louder outcry than anyone else about irregularities, and send us an inspector, a special envoy instructed to expose the malefactors, uncover abuses, and in short make a lot of noise, but ready to place himself, first and foremost, between us and the law, and screen us by muddying the waters.

If your representative arrives here by September 1st, and he has been warned about the part he has to play, and if you send us two hundred thousand francs to make good the quantities of stores that we say are deposited in remote districts, our book-keeping will be considered accurate and unimpeachable.

You can trust the soldier who will bring you this letter with a money order made out to me, payable through an Algerian bank. He is a reliable man, a relative of mine, incapable of trying to find out what he is carrying. I have taken measures to ensure the safe return of this boy. If you cannot do anything, I will die gladly for the man to whom we owe our Adeline's happiness.

The pangs and pleasures of desire, the catastrophe that had just brought his career as a gallant to an end, had prevented Baron Hulot from thinking of poor Johann Fischer, although his first letter had warned clearly enough of the danger that had now become so pressing.

The Baron left the dining-room with his mind in a turmoil, only to collapse heavily on the sofa in the drawing-room, where he lay stunned and dizzied by the violence of his fall. He stared at the pattern on the carpet, disregarding

Johann's fateful letter, that he held clutched in his hand.

From her bedroom Adeline heard her husband throw himself like a dead weight on the sofa. The sound was so singular that she thought he must have had a stroke. She looked in her glass at the scene reflected through the door, with a breath-stopping apprehension that made her incapable of movement, and saw her Hector lying like a stricken man.

The Baroness entered on tiptoe. Hector heard nothing. She was able to approach, noticed the letter, read it, and was shaken in every limb. She experienced a nervous shock of such severity that her body permanently retained the mark of it. Within a few days she had become affected by a constant tremor; for, after the first moment, the necessity for action gave her the kind of strength that is borrowed only from the very springs of vital power.

'Hector, come into my room!' she said, in a voice that was like a breath of wind. 'Don't let your daughter see you like this! Come, dear, come.'

'Where can I find two hundred thousand francs? I can have Claude Vignon sent out on a special mission. He's an astute fellow, and clever. That can be arranged in two days. . . . But two hundred thousand francs! My son has not got so much money; his house is mortgaged for three hundred thousand. My brother's savings are not more than thirty thousand. Nucingen would laugh at me! Vauvinet? . . . he was unwilling enough to lend me ten thousand francs for that scoundrel Marneffe's son. No, this is the end. I'll have to go and throw myself at the Marshal's feet, confess how things are, hear him call me a blackguard, take his broadside and go decently to the bottom.'

'But, Hector, it's not simply ruin now, it's disgrace!' said Adeline. 'My poor uncle will kill himself. Kill us, you have the right, but you cannot be a murderer! Have courage; there must be some way out.'

'None at all!' said the Baron. 'No one in the Government could find two hundred thousand francs, even to save a Ministry! Oh, Napoleon, where are you now?'

'My uncle! Poor man! Hector, we cannot let him kill himself and die in dishonour!'

'There is one chance that might be tried,' he said, 'but ...
it is very doubtful. ... Yes, Crevel is at daggers drawn with his
daughter. ... Ah! he has plenty of money, he's the only one
who could ...'

'Wait, Hector; it's better for your wife to perish than to let
our uncle, your brother, be destroyed, and the family honour!'
said the Baroness, struck by a sudden idea. 'Yes, I can save
you all. ... O God! what a dreadful thought! How could I
have thought it!'

She clasped her hands, slipped to her knees, and prayed.
As she rose again, she saw an expression of such wild
joy on her husband's face that the devil-inspired thought
returned, and Adeline fell into an almost insane vacancy of
mind.

'Go, dear, hurry to the War Office,' she exclaimed, rousing
herself from her stupor. 'Try to send out someone on a special
mission. You must! Get round the Marshal! And when you
come back at five o'clock, you may perhaps find ... yes! you
shall find two hundred thousand francs. Your family, your
honour as a man, as a Councillor of State, a Government
official, your integrity, your son, will all be saved; but your
Adeline will be lost, and you will never see her again. Hector,
my love,' she said, kneeling before him, clasping his hand
and kissing it, 'bless me and say good-bye!'

It was utterly heart-rending; and as he took his wife's
hand, raised her to her feet, and kissed her, Hulot said:

'I don't understand!'

'If you understood,' she answered, 'I should die of
shame, or perhaps I should not be strong enough to accom-
plish this final sacrifice.'

'Lunch is served, Madame,' Mariette came to announce.

Hortense came in to wish her father and mother good
morning. It was necessary to go and eat, and show serene and
cheerful faces.

'Go and start the meal without me. I'll join you later,' said
the Baroness. She sat down at her table and wrote the following letter:

My dear Monsieur Crevel,

I have a favour to ask of you, and I shall hope to see you this

295

morning, for I count on your gallantry, which is known to me, not to keep me waiting too long.

Yours very sincerely,

ADELINE HULOT

'Louise,' she said to her daughter's maid, who was serving lunch, 'take this letter down to the porter. Tell him to deliver it immediately to this address, and wait for an answer.'

The Baron, who was reading the newspapers, held out a Republican sheet to his wife, pointing to an article, and said, 'Will there be time?'

Here is the article, one of those scandal-hunting paragraphs with which newspapers spice their solid political fare:

One of our correspondents writes from Algiers that such grave abuses have come to light in the commissariat department of the province of Oran that official inquiries are being made. The malpractices are evident, and the culprits are known. If stern measures are not taken, we shall continue to lose more men by the fraudulent diversion of supplies affecting their rations, than we do by Arab steel or the torrid climate. We await fresh information, and will report further on these deplorable occurrences. The alarm excited in Algeria by the establishment of the Press there, in accordance with the 1830 Charter, no longer causes us surprise.

'I'll dress and go to the Ministry,' said the Baron, rising from the table. 'Time is so precious. A man's life hangs in the balance every minute.'

'Oh, Mama, I have no longer any hope!' said Hortense. And, unable to restrain her tears, she held out a copy of the *Revue des Beaux-Arts* to her mother. Madame Hulot saw a reproduction of the group *Delilah* by Count Steinbock, below which was the caption 'In the possession of Madame Marneffe'. The article below, signed V., gave evidence in every line of Claude Vignon's style and partial eye.

'Poor child!' said the Baroness.

Startled by her mother's almost indifferent tone, Hortense looked at her, and recognized in her expression a grief compared with which her own paled; and she came to kiss her mother and ask:

'What's the matter, Mama? What's happening? Can we be more unhappy than we already are?'

'My dear child, it seems to me that compared with what I am suffering today, my dreadful sufferings in the past are nothing. When will my suffering end?'

'In heaven, Mother!' said Hortense gravely.

'Come, my angel, you shall help me to dress. . . . Or rather, no . . . I do not want you to have anything to do with my toilet on this occasion. Send me Louise.'

Adeline, when she had returned to her room, went to the looking-glass to examine her face. She considered her reflection sadly and curiously, asking herself:

'Am I beautiful still? Am I still desirable? Have I wrinkles?'

She lifted her beautiful fair hair and uncovered her temples. . . . The skin was as fresh as a young girl's. Adeline explored further. She bared her shoulders, and was satisfied; she even felt a thrill of pride. The beauty of lovely shoulders is the last to desert a woman, especially when she has lived a pure life. Adeline chose the elements of her toilet with care; but the demure fashion of a pious and modest woman's dress is not altered by the little inventions of coquetry. Of what use was it to put on new grey silk stockings and low-cut satin slippers tied above the ankle with ribbons, when she was totally ignorant of the art of advancing a pretty foot at the crucial moment, beyond a skirt slightly raised, so opening new horizons to desire? She selected her prettiest dress, it is true, of flowered muslin, cut low in the neck and short-sleeved; but, taking fright at this bareness, she veiled her beautiful arms with transparent gauze sleeves, and hid her bosom and shoulders in an embroidered fichu. Her English ringlets seemed to her too obviously designed to captivate, so she extinguished their gaiety with a very pretty cap; but, with or without the cap, would she have had the art to play with her golden curls in order to show off her hands and hold her tapered fingers up for admiration? Her only cosmetic, her only aid to beauty, was provided by the conviction of guilt, the preparations for deliberate sin, which raised this saintly woman's emotions to a fever pitch that fleetingly gave her again the brilliancy of youth. Her eyes glittered; her cheeks glowed. But instead of assuming fascinating graces, she saw herself as appearing almost shameless, and was horrified.

Lisbeth, when Adeline had questioned her, had described the circumstances of Wenceslas's infidelity, and the Baroness had learned then, to her great surprise, that in one evening, in one instant, Madame Marneffe had successfully enticed the bewitched artist.

'How do these women do it?' the Baroness had asked Lisbeth.

The curiosity of virtuous women, on this subject, is bottomless. They would like, while remaining untouched, to possess the seductions of vice.

'Oh, they are seductive; that's their business,' Cousin Bette had replied. 'My dear, that evening, believe me, Valérie was enough to damn an angel.'

'But tell me how she set about it!'

'There's no theory in that profession; only practice,' Lisbeth had said dryly.

The Baroness, recalling that conversation, would have liked to consult Cousin Bette; but there was no time. Poor Adeline, who was incapable of inventing a beauty-patch, of setting a rosebud in the cleft of her bodice, of contriving tricks of dress calculated to fan men's smouldering desires into flame, was no more than carefully dressed. One isn't a courtesan for the wishing!

'Woman is man's meat' according to Molière's witticism, through the mouth of the judicious Gros-René.* Such a comparison implies a kind of culinary art in love. In that case, the dignified virtuous wife is the Homeric feast, flesh thrown on glowing embers. The courtesan, on the other hand, is a confection of Carême's,† with its condiments and spices, and its studied refinements. The Baroness could not, did not know how to, *serve up* her white bosom in a magnificent dish of lace, after the fashion of Madame Marneffe. The appeal of certain attitudes, the effect of certain glances, were a sealed book to her. In short, she had no magic secret weapon. This noble woman might have turned away provocatively a hundred times, but without Valérie's swing of the

*It is in fact Alain, and not Gros-René, who says this, in *L'École des femmes*.

†The famous chef, who served, amongst others, Talleyrand and the Czar Alexander.

skirts she would have had nothing to offer to the libertine's knowing eye.

To be a virtuous and even prudish woman in the world's eyes, and a courtesan to her husband, is to be a woman of genius, and there are few. In such genius lies the secret of those long attachments that are inexplicable to women without the gift of such paradoxical yet superb abilities. Imagine a virtuous Madame Marneffe ... and you have the Marchesa de Pescara! But such eminent and celebrated women, lovely and virtuous sisters of Diane de Poitiers, are rare.

The scene with which this serious and awe-inspiring study of Parisian manners began was now about to be re-enacted, with the singular difference that the afflictions foretold by the bourgeois Militia Captain had reversed the roles. Madame Hulot was waiting for Crevel with the purpose that had brought him, smiling down upon the citizens of Paris from the elevation of his *milord*, three years before. And then, most strangely, the Baroness was faithful to herself and to her love in yielding to the grossest infidelity, so unforgivable, in the eyes of some judges, that even the compelling force of passion does not justify it.

'What can I do to be a Madame Marneffe?' she asked herself, as she heard the door-bell ring.

She repressed her tears. Her face was feverishly animated as she promised herself that she would be truly a courtesan, poor noble creature!

'What the devil can the good Baroness Hulot want with me?' Crevel was wondering as he walked up the main staircase. 'Ah bah! she's going to talk to me about my quarrel with Célestin and Victorin, no doubt; but I'll not give way!'

Following Louise into the drawing-room, he said to himself as he looked around at the bareness of the 'premises' (Crevel's word):

'Poor woman! Here she is like a fine picture put in the attics by a man who knows nothing about painting.'

Crevel, seeing Count Popinot, Minister of Commerce, buy paintings and statues, wanted to be eminent himself as a Parisian Maecenas, one of those whose love of the arts consists in the search for something worth twenty francs to be bought for twenty sous.

Adeline smiled graciously on Crevel, and indicated a chair facing her.

'Here I am, fair lady, at your command,' said Crevel.

Monsieur le Maire, now a politician, had assumed black cloth. His face appeared above this garb like a full moon rising over a bank of dark clouds. His shirt, studded with three enormous pearls worth five hundred francs each, gave a high idea of his capacity . . . his thoracic capacity, that is, and he was fond of saying 'In me you see the future athlete of the Chamber!' His broad plebeian hands were clothed in yellow gloves from early morning. His patent-leather boots hinted at the little brown coupé with one spanking horse that had brought him there. In the course of three years, ambition had modified Crevel's pose. Like the great painters he had reached his second period. In society, when he called on the Prince de Wissembourg, or went to the Préfecture, or Count Popinot's house, or others of that kind, he held his hat in his hand in a negligent fashion that Valérie had taught him, and he inserted the thumb of his other hand in the armhole of his waistcoat with a captivating air, simpering and smirking meanwhile, an activity involving both eyes and head. This new manner of 'striking an attitude' was a practical joke of Valérie's, who on the pretext of rejuvenating her Mayor had endowed him with one more fashion of making himself ridiculous.

'I have asked you to come, my dear kind Monsieur Crevel,' said the Baroness nervously, 'for a matter of the greatest importance. . . .'

'I can guess it, Madame,' Crevel said, with a knowing air, 'but you are asking for the impossible. . . . Oh, I'm not an inhuman father, a pig-headed man, a solid block of stinginess, as Napoleon put it. Listen to me, fair lady. If my children were ruining themselves for their own benefit, I might come to their rescue; but to stand guarantor for your husband! That's the same as trying to fill the sieve-bottomed casks of the fifty daughters of Danaus! There they are with a house mortgaged for three hundred thousand francs, all for the sake of an incorrigible father! They've nothing left now, poor wretches, and they didn't have any fun out of spending the money either. All they have to live on now is what Victorin makes at the Law Courts. He may wag his tongue, that fine son of yours – that's all he can do! Ah! he was to be a Minister, the wise little lawyer, the bright hope of us all! A useful sort of tugboat, he is, getting in among the sandbanks in the most senseless way; for if he were borrowing to help himself along, if he had run up debts dining and wining Deputies, getting hold of votes and increasing his influence, I would say "Here's my purse; dip your hand into that, my boy!"; but to pay for Papa's follies, follies that I foretold to you! Why, his father has done for any chance he ever had of getting power ... I'm the one who'll end up as a Minister. . . .'

'I'm afraid, *dear* Crevel, it's not a question of our children, poor self-sacrificing young couple! If you harden your heart against Victorin and Célestine, I will love them enough to do something to sweeten the bitterness of your anger, in their generous hearts. You are punishing your children for a good deed!'

'Yes, a good deed in the wrong place; and that's half way to being a crime!' said Crevel, much pleased with his epigram.

'Doing good, my dear Crevel,' the Baroness went on, 'is not a matter of giving money from a purse stuffed with money! It means giving up something in order to be generous, going short oneself; and expecting nothing but ingratitude! Charity that costs nothing is unnoticed in heaven. . . .'

'Saints, Madame, have every right to go to the workhouse if they want to; they know that it's the gate of heaven for them. But I'm a worldly man. I fear God; but I find the hell of poverty much more frightening. To have empty pockets, in our present social system, is the last degree of misery. I am a man of my time. I respect money!'

'From the worldly point of view,' said Adeline, 'you are right.'

She found herself leagues away from the point, and felt like St Lawrence on his gridiron as she thought of her uncle, for she pictured him holding a pistol to his head. She lowered her eyes, and then raised them, full of angelic sweetness, to look at Crevel, but quite unprovocatively, with none of Valérie's enticingly wanton glint. Three years before, she would have fascinated Crevel with that adorable gaze.

'I have known you when you were more generous,' she said; 'you spoke of three hundred thousand francs then, with lordly openhandedness . . .'

Crevel looked at Madame Hulot, whom he saw as a lily in fading bloom; vague suspicions floated into his mind. But he felt so much respect for this saintly woman that he drove back such half-formed ideas to the more libertine regions of his heart.

'Madame, I have not changed, but a retired businessman is, and has to be, lordly with some method, and economically. He does everything systematically. He opens an account for his sprees, allows for them, earmarks certain profits for that purpose – but to make a hole in his capital . . . that would be madness! My children will have all that should be theirs, their mother's money and mine; but presumably they don't want their father to die of boredom, turn into a monk or a mummy! I lead a gay life, and go down the river joyously! I do my duty as the law requires with regard for the demands of affection and family feeling too, just as I have always scrupulously paid my debts when they fell due. If my children do as well as I have done in family life, I shall be pleased. And as for the present, so long as my follies – for I do commit some – cost nothing to anyone except *gogos* . . . (pardon me! I don't suppose you know that word we use on the Bourse for suckers), they will have nothing to reproach me with, and will find a tidy sum left for them at my death. Your children will not be able to say as much for their father – he brings off a cannon by ruining both his son and my daughter. . . .'

The more the Baroness said, the farther she seemed to be from attaining her end.

'You are very hard on my husband, my dear Crevel; and yet you would be his best friend if you had found his wife frail. . . .'

She cast a burning look at Crevel. But, like Dubois, who kicked the Regent disguised as his valet with too much enthusiasm, she over-played her part and profligate thoughts returned with such force to the 'Regency' perfumer that he said to himself:

'Can she want to revenge herself on Hulot? Does she like me better as a Mayor than in National Guard uniform? Women are such odd creatures!' And he struck an attitude in his second manner, looking at the Baroness with a Regency smirk.

'One might think,' she went on, 'that you are having your revenge on him for a virtue that resisted you, for a woman whom you loved enough . . . to . . . to buy her,' she concluded, in a whisper.

'For a divine woman,' Crevel returned, leering at the Baroness, who lowered her eyes, finding her lashes suddenly wet; 'and what a lot of bitter pills you've had to swallow . . . in the past three years . . . eh, my beauty?'

'Don't let's talk of my sufferings, *dear* Crevel; they are too much for any human being to endure. Ah, if you still loved me, you could take me from the pit I am in! Yes, I lie in hell! The regicides who were tortured with red-hot pincers, who were drawn and quartered, were on roses compared with me, for it was only their bodies that were dismembered and it is my heart that is torn asunder!'

Crevel's hand slipped from his waistcoat armhole. He laid his hat on the work-table. He broke his pose. He smiled! His smile was so idiotic that the Baroness misunderstood it: she thought it was an expression of kindness.

'You see a woman, not in despair, but suffering the death-throes of her honour, and resolved to do anything, *my dear*, to prevent a crime. . . .'

Fearing that Hortense might come in, she bolted the door; then in the same impulse cast herself at Crevel's feet, took his hand and kissed it.

'Be my deliverer!' she said.

She believed that there was generous feeling in his shop-keeper's heart, and a sudden hope flashed through her mind that she might obtain the two hundred thousand francs without losing her honour.

'Buy a soul, you who sought to buy a virtue!' she said, look-ing at him wildly. 'Trust my integrity as a woman, my honour, whose steadfastness you know! Be my friend! Save a whole family from ruin, shame, despair. Keep it from plunging into a mire whose filth will be mixed with blood! Oh, don't ask for explanations!' she went on, as Crevel made a gesture and seemed about to speak. 'Above all, don't say "I told you so!" like a person glad at a friend's misfortune. Only do as you are asked by one you once loved, a woman whose humiliation at your feet is perhaps a noble achievement. Ask her for nothing in return, but be sure that there is nothing her gratitude will withhold! No, do not give, but lend, lend to the one whom you once called Adeline!'

At this point Adeline sobbed uncontrollably, and tears came in such floods that Crevel's gloves were soaked. The words 'I need two hundred thousand francs!' were barely distinguishable amid the torrent of tears, like the boulders, substantial as they are, just breaking the surface in Alpine torrents swollen at the melting of the snows.

Such is virtue's inexperience! Vice asks for nothing, as Madame Marneffe's case has shown; it causes everything to be offered to it. Women of Valérie's kind become demanding only when they have become indispensable, or when it is a matter of extracting all that a man has left, like working a quarry when the lime becomes scarce, 'worked out', as the quarrymen say. Hearing the words 'Two hundred thousand francs!' Crevel understood everything. He gallantly raised the Baroness to her feet with the insolent words, 'Come, mother, let's keep calm,' which Adeline in her distracted state did not hear. The scene was changing its aspect. Crevel was becoming, as he put it, master of the situation. The magnitude of the sum produced such strong reaction in Crevel that his considerable emotion at seeing this beautiful woman in tears at his feet was dissipated. And then, however angelic and saintly a woman may be, when she weeps unrestrainedly her beauty disappears. Women like Madame Marneffe, as we have seen, may cry a little sometimes, let a tear roll down their cheeks; but burst into floods of tears, redden their eyes and noses ... never! They would not make such a mistake.

'Come now, *my child*, keep cool now, hang it!' Crevel said, taking the lovely Madame Hulot's hands in his and patting them. 'Why do you want two hundred thousand francs from me? What do you want it for? Who needs it?'

'Don't ask me to explain, but give it to me,' she answered. 'You will have saved the lives of three people and our children's honour.'

'And do you believe, my dear little woman,' said Crevel, 'that you could find a single man in Paris ready, at the say-so of a woman half off her head, to go, there and then, and take out of some drawer or other two hundred thousand francs, which are quietly stewing in their own juice there, waiting till she is good enough to come along and lift the gravy? Is that all you know of life and business, my pretty? Your relations are in a very bad way, better send them the Sacraments, for no one in Paris except Her Holiness the Bank, the great and illustrious Nucingen, or a few misers with a kink (as mad about gold as men like us are about a woman), could work a miracle like that. The Civil List, however civil it may be, the Civil List itself would ask you to call back tomorrow. Everybody puts out his money at interest and turns it over as best he can. You're deluding yourself, dear angel, if you imagine that it's King Louis-Philippe that we're ruled by, and he has no illusions himself on that score. He knows, as we all do, that above the Charter there stands the holy, venerable, solid, the adored, gracious, beautiful, noble, ever young, almighty, franc! Now, my fair angel, money calls for interest, and it is for ever busy about gathering it. "God of the Jews, you prevail!" as the great Racine said. In fact, the eternal allegory of the golden calf. Even in the days of Moses they had jobbers in the desert! We have returned to Old Testament ideas. The golden calf was the first great book of the national debt,' he went on. 'You live far too much in the rue Plumet, my Adeline. The Egyptians borrowed enormous sums from the Jews, and it wasn't God's chosen people they ran after, it was cash.'

He looked at the Baroness, and his expression said, 'I hope you admire my cleverness!'

'You don't know how devoted every citizen is to his sacred pile,' he continued, after this pause. 'If you'll pardon me, let me tell you this! Get hold of these facts. You want two hundred thousand francs? ... No one can give you that sort of money without selling capital. Now just reckon it up. To have two hundred thousand francs in ready money you would have to sell investments bringing in an income of about seven thousand francs, at three per cent. Well, you can't have your money in less than two days; you can't do it quicker than that. And if you mean to persuade someone to hand over a fortune, for that's a whole fortune to plenty of people – two hundred thousand francs – you'll certainly have to tell him where it's going, what you want it for. ...'

'It's a question, my kind dear Crevel, of saving the lives of two men, of whom one will die of grief and the other will kill himself! And then it affects me too, for I'll go mad! Perhaps I am a little mad already?'

'Not so mad!' he said, squeezing Madame Hulot's knees. 'Papa Crevel has his price, since you have deigned to think of him, my angel.'

'It seems it's necessary to let my knees be squeezed!' thought the noble saintly woman, burying her face in her hands. 'You offered me a fortune once!' she said, blushing.

'Ah, mother mine, three years ago!' said Crevel. 'Oh! you are more beautiful than ever!' he exclaimed, seizing the Baroness's arm and pressing it against his heart. 'You have a good memory, my child, upon my soul! Well, see how wrong you were to act the prude! Now the three hundred thousand francs that you high-mindedly refused are in another woman's purse. I loved you then and I love you still; but let's carry our minds back to three years ago. When I said to you "I mean to have you!" what was my purpose? I wanted to have my revenge on that blackguard Hulot. Well, your husband, my belle, took a jewel of a woman as his mistress, a pearl, a sly little puss, then aged twenty-three for she's twenty-six now. I thought it would be more comical, more complete, more Louis XV, more Maréchal de Richelieu, more succulent, to steal the charming creature from him, and in any case she never loved Hulot and for the past three years she has been crazy about your humble servant.'

As he said this, Crevel, from whose hands the Baroness had withdrawn her own, struck his pose again. He stuck his thumbs in his armholes and flapped his hands against his chest like a pair of wings, thinking that this made him look desirable and charming. It was a way of saying 'this is the man whom you chucked out!'

'There you are, my dear; I've had my revenge and your husband knows it! I categorically demonstrated to him that he had been made a goose of, properly what you call paid back in his own coin ... Madame Marneffe is *my* mistress, and if our friend Marneffe pops off, she will be my wife.'

Madame Hulot stared at Crevel with fixed distraught eyes.

'Hector knew that!' she said.

'And he went back to her!' Crevel replied. 'I put up with it because Valérie wanted to be the wife of a head clerk, but she swore to me that she would fix things so that our Baron should get such a drubbing that he wouldn't appear again. And my little duchess (for she was born a duchess, that woman, word of honour!) has kept her word. She has given you back your Hector "virtuous in perpetuity" as she said so wittily! He's been taught a good lesson, believe me! The Baron has had some hard knocks; he'll keep no more dancers, nor real ladies either. He's been reformed root and branch, as clean as a whistle, rinsed like a beer-glass. If you had listened to Papa Crevel instead of humiliating him, showing him the door, you would have had four hundred thousand francs, for my revenge has cost me at least that much. But I'll get my money back, I hope, when Marneffe dies ... I have invested in my future wife. That's the secret of my extravagant spending. I have solved the problem of being lordly on the cheap.'

'You would give a step-mother like that to your daughter?' exclaimed Madame Hulot.

'You don't know Valérie, Madame,' replied Crevel solemnly, striking an attitude in his first manner. 'She's a well-born woman, a well-bred woman, and a woman who enjoys the highest public esteem, as well. Why, yesterday the vicar of her parish dined at her house. We have given a magnificent monstrance to the church, for she's devout. Oh! she is clever, she is witty, she's delightful, she knows everything, she has everything. As for me, dear Adeline, I owe everything to that charming woman. She has smartened me up, improved my way of speaking, as you see; she prunes the jokes I crack, gives me words to say, and ideas. I never say anything that's not quite proper any more. One can see great changes in me; you must have noticed it. And what's more too, she has stirred up my ambition. I might be a Deputy and I should not make any bloomers, for I would consult my Egeria about every single thing. All great men in politics, like Numa and our present illustrious Prime Minister, have had their Comical ... Comfortean ... Cumaean Sibyl. Valérie entertains a score of Deputies; she's becoming very influential, and now that she's going to have a charming house and a carriage she'll be one of the secret ruling powers of Paris. She's a famous locomotive, a woman like that! Ah! I have very often thanked you for being so stubborn!'

'It's enough to make one doubt the goodness of God,' said Adeline, whose indignation had dried her tears. 'But no. Divine Justice must surely hover over that head!'

'You don't know the world, fair lady,' retorted Crevel, that great politician, deeply offended. 'The world, my dear Adeline, loves success. Well, look, does it come in search of your sublime virtue, with its price of two hundred thousand francs?'

This shot made Adeline shudder, and she was seized again with her nervous trembling. She understood that the retired perfumer was meanly revenging himself upon her, as he had revenged himself on Hulot. Disgust sickened her, and made her nerves so tense that her throat was constricted and she could not speak.

'Money! ... always money!' she said, at last.

'You certainly made me feel sorry,' Crevel went on, remembering, as he heard the exclamation, this woman's humiliation, 'when I saw you there crying, at my feet! Well, you won't believe me perhaps, but, well, if I'd had my wallet it would have been yours. You really need all that money?'

When she heard the question, big with two hundred thousand francs, Adeline forgot the abominable insults of this fine gentleman on the cheap, seeing the bait of success dangled before her with such Machiavellian cunning by Crevel, whose only motive was to penetrate Adeline's secrets in order to laugh at them with Valérie.

'Oh! I'll do anything!' cried the unfortunate woman. 'Monsieur, I'll sell myself ... I'll become, if need be, a Valérie.'

'You would find it hard to do that,' replied Crevel. 'Valérie is the supreme achievement of her kind. Dear old lady, twenty-five years of virtue are always rather off-putting, like a neglected disease. And your virtue has grown mouldy here, my child. But you are going to see just how fond I am of you. I'm going to arrange for you to have your two hundred thousand francs.'

Adeline seized Crevel's hand, held it, and laid it on her heart, incapable of articulating a word; and her eyelids were wet with tears of joy.

'Oh, wait a minute! It will have to be worked for. I'm a good-natured chap, a fellow who enjoys a good time, with no prejudices, and I'm going to tell you quite plainly just how things are. You want to be like Valérie; well and good. But that's not enough, you need a *gogo*, a sucker, a shareholder, a Hulot. Now, I know a big retired tradesman, a hosier as it happens. He's rather thick-headed and heavy in the hand, and very dull. I'm licking him into shape, and I don't know when he'll be in a state to do me credit. My man is a Deputy, a conceited boring sort of chap, who has been kept buried in the depths of the country by a female tyrant, a kind of virago, and he's a complete greenhorn with regard to the luxury and pleasures of life in Paris. But Beauvisage (he's called Beauvisage) is a millionaire, and he would give, as three years ago I would have given, my child, a hundred thousand crowns to have a lady for his mistress. Yes,' he said, thinking that he had interpreted aright the gesture that Adeline made, 'he is jealous of me, you see! Yes, jealous of my happiness with Madame Marneffe, and the lad is just the fellow to sell a piece of property in order to become proprietor of a ...'

'That's enough, Monsieur Crevel!' said Madame Hulot, no longer dissembling her disgust, and allowing all her shame to be seen on her face. 'I am punished now beyond what my sin deserves. My conscience, that has been so fiercely repressed by necessity's iron hand, cries out to me, at this supreme insult, that such sacrifices are impossible. I have no pride left; I do not blaze with anger against you as I did once before, I shall not say to you "Leave this house!" now that I have been dealt this mortal blow. I have lost the right to do so. I offered myself to you like a prostitute... Yes,' she went on, in answer to his protesting gesture, 'I have defiled my life, that was pure until now, by a vile intention, and ... I have no excuse, I knew what I was doing ... I deserve all the insults that you are heaping upon me! May God's will be done! If he desires the death of two beings worthy to go to him, may they die. I will weep for them. I will pray for their souls. If he wills the humiliation of our family, let us bow under the avenging sword, and kiss it like the Christians we are! I know how I must expiate the shame of a few moments whose memory will afflict me all my remaining days. It is not Madame Hulot, Monsieur, who is speaking to you now, it is the poor humble sinner, the Christian whose heart from now on will hold only one emotion – repentance, and for whom prayer and charity will be her only purpose in life. I can be only the humblest of women and the first among penitents with a sin of such magnitude to atone for. You have been the instrument of my return to reason, to the voice of God that now speaks in me, and I thank you for it!'

She was trembling with the nervous tremor which from that moment was not to leave her again. Her voice was gentle, in contrast with the earlier feverish utterance of a woman resolved on dishonour in order to save her family. The blood left her cheeks, she grew pale, and her eyes were dry.

'I acted my part very badly, in any case, didn't I?' she added, regarding Crevel with the same sweetness that the martyrs must have shown as they looked on the proconsul. 'True love, the holy and devoted love of a wife, offers different pleasures from those that are bought in the market from prostitutes!... Why do I use such words?' she said, reflecting, and taking another step forward on the way of perfection. 'They seem to show a wish to taunt, and I have none at all! Forgive me for them. In any case, Monsieur, it was perhaps only myself that I wanted to hurt. ...'

The majesty of virtue and its celestial light had swept away the fleeting stain upon this woman's purity, and, resplendent in the beauty that was properly her own, she appeared to Crevel to have grown taller. Adeline in that sublime moment resembled those symbolic figures of Religion, upheld by a cross, that we see in the paintings of the early Venetians. She expressed all the magnitude of her misfortune, and all the greatness of the Catholic Church to which she was taking flight for refuge like a wounded dove. Crevel was dazzled, astounded.

'Madame, I will do whatever you wish, without conditions!' he said in an inspired burst of generosity. 'We will look into things, and ... What's to be done? The impossible? Well! I'll do it! I'll deposit securities at the bank, and within two hours you shall have your money. ...'

'Oh God, a miracle!' said poor Adeline, throwing herself upon her knees.

She recited a prayer with a fervour which affected Crevel so powerfully that Madame Hulot saw tears in his eyes when she rose, her prayer ended.

'Be my friend, Monsieur!' she said to him. 'Your heart is better than your conduct and your words suggest. God gave you your heart, and you take your ideas from the world and from your passions! Oh! I will love you sincerely!' she exclaimed, with an angelic ardour which contrasted strangely with her futile attempts at coquetry.

'Don't go on trembling so,' said Crevel.

'Am I trembling?' asked the Baroness, who had not noticed the infirmity that had manifested itself so suddenly.

'Yes. Look here,' said Crevel, taking Adeline's arm and demonstrating its nervous shaking to her. 'Come, Madame,' he continued, with respect, 'keep calm. I'm going to the bank. ...'

'Come back quickly! Just think, my friend,' she said, giving up her secrets, 'it is to prevent my poor Uncle Fischer from suicide, as he has been compromised by my husband. You see I can trust you now and so I am telling you everything! Ah! if we can't raise the money in time, I know what will happen. I know the Marshal – his honour is so sensitive that he would not survive the knowledge of this for more than a day or two.'

'I'm off then,' said Crevel, kissing the Baroness's hand. 'But what has poor Hulot been up to?'

'He has robbed the state!'

'Good God! I'll be quick, Madame. I understand, and I admire you.'

Crevel bent a knee, kissed Madame Hulot's dress, and vanished with the words, 'I'll be back again soon.'

Unfortunately, on his way from the rue Plumet to get his share certificates from his own house, Crevel passed the rue Vanneau, and he could not resist the pleasure of going to see his little duchess. He arrived there with a face still showing traces of emotional storm. He went into Valérie's bedroom, and found her maid doing her hair. She studied Crevel in the glass, and even before hearing anything of the occasion, was shocked, as any woman of her kind would be, to see him showing strong emotion of which she was not the cause.

'What's the matter, my pet?' she asked him. 'Is this the way a man comes into his little duchess's room? I won't be your duchess any more, Monsieur, or even your little ducky darling, you old monster!'

Crevel answered with a sad smile, and a glance at Reine.

'Reine, my girl, that'll do for today. I'll finish my hair myself. Give me my Chinese dressing-gown, for my Monsieur looks as rum as an old Mandarin.'

Reine, a girl with a face pitted like a colander, who seemed to have been created expressly to serve as a foil for Valérie, exchanged a smile with her mistress and brought the dressing-gown. Valérie took off her wrap, under which she was wearing her vest, and slid into the dressing-gown like a snake under its tuft of grass.

'Madame is at home to no one?'

'What a question!' said Valérie. 'Come, tell me, my big pussy, have the railway shares slumped?'

'No.'

'They've raised the price of the house?'

'No.'

'You are afraid that you are not the father of your little Crevel?'

'Rubbish!' Crevel replied, in the full conviction that he was loved.

'Well, really, I'm not playing this game any longer!' said Madame Marneffe. 'When I'm forced to screw his troubles out of a friend like corks out of champagne bottles, I just give up. Go away; you annoy me. . . .'

'It's nothing,' said Crevel. 'I have to find two hundred thousand francs within two hours. . . .'

'Oh, you'll certainly find them! Well, for that matter, I haven't used the fifty thousand francs we got out of Hulot over the police business, and I can ask Henri for fifty thousand!'

'Henri! Always Henri!' said Crevel, with some heat.

'Do you imagine, my green infant Machiavelli, that I would send Henri away? Does France disarm her fleet? . . . Henri is a dagger hanging in its sheath suspended from a nail. That boy acts as a test of whether you love me or not. . . . And you don't love me this morning.'

'I don't love you, Valérie?' said Crevel. 'I love you a million!'

'That's not enough!' she retorted, jumping on to Crevel's knee and hanging on to him with both arms round his neck, like a coat on a coat-peg. 'You have to love me ten millions, all the gold in the world, and more. Henri would never leave me for five minutes in doubt as to what was weighing on his mind! Now, now, what's the matter, my old sweetie? Let's get it off our little chest. . . . Let's tell it all, and smartly too, to our little ducky darling!'

And she brushed Crevel's face with her hair, and nudged the end of his nose.

'How can a man have a nose like this,' she said, 'and keep a secret from his Vava – lélé – ririe!'

'Vava', the nose went to the right; 'lélé', to the left; 'ririe', and she pushed it gently in the centre again.

'Well, I've just seen . . .'

Crevel stopped, and looked at Madame Marneffe.

'Valérie, my jewel, do you promise me on your honour . . .

313

you know, our honour, not to repeat a word of what I'm going to tell you?'

'Agreed, Mayor! We raise our right hand so, look! ... And our foot as well!'

She struck a pose in a fashion that was enough to lay Crevel wide open, as Rabelais put it, from his brain to his heels; she was so funny and so bewitching, with her bare flesh visible through the mist of fine lawn.

'I have just seen virtue in despair!'

'Is there any virtue in despair?' she inquired, shaking her head and crossing her arms like Napoleon.

'It's poor Madame Hulot. She has to have two hundred thousand francs! Otherwise the Marshal and old Fischer will blow their brains out; and because you are a little the cause of all that, my little duchess, I'm going to mend the damage. Oh! she's a saint of a woman. I know her; she'll pay it all back.'

At the name 'Hulot', and mention of two hundred thousand francs, Valérie flashed a look between her long lashes, like the flash of a cannon amidst its smoke.

'What did the old lady do to get round you? She showed you what? Her religion?'

'Don't jeer at her, sweetheart; she's a truly saintly, very noble, very devout woman, and she deserves respect!'

'And so I don't deserve respect, don't I?' said Valérie, giving Crevel an ominous look.

'I don't say that,' replied Crevel, understanding how painful the praise of virtue must be to Madame Marneffe.

'I'm a devout woman too,' said Valérie, moving away and sitting down by herself; 'but I don't make a show of my religion. I go to church without parading the fact.'

She sat in silence, taking no further notice of Crevel. Much perturbed, he went and stood before the chair Valérie had buried herself in; but she was lost in the thoughts that he had so foolishly aroused.

'Valérie, my little angel ...!'

Profound silence. An exceedingly problematical tear was furtively wiped away.

'Say just one word, my darling duck . . .'

'Monsieur!'

'What are you thinking about, my precious?'

'Ah, Monsieur Crevel, I was thinking about the day of my first Communion! How lovely I was! How pure and saintly! Immaculate! Ah, if anyone had said to my mother: "Your daughter will be a *kept woman*; she will deceive her husband. One day a police officer will find her in a little house. She will sell herself to a Crevel in order to betray a Hulot, two horrid old men . . ." Oh, horrible! . . . Why, she would have died before the end of the sentence, she loved me so much, poor woman. . . .'

'Don't upset yourself like this!'

'You don't know how much a woman must love a man to silence the pangs of remorse that gnaw an adulterous heart. I'm sorry Reine has gone; she could have told you how she found me in tears this morning, on my knees, praying. I'm not a person, you must understand, Monsieur Crevel, who scoffs at religion. Have you ever heard me say a single wrong word on the subject?'

Crevel shook his head.

'I never allow people to talk about it in my presence. I'll make fun of anything you like: royalty, or politics, or money, everything that the world holds sacred: judges, marriage, love, young girls, old men! But not the Church! Not God! Oh, there I draw the line! I know very well that I am doing wrong, that I am sacrificing my future happiness for you. . . . And you haven't the faintest idea of what my love for you involves!'

Crevel clasped his hands.

'Ah! you would have to see into my heart, see how truly and deeply I believe, to be able to understand all I am sacrificing for you! I feel that I have in me the stuff of which a Magdalen is made. And you know what respect I show to priests! Just think of the presents I give to the Church! My mother brought me up in the Catholic faith, and I am conscious of God! It is to wrongdoers like us that he speaks most terribly.'

Valérie wiped away two tears that rolled down her cheeks. Crevel was aghast. Madame Marneffe rose to her full height, in a state of exaltation.

'Keep calm, my ducky darling! You frighten me!'

Madame Marneffe sank to her knees.

'I am not really wicked, O God!' she said, clasping her hands. 'Deign to gather in your wandering lamb. Beat and punish her to bring her back from the hands that make her a byword and adulteress, and with what joy she will hide her head upon your shoulder! How gladly she will return to the fold!'

She rose, and gazed at Crevel, and Crevel was appalled to see her wide-eyed blank stare.

'And sometimes, Crevel, do you know, I'm sometimes afraid. God's justice is effective in this world as well as in the next. What good can I hope for from God? His vengeance falls upon the guilty in every kind of way; it takes every form of ill fortune. All the misfortunes that foolish people find impossible to explain are an expiation of sin. That is what my mother told me on her death-bed, speaking of her old age. And if I were to lose you! ...' she added, hugging Crevel close in a frantic clasp. 'Ah! I should die!'

Madame Marneffe released Crevel, fell on her knees again before her chair, clasped her hands (and in what a ravishing pose!), and with unbelievable fervour recited the following prayer:

'And oh, St Valérie, my kind patron saint, why do you not come more often to visit the pillow of the child entrusted to your care? Oh, come this night as you came this morning, inspire me with good thoughts and I will leave the way of wickedness. I will renounce, like Magdalen, deceptive joys, the deluding glamour of the world, renounce even the one I love so much!'

'My darling duck!' said Crevel.

'No longer a darling duck, Monsieur!'

She turned her head proudly, like a virtuous wife; and with her eyes full of tears still looked dignified, cold, indifferent.

'Leave me,' she said, repulsing Crevel. 'Where lies my

duty? It is to be my husband's. That husband is a dying man, and what do I do? I deceive him on the very verge of the tomb! He believes your son is his. ... I shall tell him the truth, begin by begging his forgiveness and then ask for God's. We must part! Adieu, Monsieur Crevel!' and, rising, she held out a glacial hand. 'Good-bye, my friend; we shall meet again only in a better world. You owe some happiness to me, very sinful happiness, but now I want ... yes, I mean to have, your respect.'

Crevel was weeping bitter tears.

'Why, you great donkey!' she exclaimed, with a peal of diabolical laughter. 'That's the method pious women use to diddle you out of two hundred thousand francs! You talk about Maréchal de Richelieu, the original of Lovelace, and you let yourself be taken in by that tired old confidence trick, as Steinbock would call it. I could soon part you from two hundred thousand francs, if I wanted to, you great idiot! Just keep your money! If you have too much, it belongs to me! If you give two sous to that worthy dame who has taken up religion because she is fifty-seven years old, you'll never see me again, and you can have her as your mistress. You'll come back to me next morning all black and blue from her bony caresses, and saturated with her tears, and sick of her provincial little bonnets and her weeping and wailing that must make the recipient of her favours feel as if he were out in a rain-storm!'

'It's true enough,' said Crevel, 'that two hundred thousand francs – well, it's a lot of money. ...'

'Pious women open their mouths wide! Ah, it seems to me, they can sell their sermons at a better price than we can sell the most precious and most certain thing on earth – pleasure. ... And what yarns they can tell! It's incredible! Ah, I know them. I have seen them at my mother's. They think it right to go to any lengths for the sake of the Church, for ... Well, really, you ought to be ashamed of yourself, my pet – you who aren't an open-handed man at all. Why, you haven't given *me* two hundred thousand francs, all told!'

'Oh, indeed I have,' protested Crevel. 'The little house alone will cost that. ...'

'So you must have four hundred thousand francs?' she said reflectively.

'No.'

'Well then, Monsieur, you were going to lend the twc hundred thousand francs for my house to that old horror? That's high treason against your darling duck!'

'But, just listen to me!'

'If you were giving that money to some silly philanthropic scheme, you would be accepted as a coming man,' she said, warming to her theme, 'and I would be the first to urge you to do it; because, after all, you are too simple to write big books about politics to make a reputation for yourself, and you haven't a good enough style to cook up those long-winded pamphlets. You might be able to set yourself up in the way other people in your position have done, advertise yourself and write your name big, in gold letters, by leading some cause or other, social, moral, national, or what not. ... Relief Committees – that's no good; nobody thinks much of them nowadays. Young criminals saved from a life of crime and given a better chance than the poor honest devils – that's hackneyed too. For two hundred thousand francs I would like you to think up something more difficult, something really worth while. Then you would be talked about as another Edme Champion,* or a Montyon,* and I should be proud of you! But to throw two hundred thousand francs into a stoup of holy water, lend it to a religious fanatic deserted by her husband for whatever reason you like – you needn't tell me there isn't always a reason (does anyone desert me?) – that's an idiotic notion that only an ex-perfumer's noddle would think up nowadays! It smells of the shop counter. Two days after doing it you wouldn't dare to look at your face in the glass! Go away and deposit the money for the house quick, for I won't let you in here again without the receipt! Go now, at once, and be quick about it!'

She pushed Crevel out of her room by the shoulders, having seen the flame of ambition re-kindle in his face. When the outer door had closed behind him, she said:

'And there goes Lisbeth's revenge, heaped up and running

*Famous philanthropists.

over! What a pity she's at her old Marshal's! How we would
have laughed! So the old lady would like to take the bread
out of my mouth, would she? ... That'll shake her!'

*

It was necessary for Marshal Hulot to live in a style befitting
his high military rank, and he had taken a fine house in the
rue du Montparnasse, in which there are two or three princely
residences. Although he rented the whole house, he occupied
only the ground floor. When Lisbeth came to keep house for
him, she immediately wanted to let the first floor. That, as she
said, would pay for the whole place, so that the Count would
be able to live almost rent free; but the old soldier refused to
allow it.

In the past few months, sad thoughts had troubled the
Marshal. He had remarked his sister-in-law's poverty, and
was aware of her deep distress, although he had no knowledge
of the cause. The deaf old man, who had been so gay in his
deafness, became taciturn. He had it in mind that his house
might one day be a refuge for Baroness Hulot and her
daughter, and so he was keeping the first floor for them.

It was so well known that the Count de Forzheim had only
very modest means of his own that the Minister of War, Prince
de Wissembourg, had insisted on his old comrade's accepting a
grant of money for the furnishing of his house. Hulot had used
this money to furnish the ground floor fittingly, for, as he
himself put it, he had not accepted a Marshal's baton in order
to treat it as if it were not worth a brass farthing. The house
had belonged to a Senator under the Empire, and the ground
floor reception rooms had been decorated with great splendour for him, all in white and gold, with carved panelling;
they were in a very good state of preservation. The Marshal
had put in suitable good old furniture. He kept a carriage in
the coachhouse, with the two crossed batons painted on the
panels, and hired horses when he had to go anywhere *in
fiocchi*, in style, to the Minister's or the Palace, for some ceremony or reception. For the last thirty years he had had an
old soldier, now aged sixty, for his servant, whose sister was
his cook, and so he was able to save something like ten

thousand francs, and add it to a little nest-egg destined for Hortense.

Every day the old man walked along the boulevard from the rue du Montparnasse to rue Plumet; and no old pensioner from the Invalides, seeing him coming, ever failed to stand at attention and salute him, and be rewarded by the Marshal's smile.

'Who's that you come to attention for?' a young workman asked an old pensioner, a captain from the Invalides, one day.

'I'll tell you the story, boy,' the officer answered, and the 'boy' leaned back against the wall, as if resigning himself to listen to a garrulous old man.

'In 1809,' said the pensioner, 'we were covering the flank of the Grande Armée, marching on Vienna, under the command of the Emperor. We came upon a bridge defended by three batteries disposed one above the other on a projecting rocky cliff, like three redoubts, enfilading the bridge. We were commanded by Marshal Masséna. The man you see there was then Colonel of the Grenadier Guards, and I was one of them. . . . Our columns held one bank of the river; the batteries were on the other. Three times they attacked the bridge, and three times they were driven back. "Go and fetch Hulot!" the Marshal said. "No one but him and his men can make mincemeat of that mouthful!" So we marched up. The General who was pulling out of the last attack on the bridge stopped Hulot under fire to tell him what he should do, and he was blocking our way. "I don't need advice, but room to pass," our Colonel said coolly, going on to reach the bridge at the head of his men. And then -rrrattle! Booooom! Thirty guns letting fly at us!'

'Ah! by gosh!' exclaimed the workman. 'That must have brought out some of these crutches!'

'If you had heard him calmly making that remark, my boy, you would bow down to the ground before a man like that! It's not so famous as the bridge of Arcoli, but it was perhaps even finer. So we followed Hulot at the double right up to those batteries. All honour to those who did not return!' said the officer, raising his cap. 'The *kaiserlicks* were knocked out by that stroke. And so the Emperor made that veteran there a

Count – he honoured us all when he honoured our leader; and these new fellows were quite right to make him a Marshal in the end.'

'Long live the Marshal!' said the workman.

'Oh, you had better shout! The sound of gunfire has made the Marshal deaf.'

This anecdote may serve to show the respect in which the disabled pensioners held Marshal Hulot, whose unchanging Republican views, moreover, won popular affection for him in the whole neighbourhood.

It was a desolating sight to see suffering enter such a serene, pure, noble soul. The Baroness could only lie, and use all her feminine tact and skill to hide the whole dreadful truth from her brother-in-law. In the course of that disastrous morning, the Marshal, who like all old men slept little, had extracted the truth from Lisbeth about his brother's situation, promising to marry her as the price of her indiscretion. The old maid's pleasure at having confidences drawn from her, which since she entered the house she had been longing to make to her intended husband, may be imagined; for in this way she made her marriage more certain.

'Your brother is incorrigible!' shouted Lisbeth in the Marshal's good ear. Her loud clear peasant's voice made it possible for her to talk to the old man. And she strained her lungs, she was so anxious to demonstrate to her future husband that he would never be deaf to her.

'He has had three mistresses,' the old man said, 'and his wife is an Adeline! ... Poor Adeline!'

'If you take my advice,' shouted Lisbeth, 'you will use your influence with Prince de Wissembourg to find some suitable employment for my cousin. She will need it, for the Baron's salary has a claim against it for three years.'

'I'll go to the Ministry,' he replied, 'and see the Marshal, find out what he thinks of my brother, and ask him if he can do something for my sister. Try to think of some employment worthy of her.'

'The Charitable Association of Ladies of Paris has created a number of benevolent societies under the patronage of the Archbishop, and they need inspectors, who are quite well paid, to sift the genuinely needy cases. Duties of that kind would suit dear Adeline; it would be work after her own heart.'

'Order the horses,' said the Marshal. 'I'm going to dress. I'll go to Neuilly, if need be!'

'How fond he is of her! I must needs find her always in the way, wherever I go!' said Lisbeth.

Lisbeth already was the boss of that household, but behind the Marshal's back. The three servants had been intimidated and put in their places. She had engaged a personal maid, and found an outlet for her unused energy in holding all the strings in her hands, poking her nose into everything, and making it her business to see to the well-being of her dear Marshal in every possible way. Being just as Republican as her future husband, Lisbeth pleased him greatly by her democratic ideas. She flattered him, besides, with immense skill; and in the past fortnight, the Marshal, living in greater comfort and taken care of like a child by its mother, had begun to regard Lisbeth as an ideal partner.

'My dear Marshal,' she shouted, accompanying him to the steps, 'put up the windows; don't sit in a draught. Please do this, for my sake!'

The Marshal, an old bachelor who had never had any coddling in his life, went off smiling at Lisbeth, in spite of his distressed heart.

At that very moment Baron Hulot was leaving the War Office on his way to see Maréchal Prince de Wissembourg, who had sent for him. Although there was nothing unusual in the Minister's sending for one of his Directors, Hulot's conscience was so tender that he imagined something sinister and cold in Mitouflet's face.

'How is the Prince, Mitouflet?' he asked, closing his office door and overtaking the messenger, who had gone ahead.

'He must have a bone to pick with you, Monsieur le Baron,' replied the messenger, 'because his voice, his eyes, his face are set stormy.'

Hulot turned ghastly pale and said no more. He crossed the hall, the various reception rooms, and with a fast-beating heart reached the Minister's door.

The Marshal, then aged seventy, had the pure white hair and the weather-beaten skin to be expected in a veteran of his age, and a charming broad forehead of such amplitude that to the imaginative it seemed to extend like a battlefield. Under that snow-capped hoary cupola, in the shadow of very bony projecting eye-sockets, shone eyes of a Napoleonic blue, usually sad in expression, full of bitter thoughts and regrets. This rival of Bernadotte's had hoped to attain a throne. But those eyes could flash formidable lightning when animated by strong feeling, and then his voice, always deep, rang out stridently. In anger, the Prince was a soldier again; he spoke the language of Sub-Lieutenant Cottin; he spared no one's feelings. Hulot d'Ervy found this old lion, his hair shaken back like a mane, standing frowning with his back to the fireplace, his eyes remote, apparently lost in abstraction.

'You sent for me, Prince?' Hulot said deferentially, affecting nonchalance.

The Marshal kept his eyes fixed on the Director, in silence, during the time he took to walk towards him from the door. This oppressive stare was like the eye of God. Hulot did not sustain it; he lowered his eyes in embarrassment.

'He knows everything,' he told himself.

'Has your conscience nothing to say to you?' asked the Marshal in his grave deep voice.

'It tells me that I was probably wrong, Prince, to have levies made in Algeria without referring the matter to you. After forty-five years of service, at my age and with my tastes, I have no private fortune. You know the principles that guide the four hundred elected representatives of France. Those gentlemen are envious of anyone holding a high position. They have cut Ministers' salaries – that's typical! ... Is it possible to ask them for money for an old servant of the state? ... What are we to expect from people who pay judges and magistrates so badly? They give the dock labourers of Toulon thirty sous a day, when it is a physical impossibility for a family to exist on less than forty, and it never occurs to them that it's outrageous to pay clerks in Paris no more than six hundred or ten or twelve hundred francs! They want our places themselves when the salary amounts to forty thousand francs! And those are the people who now refuse to restore to the Crown a piece of property confiscated from the Crown in 1830, one Louis XVI bought from his privy purse, moreover, when they are asked for it on behalf of an impoverished Prince! . . . If you had not a fortune of your own, Prince, they might well have left you, like my brother, high and dry with nothing but your salary, never remembering that you saved the Grande Armée (and I was there) in the swampy wastes of Poland.'

'You have robbed the state! You have made yourself liable to be tried in the law-courts,' said the Marshal, 'like that clerk in the Treasury! And you treat the matter so lightly, Monsieur?'

'Oh, but there's a great difference, Monseigneur!' exclaimed Baron Hulot. 'Have I dipped my hands in a cash-box entrusted to me? . . .'

'When a man in your position commits a vile crime like this,' said the Marshal, 'he doubles the crime by acting with blundering clumsiness. You have disgracefully compromised our administration, which until now had the cleanest hands in Europe! And that, Monsieur, for two hundred thousand francs for a whore!' said the Marshal in a terrible voice. 'You are a Councillor of State, and the punishment of an ordinary soldier who sells regimental property is death. Colonel Pourin, of the Second Lancers, once told me this story. At Saverne, one of his men fell in love with a little Alsatian girl who wanted him to give her a shawl. The hussy made so much fuss about it that the poor devil, who was about to be promoted to quartermaster after twenty years' service, and was respected by the whole regiment, sold some things belonging to his company to get the shawl. Do you know what that lancer did, Baron d'Ervy? He ground up glass from a window and swallowed it, and died in hospital eleven hours later. . . . Try, you, to die of a stroke, so that we can save your honour. . . '

The Baron looked at the old soldier with haggard eyes, and as the Marshal saw his expression, which betrayed the coward, colour rose to the old man's cheeks and his eyes blazed.

'Would you fail me? . . .' stammered Hulot.

At that moment, Marshal Hulot, who had been told that his brother was alone with the Minister, ventured to enter the room, and, in the manner of deaf men, walked right up to the Prince.

'Oh!' cried the hero of the Polish campaign. 'I know what you have come for, my old comrade! But it is quite useless!'

'Useless?' repeated Marshal Hulot, hearing only that word.

'Yes, you have come to speak on behalf of your brother; but do you know what your brother is?'

'My brother?' said the deaf man.

'Yes,' shouted the Marshal, 'your brother is a dastardly scoundrel, utterly unworthy of you!'

And in his wrath the Marshal's eyes flashed fulgurating glances, like those looks with which Napoleon broke men's wills and nerve.

'You lie, Cottin!' returned Marshal Hulot, ashen pale. 'Throw down your baton as I throw down mine! I am at your service.'

The Prince went up to his old comrade, looked straight into his eyes, and as he clasped his hand, said in his ear:

'Are you a man?'

'You shall see. . . .'

'Well, stand firm! You have to bear the worst disaster that could befall you.'

The Prince turned, took a file of documents from the table and put it in Marshal Hulot's hands, crying:

'Read this!'

The Comte de Forzheim read the following letter from the top of the file:

To His Excellency the President of the Council

Confidential

Algiers

My dear Prince,

We have a very bad business on our hands, as you will see from the accompanying papers.

Briefly, the matter is this: Baron Hulot d'Ervy sent one of his uncles into the province of Oran in order to make purchases of grain and forage as a speculation, with a storekeeper as accomplice. The storekeeper gave away certain information in order to save his own skin, and has since escaped. The Public Prosecutor handled the affair summarily, thinking it involved two minor officials only; but Johann Fischer, your Director general's uncle, finding himself about to be brought before a court, stabbed himself fatally with a nail, in prison.

That would have been the end of the matter, if this worthy and honourable man, who was apparently betrayed by both his accomplice and his nephew, had not taken it into his head to write to Baron Hulot. This letter, seized by the police, startled the Public Prosecutor so much that he came to see me. It would be such a terrible thing to arrest and try a Councillor of State, a Director general with such a long record of loyal service (for he saved us all after Beresina by his reorganization of the administration), that I had the papers sent to me.

Must we let the affair take its course? Or should we, as the apparent chief culprit is dead, kill the case, after sentencing the storekeeper in default?

The papers are sent to you by permission of the Attorney General; and as Baron d'Ervy is domiciled in Paris, proceedings will be within the competence of your superior court. We have found this, rather backstairs, means of disposing of the problem for the moment.

Only, my dear Marshal, act quickly. This deplorable affair is being far too much talked about already, and it will do twice as much damage if the complicity of the eminent man chiefly concerned, which at present is known only to the Public Prosecutor, the examining judge, the Attorney General, and me, should leak out.

There, the paper fell from Marshal Hulot's fingers. He looked at his brother, and saw that there was no need to examine the documents; but he looked for Johann Fischer's letter, and held it out to him after scanning it rapidly.

From Oran Prison

Dear Nephew,

When you read this letter, I shall no longer be alive.

Set your mind at rest; nothing will be found to implicate you. With me dead, and your Jesuit Chardin escaped, the case will be stopped. When I think of the happiness of our Adeline's face, that we owe to you, I feel that it is very easy to die. It is unnecessary, now, to send the two hundred thousand francs. Farewell.

This letter will reach you through a prisoner whom I believe I can trust. JOHANN FISCHER

'I make my apologies to Your Excellency,' Marshal Hulot said to Prince de Wissembourg, with a pathetic pride.

'Come, don't be ceremonious with me, Hulot,' the Minister replied, grasping his old friend's hand. 'It was only himself that the poor lancer killed,' he said, with a withering look at Hulot d'Ervy.

'How much did you take?' Count de Forzheim said sternly to his brother.

'Two hundred thousand francs.'

'My dear friend,' said the Count, addressing the Minister, 'you shall have the two hundred thousand francs within forty-eight hours. It shall never be said that a man bearing the name of Hulot defrauded the state of a sou.'

'What nonsense!' said the Marshal. 'I know where those two hundred thousand francs are, and I'll have them returned. Send in your resignation and apply for your pension!' he added, tossing a double sheet of foolscap in the direction of the Councillor of State, who, his legs giving way beneath him, had sat down at the table. 'Proceedings against you would disgrace us all, so I have obtained the consent of the Council of Ministers to taking this course. Since you accept life without honour, without my esteem, can consent to exist in degradation, you shall have the pension that you are entitled to. Only, see to it that you are soon forgotten.'

The Marshal rang.

'Is the clerk Marneffe there?'

'Yes, Monseigneur,' said the attendant.

'Send him in.'

'You and your wife,' exclaimed the Minister, when Marneffe appeared, 'have deliberately ruined the Baron d'Ervy, whom you see here.'

'Monsieur le Ministre, I beg your pardon, we are very poor. I have only my salary to live on, and I have two children, of whom the one that is to come has been put in my family by Monsieur le Baron.'

'What a rascally face!' said the Prince to Marshal Hulot, indicating Marneffe. 'That's enough of this Sganarelle* talk,'

*Name of several Molière characters, but especially the hero of *Le Médecin malgré lui*.

he answered the man. 'You must return two hundred thousand francs, or you will go to Algeria.'

'But, Monsieur le Ministre, you don't know my wife; she has squandered everything. Monsieur le Baron invited six people to dinner every day. ... Fifty thousand francs were spent in my house every year.'

'Leave the room!' thundered the Minister in the voice that once cried the *Charge* at the height of battles. 'You will receive notice of your transfer within two hours. ... Go!'

'I prefer to hand in my resignation,' said Marneffe insolently. 'It's a bit too thick to stand in my shoes and be bullied into the bargain; it's not to my taste at all!'

And he left the room.

'What an impudent rogue!' said the Prince.

Marshal Hulot, who during this scene had stood motionless, pale as death, turning his eyes from time to time as if impelled to scrutinize his brother's face, came forward to shake the Prince's hand, saying:

'Within forty-eight hours reparation shall be made for the loss of the money; but as for honour! ... Farewell, Marshal! The last blow is the one that kills. ... Yes, I shall not survive it,' he said quietly.

'Why the devil did you have to come this morning?' the Prince said with some feeling.

'I came for his wife's sake,' the Count replied, with a glance at Hector. 'She has no means of livelihood ... especially after this.'

'He has his pension.'

'He has borrowed money on it.'

'He must have the devil in him!' said the Prince, with a shrug. 'What philtre do these women make you swallow to take away your wits?' he demanded of Hulot d'Ervy. 'How could you, who know the meticulous exactness with which the French administration writes everything down, makes out endless reports about every detail, covers reams of paper recording the outlay or receipt of a few centimes, you who used to complain that hundreds of signatures were needed for the most trivial transactions – to discharge a soldier, to buy a curry-comb – how could you hope to conceal theft for long?

And what about the Press? And people who covet your place? And others who would like to steal too? Do these women rob you of ordinary common sense? Have they put blinkers on your eyes? Or are you made of different stuff from the rest of us? You should have given up administration as soon as you became not a man but a temperament! If you can add such utter blind folly to your crime, you will end up ... I would rather not say where. ...'

'Promise me to do something for her, Cottin!' said Count de Forzheim, hearing nothing and thinking only of his sister-in-law.

'Set your mind at rest about that!' said the Minister.

'Thank you, then, and good-bye! – Come, sir,' he said to his brother.

The Prince considered the two brothers with apparent detachment, two so dissimilar in attitude, in essential structure, in character: the brave man and the coward, the sensualist and the self-disciplined, the honest man and the peculator, and he said to himself:

'This coward will not know how to die! And my poor Hulot, so upright, has death in his knapsack!'

He sat down at his table and took up the reading of the dispatches from Africa again, with a gesture which expressed both a soldier's nonchalance and the profound compassion that the sight of battlefields makes part of his nature. For, in fact, no one is more humane than the soldier, to all appearance so tough, and trained by war to possess the icy cold inflexibility indispensable on the battlefield.

On the following day several newspapers carried these items of news under various headlines:

Monsieur le Baron Hulot d'Ervy has requested permission to send in his resignation. The irregularities in the books of the Algerian Administration, recently brought to light by the death and flight respectively of two officials, have influenced this highly placed administrator's decision. Learning of the crimes committed by these employees, in whom he had had the ill-fortune to place some trust, Monsieur le Baron was stricken with a seizure in the War Minister's office.

Monsieur Hulot d'Ervy, brother of the Marshal, has completed forty-five years of service. His decision, which he cannot be persuaded to alter, has been received with regret by all who know Monsieur Hulot, whose qualities in private life are no less outstanding than his talents as an administrator. No one will have forgotten the devotion of the Commissary general of the Imperial Guard at Warsaw, nor the energy and skill with which he organized the supply services of the army raised in 1815 by Napoleon.

Yet another of the notable figures of the Empire is about to pass from the scene. Since 1830, Monsieur le Baron Hulot has been one of the unfailing, indispensable lights of the Council of State and the War Office.

Algiers: The affair referred to as the forage scandal, which has been absurdly inflated in certain newspapers, is now brought to a close by the death of the chief culprit. The man Johann Wisch has committed suicide in prison, and his accomplice is in hiding, but the charges against him will be heard in his absence.

Wisch, a former army contractor, was an honest man, greatly respected, who did not survive the knowledge that he had been duped by Chardin, the storekeeper who has absconded.

And in the Paris news there was this:

The Minister of War, in order to prevent any future irregularity, has decided to create a commissariat department in Africa. It is reported that Monsieur Marneffe, a senior clerk, is to be placed in charge of this organization.

The question of who is to succeed Baron Hulot is exercising many ambitious minds. We hear that this Directorship has been offered to Comte Martial de la Roche-Hugon, the Deputy, who is brother-in-law to Comte de Rastignac. Monsieur Massol, Master of Requests, is to be appointed Councillor of State, according to report, and Monsieur Claude Vignon may become Master of Requests.

Of all the kinds of political rumours the most full of pitfalls for opposition newspapers is the official rumour. However wary journalists may be, the skilful leakage of news may make them the acquiescent or unconscious mouthpieces of men like Claude Vignon who have left journalism for the higher spheres of politics. It takes a journalist to make use of a journal for an undisclosed purpose. So, to misquote Voltaire, we may say:

The people vainly take the Paris news for truth.

*

Marshal Hulot drove home with his brother, the Baron sitting in front, respectfully leaving the elder brother alone inside the carriage. The two brothers did not exchange a word. Hector was shattered. The Marshal remained absorbed in his own thoughts, like a man putting forth all his strength, concentrating all his forces, to hold up a crushing weight. When they reached his house, the Marshal, without speaking, imperatively motioned the Baron to his study. The Count had been presented by the Emperor Napoleon with a magnificent pair of pistols of Versailles workmanship. He took the box, engraved with the inscription 'Presented by the Emperor Napoleon to General Hulot', from his desk, laid it in full view, and indicating it to his brother said:

'There is your medicine.'

Lisbeth, who was watching through the half-open door, ran to the carriage and ordered the coachman to take her at top speed to the rue Plumet. Within about twenty minutes she returned with the Baroness, whom she had told of the Marshal's threat to his brother.

The Count, without a glance at his brother, rang for his factotum, the old soldier who had served him for thirty years.

'Beau-Pied,' he said, 'fetch my lawyer and Count Steinbock, my niece Hortense, and the Treasury stockbroker. It is half past ten now – I want them all here by twelve o'clock. Go by cab ... and go faster than that! ...' he said, reverting to a Republican expression that had been often on his lips in earlier days. And the lines of his face hardened into the awe-inspiring frown that his soldiers had known and respected when he was searching the furze thickets of Brittany in 1799 [see *Les Chouans*].

'As you command, Marshal,' said Beau-Pied, saluting.

Ignoring his brother, the old man returned to his study, took a key from his writing-desk and opened a malachite cash-box mounted in steel, the gift of the Emperor Alexander. By the Emperor Napoleon's orders, he had gone to return to the Russian Emperor personal effects taken at the battle of Dresden, in exchange for which Napoleon was hoping to get Vandamme. The Czar had presented this splendid gift to

General Hulot in acknowledgement of his services, telling him that he hoped one day to be in a position to render a similar courtesy to the French Emperor; but he kept Vandamme. The imperial arms of Russia were inlaid in gold on the cover of the box, which was richly ornamented with gold. The Marshal counted the notes and gold coins it contained. He had a hundred and fifty-two thousand francs, and he nodded as if satisfied.

At that moment Madame Hulot appeared, in a state that would have melted the heart of the most case-hardened judge. She threw herself into Hulot's arms, looking frantically from the case of pistols to the Marshal and back at the pistols again.

'What have you against your brother? What has my husband done to you?' she said, in such a ringing voice that the Marshal heard her.

"He has cast dishonour upon us all!' said the old Republican soldier, with an effort that reopened one of his old wounds. 'He has embezzled from the state! He has made my name hateful to me; he makes me long for death, he has killed me. ... I only live now to make restitution. ... I have been humiliated before the Condé of the Republic, the man I most venerate, to whom I unjustly gave the lie, the Prince de Wissembourg! Is all that nothing? That is how his account stands with his country!'

He wiped away a tear.

'And now for his account with his family!' he went on. 'He robs you of the bread that I was keeping for you, the fruit of thirty years of saving, the money hoarded through an old soldier's life of privation! This was meant for you!' he said, pointing to the notes. 'He has killed your Uncle Fischer, a noble and worthy son of Alsace, a working man who could not bear, as he can, the thought of a stain on his name. And that is not all. God in his wonderful mercy allowed him to choose an angel among women! He had the ineffable good fortune to marry an Adeline! And he has betrayed her, filled her cup with sorrow, left her for harlots, strumpets, dancers, actresses, Cadines, Joséphas, Marneffes! ... And this is the man whom I made my son, my pride! ... Go, wretched man, if you can accept the life you have disgraced! Leave this house! I have not the strength to curse a brother whom I have loved so dearly; I am as weak where he is concerned as you are, Adeline; but let me never see his face again. I forbid him to attend my funeral, to follow my coffin. Let him at least bear the shame of his crime, if he feels no remorse!'

The Marshal, who had turned ghastly pale, sank back on the sofa, exhausted, after these solemn words. And for the first time in his life, perhaps, tears fell from his eyes and traced furrows down his cheeks.

'Poor Uncle Fischer!' exclaimed Lisbeth, putting her handkerchief to her eyes.

'My brother!' said Adeline, kneeling at the Marshal's feet. 'Live for my sake! Help me in the task that I must undertake, to reconcile Hector with life, to make him atone for his crimes!'

'Make him atone?' said the Marshal. 'If he lives, he has not reached the end of his crimes! A man who could not appreciate an Adeline, who has destroyed in his own soul the feelings of a true Republican, that love of his country, his family, and the unfortunate, that I tried to inculcate in him – such a man is a monster, not a human being. ... Take him away if you still love him, for I hear a voice within me crying to me to load my pistols and blow his brains out! By killing him I should save you all, and I should save him from himself.'

The old Marshal rose with such a menacing gesture that poor Adeline exclaimed:

'Come, Hector!'

She seized her husband's arm, drew him with her and left the house, supporting the Baron, for he was in such a state of collapse that she had to put him into a cab to get him to the rue Plumet, where he took to his bed. Utterly broken, he remained there for several days, refusing all food, saying nothing. Then by dint of tears Adeline persuaded him to swallow some broth. She watched over him, sitting by his bed, no longer feeling, of all the emotions that had once filled her heart, anything but profound pity.

At half past twelve Lisbeth showed the lawyer and Count Steinbock into her dear Marshal's study, where she had stayed with him, in great alarm at the change visibly taking place in him.

'Monsieur le Comte,' said the Marshal, 'I ask you to sign an authorization which would enable my niece, your wife, to sell a bond for certain stock of which she at present possesses only the capital. Mademoiselle Fischer, you will consent to this sale, giving up the interest you receive.'

'Yes, dear Count,' said Lisbeth, without hesitating.

'Good, my dear,' said the old soldier. 'I hope I shall live long enough to recompense you. I had no doubt of your agreement. You are a true Republican, a woman of the people.'

He took the old maid's hand, and kissed it.

'Monsieur Hannequin,' he said to the lawyer, 'draw up the necessary document for the sale by power of attorney, and let me have it here by two o'clock, so that the stock may be sold on the Bourse today. My niece, the Countess, holds the certificates. She will be here presently, and will sign the power of attorney when you bring it, and so will Mademoiselle. Monsieur le Comte will go back with you and give you his signature in your office.'

The artist, at a sign from Lisbeth, bowed respectfully to the Marshal and left the room.

Next morning, at ten o'clock, Count de Forzheim sent in his name to Prince de Wissembourg, and was at once admitted.

'Well, my dear Hulot,' said Marshal Cottin, holding out newspapers to his old friend, 'we have saved appearances, you see. ... Read this.'

Marshal Hulot laid down the newspapers on his old comrade's desk, and handed him two hundred thousand francs.

'This is the sum that my brother took from the state,' he said.

'But this is folly!' exclaimed the Minister. 'It's not possible,' he added, speaking into the ear-trumpet that the Marshal held out towards him, 'for us to arrange the restitution of this money. We should be obliged to admit your brother's peculation, and we have done everything possible to cover it. ...'

'Do what you like with it; but I do not wish the Hulot family to hold one farthing that has been stolen from the state,' said the Count.

'I'll lay the matter before the King. We need say no more about it,' replied the Minister, realizing the impossibility of overcoming the old man's sublime determined obstinacy.

'Good-bye, Cottin,' said the old man, taking Prince de Wissembourg's hand. 'I feel as if my soul were frozen. . . .'

Then when he had taken a step towards the door, he turned again, and gazed at the Prince, whom he saw to be deeply moved; he opened his arms to clasp him, and the two old soldiers embraced each other.

'It seems to me,' he said, 'that I am saying good-bye to the whole Grand Army in your person. . . .'

'Good-bye then, my dear old comrade!' said the Minister.

'Yes, it is good-bye indeed, for I am going the way of all those soldiers of ours whom we have mourned. . . .'

As he finished speaking, Claude Vignon came in. The two old survivors of the Napoleonic armies gravely saluted each other, effacing all sign of emotion.

'I hope you were pleased with the notices in the papers, Sir,' said the future Master of Requests. 'I went to work on the Opposition sheets to plant the idea that they were publishing our secrets.'

'It is all useless, unfortunately,' the Minister replied, as he watched the Marshal making his way out across the room beyond. 'I have just said a last good-bye which I found most painful. Marshal Hulot has not three days to live; I saw that plainly yesterday. That man, a model of integrity, a soldier that the very bullets respected in spite of his daring . . . there . . . sitting there, in that chair . . . was given his death-blow, and from my hand, by a piece of paper! Ring and order my carriage. I am going to Neuilly,' he said, locking the two hundred thousand francs in his ministerial portfolio.

In spite of all Lisbeth's care and attention, three days later Marshal Hulot was dead. Such men are the pride of the causes they have embraced. To Republicans the Marshal was the ideal patriot, and they all came to take part in his funeral procession, which was followed by an enormous crowd. The

Army, the Government, the Court, the ordinary people, all came to render homage to his high virtue, his untouched integrity, his undimmed glory. Not for the asking do the representatives of a whole nation follow a man's coffin. This funeral was marked by one of those gestures, showing the greatest delicacy, good taste, and true feeling, that from time to time recall the qualities and the glory of the French aristocrats. For, following the Marshal's coffin, the old Marquis de Montauran was to be seen, the brother of the man who in the rising of the Chouans in 1799 had been the opponent, the defeated and fatally wounded opponent, of Hulot. The Marquis, falling under the bullets of the Republican bluecoats, the Blues, had entrusted his young brother's interests to the Republican soldier [see *Les Chouans*]. Hulot had accepted the nobleman's charge thus laid upon him, and executed it so well that he had succeeded in preserving his estates for the young man, who was at that time an *émigré*. And for that reason the old French nobility, too, paid their homage to the soldier who nine years before, in 1832, had vanquished Madame, when she tried to recover the throne for her son, the Duc de Berry, by force of arms.

For Lisbeth, this death, falling four days before the last publication of the banns of her marriage, was the bolt from heaven that destroys the harvest in the barn. The peasant woman had succeeded, as often happens, only too well. The Marshal had died of the blows struck at the family by herself and Madame Marneffe. The old maid's hatred, that had seemed to be quenched by success, had fresh fuel added in the disappointment of all her hopes. Lisbeth went to weep with rage to Madame Marneffe's, for she no longer had a place to live, the Marshal's lease of his house terminating with his death. Crevel, to console his Valérie's friend, took her savings and considerably increased them, and invested this capital in five-per-cents in Célestine's name, giving Lisbeth the life interest. Thanks to him, Lisbeth possessed an annuity of two thousand francs. When the inventory of the Marshal's property came to be taken, a note from the Marshal was found addressed to his sister-in-law, his niece Hortense, and his nephew Victorin, charging them with the payment, between them, of twelve hundred francs a year to Mademoiselle Lisbeth Fischer, who was to have been his wife.

Adeline, seeing the Baron lying between life and death, managed to keep the Marshal's death from him for several days; but then Lisbeth came in, in mourning, and he discovered the fatal truth, eleven days after the funeral. This terrible blow galvanized the sick man into new energy. He rose from his bed and went to find his family. They were gathered in the drawing-room, dressed in black, and fell silent when he appeared. In a fortnight, Hulot, grown as thin as a spectre, seemed to his family to have become only a shadow of himself.

'We must decide what we are going to do,' he said in a colourless voice, sitting down and looking at the family group, from which only Crevel and Steinbock were absent.

'We can't stay here any longer,' Hortense was saying as her father came in; 'the rent is too high.'

'As to rooms,' said Victorin, breaking the painful silence, 'I can offer my *mother* . . .'

When he heard these words, which seemed meant to exclude him, the Baron raised his eyes which had been bent unseeingly on the floor, gazing at the pattern on the carpet, and looked miserably at the lawyer. A father's rights are still so sacred, even when he is disgraced and stripped of all honour, that Victorin stopped.

'Your mother . . .' repeated the Baron. 'You are quite right, my son!'

'The rooms above ours, in our house,' Célestine finished her husband's sentence.

'Do I stand in your way, children?' said the Baron, with the gentleness of a man self-condemned. 'Oh, you need not worry about the future. You will have no more cause to complain of your father, and you shall not see him again until you need no longer blush for him.'

He took Hortense by the hand and kissed her brow. He opened his arms to his son, who despairingly threw himself into them, guessing what his father intended to do. The Baron beckoned Lisbeth, who came to him, and he kissed her forehead. Then he returned to his room, where Adeline, acutely anxious, followed him.

'My brother was right, Adeline,' he said to her, taking her hand. 'I am not worthy to live with my family. I did not dare to bless my children, except in my heart. They have behaved wonderfully. Tell them that I could only embrace them; for from a disgraced man, a father who becomes his family's murderer and scourge, instead of being its protector and its pride, a blessing would be inappropriate. But I will bless them, all the same, every day, when I am separated from them. As for you, only almighty God can reward you as you deserve! ... I beg your forgiveness,' he said, kneeling before his wife, taking her hands, and shedding tears.

'Hector! Hector! You have sinned greatly, but Divine mercy is infinite, and it is possible to atone for everything, if you stay with me. ... Don't kneel; rise with Christian faith and hope in your mind, my dear. I am your wife, not your judge. I am yours, to do as you will, to go where you go. I am, I know, strong enough to console you. My love, respect, and care will make life endurable for you! Our children are established in life; they no longer need me. Let me try to distract your mind from your troubles and seek new interests with you. Allow me to share the hardships of your exile and your poverty, to soften their edge. I shall always be of some use to you, even if only to spare you the expense of a servant. ...'

'Do you forgive me, my dear beloved Adeline?'

'I do; but get up, dear!'

'Well, with your forgiveness I can live!' he said, rising. 'I came back to our room so that our children should not witness their father's humiliation. Ah! to have a father as guilty as I before their eyes every day – I cannot let them suffer such a shocking reversal of the proper order of things. The debasement of paternal authority means the disintegration of the family. So I cannot remain here; I must go, to spare you the odious spectacle of a father deprived of his dignity. Do not try to prevent my going, Adeline. You would be loading with your own hands the pistol I would use to blow my brains out. And do not follow me into hiding; you would make me lose the only strength remaining in me, the strength brought by remorse.'

Hector's emphasis silenced his wife, who saw her life failing. It was from her close union with her husband that this wife, so great, with so much lying in ruins about her, derived her courage. She had dreamed of his being all hers, seen opening before her the sublime mission of comforting him, of bringing him back to family life and reconciling him with himself.

'Hector, do you mean to leave me to die of despair, fretting and anxious about you?' she said, as she saw the mainspring of her existence about to be taken from her.

'I will come back to you, my angel, come from heaven, expressly, I think, for my sake. I will come back, if not rich, at least with money enough. Listen, my dear Adeline. I cannot stay here, for a host of reasons. To begin with, my pension, which will be about six thousand francs, is held for four years for repayment, so that I have nothing. And that's not all! I shall be in danger of arrest for debt in a few days, because of the notes of hand held by Vauvinet. So I must keep out of sight until my son – I'll leave precise instructions with him – has redeemed them. My disappearance will make that much easier. When my pension is free of claims, when Vauvinet is paid, I'll come back to you. ... With you I could not hope to keep the secret of my hiding-place. Don't worry, Adeline, don't cry. It's only a matter of a month. ...'

'Where will you go? What will you do? What will become of you? Who will look after you, now that you're no longer young? Let me disappear with you – we will go abroad,' she said.

'Well, we'll see,' he replied.

The Baron rang, and ordered Mariette to collect his things and pack them at once in secret. Then, after embracing his wife with a demonstrative tenderness to which she was little accustomed, he begged her to leave him alone for a few moments to write out the instructions that Victorin needed, promising her not to leave the house before nightfall, nor without her. As soon as the Baroness had returned to the drawing-room, the experienced old campaigner walked through the dressing-room to the hall and went, leaving a piece of paper with Mariette, on which he had written: 'Send on my baggage, by rail, addressed to Monsieur Hector, at Corbeil, to be left till called for.' The Baron was already in a cab on his way across Paris when Mariette went to show this note to the Baroness, saying that Monsieur had just gone out. Adeline, increasingly shaken by her tremulous agitation, rushed to the bedroom, where her children followed her in alarm, on hearing a piercing cry. They found the Baroness unconscious. She had to be put to bed, and lay there for a month in a nervous fever, between life and death.

'Where is he?' That was all anyone could induce her to say.

Victorin's search for him, and inquiries, produced no result, because the Baron had confused the trail. He had driven to the place du Palais-Royal. Then, summoning up all his old ability to get out of a tight corner, he proceeded to put into effect a scheme that he had thought out during the days when he lay, crushed by grief and chagrin, in bed. He crossed the Palais-Royal, and hired a splendid carriage in the rue Joquelet. The coachman, as he was ordered, drove to the rue de la Ville-l'Éveque and into the courtyard of Josépha's house, whose gates opened for this showy vehicle at the coachman's shout. Curiosity brought Josépha to investigate, when her footman carried the message that an invalid old gentleman, unable to leave his carriage, asked her to come down for a moment.

'Josépha! Don't you know me?'

The famous singer recognized Hulot only by his voice.

'What! It's you, poor old soul! Word of honour, you look like one of those twenty-franc pieces clipped by the German Jews that the money-changers won't take.'

'Yes, unfortunately,' said Hulot. 'I've been at death's door. But you are as beautiful as ever. Are you as kind, I wonder?'

'That's according. Everything is relative!' she said.

'See here,' Hulot went on; 'can you put me up in a servant's room in the attics for a few days? I haven't a farthing. I have no hope, no way of earning a living, no pension, no wife, no children, no place of refuge, no honour, no courage, no friend, and, worst of all, I'm threatened with arrest for debt. ....'

'Poor old chap! That's a lot of things to have none of! Have you lost your breeches too – *sans culotte*?'

'If you mock, I'm done for!' exclaimed the Baron. 'And I counted on you, like Gourville counting on Ninon de Lenclos.'

'They tell me that it was a society lady that left you in this pickle?' said Josépha inquiringly. 'Those jokers know how to pluck the turkey better than we do! Oh! you're just like a carcass the crows have done with. One can see daylight through you!'

'The matter's urgent, Josépha!'

'Come in, old dear! I'm alone, and my servants don't know you. Send away your carriage. Is it paid for?'

'Yes,' said the Baron, getting down with the help of Josépha's arm.

'You can say you're my father, if you like,' said the singer, with a sudden access of pity.

She took Hulot to sit in the magnificent drawing-room where he had seen her last.

'Is it true,' she began again, 'that you have killed your brother and your uncle, ruined your family, mortgaged your children's house, and run off with the money-bags of the Government in Africa, you and the princess between you?'

The Baron sadly bowed his head.

'Well, I really like that!' cried Josépha, jumping up, full of enthusiasm. 'That's a real bust-up! You're just like Sardanapalus over again! It's grand! It's going the whole hog! You may be a blackguard, but you have a heart. If you ask me, I'd rather have a proper spendthrift, mad about women, like you, than one of those cold soul-less bankers who are supposed to be so virtuous, and ruin thousands of families with their golden railways – golden for them, and iron for their unlucky suckers, their *gogos*! You have only ruined your own family; the only property you've sold is you! And then, you have excuses, physical and moral'

She struck a tragic pose and declaimed:

341

'"Venus, with teeth and claws fast fixéd in her prey.". . . That's how it is!' she concluded, with a pirouette.

So Hulot found that he was absolved by vice; vice smiled at him from its surroundings of sumptuous luxury. The immensity of the crimes was there, as it is for members of a jury, an extenuating circumstance.

'Is your society lady pretty, at least?' the singer asked, seeking as a first kindness to distract Hulot, for his despondent sadness was distressing.

'Indeed, nearly as pretty as you,' replied the Baron tactfully.

'And . . . good fun, so they say? What did she do? Is she more of a comic turn than me?'

'Don't let's talk about her,' said Hulot.

'They say that she has caught my Crevel, and little Steinbock, and a marvellous Brazilian?'

'Very likely . . .'

'And she's living in a house as fine as this one, that Crevel gave her. That hussy is my first assistant chief scullery-maid and disher-up, she finishes off the men that I've made the first cut in! That's why I'm so anxious to know what she's like, old dear. I've seen her driving in the Bois de Boulogne, in an open carriage, but only in the distance. . . . She's an accomplished gold-digger, so Carabine says. She's trying to make a meal of Crevel! But she won't be able to do more than nibble at him. Crevel is a tough old piece of cheese! A jolly good sort who always says *yes*, and does just what he wants to do and no more. He's as vain as you like, and hot-blooded, but his cash is frozen cold. You can get nothing more out of that kind than about a thousand to three thousand francs a month, and they stick their feet in and baulk before anything big, like donkeys before a river. They're not like you, old boy; you're a man of passions – anyone could set you on to sell your country! And so, you see, I'm willing to do anything for you! You are my father; you started me out in the world! It's a pious duty! How much do you need? What about a hundred thousand francs? I would work like a cart-horse, till I dropped, to get it for you. As for a crust of bread and a spot to tuck yourself up in, that's nothing. You shall have your place laid for you here every day, you can take a nice room on the second floor, and there'll be a hundred crowns a month to put in your pocket.'

The Baron, touched by this reception, had a last honourable scruple.

'No, my dear child, no. I didn't come here to sponge on you,' he said.

'At your age it's a rare triumph to be able to!' she said.

'This is what I want, child. Your Duc d'Hérouville has large estates in Normandy, and I would like to be his steward, under the name of Thoul. I have the ability for the job, and the trustworthiness, for though a man may diddle the Government, one doesn't pilfer money from a cash-box. . . .'

'Aha!' mocked Josépha. 'He who once drinks of that well will drink again!'

'In fact, all I want is to live out of sight and mind for three years. . . .'

'Oh, that's soon arranged,' said Josépha. 'This evening, after dinner, I only have to ask him. The Duke would marry me, if I wanted him to; but I have his money, and I want something more ... his esteem! He's a duke from the top of the tree. He's noble. He's distinguished. He's as big a man as Napoleon and Louis XIV put together, although he's a dwarf. And then I have played the part Schontz played with Rochefide: what I told him has just earned him two millions. But listen to me, my old son of a gun ... I know you, you've a weakness for women, and away there in Normandy you would always be chasing after the little Norman girls – they're wonderful-looking. You would have your bones broken by sweethearts or fathers, and the Duke would be forced to throw you out. Can't I just see by the way you look at me that the young man inside you is not dead, as Fénelon said! That job isn't what you want. You can't break away from Paris and us girls just for the wanting to, you know, old boy! You would die of boredom at Hérouville!'

'But what am I to do?' said the Baron. 'I want to stay with you only until I can find the next step to take.'

'See here, would you like me to fix you up according to my notion? Listen, my old fireman! You need women. They're a consolation for everything. Listen to me now. Down in La Courtille, in the rue Saint-Maur-du-Temple, I know a poor family who possess a treasure: a little girl, prettier than I was at sixteen! Ah! there's a glint in your eye already! The creature works sixteen hours a day embroidering fine materials for the silk merchants, and earns sixteen sous a day, a sou an hour, a pittance! And all she has to eat, like the Irish, is potatoes; and potatoes fried in rat grease, with bread five times a week, perhaps. She drinks water from the Ourcq out of the town taps, because Seine water is too dear, and she can't have her own workshop for want of six or seven thousand francs. There's nothing she wouldn't do to get hold of seven or eight thousand francs. Your family and your wife are a nuisance, aren't they? ... Besides, one can't see oneself a nobody where one has been set up as a god. A father with no money, who has lost everyone's respect, is only good for stuffing with straw and putting in a glass case ...'

The Baron could not help smiling at these outrageous sallies.

'Well, little Bijou is coming tomorrow to bring me an embroidered dressing-gown, a perfect dream! They have been working on it for six months; no one else will have anything like it! Bijou is fond of me because I give her sweets and my old dresses. And besides I send the family notes for the shopkeepers, good for bread, firewood, and meat, and they would break a leading citizen's two shin bones for me, if I wanted them to. I try to do a little good if I can! Oh, I know what it is like to go hungry! Bijou pours out her heart to me, and confides all her little secrets. There's the stuff of a character actress at the Ambigu-Comique in that little girl. Bijou has rosy dreams of wearing fine dresses like mine, and, more wonderful than anything, going about in a carriage. I'll say to her: "Child, how would you like a gentleman of ..." How old are you? ...' she interrupted her flow of words to ask. 'Seventy-two? ...'

'I have stopped counting.'

'"How would you like," I'll say to her, "a gentleman of seventy-two, very natty, who doesn't take tobacco, as sound as my eye, as good as a young man? You'll marry him, without a licence, of course, and you'll live very nicely together; he'll give you seven thousand francs to set up for yourself; he'll furnish a flat for you, all in mahogany. Then if you're good, he'll take you sometimes to the theatre. He'll give you a hundred francs a month for yourself, and fifty francs for the housekeeping!" I know Bijou, she's like me at fourteen. I jumped for joy when that abominable Crevel made me those very same atrocious propositions. Well, old boy, you will be snugly stowed away there for three years. That's sensible and straightforward; and the arrangement will hold illusions for three or four years, though not longer.'

Hulot had no hesitation, his mind was made up to refuse; but in order not to seem ungrateful to the kind-hearted singer who was doing her best for him in her own fashion, he pretended to waver between vice and virtue.

'Bless me! You're as slow to warm up as a paving-stone in December!' she said, astonished. 'Look, you will be creating the happiness of a whole family, a grandfather who totters about, a mother who wears herself out working, and two sisters, one of them no beauty, who between them earn thirty-two sous by ruining their eyes. That will make up for the unhappiness you have caused in your own home. You will be redeeming your sins, and having a good time like a tart at Mabille.'

Hulot, to put an end to this temptation, made the gesture of counting money.

'Don't worry about ways and means,' Josépha took him up. 'My duke will lend you ten thousand francs: seven thousand for an embroidering workshop in Bijou's name, three thousand for furnishing; and every three months you will find six hundred and fifty francs here, on your note of hand. When you get your pension back, you can repay the seventeen thousand francs to the Duke. Meantime you'll be as well off as a pig in clover, and hidden away in a corner the police will never find. You can dress yourself up in a big beaver overcoat and look like a comfortable householder of the district. Call yourself Thoul, if that's your fancy. I'll introduce you to Bijou as an uncle of mine, gone bankrupt in Germany, and you'll be pampered like a little tin god. There you are,

'Papa! ... Who knows? Perhaps you'll have no reason to regret anything that's happened. And in case by any chance you might ever feel bored, you should keep one of your fine onionskins, and then you can come and invite yourself to dinner and spend the evening here.'

'But I'm the man who only asked to reform and lead a virtuous life! Here, borrow twenty thousand francs for me and I'll be off to America to make my fortune, like my friend d'Aiglemont when Nucingen ruined him. ...'

'You!' cried Josépha. 'Leave orderly living to shopkeepers and simple soldier-boys and good Fr-r-r-rench citizens who have only their virtue to distinguish them! But you were born for something better than to be a milk-and-water ninny. You are just like me, in a man's shape: a bad lot with a talent and a bent that way!'

'I had better sleep on it. We can talk about this tomorrow.'

'You shall dine with the Duke. My Hérouville will receive you as politely as if you had saved the state! And tomorrow you can make up your mind. Come, cheer up, old boy! Life is an overcoat: when it's dirty, we brush it; when there are holes in it, we patch them; but we keep ourselves covered as well as we can!'

This philosophy of vice, and her spirited gaiety, dissipated Hulot's bitter griefs.

Next day, at midday, after a delicious meal, Hulot saw walk in one of those living masterpieces that only Paris in the whole world can create; for only in Paris exists the endless concubinage of luxury and want, of vice and sober virtue, of repressed desire and ever-renewed temptation, which makes this city the heir of Nineveh, Babylon, and Imperial Rome. Mademoiselle Olympe Bijou, a girl of sixteen, had the exquisite face that Raphael found for his Virgins, with innocent eyes saddened by overwork, dreamy dark eyes, shaded by long lashes, their limpidity suffering from long nights of toil, eyes heavy with fatigue; and a complexion with the fineness of porcelain and an almost chlorotic transparency; and a mouth like a half-burst pomegranate, a passionate breast, a rounded figure, pretty hands, dazzlingly pretty white teeth, luxuriant black hair: and all this beauty was done up in cotton at seventy-five centimes a metre, adorned with an embroidered collar, mounted on stitched leather slippers, and garnished with gloves at twenty-nine sous. The child, quite unconscious of her rare value, had put on her best to come to the grand lady's house. The Baron, seized afresh in the taloned grip of sensuality, felt his whole life centred in his eyes. He forgot everything before this divine creation. He was like a hunter sighting the game: not even the presence of an emperor will prevent him from taking aim!

'And,' Josépha whispered in his ear, 'it's guaranteed mint-new; it's a decent girl! And with no bread to eat. That's Paris! I was just like her!'

'It's a bargain,' replied the old man, rising to his feet and rubbing his hands.

When Olympe Bijou had gone, Josépha looked at the Baron slyly.

'If you don't want trouble, Papa,' she said, 'be as strict as the High Court Judge on his judgement seat. Keep the little girl on a short rein. Be a Bartholo! Beware of the Augustes and Hippolytes and Nestors and Victors and all the other *ors*, including gold ore! ... Bless you, once the creature is properly dressed and fed, if it raises its head you'll be led a dance just like one of the Russian dances. ... I'll look after your settling in. The Duke does things in proper style; he is going to lend you, that is to say give you, ten thousand francs, and he is depositing eight thousand of them with his lawyer, who will be told to hand you out six hundred francs every three months, for I don't trust you ... Now, don't you think I'm a nice girl?'

'Adorable!'

Ten days after deserting his family, while they, in tears, were gathered round Adeline's bed, where she lay apparently dying, and while her faint whisper asked 'Where is he?', Hulot, now Thoul of the rue Saint-Maur, was established with Olympe at the head of an embroidery business, under the odd style of *Thoul and Bijou*.

From the misfortunes implacably pursuing his family, Victorin Hulot received the hammering that makes a man or breaks him. It perfected Victorin. In the great storms of life we act like

347

ships' captains at sea, and lighten ship by throwing the heavy cargo overboard. The lawyer abandoned his inner arrogance, his air of complacency, his pride in his eloquence, and his political pretensions. He grew to be Adeline's masculine counterpart. He resolved to make the best of his Célestine, although she was certainly not the wife he had dreamed of, and achieved a balanced view of life, realizing that we are obliged by the universal law to be content with a more or less imperfect approximation to the ideal. He solemnly vowed, in his profound sense of shock at his father's behaviour, to do all his duty. His resolution was confirmed as he sat at his mother's bedside on the day that she passed the crisis of her illness. That stroke of good fortune did not come singly. Claude Vignon, who called to inquire after Madame Hulot's health, every day, on behalf of Prince de Wissembourg, asked the Deputy, now re-elected, to go with him to see the Minister.

'His Excellency,' he told him, 'wants to confer with you about your family affairs.'

The Minister had known Victorin Hulot for a long time, and received him with an affability characteristic of him and auguring well.

'My boy,' said the old warrior, 'I solemnly promised your uncle, the Marshal, in this very room, that I would look after your mother. That saintly woman, they tell me, is on the way to recovery, so now is the time to bind up your wounds. I have two hundred thousand francs for you here, and I am going to give you the money now.'

The lawyer made a gesture worthy of his uncle, the Marshal.

'Don't worry,' said the Prince, smiling. 'It's a *fidei-commissum* – money left in trust. My days are numbered. I shall not be here for ever, so take the money and take over my duty with regard to your family. You may use the money to pay off the mortgage on your house. This two hundred thousand francs belongs to your mother and your sister. But Madame Hulot's devotion to her husband leads me to fear that if I gave this money to her I should see it wasted; and the intention of those who return it is that it should be used for the maintenance of Madame Hulot and her daughter, Countess Steinbock. You are a man of practical good sense, the worthy

348

son of your noble mother and the true nephew of my friend the Marshal. You are appreciated at your true worth here, my dear boy, as you are elsewhere. So be your family's guardian angel, accept your uncle's legacy and mine.'

'Your Excellency,' said Hulot, grasping the Minister's hand, 'men like you know that words of thanks mean nothing; gratitude has to be proved.'

'Prove yours then!' said the old soldier.

'Show me how I may.'

'Accept my proposals,' said the Minister. 'We want to appoint you as legal adviser to the War Office, which on the engineering side has more litigation than it can deal with, arising from the plans for the Paris fortifications; and also as consultant lawyer to the Préfecture of Police, and adviser to the Civil List Board. These three appointments would give you a salary of eighteen thousand francs, and your political independence would not be in the least affected. You must vote in the Chamber in accordance with your political views and your conscience. ... Feel perfectly free to act as you please! We should be in a very bad way, you know, if we had no Opposition!

'And now, there is one other matter. I had a letter from your uncle written a few hours before he died, indicating what I should do in order to help your mother, whom the Marshal was very fond of. A number of ladies, presidents of charitable societies, Mesdames Popinot, de Rastignac, de Navarreins, d'Espard, de Grandlieu, de Carigliano, de Lenoncourt, and de La Bâtie, have created the post of Lady Welfare Visitor for your dear mother. The ladies cannot do everything in the administration of their charities themselves; they need a lady they can trust, able to act as a whole-time representative for them, to go and visit unfortunate people, see that their charity is not being misused, make sure that help has been properly given to those who have asked for it, seek out needy people who are too proud to apply for assistance, and so on. Your mother will act as a good angel; she will be answerable only to the clergy and the charitable ladies; her salary will be six thousand francs a year, and her cab expenses will be paid. You see, young man, how an honourable and upright man can still protect his family beyond the grave. In properly constituted societies, such names as your uncle's are, and rightly so, a shield against misfortune. Follow in your uncle's footsteps then, continue steadfastly in his way, for you have made a good beginning, I know.'

'So much kindness and consideration, Sir, do not surprise me in my uncle's friend,' said Victorin. 'I will do my best to live up to what you expect of me.'

'Go and be a consolation to your family, then! ... Ah, by the way,' the Prince added, as he shook hands with Victorin, 'I hear that your father has disappeared?'

'Yes, I'm afraid so.'

'That's all the better. The unhappy man has shown some tact and enterprise – they are not qualities that he ever lacked.'

'He has some creditors to avoid.'

'Ah, I see,' said the Marshal. 'You shall be given six months' salary, from the three new appointments. That advance will no doubt help you to withdraw the notes-of-hand from the moneylender's hands. I'll see Nucingen, in any case, and perhaps I may be able to free your father's pension without its costing you or my Ministry anything. The Peer of France has not killed the banker in Nucingen, however; he's insatiable, and he'll want some concession or other ...'

When he returned to the rue Plumet, then, Victorin was in a position to carry out his plan of taking his mother and sister to live with him.

The distinguished young barrister possessed as his sole fortune one of the loveliest properties in Paris, a house bought in 1834 in anticipation of his marriage, situated on the boulevard between the rue de la Paix and the rue Louis-le-Grand. A speculator had built two houses, one facing on the street and the other on the boulevard, and between them, with a garden and a court on either side, there stood a pavilion, the noble wing of an old house, all that remained of the magnificent Hôtel de Verneuil. Young Hulot, relying on Mademoiselle Crevel's dowry, had bought this superb property for a million francs when it was put up for auction, paying five hundred thousand francs down. He lived on the ground floor of the old building, and planned to pay off the money he still owed with the rents of the others; but if speculation in house property is a safe investment in Paris, it may show a very slow or erratic return, depending on unforeseeable circumstances. As strollers about Paris may have observed, the boulevard between the rue Louis-le-Grand and the rue de la Paix was for a long time left undeveloped. In fact it was cleared up and beautified with such tedious slowness that it was not until 1840 that trade came to it, with its splendid shop-fronts, the moneychangers' gold, the fairy display of fashion's creations, and the extravagant ornate luxury of its expensive shops.

In spite of the two hundred thousand francs that Crevel had given his daughter, at a time when his vanity had been flattered by the marriage and before the Baron had stolen Josépha from him, and although a further two hundred thousand francs had been paid off by Victorin over seven years, the debt on the property still stood at five hundred thousand francs, as a result of the money he had raised on it, as a dutiful son, to pay off his father's debts.

Fortunately, the steady rise in rents, and the beauty of the situation, began at this time to give the houses a greatly increased value. The speculation was paying off after eight years, during which the lawyer had toiled to pay interest and an insignificant amount of the capital. The shopkeepers of their own accord were offering satisfactory rents for the shops, on condition of having eighteen-year leases. The flats were rising in value because of the shift in the business centre of Paris, by then becoming settled between the Bourse and the Madeleine, a district which was in future to be the seat of political and financial power.

The trust money placed in Victorin's hands by the Minister, together with the salary paid in advance, and the additional sums agreed to by his tenants, would reduce his debt to two hundred thousand francs. The two houses, fully let, would bring in a hundred thousand francs a year. In another two years, during which he could live on his professional fees augmented by the salaries of the appointments that the Minister had given him, Hulot would be in a splendid position. It was manna fallen from heaven.

Victorin would now be able to give his mother the whole first floor of his *pavillon*, and the second floor, apart from two rooms for Lisbeth, to his sister. And this triple household, run by Lisbeth, could meet its expenses and honourably maintain the establishment expected of a rising lawyer. The luminaries of the Palais de Justice were rapidly disappearing; and Hulot, eloquent but judicious and discreet, and a man of strict probity, was listened to by Judges and Councillors. He worked hard at his cases, said nothing that he could not prove, and was selective in the causes he undertook to plead; he was, in sum, a credit to his profession.

Her home in the rue Plumet was so hateful to the Baroness that she did not hesitate to leave it for the rue Louis-le-Grand. Through her son's kindness, she now occupied a beautiful set of rooms. She was spared all domestic cares, for Lisbeth had agreed to work the same housekeeping miracles for the Hulots that she had achieved at Madame Marneffe's, foreseeing that she would thus be in a position to bring the heavy weight of her vengeance to bear upon the lives of these three upright persons, for whom her hatred had been inflamed by the overthrow of all her hopes. Once a month Lisbeth went to see Valérie, sent there both by Hortense, anxious for news of Wenceslas, and by Célestine, who was exceedingly uneasy about her father's open and acknowledged liaison with a woman who had ruined the lives of her husband's mother and sister, and wrecked their happiness. As may be imagined, Lisbeth took advantage of their desire for information to visit Valérie as often as she pleased.

About twenty months went by, in the course of which the Baroness's health improved, although her nervous trembling persisted. She acquainted herself with her duties, which offered her a means of distracting her mind from her grief, useful to others, as well as nourishment for the divine faculties of her soul. She saw in them, moreover, a way by which she might find her husband, because of the chances afforded by the calls for her services that led her into every part of Paris.

During this time, the notes of hand held by Vauvinet were redeemed, and the pension of six thousand francs due to Baron Hulot almost cleared of the charge upon it. Victorin 'paid all his mother's expenses, and Hortense's, with the ten thousand francs interest on the capital left in trust for them by the Marshal. Adeline's salary was six thousand francs, so that when they had the Baron's pension mother and daughter would be assured of a clear income of twelve thousand francs. The poor woman would have been almost happy, if it had not been for her unremitting anxiety about the fate of her Baron, whom she would have liked to share in the brightening family fortunes, and the sight of her deserted daughter, and the terrible blows that Lisbeth struck her, in apparent innocence, giving free rein to the promptings of her diabolical spirit.

A scene which took place at the beginning of March 1843, will show Lisbeth's persistent smouldering hate at work, and the effects of the old maid's continuing partnership with Madame Marneffe. Two notable events had taken place in Madame Marneffe's life. First, she had given birth to a still-born child, whose coffin was worth two thousand francs a year to her. Then, eleven months before, Lisbeth had brought back a sensational piece of news about Marneffe, from a reconnaissance expedition to the Marneffe household.

'This morning,' she had reported, 'that dreadful Valérie called in Doctor Bianchon to make quite sure that the doctors who said yesterday that there was no hope for her husband had made no mistake. Doctor Bianchon said that the unspeakable creature is going to be claimed this very night by the hell that's waiting for him. Old Crevel and Madame Marneffe escorted the Doctor to the door, and your father, my dear Célestine, gave him five gold pieces for the good news. When he got back to the drawing-room Crevel twirled on his toes like a ballet dancer, and he hugged that woman, crying "You'll be Madame Crevel at last!" And when she went back to her place at the bedside of her husband with the death-rattle in his throat, and left us together, your fine father said to me "With Valérie as my wife, I'll be a Peer of France! I'll buy an estate I have my eye on – Presles. I'll be a member of the Council of Seine-et-Oise, and a Deputy. I'll have a son! I'll be anything in the world I want to be." "All very well," I said to him; "and what about your daughter?"

"Bah, she's only a daughter!" was what he answered. "And she's become far too much of a Hulot, and Valérie can't bear that lot. My son-in-law has always refused to come here. Why should he play the mentor, the Spartan, the puritan, the slum visitor? Besides I've settled my reckoning with my daughter; she's had all her mother's fortune and two hundred thousands francs besides. So I'm free to do as I like. I'll consider how my son-in-law acts when my marriage comes off; I'll give them tit-for-tat. If they behave well to their stepmother, I'll see! I'm a man, you know!" And plenty more of the same stuff! And he struck a pose like Napoleon on his column!'

The ten months of formal widowhood ordained by the Code Napoléon had run out a few days since. The Presles estate had been bought. And that very morning Victorin and Célestine had sent Lisbeth to Madame Marneffe's to look for news about the charming widow's marriage to a Mayor of Paris, now a member of the Council of Seine-et-Oise.

Célestine and Hortense had been drawn closely together in affection since they had come to live under the same roof, and they formed virtually one household. The Baroness was so conscientious about fulfilling the duties attached to her post that she spent even more time than was necessary at her charities, and was out of the house every day between eleven o'clock and five. The two sisters-in-law stayed at home and looked after their children together, and this had created a bond between them. They had come to be so close to each other that they spoke their thoughts aloud. They presented a touching picture of two sisters in harmony, one happy, the other sad. The unhappy sister, beautiful, charged with overflowing vitality, lively, gay, and quick-witted, in appearance belied her actual situation; while the sober Célestine, so gentle and calm, as equable as reason itself, habitually reflective and thoughtful, would have made an observer believe that she had some secret sorrow. Perhaps the contrast between them contributed to their warm friendship: each found in the other what she herself lacked.

Sitting in a little summer-house in the middle of a garden that the trowel of speculative building had spared, by a whim of the builder who had thought of keeping this patch a hundred feet square for himself, they were enjoying the first green shoots of the lilacs, an occasion in spring only properly and fully savoured in Paris, where for six months of the year the Parisians live oblivious of green leaves, among the stone cliffs round which their human ocean ebbs and flows.

'Célestine,' Hortense was saying, in answer to an observation of her sister-in-law's, lamenting her fate in having a husband shut up in the Chamber on such a fine day, 'I don't believe you know how well off you are. Victorin is an angel, and you often plague him.'

'Men enjoy being plagued, my dear! Teasing is a mark of affection sometimes. If your poor mother had been – not exactly demanding, but nearer to it, harder to please, you would certainly have had fewer troubles to put up with.'

'Lisbeth's not back yet! I may sing the song of Marlborough going to the war and never returning, for her,' said Hortense. 'I can't wait to have news of Wenceslas! What is he living on? He has done no work for two years.'

'Victorin saw him the other day, so he told me, with that hateful woman, and he thinks she must keep him in idleness. Ah, if you wanted to, Hortense dear, you could still bring your husband back.'

Hortense shook her head.

'Believe me, your situation will soon become intolerable,' Célestine went on. 'Your anger and despair and indignation helped you to bear up at first. And then you had the frightful misfortunes that have overtaken our family since – two deaths, financial ruin, and Baron Hulot's catastrophe – to occupy your mind and heart. But now, when you are living in peace and quiet, you will not find the emptiness of your life easy to endure. And as you cannot, and would never want to, turn aside from the path of virtue, you will simply have to seek a reconciliation with Wenceslas. That's what Victorin thinks, and he's so fond of you. There is something stronger than our personal feelings, and that's nature.'

'A man so spineless!' exclaimed the proud Hortense. 'He's that woman's lover because she keeps him. Has she even paid his debts, I wonder? Heavens, I think night and day of the position he's in! He's my child's father, and he lets himself fall so low. ...'

'Look at the example your mother gives you, dear child ...' said Célestine. Célestine belonged to the type of woman who, given reasons of sufficient force to convince a Breton peasant, reiterates her original argument for the hundredth time. The rather insipid, cold and commonplace character of her face, the stiff braids of her light brown hair, her colouring, were indicative of the down-to-earth, sensible woman she was, with no charm, but with no weakness either.

'The Baroness would like nothing better than to be with her disgraced husband, to console him, and wrap him in her love, and hide him from all eyes,' Célestine went on. 'She has had Monsieur Hulot's room made ready for him upstairs, as if she might find him any day and bring him home to it.'

'Oh, my mother is sublime!' answered Hortense. 'She has been sublime every moment of every day for twenty-six years; but I'm not that kind, I haven't got her temperament ... I get angry with myself sometimes, but what can I do? Oh, you don't know what it's like, Célestine, to have to come to terms with sordid degradation!'

'You forget my father ...' said Célestine, without emotion. 'He is certainly travelling the road on which yours came to grief. My father is ten years younger than the Baron, and he's a businessman, it's true; but where will it end? That Madame Marneffe has turned my father into her lap-dog. Both his money and his ideas are hers to do what she likes with; and there's no way of opening his eyes. And now we may hear that the banns of marriage have been published, and, I can tell you, I tremble! My husband means to do everything possible; he looks upon it as a duty to strike back, on behalf of society as well as the family, and to call that woman to account for all her crimes. Ah! dear Hortense, minds like Victorin's are too noble, and you and I have hearts too idealistic, for the ways of the world. We come to realize what it is like too late! I am telling you a secret, dear sister, in confidence, because it concerns you; but don't give it away by a word or a sign to Lisbeth, or your mother, or anyone, for ...'

'Here is Lisbeth!' said Hortense. 'Well, Cousin, how do things go in the little inferno in the rue Barbet?'

'Not well for you, my dears. Your husband, my dear Hortense, is more infatuated than ever with that woman, and I must admit that she's madly in love with him. And your father, dear Célestine, is as blind drunk with love as a lord. There's nothing new in that sort of thing – I see it happening all the time. Thank heaven I have never had anything to do with men ... they really are just animals! In five days from now, Victorin and you, my dear child, will have lost your father's fortune!'

'The banns have been published?' asked Célestine.

'Yes,' answered Lisbeth. 'I have been pleading your cause. I said to that monster, who is following in the other one's footsteps, that if he cared to get you out of your difficulties and pay off the debt on your house, you would be grateful to him, and receive your stepmother ...'

Hortense raised her hands in dismay.

'Victorin will decide,' Célestine said coldly.

'And do you know what Monsieur le Maire replied?' Lisbeth went on. '"I don't mind leaving them in a bit of trouble. The only way to break a horse is by hunger, lack of sleep, and sugar!" Monsieur Crevel is worse than Baron Hulot. ... So you poor children may put on mourning for your chances of inheriting that fortune. And what a fortune too! Your father has paid three millions for Presles, and he still has an income of thirty thousand francs! Oh, he has no secrets from me! He is talking of buying the Navarreins town house, in the rue du Bac. Madame Marneffe has forty thousand a year of her own. ... Ah, here comes our angel, here's your mother!' she exclaimed, as they heard the sound of wheels.

And the Baroness presently came down the steps to join the family group. At fifty-five years of age, tried by so many sorrows, incessantly trembling as if shaking with fever, grown pale and wrinkled, Adeline still preserved her fine figure, noble carriage, and natural dignity. Seeing her, people said: 'She must have been lovely!' Fretted as she was by her devastating ignorance of her husband's fate, by her inability to let him share the prosperity that the family was beginning to enjoy in the peace and seclusion of this oasis of Paris, she had the imposing charm of timeworn ruins. With the extinguishing of each new gleam of hope, after each fruitless search, Adeline fell into a dark fit of melancholy that was the despair of her children.

The Baroness's return was eagerly awaited that day, for she had set off in the morning with some hope. An official, under an obligation to Hulot for advancement in his career, had said that he had seen the Baron in a box at the Ambigu-Comique Theatre, with a strikingly beautiful woman. Adeline had gone to call on Baron Vernier. That high official, while confirming that he had indeed seen his former patron, and saying that from the Baron's manner and behaviour towards the woman during the play he had received the impression that there was a clandestine bond between them, had told Madame Hulot that her husband had left well before the end of the performance, in order to avoid meeting him.

'He looked like a man on a family outing, and his appearance suggested straitened circumstances,' he said in conclusion.

'Well?' the three women interrogated the Baroness.

'Well, Monsieur Hulot is in Paris,' replied Adeline; 'and it's some happiness even to know that he is near us.'

'He does not appear to have mended his ways!' said Lisbeth, when Adeline had given them an account of her interview with Baron Vernier. 'He must have set up house with some little work-girl. But where can he be getting money from? I'll lay a wager he asks his former mistresses for it – Mademoiselle Jenny Cadine or Josépha.'

The nervous trembling that constantly shook the Baroness increased in violence. She wiped away tears that rose to her eyes, and looked sadly up.

'I do not believe that a Grand Officer of the Legion of Honour would have fallen so low,' she said.

'For the sake of his pleasure,' returned Lisbeth, 'is there anything that he would not do? He has embezzled from the state, so he will steal from individuals; he may come to commit murder perhaps . . .'

'Oh! Lisbeth!' exclaimed the Baroness. 'Keep such thoughts to yourself.'

Just then Louise approached the family group, which had been joined by the two little Hulots and little Wenceslas, come to see if there were sweets in their grandmother's pockets.

'What is it, Louise?' someone asked.

'There's a man asking for Mademoiselle Fischer.'

'What kind of man?' asked Lisbeth.

'Mademoiselle, he's all in rags, with fluff all over him like a mattress-maker. He has a red nose, and smells of wine and brandy. . . . He's like one of those workmen who don't work more than half the week.'

The effect of this not very attractive description was to send Lisbeth hurrying to the court of the house in the rue Louis-le-Grand. There she found a man smoking a pipe obviously coloured by someone practised in that smoker's art.

'Why have you come here, Chardin?' she said. 'It was arranged that you should be at the door of Madame Marneffe's house in the rue Barbet-de-Jouy on the first Saturday of every month. I have just come back after staying five hours there, and you didn't appear!'

'I did go, respected and kind young lady!' answered the mattress-maker; 'but there was a prize game of pool on at the café des Savants, in the rue du Coeur-Volant, and everybody has his weaknesses. Mine is billiards. Without billiards, I might have silver plates to eat off. Because I'll tell you this!' he said, as he fumbled in the pocket of his torn trousers and took out a scrap of paper. 'Billiards means a dram of spirits here and a drop of plum brandy there. . . . It ruins a man, just like everything good does, because of the things that go with it. I know what the orders are, but the old man is in such a corner that I tried my chance on forbidden ground. . . . If our horsehair were all horsehair, we might sleep on it, but it's a mixture! God isn't on everyone's side, as they say; he helps the ones he likes best – he has a right to, after all. Here's the writing of your esteemed relation; very friendly to the mattress trade, he is . . . . It goes with his political opinions.'

And old Chardin sketched shaky zigzags in the air with his right forefinger.

Lisbeth, unheeding, read the following note:

Dear Cousin,

Be my Providence! Send me three hundred francs, today.

HECTOR

'Why does he need so much money?'

'It's for the landlord!' said old Chardin, still trying to work out his squiggles. 'And then there's my son has come back from Algeria, through Spain and Bayonne, and ... he hasn't knocked off anything, which isn't like him at all, for he's a sharp knocker-off, saving your presence, my son is. That's the way it is! The boy has to eat. But he'll give you back all we lend him, for he means to start up a what-you-may-call-it; he's got ideas that will take him far. ...'

'To the police courts!' returned Lisbeth. 'He murdered my uncle! I'll not forget it.'

'Him? He wouldn't wring a hen's neck; he couldn't do it, respected miss!'

'Here, take this – three hundred francs,' said Lisbeth, taking fifteen coins from her purse. 'Be off with you, and don't ever come here again.'

She went to the gate with the father of the storekeeper from Oran, and pointed out the tipsy old man to the porter.

'If that man should ever come back, don't let him in, and tell him that I am not here. If he asks whether Monsieur Hulot or Madame la Baronne Hulot lives here, say that you do not know anyone of that name.'

'Very well, Mademoiselle.'

'It might cost you your place if you did anything stupid, even by accident,' the spinster added in a low voice, to the man's wife.

'Cousin,' she said, turning to meet the lawyer as he came in, 'there's a serious misfortune threatening.'

'What misfortune?'

'In a few days your wife will have Madame Marneffe for her step-mother.'

'We'll see about that!' replied Victorin.

For the past six months Lisbeth had been paying a small

360

pension regularly to her patron, Baron Hulot, of whom she was now the patroness. She was in the secret of his whereabouts; and she relished the sight of Adeline's tears, saying, as we have seen, whenever she saw her cousin gay and hopeful: 'You may be prepared to read my poor cousin's name in the papers, in the police court news, any day'.

In this she overreached herself, as she had done once before. She had awakened Victorin's suspicions. Victorin had made up his mind to get rid of the sword of Damocles for ever being pointed out by Lisbeth, and of the she-devil who had brought so much misfortune on his mother and his whole family. Prince de Wissembourg, who knew the damage Madame Marneffe had wreaked, supported the lawyer in his resolve; and he had promised him, as President of the Council, the secret help of the police, in order to disillusion Crevel and save a fortune from the talons of the diabolical courtesan, whom he had not forgiven for Marshal Hulot's death and the destruction of the Councillor of State.

Lisbeth's words 'He gets money from his former mistresses' echoed in the Baroness's mind all night. Clutching at any hope, like drowning men at straws, or the doomed sick flying to quack doctors, or the souls fallen to Dante's nethermost circle of despair, she came in the end to believe in the degradation, the bare suggestion of which had at first aroused her indignation; and it occurred to her that she might call on one of those odious women to help her.

Next morning, without consulting her children, without a word to anyone, she went to the house of Mademoiselle Josépha Mirah, *prima donna* of the Royal Academy of Music, in order to grasp at last or finally lose the hope that had appeared and glimmered before her like a will o' the wisp. At noon the great singer's maid brought her Baroness Hulot's card, saying that the lady was waiting at the door, having asked if Mademoiselle could receive her.

'Have the rooms been tidied?'

'Yes, Mademoiselle.'

'Are there fresh flowers?'

'Yes, Mademoiselle.'

'Tell Jean to go through the rooms to see that everything

is in order before showing the lady in, and say that she is to be treated with the greatest respect. When you have done that, come back to help me dress, because I mean to look my smartest!'

And she went to survey herself in her cheval-glass.

'It's a time to put on all we've got,' she told herself. 'Vice needs to be well-armed before confronting virtue! Poor woman! What can she want of me? It disturbs me to see

The noble sacrifice, struck down by ruthless fate! . . .'

She was still singing the well-known aria when her maid returned.

'Madame,' the maid said, 'the lady has had a nervous attack, a fit of trembling.'

'Offer her something: orange-flower water, rum, soup!'

'I did do that, Mademoiselle; but she won't take anything. She says it's a weakness she has, because of her nerves.'

'Which room did you show her into?'

'The large drawing-room.'

'Hurry, girl! Bring me my prettiest slippers, the flowered wrap that Bijou embroidered, all the lace frills we can muster. Do my hair up in an imposing style. We have to impress a woman who . . . That woman is playing the role opposite mine! And send someone to tell the lady . . . (for she is a great lady, girl! She's more than that, she's what you can never be: a woman whose prayers are able to deliver souls from the purgatory you talk of!) . . . let someone tell her that I'm resting, that I was singing last night, that I'm just getting up. . . .'

The Baroness, in Josépha's large drawing-room, did not notice time passing, although she waited there a good half hour. This room, already redecorated since Josépha had come to live in her little residence, was hung with purple and gold silk. It was one of four intercommunicating rooms, kept at a mild temperature by warm air circulating from hidden vents; and they were a perfect example, in a modern setting, of the kind of luxury formerly lavished by aristocrats on such little dwellings, many of whose splendours still survive in aptly named 'follies'.

The Baroness, taken completely by surprise, examined all the objects and works of art about her in utter astonishment. In this room she found an explanation of the wasting of great fortunes in the melting-pot under which Pleasure and Vanity blow up a consuming flame. The woman who for twenty-six years had lived among the cold relics of Empire luxury, whose eyes habitually rested on faded carpets, tarnished bronzes, silk hangings as worn and tired as her heart, caught an impression of the strength of the seductive power of vice as she saw what it had accomplished in this place. It was impossible not to envy the possession of such things, such beautiful and admirable creations, among which were represented all the great anonymous artists whose work makes Paris and its contribution to Europe what it is.

It was *unique* perfection that here held the eye. The models had been broken; the ornaments, statuettes, sculptures, were all original works. That is the gift most worth having of modern luxury. To possess things not vulgarized by the taste of two thousand rich bourgeois citizens, who think splendid living is the display of the expensive objects that cram the shops: that is true luxury, the luxury of modern aristocrats, those ephemeral stars in the Parisian firmament.

The Baroness, as she examined the flower-stands inlaid with bronze cut in ornamental patterns in the style called Boule, holding rare exotic flowers, was frightened to think how much wealth these rooms contained. Her wonder was inevitably transferred to the person about whom all this profusion was heaped up. Adeline thought that Josépha Mirah, whose portrait, by Joseph Bridau, adorned the adjoining boudoir, must be a singer of genius, a Malibran, and she was prepared to see an idolized star. She regretted having come. But she was driven on by an emotion so powerful and so natural, by a devotion so little self-regarding, that she summoned up all her courage to go through with the interview. Then, too, she would satisfy her piercing curiosity to see the attractions that kind of woman must possess to be able to mine so much gold from the unyielding measures of Parisian soil.

The Baroness considered her appearance, wondering whether she did not seem a blot upon all this luxury; but she looked well in her velvet dress with its high-necked inset and deep collar of beautiful lace, and her velvet bonnet of the same colour suited her. Seeing herself to be still as imposing as a queen, who is still a queen even when dethroned, she reflected that the dignity of suffering must equal the dignity conferred by talent. She heard doors open and shut, and at last saw Josépha.

The singer resembled Allori's *Judith*, which remains graven in the memory of those who have seen it in the Pitti Palace, by the door of one of the great galleries. She had the same proud pose, the same sublimity of face, black hair knotted without ornament, a yellow loose gown embroidered with innumerable flowers, exactly like the brocade worn by the immortal murderess as Bronzino's nephew depicted her.

'Madame la Baronne, you find me overwhelmed by the honour you have done me in coming here,' said the singer, who had promised herself to play her role of great lady with an air.

She pushed forward an easy-chair for the Baroness, and herself took a folding-chair. She saw that this woman had been beautiful, and was moved by profound pity as she watched her nervous shaking, that the least agitation made convulsive. She could read in a single glance the saintly life that Hulot and Crevel had long ago described for her; and she not only lost all idea of matching herself against this woman, but bowed before a greatness that she could recognize. The sublime artist admired what the courtesan might have mocked.

'Mademoiselle, I am brought here by despair, which drives one to use any means . . .'

Josépha's gesture made the Baroness realize that she had wounded the woman of whom she was hoping so much, and she looked at the singer. The supplication of her eyes quenched the flame in Josépha's, and the singer finally smiled. The silent play of glances between the two women was devastatingly eloquent.

'It is two and a half years since Monsieur Hulot left his family, and I have no idea where he is, although I know that he is living in Paris,' the Baroness went on, in a voice that shook. 'It came to me in a dream, perhaps absurdly, that you must have taken an interest in Monsieur Hulot. If you could enable me to see Monsieur Hulot again, oh, Mademoiselle, I would pray to God for you, every day of the days that still remain to me on this earth!'

Two great tears in the singer's eyes showed her responsive feeling.

'Madame,' she said, in a tone of profound humility, 'I wronged you before I knew you; but now that I have had the good fortune to behold in you the most perfect image of virtue that exists on earth, believe me I know how great my fault was, and do sincerely repent it, and you may count on my doing my utmost to repair it! ...'

She took the Baroness's hand, before the Baroness could prevent her, and kissed it with the utmost respect, even humbling herself by kneeling. Then she rose as proudly as if she were playing Mathilde at the Opera, and rang the bell.

'Go at once,' she said to her footman, 'on horseback, and flog the horse if you have to, but at all costs find the girl Bijou, of the rue Saint-Maur-du-Temple, and bring her here. Take a cab for her, and tip the driver to make all the speed he can. Don't lose a moment, if you want to keep your place. Madame,' she said, returning to the Baroness, and speaking with profound respect, 'I ask you to forgive me. As soon as I had the Duc d'Hérouville for my protector I sent the Baron back to you, when I learned that he was ruining his family for me. What more could I do? In the theatre we all must needs have a protector when we start our career. Our salary doesn't cover even half our expenses, so we take temporary husbands. ... It was not that I wanted Baron Hulot, who made me leave a rich man, a vain creature. Old Crevel would certainly have married me. ...'

'So he told me,' the Baroness interrupted her.

'Well, so you see, Madame, that I might have been a respectable woman today! I should have had only one lawful husband!'

'You have excuses, Mademoiselle,' said the Baroness. 'God will take them into account. But I am not here to reproach you, far from that; I am anxious to put myself in your debt.'

'Madame, I have been helping Monsieur le Baron for nearly three years. . . .'

'You!' exclaimed the Baroness, with tears in her eyes. 'Oh, what can I do for you? I have only my prayers to give you. . . .'

'Monsieur le Duc d'Hérouville and I,' the singer continued, 'a noble heart, a true aristocrat. . . .'

And Josépha told the story of how Monsieur Thoul had set up house and 'married'.

'So, Mademoiselle,' said the Baroness, 'my husband, thanks to you, has wanted for nothing?'

'We did what we could to help, Madame.'

'And where is he?'

'Monsieur le Duc told me, about six months ago, that the Baron, who was known to his lawyer as Monsieur Thoul, had drawn the whole sum of eight thousand francs that he was to have in instalments every three months,' said Josépha. 'But neither I nor Monsieur d'Hérouville has had any news of the Baron. People like us lead such a full, such a busy, life that I could not run after old Thoul. And it so happens that in the last six months, Bijou, who does my embroidery, his . . . what shall I call her?'

'His mistress,' said Madame Hulot.

'His mistress,' repeated Josépha, 'has not been here. Mademoiselle Olympe Bijou may very well have got divorced. Divorce is quite common in our district.'

Josépha rose, chose exotic flowers from her flower-stands, and made a charming, sweet-scented bouquet for the Baroness, who, we may as well say, had found her expectations quite disappointed. The Baroness, like those good bourgeois folk who take talented people for some kind of monster, eating and drinking, walking and speaking, quite differently from other human beings, had been hoping to see Josépha the fascinating man-eater, the opera singer, the dazzling and voluptuous courtesan; and she had found a serene and well-poised woman, with the noble dignity given her by her talent, the simplicity of an actress who knows that every evening she is a queen; and, even more unexpectedly, a courtesan who in her looks, her attitude and manner, was paying full and unreserved homage to the virtuous wife, to the *Mater dolorosa* of the holy hymn, and making an offering of flowers to her sorrows, as in Italy they adorn the Madonna.

'Madame,' said the footman, returning after half an hour, 'old Madame Bijou is on her way; but it is not sure that her daughter Olympe can be counted on to come. Madame's embroideress has become a respectable woman; she is married. ...'

'A make-believe marriage?' asked Josépha.

'No, Madame, really married. She is in charge of a fine business. She has married the owner of a large fancy goods shop that thousands have been spent on, on the boulevard des Italiens, and she has left her embroidering business to her sister and mother. She is Madame Grenouville. The fat shopkeeper ...'

'A man like Crevel!'

'Yes, Madame,' said the servant. 'He has made a marriage settlement of thirty thousand francs on Mademoiselle Bijou. Her elder sister too, they say, is going to marry a rich butcher.'

'Your affair is not going so well, seemingly,' the singer said to the Baroness. 'Monsieur le Baron hasn't stayed where I settled him.'

Ten minutes later Madame Bijou was announced. Josépha prudently showed the Baroness into her boudoir and drew the curtains across.

'You would scare her,' she told the Baroness. 'She wouldn't give anything away if she guessed that you were interested in her confidences. Let me draw her confession from her! If you hide here, you will hear everything. This kind of scene is played just as often in real life as it is in the theatre.

'Well, Mother Bijou,' said the singer to an old woman bundled in tartan cloth, who looked like a portress in her Sunday best, 'so you are all well off? Your daughter has been lucky!'

'Oh, well off! ... My daughter gives us a hundred francs a month, and she goes in her carriage, and she eats off silver; she's a millionairess, she is! ... Olympe could easily have made me comfortable. To have to work at my age! ... Do you call that well off?'

'She is wrong to be ungrateful, for she owes her beauty to

you,' said Josépha. 'But why has she not come to see me? It was I who saved her from want by marrying her to my uncle.'

'Yes, Madame, old Thoul! ... But he's very old, worn out. ...'

'What have you done with him then? Is he with you? She was very silly to leave him, he's worth millions now. ...'

'Ah, bless my soul!' said old Madame Bijou. 'Isn't that what we told her when she treated him so badly, and him as soft as could be with her, poor old soul! Ah, she fairly kept him on the trot! Olympe has gone to the bad, Madame!'

'How's that?'

'She got to know, saving your presence, Madame, one of those fellows paid to clap at the theatre, the grand-nephew of an old mattress-maker of the Faubourg Saint-Marceau. He's a *good-for-nothing*, and a *hanger-on* at the theatre, like all those boys with looks. Well, he's a cock of the side-walk in the boulevard du Temple, where he's taken on to make a fuss of new plays, and work up the actresses' entrances, as he calls it. He spends the morning over lunch, and before the show he has dinner to keep himself in good fettle like. Well, he's been fond of the drinking and the billiards ever since he could walk, as you might say. As I said to Olympe, "It's not a way to live, that!"'

'It is, unfortunately, a way that some men live,' said Josépha.

'Anyhow, Olympe lost her head over the fellow, who kept bad company, Madame, and a proof of it is that he nearly got himself arrested in a bar thieves use, but Monsieur Braulard, the head of the *claque*, got him out of it that time. And so he's one of the lot that wears gold rings in their ears, and earns their living doing nothing, and hangs round the women who go mad about good-looking chaps like him. Well, all the money that Monsieur Thoul gave her went into his games. The business was doing very badly. Whatever came in from embroidery went on billiards. And so this chap here had a pretty sister, about as much use as her brother was, not up to any good, living in the students' quarter.'

'A tart from La Chaumière,' said Josépha.

'Yes, Madame,' said Bijou. 'And so Idamore – that's what

he calls himself for business, for his real name's Chardin – well, Idamore thought that your uncle must have far more money than he said, and he found a way of sending his sister Élodie – that's the theatre name he gave her – to us as a work-girl without my daughter thinking anything of it. Well, bless us all! She turned the whole place upside down, she taught all those poor girls bad ways, you couldn't do a thing with them, quite shameless they got, saving your presence. ... And she didn't rest till she had got old Thoul for herself, and she's took him away we don't know where, and that's put us in a fine fix because of all those bills. And we're still left from hand to mouth not able to pay them, except that my daughter, whose name is in it, keeps an eye on them. ... Well, when Idamore saw that he had hooked the old fellow because of his sister, he left my poor daughter standing there, and he's now with a young leading lady in the Funambules. And so my daughter got married, as you'll see. ...'

'But do you know where the mattress-maker lives?' asked Josépha.

'Old Papa Chardin? Does that lot live anywhere! He's drunk from six o'clock in the morning. He makes a mattress about once a month. He spends the whole day in low sort of tap-rooms. He plays pools ...'

'What, pullets? He's a proud cock!'

'You don't understand, Madame; pools at billiards. He wins three or four every day, and he drinks ...'

'Egg flip!' said Josépha. 'But if Idamore's playground is the boulevard, we could find him through my friend Braulard.'

'I don't know, Madame, seeing as all this happened six months ago. Idamore is one of those ones taking the road to gaol, and from there to the central prison at Melun, and from there ... save us! ...'

'To the hulks!' said Josépha.

'Ah! Madame knows it all,' said Madame Bijou, with a smile. 'If my daughter had never have met that fellow, she would have been ... But she's been very lucky, all the same, you'll tell me; for Monsieur Grenouville got so crazy about her that he's married her.'

'And how was that marriage made?'

'Because Olympe was in such a taking, Madame. She saw herself thrown over for the young leading lady – ah! she didn't half give her a trouncing, she properly what you call walloped her – and then she had lost old Thoul who adored her, too, and she said she was through with men. And so, Monsieur Grenouville, him who used to come and buy a lot from us, two hundred embroidered Chinese shawls a quarter, he wanted to console her; but believe it or not, she wouldn't hear a word, it was the Registrar's Office and the church for her or nothing. "I'm going to be respectable!" that's what she kept on saying. "I'll be respectable or I'll die first!" And she stuck to it. Monsieur Grenouville said he would marry her if she would have nothing more to do with us, and we said we would let her ...'

'If money passed?' said Josépha shrewdly.

'Yes, Madame, ten thousand francs, and a bit every year for my father, who isn't able to work any more.'

'I asked your daughter to look after old Thoul and make him happy, and she's thrown him into the gutter! It really is a shame. I'll never try to help anyone again! That's what happens when you try to give a helping hand to someone! You always have reason to regret a kindness. It's throwing money away – you don't know how it may turn out. Olympe might at least have let me know what she was up to! If you can find old Thoul again within a fortnight, I'll give you a thousand francs. ...'

'That's not an easy job, Madame, though you're so kind. But there's a lot of money in a thousand francs, and I'll see what I can do.'

'Good-bye, Madame Bijou.'

When she went into her boudoir, the singer found Madame Hulot in a dead faint; but even in unconsciousness she was shaken by her nervous trembling, like a snake still twitching with its head cut off. Strong smelling salts, cold water, all the usual remedies, were applied, and the Baroness was recalled to life, or, more precisely, to memory of her sorrows.

'Ah! Mademoiselle, how low he has fallen!' she said,

recognizing the singer and seeing that she was alone with her.

'Have courage, Madame,' answered Josépha, who had seated herself on a cushion at the Baroness's feet, and was kissing her hands. 'We'll find him; and if he is in the mire, well, it'll wash off. Believe me, for well-bred people, it's only a matter of clothes. . . . Let me make amends for the wrong I did you, for I can see how much your husband means to you, in spite of his behaviour, since you came here for him! True enough, poor man, he's fond of women. . . . Well, if only you could have had a little of our knack, you know, you would have kept him from running after us. You would have been what we know all about being – *every kind of woman* to a man. The government ought to start a school for respectable women! But governments are so prudish! And yet it's the men that run the governments that we lead by the nose – I'm sorry for the nations. . . . But we must think of what's to be done for you instead of gibing at them. . . . Well, don't worry, Madame; go home, and set your mind at rest. I'll bring you back your Hector, as good as he was thirty years ago.'

'Oh, Mademoiselle, let us go and see this Madame Grenouville!' said the Baroness. 'She is bound to know something. I might see Monsieur Hulot today, and rescue him from poverty and shame at once. . . .'

'Madame, I shall prove to you, here and now, the deep gratitude I shall always feel for the honour you have done me. I will not allow the singer Josépha, the Duc d'Hérouville's mistress, to be seen in the same carriage as the beautiful and saintly image of virtue. I respect you too much to appear in public with you. I am not affecting humility, like an actress: this is homage that I properly pay you. You make me sorry, Madame, that I cannot follow your path, in spite of the thorns in your bleeding hands and feet! But what can one do? I belong to Art, as you belong to Virtue. . . .'

'Poor girl!' said the Baroness, moved, in the midst of her own sorrows, by an unusual sympathy and compassion. 'I will pray for you. You are the victim of our society, which has to have its entertainment. When old age comes, your penitent voice will be hearkened to ... if God deigns to hear the prayers of a ...'

'Of a martyr, Madame,' said Josépha, reverentially kissing the hem of the Baroness's dress.

But Adeline took the singer's hand, drew her to her, and kissed her forehead. Blushing with pleasure, the singer saw Adeline to her cab, with every mark of the deepest respect.

'It must be some lady of charity,' said the man-servant to the maid. '*She* doesn't treat anybody like that, not even her best friend, Madame Jenny Cadine!'

'Wait a few more days, Madame,' Josépha said, 'and you shall see him, or I'll deny the God of my fathers; and for a Jewess to say that, you know, is to promise success.'

About the time of the Baroness's arrival at Josépha's house, Victorin was interviewing an old woman of about seventy-five, who in order to obtain admission to the distinguished lawyer had made use of the awful name of the chief of the Sûreté. The attendant announced:

'Madame de Saint-Estève!'

'That's just one of the names I use,' she said, as she sat down.

Victorin felt something like an inner shudder at the sight of that hideous beldame. Her expensive dress did nothing to soften the effect of the cold malignity of her horribly wrinkled, pallid, sinewy face. Marat, if he had been a woman of her age, would have looked like her, a figure of the Terror incarnate. The sharp little eyes of the sinister old hag showed a tiger's blood-thirsty greed. Her flattened nose, the nostrils elongated to oval holes that seemed to exhale the fires of hell, suggested the purposefully evil beaks of birds of prey. Behind her low cruel forehead manifestly lay an intriguing mind. The long hairs springing haphazard from every crevice of her face seemed to indicate a masculine enterprise and capacity for organization. Anyone seeing this woman would have reflected that none of the painters ever found the right model for Mephistopheles.

'My dear Monsieur,' she said patronizingly, 'it's a very long time since I took a hand in any business. Anything I do for you I'm doing for the sake of my dear nephew, who means more to me than a son. The President of the Council dropped a couple of words in the ear of the Prefect of Police about you, but he, after conferring with Monsieur Chapuzot, is of the opinion that the police should not appear at all in an affair of this kind. My nephew has been given a free hand, but my nephew will only act in an advisory capacity, he must not be compromised....'

'Your nephew is ...?'

'Quite so, and I'm rather proud of the fact,' she cut the lawyer short; 'for he's my pupil, a pupil who soon surpassed his master. ... We have considered your business, and we have taken its measure! Will you give thirty thousand francs to be rid of this matter, once for all? I liquidate the business for you, and you pay only when the thing is done. ...'

'You know the persons concerned?'

'No, my dear Monsieur, you must inform us further. We've been told: "There's a moonstruck old man that a widow's got her hooks in. The widow, aged twenty-nine, knows how to play her cards, and she has cleaned up forty thousand francs a year from two heads of families. Now she's on the point of raking in eighty thousand francs a year by marriage with an old fellow of sixty-one. She will ruin an entire respected family, and pass that enormous fortune on to some lover's child by getting rid of her old husband as soon as may be ...". That is the situation.'

'That is correct,' said Victorin. 'My father-in-law, Monsieur Crevel ...'

'A former perfumer, a Mayor. I live in his district, under the name of Ma'am Nourrisson,' she took him up.

'The other person is Madame Marneffe.'

'I don't know her,' said Madame de Saint-Estève; 'but in three days I'll be in a position to count her shifts.'

'Could you prevent the marrage?' asked the lawyer.

'How far have things gone?'

'The second reading of the banns.'

'The woman would have to be kidnapped. Today's Sunday ... there are only three days, for they'll marry on Wednesday. No, it's impossible! But we could kill her for you. ...'

Victorin Hulot jumped, with any law-abiding citizen's reaction to hearing those six words spoken in a business-like tone.

'Murder! . . .' he said. 'And how would you do it?'

'For the last forty years, Monsieur, we have played the part of fate,' she answered with a formidable pride, 'and have done just as we please in Paris. More families than one, and many from the faubourg Saint-Germain, have told me their secrets, believe me! I have made and broken many a marriage, and torn up many a will, and saved many a threatened reputation. I keep a flock of secrets tucked away in their pen in here,' and she tapped her forehead; 'and they're worth thirty-six thousand francs a year to me. And you'll be one of my lambs, naturally! A woman like me, would she be what I am if she talked about how she did things? I don't talk, I act! Everything that happens, my dear Monsieur, will be an accident, and you will not feel the slightest remorse. You will be like people cured by hypnotists; at the end of a month they believe that nature did it all.'

A cold sweat broke out on Victorin. Sight of the headsman would have disturbed him less than this sententious and portentous sister of the hulks. Looking at her dress, the colour of wine lees, he fancied her clothed in blood.

'Madame, I cannot accept the assistance of your experience and energy if success is to cost a life, or if any action in the least criminal is implied.'

'You are a great baby, Monsieur!' replied Madame de Saint-Estève. 'You want to preserve your rectitude whole in your own eyes, and at the same time you want your enemy to die.'

Victorin shook his head.

'Yes,' she went on. 'You want this Madame Marneffe to release the prey she's holding in her jaws! And how would you set about making a tiger drop his chunk of meat? . . . Would you do it by rubbing your hand along his back and saying "*Pussy! . . . Pussy! . . .*"? You are not logical. You declare war, and don't want any bloodshed! Very well, I'll make you a present of your innocence since it's so dear to you. I have always seen that rectitude is the raw material of which hypocrisy is made! One day within the next three months a poor priest will come to ask you for forty thousand francs for a benefaction – for a ruined monastery in the desert, in the Levant! If you are pleased with the way things have fallen out, give the fellow the forty thousand francs. It's not any more than you'll pay, anyway, to the Inland Revenue! It's a trifle, come now, compared with what you'll gain.'

She got to her feet – broad feet, the flesh bulging over the satin slippers that barely contained them. She smiled, and bowed, and moved towards the door.

'The devil has a sister,' said Victorin, as he rose.

He went to the door with this horrifying stranger, conjured up from the haunts of the secret agents of espionage as a monster rises from subterranean depths at the Opera in a ballet, at the wave of a fairy's wand.

When he had finished his business in the law courts, Victorin went to see Monsieur Chapuzot, head of one of the most important departments of the Prefecture of Police, in order to make some inquiries about the stranger. Finding Monsieur Chapuzot alone in his office, Victorin Hulot thanked him for his help.

'You sent me an old woman,' he said, 'who might be called criminal Paris personified.'

Monsieur Chapuzot laid his spectacles down on his papers, and looked at the lawyer with raised eyebrows.

'I should certainly not have taken the liberty of sending you anyone without letting you know beforehand, or sending a note of introduction,' he replied.

'It must have been Monsieur le Préfet then . . .'

'That is unlikely,' said Chapuzot. 'The last time that Prince de Wissembourg dined with the Minister of Home Affairs, he saw the Prefect and spoke to him about your position, a most deplorable situation, and asked him if it was possible in a friendly way to come to your assistance. The concern His Excellency showed about this family matter naturally enlisted Monsieur le Préfet's keen interest, and he was good enough to consult me. Ever since Monsieur le Préfet took over the administration of this department, which has been so much reviled and does so much useful work, he has made it a rule not to intervene in any way in family matters. He was right in principle and theory; although he was going contrary to traditional practice. Speaking of the forty-five years of my experience, the police between 1799 and 1815 rendered great services to families, but since 1820 the Press and constitutional government have completely altered the conditions of our service. So my advice was not to have anything to do with an affair of this kind, and Monsieur le Préfet was so good as to concur with my observations. The chief of the Sûreté, in my presence, received the order not to take any steps in the matter; and if it is true that you have had a visit from someone sent by him, I shall reprimand him – it would be grounds for his dismissal.

'It is easy to say "That's a matter for the police!" The police! They all call for the police! But, my dear sir, the Marshal, the Council of Ministers, simply do not know what the police are. Only the police themselves know their powers. The kings, Napoleon, Louis XVIII, knew their own police; but as for ours, only Fouché, Monsieur Lenoir, Monsieur de Sartines, and a few perspicacious Prefects, have realized how it has been limited. . . . Nowadays everything is changed. We have been diminished, disarmed!

'I have seen many an abuse spring up in private affairs that I could have swept away with just five scruples of arbitrary action! We shall be regretted by the very men who have cut us down when, like you, they find themselves faced with some monstrous wrong that we ought to have the same power to put right as we have to clear away dirt! In public affairs the police are held responsible for anticipating anything that may affect public security; but the family is sacred. I would do everything possible to discover and prevent an attempt against the King's life – I would look into a house as if its walls were transparent. But to go and lay our fingers on family affairs, concern ourselves with private interests! Never, so long as I sit in this office – because I'm afraid. . . .'

'Of what?'

'Of the Press, Monsieur le Député, of the Left Centre Party!'

'What ought I to do?' said Hulot, after a pause.

'Well, you represent the family!' returned the departmental chief. 'That says all there is to say. Act as you think best. But as to helping you, making the police the instrument of private passions and private interests, do you imagine that is possible? That, do you know, was the reason behind the inevitable prosecution, which the magistrates found illegal, of the predecessor of our present Sûreté chief. Bibi-Lupin used the police on behalf of private individuals. There was a far-reaching social danger implied in that! With the powers he could use, that man would have been formidable, he would have been the hand of Fate!'

'But, in my place ...?' said Hulot.

'Ah! You're asking me for advice, you – a man who sells it!' replied Monsieur Chapuzot. 'Come, now, my dear sir, you're making fun of me.'

Hulot bowed to the departmental chief and went away, without noticing that official's almost imperceptible shrug as he rose to show him out.

'And that man aspires to be a statesman!' said Monsieur Chapuzot to himself, taking up his reports again.

Victorin returned home, his perplexities unresolved, unable to confide them to anyone. At dinner, the Baroness joyfully announced to her family that within a month their father might be sharing their prosperity, and ending his days peacefully with them all.

'Ah, I would gladly give my three thousand six hundred francs a year to see the Baron here!' cried Lisbeth. 'But dear Adeline, do not count on such happiness too soon, I beg of you!'

'Lisbeth is right,' said Célestine. 'My dear Mother, wait until it happens.'

The Baroness, her heart overflowing with tenderness and hope, told the story of her visit to Josépha, said that she thought poor creatures like her unhappy, in spite of all their success, and spoke of Chardin, the mattress-maker, father of the Oran storekeeper, as proof that she was not cherishing empty hopes.

Next morning, by seven o'clock, Lisbeth was in a cab on her way to the quai de la Tournelle. She stopped the vehicle at the corner of the rue de Poissy.

'Go to the rue des Bernardins, number seven,' she said to the driver. 'It is a house with an entry and no porter. Go up to the fourth floor and ring at the door to the left, on which you will see a notice "Mademoiselle Chardin. Lace and cashmere shawls mended". When someone comes to the door, you will ask for the *gentleman*. You will get the reply "He is out". You will say "I know, but find him. His *maid* is waiting in a cab on the quai, and wants to see him".'

Twenty minutes later, an old man who looked about eighty, with perfectly white hair, and a nose reddened by the cold in a pale and wrinkled face like an old woman's, shuffled up in carpet slippers, his back bent. He was wearing a threadbare alpaca coat with no decoration, and at his wrists protruded the sleeves of a knitted woollen garment, and shirt-cuffs of doubtful cleanliness. He came timidly up, looked at the cab, recognized Lisbeth, and appeared at the door.

'Ah, my dear Cousin,' she said. 'What a sad state you are in!'

'Élodie takes all the money for herself!' said Baron Hulot. 'Those Chardins are low scum. ...'

'Do you want to come back to us?'

'Oh, no, no!' said the old man. 'I wish I could go to America. ...'

'Adeline is on your track.'

'Ah, if my debts could only be paid!' said the Baron questioningly, with a furtive look. 'For Samanon is after me.'

'We haven't yet paid off your arrears. Your son still owes a hundred thousand francs.'

'Poor boy!'

'And your pension will not be free for seven or eight months. ... If you'll wait, I have two thousand francs here!'

The Baron held out his hand in a gesture of shocking avidity.

'Give it to me, Lisbeth! God bless you for it! Give it to me! I know where I can go!'

378

'But you will tell me where, you old monster?'

'Yes, I can wait eight months, because I have found a little angel, a good creature, an innocent soul, not old enough yet to have been corrupted.'

'Remember the police court,' said Lisbeth, who cherished the hope of seeing Hulot there one day.

'Oh, she lives in the rue de Charonne!' said Baron Hulot. 'That's a quarter where there's no scandal, whatever happens. Oh, no one will ever find me there. I'm disguised, Lisbeth, as Père Thorec; they think I'm a retired cabinet-maker. The child loves me, and I'm not going to let them shear me like a sheep any more.'

'No, that's been done!' said Lisbeth, looking at his coat. 'Suppose I drive you there, Cousin? ...'

Baron Hulot climbed into the cab, casting off Mademoiselle Élodie, like a novel read and thrown away, without even saying good-bye.

Half an hour later, a half hour spent by the Baron in talking to Lisbeth uninterruptedly of little Atala Judici, for he had by degrees become the victim of the terrible obsessive passions that destroy old men, his cousin set him down with two thousand francs in his pocket in the rue de Charonne, in the faubourg Saint-Antoine, at the door of a dubious and sinister-looking house.

'Good-bye, Cousin. You will be Père Thorec now, is that right? Don't send anyone to me except porters, and always hire them from different places.'

'Agreed. Oh! I'm very lucky!' said the Baron, his face alight with anticipation of a quite new happiness.

'They'll not find him there!' said Lisbeth to herself; and she stopped her cab on the boulevard Beaumarchais, and from there returned by omnibus to the rue Louis-le-Grand.

*

On the following day, when the whole family was gathered in the drawing-room after lunch, Crevel was announced. Célestine ran to throw her arms round her father's neck, and behaved as if he had been there only the evening before, although this was his first visit in two years.

'How do you do, Father?' said Victorin, holding out his hand.

'Good morning, my children,' said Crevel pompously. 'Madame la Baronne, I lay my homage at your feet. Heavens, how these children grow! This crowd is treading on our heels! They're saying to us "Grandpapa, I want my place in the sun!" Madame la Comtesse, you are still as wonderfully beautiful as ever!' he went on, looking at Hortense. 'Ah, and here's the balance of our pocketful, Cousin Bette, the wise virgin! Well, you are all very comfortable here . . .' he said, after he had handed out these remarks to each in turn, with an accompaniment of hearty laughs that moved the rubicund flesh of his heavy cheeks only with difficulty. And he looked round his daughter's drawing-room with some contempt.

'My dear Célestine, I'll make you a present of all my furniture from the rue des Saussayes; it will do very well here. Your drawing-room is in need of a bit of furbishing up. . . . Ah, here's Wenceslas, funny little chap! Well, now, grandchildren, are we all good children? We must mind our manners and morals, you know.'

'To make up for those who haven't any,' said Lisbeth.

'That sarcasm, my dear Lisbeth, doesn't affect me now. I am going to put an end to the false position I have been in for so long, my children. I am here, like a proper father and head of the family, to announce to you that I am going to be married, just like that, without any bones about it.'

'You have a perfect right to get married,' said Victorin. 'And for my part I release you from the promise you made me when you gave me my dear Célestine's hand. . . .'

'What promise?' demanded Crevel.

'A promise that you would not remarry,' answered the lawyer. 'You will do me the justice of agreeing that I did not ask you to give such a promise, that you made it quite voluntarily, in spite of what I said, for at the time I pointed out that you ought not to bind yourself in that way.'

'Yes, I remember, my dear fellow,' said Crevel, rather taken aback. 'And see here, bless me, upon my word! . . . my dear children, if you will only get on well with Madame Crevel, you will have no reason to regret it. I am grateful for your proper feeling, Victorin. No one treats me with generosity without having his reward. ... See here, now, come on! Accept your stepmother in a friendly way and come to the wedding!'

'You don't tell us, Father, who your fiancée is?' said Célestine.

'Why that's no secret to anyone,' returned Crevel. 'Let's not play hide and seek! Lisbeth must have told you ...'

'My dear Monsieur Crevel,' answered Lisbeth, 'there are names that are not mentioned here. ...'

'Well, it's Madame Marneffe!'

'Monsieur Crevel,' said the lawyer sternly, 'neither I nor my wife will be present at that marriage, not because it affects our interests, for what I said just now was meant sincerely. Yes, indeed, I should be very glad to know that you would find happiness in marriage. But there are considerations of honour and delicacy that you will understand, which I must not put into words, because it would mean reopening wounds here that are still fresh.'

The Baroness made a sign to the Countess, who picked up her son, saying:

'Come, it's time for your bath, Wenceslas! Good-bye, Monsieur Crevel.'

The Baroness bowed to Crevel silently. Crevel could not help smiling at the child's surprise at finding himself threatened with this unexpected bath.

'The woman you intend to marry, Monsieur,' said the lawyer sharply, when he was alone with Lisbeth, his wife, and his father-in-law, 'is a woman loaded with spoils from my father, who in cold blood has brought him to his present state, who after destroying him is living with his son-in-law, and has caused my sister intense suffering. ... And do you imagine that we will publicly approve your folly by my presence? I am sincerely sorry for you, my dear Monsieur Crevel! You lack family feeling; you do not understand the solidarity that in honour binds a family's several members. One cannot reason with the passions – I know that, unfortunately, only too well. Men swept by passion are both deaf and blind. Your daughter Célestine's sense of filial duty is too strong to allow her to reproach you.'

'It would be a pretty thing if she did!' said Crevel, endeavouring to stem this harangue.

'Célestine would not be my wife if she made a single protest,' the lawyer went on; 'but I am free to try to stop you when you are about to step over a precipice, especially as I have given you proof of my disinterestedness. It is certainly not your fortune, it is yourself that I am concerned about. . . . And in order to make my feelings quite clear to you, I may add, if only to set your mind at rest in the matter of your future marriage contract, that my position now leaves nothing to be desired.'

'Thanks to me!' exclaimed Crevel, whose face had turned purple.

'Thanks to Célestine's fortune,' the lawyer replied; 'and if you regret having given your daughter, as your share of her dowry, a sum that is less than half of what her mother left her, we are quite prepared to return it to you. . . .'

'Do you know, my learned son-in-law,' said Crevel, striking his pose, 'that when I give Madame Marneffe the protection of my name, she is not required to answer to the world for her conduct, otherwise than as Madame Crevel?'

'That is perhaps very chivalrous,' said the lawyer; 'it is treating matters of the heart, the aberrations of passion, generously. But I do not know a name, or law, or title, that can cover the theft of three hundred thousand francs meanly extorted from my father! I tell you plainly my dear father-in-law, that your future wife is unworthy of you, that she is deceiving you, that she is madly in love with my brother-in-law, Steinbock, whose debts she has paid.'

'I paid them!'

'Very well,' returned the lawyer; 'I'm happy to hear it, for Count Steinbock's sake – he may be able to pay what he owes some day. But he is the lover, very much loved, very often loved. . . .'

'He is her lover!' said Crevel, whose face showed how upset he was. 'It is cowardly and filthy and mean and vulgar to slander a woman! When a man says that sort of thing, Monsieur, he must be prepared to prove it.'

'I will give you proofs.'

'I'll wait to see them!'

'The day after tomorrow, my dear Monsieur Crevel, I'll tell you the day and the hour and the minute when I shall be in a position to expose the dreadful depravity of your future wife.'

'Very well, I shall be charmed,' said Crevel, recovering his composure. 'Good-bye, my children, *au revoir*. Good-bye, Lisbeth ...'

'Go after him, Lisbeth,' said Célestine in Cousin Bette's ear.

'Well, well, is that how you go off?' Lisbeth cried after Crevel.

'Ah!' Crevel said to her. 'He takes a high and mighty line nowadays, my son-in-law; he's outgrown his boots. What with the law courts, the Chamber, the sharp practice of lawyers, and the sharp practice of politicians, they've put a keen edge on him. Aha! he knows that I'm getting married next Wednesday, and on Sunday this gentleman claims that in three days he'll be able to fix the day on which he'll demonstrate to me that my wife is unworthy of me ... that's a good one! I'm going back now to sign the contract. Well, you can come with me, Lisbeth; come on! They won't know anything about it! I meant to leave forty thousand francs a year to Célestine; but after the way Hulot has just behaved, how can I ever feel any affection for them again?'

'Give me ten minutes, Papa Crevel. Wait for me in your carriage at the door. I'll find some excuse for going out.'

'Well, I'll do that. ...'

'My dears,' said Lisbeth, returning to the family, now together again in the drawing-room, 'I'm going with Crevel. The contract is to be signed this evening, and I'll be able to tell you what its terms are. It will probably be my last visit to that woman. Your father is furious. He is going to disinherit you. ...'

'His vanity will prevent that,' the barrister replied. 'He was determined to possess Presles, and he will want to keep it in the family; I know him. Even if he should have children,

Célestine would still inherit half of what he leaves; legally it's not possible for him to give away his whole fortune. ... But these questions really do not interest me; all I'm thinking about is our honour. Go with him, Cousin,' he said, pressing Lisbeth's hand, 'and listen to the contract carefully.'

Twenty minutes later, Lisbeth and Crevel walked into the house in the rue Barbet, where Madame Marneffe was waiting in a gentle impatience to hear the result of the overtures that she had commanded Crevel to make.

Valérie had in the end fallen victim to the kind of infatuation that takes a woman's heart by storm once in a lifetime. Only doubtfully successful as an artist, Wenceslas, in Madame Marneffe's hands, became a lover so perfect that he was for her all she had been for Baron Hulot.

Valérie held slippers in one hand and the other was in Steinbock's possession, as she rested her head on his shoulder. Some conversations, such as that they had embarked on after Crevel's departure, of broken sentences and disconnected phrases, are rather like the rambling literary works of our time, on the title-page of which are set the words: *Copyright Reserved.* The intimate poetry of this duologue had led the artist to utter a natural regret, not unmixed with bitterness.

'Oh, what a pity that I ever married!' said Wenceslas. 'For if I had waited, as Lisbeth told me to, I could marry you now!'

'Only a Pole could want to turn a devoted mistress into a wife!' exclaimed Valérie. 'To exchange love for duty! Pleasure for boredom!'

'I know how fickle you are!' said Steinbock. 'Haven't I heard you talking to Lisbeth about Baron Montès, that Brazilian. ...'

'Would you like to get rid of him for me?' said Valérie.

'I suppose that's the only way to keep you from seeing him,' the ex-sculptor retorted.

'Let me tell you, my pet,' said Valérie. 'I was keeping him in the larder to make a husband of him. You see I have no secrets from you! The things I have promised that Brazilian! Oh! long before I knew you,' she added quickly, as Wenceslas made a gesture. 'Well, he uses those promises against me as a kind of torture, and they mean that I'll have to be married practically in secret; for if he hears that I am marrying Crevel, he is a man who would think nothing of ... of killing me!'

'Oh! you don't need to worry about that!' said Steinbock, with a scornful gesture, signifying that for a woman loved by a Pole such danger must be negligible.

Note that, in matters involving courage at least, Poles can never be accused of empty boasting; they are so truly and unquestionably brave.

'And Crevel is such an idiot, wanting to have a party and get full value for his money, as usual, in a big show at my wedding. He puts me in a fix that I don't know how to get out of!'

How could Valérie confess to the man whom she adored that Baron Henri Montès had, since Baron Hulot's dismissal, succeeded to the privilege of visiting her at any hour of the night, and that, for all her adroitness, she had still not managed to find a plausible pretext for a quarrel that would throw all the blame on the Baron? She was well aware of the primitive savage underlying the civilized veneer in the Baron, who in some ways was very like Lisbeth, and her thoughts about that Othello from Rio de Janeiro made her shudder.

At the sound of wheels, Steinbock took his arm from Valérie's waist, left her side, and picked up a newspaper. Crevel and Lisbeth found him absorbed in it, while Valérie's attention was concentrated on a pair of slippers that she was embroidering for her future husband.

'How she's slandered!' whispered Lisbeth at Crevel's ear, on the threshold, pointing out this tableau to him. 'Just look at her hair! Is there a hair out of place? To hear Victorin you might have expected to surprise a pair of nesting turtle-doves.'

'My dear Lisbeth,' replied Crevel, striking his pose, 'take it from me that to turn Aspasia into Lucretia, one only has to inspire a passion in her!'

'Haven't I always told you,' said Lisbeth, 'that women love fat libertines like you?'

'She would be very ungrateful besides if she didn't love me,' Crevel went on, 'considering all the money I have spent on this place. Only Grindot and I know how much!'

And he waved a hand in the direction of the staircase. In the planning of this house, which Crevel regarded as his own, Grindot had tried to rival Cleretti, the fashionable architect whom the Duc d'Hérouville had employed on Josépha's house. But Crevel, who had no capacity for appreciating the arts, had determined, in the fashion of all bourgeois patrons, to spend only a fixed sum, specified in advance. And Grindot, so limited, had found it impossible to realize his artistic conception of the whole.

To compare Josépha's house with the house in the rue Barbet was to understand the gulf between distinctive individual style and the vulgar taste. The admirable objects in Josépha's house were to be found nowhere else: those that caught the eye in Crevel's could be bought anywhere. These two different kinds of luxury are distinct and separate, and the river of a million reproductions flows between. A unique mirror is worth six thousand francs; the mirror designed by a manufacturer, who sells as many as he can, costs five hundred francs. A genuine boule lustre may fetch three thousand francs at a public auction: the same thing cast in a mould can be manufactured for ten or twelve hundred. Among antiques, the one holds the place of a Raphael in the world of art: the other is a copy. How much would you give for a copy of a Raphael? Crevel's house, in short, was a splendid illustration of a fool's idea of luxury, while Josépha's was a very fine example of an artist's work.

'War is declared,' said Crevel, as he entered the room, to his future wife.

Madame Marneffe rang.

'Go and fetch Monsieur Berthier,' she said to the footman, 'and don't come back without him. If you had been successful, dear old thing,' she said, with a kiss, to Crevel, 'we would have delayed my happiness, and had a dazzling reception; but when a whole family opposes a marriage, my dear, the only proper thing is to do it quietly without any fuss, expecially when the bride is a widow.'

'Nonsense! What I want is to make a display in the Louis XIV style,' said Crevel, who for some time had been finding the eighteenth century cramping. 'I have ordered new carriages: there is a carriage for the bridegroom, and a carriage for the bride, two smart coupés, a barouche, and a coach made for state occasions with a superb seat on springs that shakes like Madame Hulot.'

'Oh, so that's what *you want*! ... So you're not my lamb any more? No, no, my pet, you'll do what I want. We'll sign our marriage contract here in private, this evening. Then on Wednesday we'll have the official marriage, as people really do marry, under the rose, as my poor mother used to say. We'll walk to the church, dressed quite simply, and there will be low mass. We'll have Stidmann, Steinbock, Vignon, and Massol for our witnesses. They're all lively spirits, who'll just happen to be there at the registrar's office at your Mairie, and they'll sit out a mass for our sakes. Your colleague will marry us, as a favour to you, at nine in the morning; mass at ten o'clock; and we'll be back here for lunch at half past eleven. I have promised our guests that we shan't rise from table until the evening. ... We'll have Bixiou and your old companion at Birotteau's place, du Tillet, and Lousteau, Vernisset, Léon de Lora, Vernou, the brightest of the bright sparks, and they won't know we've been married. We'll mystify them, we'll get just a trifle tipsy, and we'll have Lisbeth with us. I mean her to learn what marriage is. Bixiou must make a pass at her and ... and open her eyes.'

For a couple of hours Madame Marneffe prattled on in a stream of light-hearted nonsense that led Crevel to make this discerning reflection:

'How could a woman so gay be depraved? Frivolous, yes! but perverse ... what nonsense!'

'What did your children say about me?' Valérie asked Crevel at one point, as he sat beside her on her little sofa. 'Lots of horrors?'

'They declare,' he answered, 'that you are an immoral woman, in love with Wenceslas – you who are virtue's own self!'

'Of course I love him, my little Wenceslas!' cried Valérie, calling the artist to her, pulling down his head, and planting a kiss on his forehead. 'Poor boy, with no one to help him and no cash, despised by a carrot-haired giraffe! What do you think, Crevel? Wenceslas is my poet, and I love him openly by broad daylight as if he were my own child! These virtuous women see evil everywhere and in everything. Tell me, can they not be in a man's company without doing wrong? I can only speak for myself, and I'm like a spoiled child who has never been refused anything: bonbons don't tempt me any more. Poor women, I'm sorry for them! ... And who was it that had such nasty things to say?'

'Victorin,' said Crevel.

'Well, why didn't you shut the poll parrot lawyer's mouth with the story of his mama's two hundred thousand francs?'

'Oh, the Baroness had fled,' said Lisbeth.

'Let them be warned, Lisbeth,' said Madame Marneffe, knitting her brows. 'Either they'll receive me, and in proper fashion too, and call on their stepmother, all of them, or I'll set them lower than the Baron! Tell them I said so. I'll end by turning nasty, see if I don't! Upon my word, I think evil minds are like a scythe, perpetually cutting back the good.'

At three o'clock, Maître Berthier, Cardot's successor, read the marriage contract, after a short consultation with Crevel, for certain provisions had depended on the attitude adopted by Monsieur and Madame Hulot. Crevel settled on his future wife a fortune comprising, first, an income of forty thousand francs from certain designated securities; secondly, the house and all its contents; thirdly, a capital sum of three million francs. In addition, he made over to his future wife, by deed of gift, all that the law allowed; the money left to her was left unconditionally, and tax paid; and if the parties should die without issue, each made the other residuary legatee of all property, estates, and possessions. This contract reduced Crevel's fortune to a capital of two millions. If he had children by his new wife, Célestine's share was to be reduced to five hundred thousand francs, and Valérie would have a life interest in the remainder. This was about a ninth part of his entire fortune.

Lisbeth returned to dinner at the rue Louis-le-Grand with despair written on her face. She explained and commented upon the marriage contract, but found both Célestine and Victorin indifferent to the disastrous news.

'You have set your father against you, my dears. Madame Marneffe has sworn that you shall receive Monsieur Crevel's wife, and call on her,' she said.

'Never!' said Hulot.

'Never!' said Célestine.

'Never!' exclaimed Hortense.

The urge to take the proud Hulots down a peg got the better of Lisbeth.

'She appears to hold a weapon against you!' she answered. 'I don't yet know exactly what it is, but I'll find out. . . . She spoke vaguely of some story of two hundred thousand francs that concerns Adeline.'

The Baroness slid gently down on the divan where she was sitting, and was seized with appalling convulsions.

'Go there, children!' she shrieked. 'Receive that woman! Monsieur Crevel is abominable! No torture would be too vile. . . . Do what that woman wants. . . . Oh, he's a monster! *She knows everything!*'

After these words, uttered with tears and sobs, Madame Hulot had just sufficient strength to go up to her room, supported by her daughter and Célestine.

'What's the meaning of all this?' exclaimed Lisbeth, left alone with Victorin.

The lawyer, standing nailed to the spot in understandable stupefaction, did not appear to hear her.

'What is it, dear Victorin?'

'I am appalled!' said the lawyer, with a dark and lowering face. 'Let whoever threatens my mother beware! I have done with scruples! If I had the power, I would crush that woman like a viper. Ah! let her dare attack the life and honour of my mother!'

'She said – don't repeat this, my dear Victorin – she said that she would see you all humbled and brought lower than your father. She sharply reproached Crevel with not having shut your mouths with this secret that seems to terrify Adeline so much.'

A doctor was sent for, as the Baroness's state grew worse. He prescribed a heavy dose of opium, and when she had taken it

Adeline fell deeply asleep; but the minds of the whole family were filled with dire forebodings.

Next day, the barrister left early for the law courts, and on his way called at the police headquarters, where he begged Vautrin, chief of the Sûreté, to send Madame de Saint-Estève to him.

'We've been forbidden to concern ourselves with your affairs, Monsieur; but Madame de Saint-Estève is a free-lance, she's at your service,' the famous chief replied.

On his return home the unhappy lawyer heard that they feared for his mother's reason. Doctor Bianchon, Doctor Larabit, and Professor Angard, in consultation, had just decided to use drastic measures to draw away the blood flowing into the brain. As Victorin was listening while Doctor Bianchon enumerated the reasons he had to hope that the crisis might pass, although his colleagues were more pessimistic, the man-servant came to announce that the lawyer's client, Madame de Saint-Estève, was below. Victorin left Bianchon in mid-sentence and ran down the stairs like a lunatic.

'Is there perhaps some contagious source of madness in this house?' said Bianchon, turning to Larabit.

The doctors departed, leaving a young doctor from the hospital, instructed by them, to look after Madame Hulot.

'A life-time of virtue!' were the only words that the stricken woman had uttered since the catastrophe.

Lisbeth never left Adeline's bedside, sitting up all night with her. She was the admiration of the two younger women.

'Well, my dear Madame de Saint-Estève!' said the lawyer, showing the horrible old hag into his study and carefully closing the doors. 'How far have we got?'

'Well, my dear friend,' she said, regarding Victorin with a coldly ironical eye, 'so you have considered matters and made your little reflections?'

'Have you done anything?'

'Will you give fifty thousand francs?'

'Yes,' Hulot answered, 'for we have to act. Do you know that with one single sentence that woman has endangered my mother's life and reason? So, proceed!'

'We have proceeded!' replied the old woman.

'Well? ...' said Victorin, with an uncontrollable gesture.

'Well, you don't stick at the expenses?'

'Not at all.'

'Because twenty-three thousand francs has already been spent.'

Hulot stared at Madame de Saint-Estève in amazement.

'Ha! you are not a simpleton, are you? You, a leading light of the law courts! With that money we've bought a chambermaid's conscience and a picture by Raphael. That's cheap enough. ...'

Hulot stood speechless, and could only stare.

'Well,' the old woman went on, 'we've bought Mademoiselle Reine Tousard. Madame Marneffe has no secrets from her.'

'I see. ...'

'But if you're going to be tight-fisted, say so!'

'I'll pay the money blind, don't worry,' he said. 'My mother said that these people deserved the worst kind of torture. ...'

'We don't break people on the wheel now,' said the hag.

'You guarantee success?'

'Leave it to me,' said the beldame. 'Your vengeance is a-brewing.'

She looked at the clock. It was six.

'Your vengeance is preparing; the furnaces of the Rocher de Cancale are alight; the carriage horses stamp; my irons grow hot. Ah! I know your Madame Marneffe inside out. All is ready, ha! There is poisoned bait in the rat-trap. I'll tell you tomorrow if the mouse is taken. I think she will be! Good-bye, my son.'

'Good-bye, Madame.'

'Do you speak English?'

'Yes.'

'Have you seen *Macbeth* played in English?'

'Yes.'

'Well, my son, thou shalt be King hereafter! That is to say you shall inherit!' said that appalling witch, foreshadowed by Shakespeare, who apparently was acquainted with Shakespeare's works.

She left Hulot, stunned, at the door of his study.

'Don't forget that the consultation is to be tomorrow,' she said graciously, in an accomplished version of a client's manner, as she saw two persons approaching, posing for their benefit with the airs and graces of a confidence-trick countess.

'What cool effrontery!' said Hulot to himself, as he bowed his pretended client out.

Baron Montès de Montejanos was a social lion, but a lion of an unaccountable kind. Fashionable Paris, and the Paris of the turf and the *demi-monde*, admired this foreign aristocrat's ineffable waistcoats, his impeccable patent-leather boots, his incomparable walking-sticks, his covetable horses, his carriage driven by Negroes who were patently slaves, and well-beaten slaves at that. It was known that he had an enormous fortune: he had seven hundred thousand francs in current account with du Tillet, the well-known banker. Yet he was always alone. If he went to a first night, he sat in the stalls. He frequented no *salon*. He had never given his arm to a courtesan! And his name could not be coupled, either, with that of any pretty woman in high social circles. His chief amusement was playing whist at the Jockey Club. For want of material, people were reduced to malicious comment on his ways and habits, or, infinitely more amusingly, so it seemed, on his person. They called him Combabus!

It was Bixiou, Léon de Lora, Lousteau, Florine, Mademoiselle Héloïse Brisetout, and Nathan, having supper one evening with the celebrated Carabine, with lots of lions and lionesses in the company, who had invented an exceedingly diverting explanation of his behaviour. Massol, as a learned Councillor of State, and Claude Vignon, in his capacity as an ex-professor of Greek, had related to the ignorant girls the famous anecdote, narrated in Rollin's *Ancient History*, concerning Combabus, the voluntary Abelard appointed to guard the wife of a King of Assyria, Persia, Bactria, Mesopotamia, and other geographical regions particularly the province of old Professor du Bocage, d'Anville's successor in the work of bringing the East of antiquity to life. The nickname, which set Carabine's guests and boon companions laughing for a quarter of an hour, was the subject of a number of very unseemly jests in a symposium, to which the Académie might very probably not award a Montyon Prize, in which the name became, and remained, a crown set on the luxuriant mane of the handsome Baron, whom Josépha called a 'magnificent Brazilian', as one might speak of a 'magnificent catoxantha'.

Carabine, the most renowned of courtesans, with her refined beauty and ready wit had snatched the sceptre of the *demi-monde* from the hands of Mademoiselle Turquet, better known as Malaga. Mademoiselle Séraphine Sinet, for that was her real name, stood in the same relation to the banker, du Tillet, as Josépha Mirah did to the Duc d'Hérouville.

Now, at about seven o'clock on the morning of that day on which the beldame Saint-Estève had prophesied success to Victorin, Carabine had said to du Tillet:

'If you were a nice man you would give a dinner for me at the Rocher de Cancale, and bring Combabus. We want to find out whether he has a mistress. ... I have a bet on it, that he has, and I want to win. ...'

'He's still staying at the Hôtel des Princes. I'll call there,' du Tillet answered. 'We'll have some fun. Invite the whole crowd – that lad Bixiou, Lora, all our set, in fact!'

At half past seven, in the best private room of the restaurant which has seen the whole of Europe dine within its walls, the table glittered with a magnificent service of silver plate, designed and ordered for occasions when the bill was to be paid with Vanity's banknotes. A blaze of light brought scintillating reflections from its chased surfaces. Waiters, whom a provincial visitor would have mistaken for diplomats but for their youth, stood about with the grave deportment of men who know themselves to be grossly overpaid.

Five persons had arrived, and nine more were expected. First came Bixiou, the salt of every intellectual dish, still holding his place in 1843, with an arsenal of shafts of wit that were always original, a phenomenon as rare in Paris as virtue. Then Léon de Lora arrived, the greatest living painter of sea and landscape, who, unlike some of his rivals, has never let the standard of his later work fall below that of his earliest paintings. To the girls, these two kings of wit were indispensable. A supper, or dinner, or party without them was unthinkable.

Séraphine Sinet, known as Carabine, in her capacity as acknowledged mistress of the Amphitryon of the party, was among the first to arrive, and stood radiant under the floods of light, her face roguish above her dazzling shoulders, the loveliest in Paris, her neck looking as if it had been turned on a lathe, it was so smooth! She was wearing a gown of satin brocade in two shades of blue, trimmed with enough English lace to keep a village supplied with food for a month. Pretty Jenny Cadine, who was not playing this evening, and who is too well known to need description, arrived in a fabulous gown. For these ladies a party is always a Longchamps of fashion at which each endeavours to carry off the prize for her millionaire, saying in this way to her rivals:

'The most discriminating judges award a Gold Cup to me!'

A third woman, evidently just beginning her career, was observing the splendid array of her two rich, established, companions, and looking rather abashed. She was simply dressed in white cashmere with blue lace, and had had her hair piled up and adorned with flowers by a back-street hairdresser, whose prentice hand had, without meaning to, lent a charming silliness to the masses of her lovely fair hair. Still feeling awkward in her evening dress, she had, in the well-worn phrase, 'the shyness inseparable from a first appearance'. She had come from Valognes to find a market in Paris for a freshness to make any rival despair, an ingenuous candour that might stir desire in a dying man, and a beauty equal to that of any of the lovely girls from Normandy who fill the various theatres of the capital. The lines of her unblemished face had the ideal purity of angels' faces. Her milky skin reflected the light like a mirror. The subtle colour seemed to have been laid upon her cheeks by an artist's brush. She was called Cydalise; and, as will appear, was a necessary pawn in the game of 'Ma'am Nourrisson' against Madame Marneffe.

'Your arms don't go with your name, child,' Jenny Cadine had said when Carabine, who had brought her, introduced this sixteen-year-old masterpiece. And it was true that the fine-textured skin of Cydalise's arms, now displayed to public admiration, was reddened by the vigorous surge of country blood.

'How much is she worth?' Jenny Cadine asked Carabine, under her breath.

'A fortune.'

'What do you mean to make of her?'

'Why, Madame Combabus!'

'And what are you going to get out of it?'

'Guess!'

'A silver service?'

'I have three already!'

'Diamonds?'

'I have diamonds galore. . . .'

'A green monkey?'

'No, a picture by Raphael!'

'What crazy fancy have you got in your head?'

'Josépha bores me to the marrow with her pictures,' answered Carabine. 'And I want to have far finer ones than she has. . . .'

Du Tillet came in with the guest of honour, the Brazilian. The Duc d'Hérouville followed with Josépha. The singer wore a simple velvet dress; but a necklace worth a hundred and twenty thousand francs gleamed on her neck, its pearls almost indistinguishable from her camellia-petal skin. She had placed one red camellia (a beauty patch!) among her dark tresses, with dazzling effect, and had amused herself by setting eleven rows of pearls, one above the other, on each arm. She came up to shake hands with Jenny Cadine, and Jenny said:

'Oh, do lend me your mittens!'

Josépha unfastened her bracelets and presented them to her friend on a plate.

'What style!' said Carabine. 'Just like a duchess! Did you ever see so many pearls? Did you plunder the whole sea to deck this girl, Monsieur le Duc?' she added, turning to the little Duc d'Hérouville.

The actress took just two bracelets, clasped the twenty others on the singer's lovely arms, and set a kiss above them.

Lousteau, the literary sponge, La Palférine and Malaga,

Massol and Vauvinet, and Théodore Gaillard, a proprietor of one of the leading political newspapers, completed the party. The Duc d'Hérouville, whose polished aristocratic courtesy was shown to everyone alike, gave the Comte de La Palférine that special nod which, without implying any particular esteem or intimacy, proclaims to the world: 'We belong to the same class, the same breed. We are equals!' That greeting, the aristocratic shibboleth, was created to be the despair of intellectuals and upper-middle-class climbers.

Carabine placed Combabus on her left, and the Duc d'Hérouville on her right. Cydalise sat on the Brazilian's left, with Bixiou on her other side. Malaga took her place beside the Duke.

At seven o'clock they attacked the oysters. At eight, between two courses, they were sipping iced punch. Everyone knows the menu of these parties. At nine there was the babble of talk to be expected after the consumption of forty-two bottles of different wines shared among fourteen people. Dessert, the wretched dessert of the month of April, was on the table. The heady atmosphere had affected only the girl from Normandy, who was humming a carol. With the exception of that poor child, no one had lost full use of his faculties, for the men there, and the women, were the *élite* of Paris diners-out. Wit struck sparks, eyes were brilliant but remained full of intelligence, and tongues turned to satire, anecdote, and indiscreet sallies. The conversation – that had followed the usual round: racecourses and horses, the stock exchange, the comparative merits of social stars, and current scandal – threatened to grow intimate, to break the company up into little groups of two kindred souls.

It was then, following meaning glances from Carabine at Léon de Lora, Bixiou, La Palférine, and du Tillet, that the subject of love was introduced.

'Correct doctors never talk medicine, aristocrats never discuss their blue blood, talented people never talk about their works,' said Josépha; 'so why should we talk shop? ... I've had the Opera performance cancelled to be here, and I'm certainly not going to *work* now. So let's not have any stage attitudinizing, dear friends.'

'They're talking about real love, my sweet!' said Malaga. 'The kind of love that swallows up a man, makes him send his father and mother, wife and children, to the bottom, and himself to finish up in Clichy. . . .'

'Well, *you* may tell us all about it, then!' returned the singer. 'I don't know no such creature!'

I don't know no such creature! . . . A phrase picked up from the Paris guttersnipes, on a courtesan's lips, with her eyes and expression to give it beauty, can be a whole poem.

'So I don't love you, Josépha?' said the Duke, in a low voice.

'Perhaps you do truly love me,' the singer answered in a whisper, smiling; 'but I haven't the kind of emotion they are talking about, love that makes the entire universe dark without the beloved one. I am very fond of you, and you are so useful to me. . . . But you are not indispensable; and if you deserted me tomorrow, I should exchange one duke for three. . . .'

'Does love exist in Paris?' said Léon de Lora. 'There's no time even to make a living here, so how can anyone give himself up to real love, which takes hold of a man as water takes hold of sugar? You have to be enormously rich to fall in love, for love annihilates a man, as, for instance, it seems to have done to our Brazilian friend. It's just as I have always said, *extremes meet!* A true lover is like a eunuch; there are no longer any women on earth for him! He is a mystery; he's like a true Christian, solitary in his desert hermitage! Rather like this gallant Brazilian! . . .'

The whole table turned to look at Henri Montès de Montejanos, who was embarrassed to find himself the centre of attention.

'He's been sitting there for the past hour like an ox in a field, as unaware as any ox would be that he has sitting beside him . . . in this company I can't say the most beautiful woman, but the freshest woman in Paris.'

'Everything is fresh here, even the fish. That's what this place is noted for,' said Carabine.

Baron Montès de Montejanos looked at the landscape painter amicably, and said:

'Very good! Your good health!'

And he bowed to Léon de Lora, raised his glass of port, and drank with ceremonial gravity.

'So you are really in love?' Carabine said to her neighbour, interpreting the toast in her own fashion.

The Brazilian Baron refilled his glass, bowed to Carabine, and repeated the toast.

'To Madame's health!' the courtesan repeated, with such a droll intonation that du Tillet, Bixiou, and the landscape painter burst out laughing.

The Baron remained as inscrutable as a bronze statue. His self-possession vexed Carabine. She knew perfectly well that Montès was in love with Madame Marneffe; but she had not expected this uncompromising fidelity, this determined silence, the attitude of a man with no doubts in his mind. A woman gains esteem by her lover's regard for her, just as a lover does by his mistress's bearing. Proud of loving Valérie, and being loved by her, the Baron seemed to smile a little ironically at these experienced connoisseurs. He looked superbly handsome; wine had not altered his colour, and his eyes, with their peculiar golden-brown brilliancy, guarded his soul's secrets. And in her own mind Carabine said:

'What a woman! How closely she has sealed that heart of yours!'

'He's a rock!' said Bixiou, under his breath. He thought the whole thing was a joke, and had no suspicion of the importance attached by Carabine to the demolition of the fortress.

While this conversation, apparently so frivolous, was going on on Carabine's right, on her left the discussion about love continued between the Duc d'Hérouville, Lousteau, Josépha, Jenny Cadine, and Massol. They were considering whether this rare phenomenon were the product of passion, obstinacy, or infatuation. Josépha, completely bored by all this theory-spinning, was anxious to change the subject.

'You're talking of something you know absolutely nothing about! Is there a single person here who has ever loved a woman, and a woman quite unworthy of him, enough to run through all his money and his children's money for her, to pawn his future and tarnish his past, risk prison hulks for robbing the state, to kill an uncle and a brother, and let the wool be pulled over his eyes so completely that it never even occurs to him that he is being blindfolded to prevent him from seeing the abyss into which he is being pushed as a crowning jest? Du Tillet has a cash-box under his left breast; Léon de Lora keeps wit there; Bixiou would think himself a fool to care for anyone but himself; Massol has a Minister's portfolio for a heart; Lousteau has nothing there but a stomach, or he could never have let Madame de la Baudraye leave him; Monsieur le Duc is too rich to be able to prove his love by ruining himself; Vauvinet does not count, because I can't think a moneylender really a member of the human race. So none of you has ever loved, and neither have I, nor has Jenny, nor Carabine. . . . For my part, I have seen the phenomenon I've been describing only once. It was our poor Baron Hulot,' she said, turning to Jenny Cadine; 'and I'm advertising for him as if he were a lost dog, for I want to find him.'

'Well, well!' said Carabine to herself, looking at Josépha out of the corners of her eyes. 'Can Madame Nourrisson have two Raphael pictures, or what's making Josépha play my game?'

'Poor fellow!' said Vauvinet. 'He was a fine man, very impressive. He carried himself with such dignity, such style! He looked like François I. What a volcano he was! And so ingenious, with a real talent for getting hold of money! Wherever he is, he must be looking for money now; and he's quite capable of finding it too, extracting it from those walls of bones you see on the outskirts of Paris, near the city gates, where he is probably hiding. . . .'

'And all that,' said Bixiou, 'for that little Madame Marneffe! There's a sly baggage, if ever there was one!'

'She's going to marry my friend Crevel!' observed du Tillet.

'And she's crazy about my friend Steinbock!' added Léon de Lora.

These three remarks were three pistol-shots that struck Montès full in the chest. He turned pale, so shocked that he stumbled to his feet with some difficulty.

'You utter swine!' he said. 'How can you dare even speak an honourable lady's name in the same breath with all your fallen women, much less make her a target for your slanders?'

Shouts of 'Bravo!' and applause from all sides cut Montès short. Bixiou, Léon de Lora, Vauvinet, du Tillet, and Massol gave the signal, and a chorus followed.

'Long live the Emperor!' said Bixiou.

'Give him a crown!' exclaimed Vauvinet.

'*Groans* for *Médor, hurrah* for Brazil!' cried Lousteau.

'Ah! my copper Baron, so you love our Valérie?' said Léon de Lora. 'Does it not make you sick?'

'What he said was not exactly parliamentary, but it was magnificent!' observed Massol.

'But my dear honoured client, you're under my wing as your banker. Your innocence is going to damage my reputation!'

'Ah, tell me – you are a reasonable man ...' the Brazilian implored du Tillet.

'Thank you, on behalf of the company,' said Bixiou, bowing.

'Tell me, is there any truth in this at all? ...' Montès went on, taking no notice of Bixiou's interruption.

'Well,' replied du Tillet, 'I have the honour to inform you that I am invited to Crevel's wedding.'

'Ah! Combabus takes on the defence of Madame Marneffe!' said Josépha, rising solemnly.

She moved with an air of mock tragedy towards Montès, gave him a friendly little pat on the head, regarded him for a moment with a comical expression of admiration, and shook her head.

'Hulot is my first example of love through hell and high water; behold the second!' she said. 'But we really shouldn't count him, because he comes from the tropics!'

As Josépha gently tapped his forehead, the Brazilian sank back into his chair again and looked in appeal towards du Tillet.

'If I am the victim of one of your Paris jokes,' he said; 'if you have done this to induce me to give away my secret ...' –

and his stare ringed the table with flame, transfixing the circle of guests with eyes behind which the fires of a Brazilian sun were blazing – '. . . for God's sake, tell me so,' he concluded, in almost childish supplication, 'but do not blacken the name of the woman I love. . . .'

'Well, then!' Carabine said in a low voice, in reply. 'Supposing it's true that you have been shamefully betrayed, tricked, and deceived by Valérie, and I give you proofs of it, within an hour, at my house, what will you do?'

'I can't tell you here, before all these Iagos . . .' said the Brazilian baron.

Carabine thought he said *magots* – apes.

'Ah, hush!' she answered, smiling. 'Don't give darts they can turn against you to the wittiest men in Paris. Come home with me, and we can talk.'

Montès was shattered.

'Proofs!' he stammered. 'Consider . . .'

'You shall have only too many, answered Carabine; 'and if the mere suspicion affects you like this, I fear for your reason. . . .'

'He isn't half obstinate, this fellow; he's worse than the late King of Holland. See here, Lousteau, Bixiou, Massol – listen all of you. Aren't you all invited to lunch by Madame Marneffe the day after tomorrow?' demanded Léon de Lora.

'*Ja*,' replied du Tillet. 'With all respect, I repeat, Baron, that if by any chance you had the idea of marrying Madame Marneffe, you are thrown out like a Bill in Parliament, black-balled, by a fat ball called Crevel. My old comrade Crevel has eighty thousand livres a year, and you, my friend, have not flashed so much money, or so I imagine, for if you had, then you, no doubt, would have been the preferred one.'

Montès listened with a half-absent air, with a half-smile on his lips, that everyone there found terrifying. The head waiter came in just then to announce discreetly to Carabine that a relative of hers was in the hall and wished to speak to her. The girl rose, went out, and found Madame Nourrisson waiting, swathed in black lace.

'Well, am I to go to your house, daughter? Has he taken the bait?'

'Yes, Mother. The pistol is rammed so full that I'm afraid of its exploding.'

An hour later, Montès, Cydalise, and Carabine, returning from the Rocher de Cancale, walked into Carabine's little drawing-room in the rue Saint-Georges. The courtesan found Madame Nourrisson sitting in a low chair by the fire.

'Ah, here's Aunt . . .' she said.

'Yes, girl. I've come to fetch my bit of money myself. You might forget all about me, although you are a good-hearted child, and I have bills to pay tomorrow. A ladies' wardrobe-dealer, you know, is always pinched for cash. Who's this you've got lagging behind you? This gentleman looks as if he were in some sort of trouble.'

The hideous Madame Nourrisson, who had undergone a complete metamorphosis and now looked like a respectable old woman, rose to kiss Carabine, one of the hundred and one prostitutes whom she had launched in their horrible profession of vice.

'He's an Othello who has made no mistake about the grounds for his jealousy. I have the honour to present to you Monsieur le Baron Montès de Montejanos . . .'

'Oh, I know Monsieur, I've heard such a lot about him. They call you Combabus because you love only one woman; in Paris that's just the same as having none at all. Now is it by any chance the object of your affection that's the trouble? Madame Marneffe, Crevel's woman? Well, my dear sir, you ought to bless your lucky stars instead of blaming them. She's a complete bad lot, that little woman. I know her goings-on!'

'Ah, bah!' said Carabine, into whose hand Madame Nourrisson had slipped a letter as she kissed her. 'You don't know these Brazilians. They're fire-eaters, absolutely set on having knives stuck in their hearts! The more jealous they are, the more jealous they want to be. Monsieur here is talking of wading through blood, but he's in love so he's not likely to massacre anyone. Well, I've brought Monsieur le Baron here to give him proofs of his bad luck that I got from little Stein-bock.'

Montès was drunk. He listened as if the matter concerned

someone else. Carabine went to take off her short velvet cape, and read a facsimile of the following note:

My pet, *he* is going to dinner with Popinot this evening, and is to call for me at the Opera at eleven. I will leave the house at half past five, and count on finding you in our paradise; you can have dinner sent in from the Maison d'Or. Dress, so that you can escort me to the Opera. We shall have four hours together. Send me back this little note – not that your Valérie doesn't trust you, for you know I would give you my life, my fortune, and my honour, but I am afraid of some trick that accident may play us.

'Well, Baron, this is the *billet doux* sent this morning to Count Steinbock; read the address! The original has been burned.'

Montès turned the note over and over, recognized the hand-writing, and was struck by a thought, suggesting a gleam of hope, which showed the perturbed state of his mind.

'Ah, indeed? And what is your motive? What do you get out of inflicting this misery on me? For you must have paid solid cash to have this note in your hands long enough to get it lithographed!' he said, staring at Carabine.

'Idiot!' said Carabine, at a nod from Madame Nourrisson. 'Don't you see poor Cydalise ... only sixteen, and so much in love with you that neither a bite nor a sup has passed her lips in three months, and breaking her heart because you won't even give her a glance?'

Cydalise held her handkerchief to her eyes.

'She's furious, even though she *looks* as if butter wouldn't melt in her mouth, to see the man she's mad about given the run around by a crafty bitch,' Carabine went on, 'and she could kill Valérie. ...'

'Oh, that!' said the Brazilian. 'That's my business!'

'Kill her? You, my lad? We don't do that sort of thing here, these days.'

'Oh!' returned Montès. 'I don't belong here! I live in a jurisdiction where the law is in my hands, where I bite my thumb at your laws, and if you give me proof ...'

'Why, is this note not proof enough?'

'No,' said the Brazilian. 'I don't trust writing. I must see ...'

'Oh, as to seeing!' said Carabine, interpreting another nod

from her so-called aunt. 'We'll let you see as much as you want to, dear tiger, but on one condition. ...'

'What condition?'

'Look at Cydalise!'

Madame Nourrisson signed to Cydalise, who looked languishingly at the Baron.

'Will you be her lover? Will you set her up in life?' demanded Carabine. 'A girl as beautiful as that is worth a house and a carriage. It would be a crying shame to let her go about on foot. And she has ... a few debts. How much do you owe?' asked Carabine, pinching Cydalise's arm.

'She's worth what she's worth!' said the old woman. 'So long as the condition is agreed, let that do!'

'Listen!' exclaimed Montès, at last waking up to the girl's beauty. 'You will show me Valérie? ...'

'And Count Steinbock, naturally!' agreed Madame Nourrisson, nodding again.

During the past ten minutes, as the old woman watched, he had seen that the Brazilian was the instrument tuned to murderous pitch that she required. She saw that he was sufficiently blinded, too, to be no longer on his guard against those who were leading him on; and now she intervened.

'Cydalise, my dear friend from Brazil, is my niece, so I must take an interest in this arrangement. All the old affair can be cleared up and swept off in ten minutes, because it's one of my friends who lets the furnished room to Count Steinbock, where Valérie is taking her coffee at this moment – odd coffee, but that's what she calls it, her coffee. So now let's come to business, Brazil! I like Brazil, a hot country. What are you going to do about my niece?'

'Old ostrich!' said Montès, struck by the feathers in the woman's hat. 'Don't interrupt me. If you show me ... show me Valérie and that artist together ...'

'As you would like to be with her yourself,' said Carabine. 'That's understood.'

'Well, I'll take this Norman girl, I'll take her ...'

'Take her where? ...' demanded Carabine.

'To Brazil!' replied the Baron. 'I'll marry her. My uncle left me an estate twenty-five miles square, entailed, which is why I still possess the place. I have a hundred Negroes there, no one but Negroes, and Negresses, and piccaninnies, bought by my uncle ...'

'A slave-dealer's nephew! ...' said Carabine, making a face. 'That needs thinking about. Cydalise, my child, are you fond of black men?'

'That's enough, Carabine; no more tomfoolery, now,' said Madame Nourrisson. 'A nice way to behave! This gentleman and I are talking business.'

'If I take a Frenchwoman again, I intend her to be entirely mine,' the Baron went on. 'I warn you, Mademoiselle, I am a king, but not a constitutional monarch. I am a czar. All my subjects have been bought, and no one ever leaves the confines of my kingdom, which is two hundred and fifty miles away from any inhabited place. Savages live beyond it in the interior, and it is separated from the coast by a wilderness as large as the whole of your France. ...'

'Give me an attic here!' said Carabine.

'That's what I thought,' said the Brazilian, 'and I sold all my property and possessions in Rio de Janeiro to come back to Madame Marneffe.'

'Journeys like that are not made for nothing,' said Madame Nourrisson. 'You have a right to be loved for yourself, especially being so handsome. ... Oh! isn't he handsome?' she said to Carabine.

'Handsome! He's handsomer than the postilion at Long-jumeau,' replied the girl.

Cydalise took the Brazilian's hand, and he disengaged himself as politely as he could.

'I came back to carry Madame Marneffe off!' said the Baron, going on with his story. 'And do you know why I was away three years?'

'No, dear savage,' said Carabine.

'Well, she had told me so many times that she wanted to live with me, alone, in some wilderness! ...'

'Oh, not a savage after all,' said Carabine, bursting out laughing; 'just a member of the tribe of civilized innocents.'

'She had said it so often,' went on the Baron, not even hearing Carabine's gibes, 'that I had a delightful place to live

405

made ready, in the middle of that immense estate. I came back to France to fetch Valérie, and on the night when I saw her again ...'

'*Saw her again* is proper,' said Carabine. 'I'll remember the expression!'

'... She told me to wait until that wretched Marneffe died, and I agreed, and forgave her for accepting Hulot's attentions. I don't know whether the devil has put on petticoats, but from that moment that woman was all I could ask, all I could wish for; and truly never for a moment has she given me any cause to suspect her!'

'Now, that's piling it on a bit!' said Carabine to Madame Nourrisson.

Madame Nourrisson nodded in agreement.

'My faith in that woman,' said Montès, giving way to tears, 'was as strong as my love. I nearly slapped the faces of all those people round the table, just now. ...'

'So I noticed!' said Carabine.

'If I have been betrayed, if she is going to marry, if she is in Steinbock's arms at this minute, she has earned death a thousand times over, and I will kill her as I would crush a fly. ...'

'And what about the gendarmes, my boy?' said Madame Nourrisson, with an old crone's leer that made the flesh creep.

'And the police superintendent, and the magistrates, and the assize court, and the whole boiling!' said Carabine.

'You're talking big, dearie!' went on Madame Nourrisson, for she was anxious to learn what the Brazilian's plans for vengeance were.

'I will kill her!' the Brazilian coldly repeated. 'You called me a savage, did you? ... Do you imagine that I mean to imitate your countrymen's stupidity and buy poison from the druggists? ... I was planning, on the way here, how I should execute my vengeance if you were right about Valérie. One of my Negroes carries on him the most deadly of animal poisons, a terrible disease much more effective than any vegetable poison and that can only be cured in Brazil. I will give it to Cydalise to take, and she shall infect me. Then when death is in the veins of Crevel and his wife, I shall be beyond the Azores with your cousin, whom I shall cure, and take for my wife. We savages have our own methods! Cydalise,' he said, looking at the Norman girl, 'is the simple creature that I need. How much money does she owe?'

'A hundred thousand francs!' said Cydalise.

'She doesn't talk much, but when she does she says a mouthful,' Carabine whispered to Madame Nourrisson.

'I am going mad!' groaned the Brazilian hollowly, collapsing on a sofa. 'I cannot survive it! But I must see for myself – it's not possible! A lithographed note. ... Who can say that it isn't a forgery? ... Baron Hulot – Valérie's lover? ...' He recalled what Josépha had said. 'But the proof that he could not have been is that she's still alive! ... But I will not leave her alive if she is not mine. ... She shall not be another man's!'

Montès was a terrifying sight, and it was even more frightening to hear him. He roared like a lion, and threw himself about the room. Everything he laid hands on was broken; the rosewood splintered like glass.

'How he breaks up the place!' said Carabine, looking at Madame Nourrisson. 'My child,' she went on, tapping the Brazilian on the arm, '*Orlando furioso* sounds very well in a poem; but in a flat he's just Roland in a rage, plain prose – and plain expensive!'

'I am of your way of thinking, son!' said Nourrisson, rising and moving to stand facing the exhausted Brazilian. 'When two people have that kind of love, when they are fatally, inextricably, *hooked together*, they must answer for love with their lives. The one who pulls away tears everything asunder, that's plain! It's total ruin. You have my esteem, my admiration, and above all my approval of the way you refuse to take things lying down, and from now on I'm going to be a firm friend of Negroes. But then, after all, you're in love! You'll stop on the brink!'

'I ... If she's a trollop, I'll ...'

'See here, you talk too much. Better cut the cackle and come to business!' returned Madame Nourrisson, speaking now as her practical down-to-earth self. 'A man who means vengeance and calls his methods savage should not behave

407

like this. We'll let you see your loved one in her paradise, but you must take Cydalise and go in there with your sweetheart on your arm, as if a maid had given you the wrong room by mistake. And you must not make a scene! If you want your revenge, you must sing small, look as if you are in despair, and let yourself be bowled over by your mistress! Isn't that the right way to do it?' she asked, seeing the Baron look surprised at such an elaborate, well-plotted scheme.

'Very well, old ostrich,' he replied; 'so be it. . . . I understand.'

'Good-bye, love,' said Madame Nourrisson to Carabine. She signed to Cydalise to go downstairs with Montès, and remained alone for a moment with Carabine.

'Now, pet, I'm afraid of only one thing – that he may strangle her! I should be in a fine pickle if he did; we can only get along by keeping things quiet. Oh, I think you have won your Raphael picture, only they do say it's a Mignard. Never mind; that's much finer. They told me that Raphaels are all blackened, and the one I've got is just as nice as a Girodet.'

'All I care about is going one better than Josépha,' declared Carabine, 'and it's all the same to me whether it's with a Mignard or a Raphael. You wouldn't believe the pearls that gold-digger had on this evening. . . . You would have bartered your soul for them!'

Cydalise, Montès, and Madame Nourrisson took a cab that was standing by Carabine's door. Madame Nourrisson, in a low voice, directed the driver to a house in the same block as the Italian Opera, only seven or eight minutes' drive from the rue Saint-Georges, but she told the man to go along the rue Lepelletier, and very slowly, so that they could examine the waiting carriages.

'Brazilian!' Madame Nourrisson commanded. 'Look out for your angel's carriage and servants.'

The Baron pointed out Valérie's carriage as the cab drove past.

'She told her servants to be here at ten o'clock and took a cab to the house, and she's there now with Count Steinbock. She has had dinner there, and in half an hour she'll be on her way to the Opera. It's very neatly worked out! It shows you how she has been able to keep the blinkers over your eyes for so long,' said Madame Nourrisson.

The Brazilian did not answer. He had reassumed, together with a tiger's savage ferocity, the imperturbable composure that had been so much admired at the dinner party. His calm now, however, was that of a bankrupt the day after his bankruptcy has been declared.

At the door of the fateful house a hackney-carriage with two horses was standing, one of those called a 'General Company' from the name of the firm that runs them.

'Stay in your box,' Madame Nourrisson commanded Montès. 'You can't walk in there as if it were a tap-room. You'll be fetched.'

The paradise that was shared by Madame Marneffe and Wenceslas was not in the least like Crevel's little house, which Crevel had sold to the Comte Maxime de Trailles, as it seemed to him that he had no further use for it. This paradise, by no means their exclusive possession, was a room on the fourth floor, opening on the staircase, in a house in the same block as the Italian Opera. On each floor of this house, on every landing, there was a room once intended to serve as a kitchen for each set of rooms. When the house had become a place of assignation, with rooms let out at an exorbitant rent, the owner, the real Madame Nourrisson, second-hand-clothes dealer in the rue Neuve-Saint-Marc, had realized the enormous potential value of these kitchens, and converted them into something like private dining-rooms. Each of these rooms, shut off on two sides by thick party-walls, with windows looking on the street, was completely isolated by heavy double doors on the fourth side, on the landing. Important secrets could therefore be discussed over dinner in this place without risk of being overheard. For greater security, the windows were provided with sun-blinds on the outside and shutters within. The privacy of the rooms was worth a rent of three hundred francs a month. The entire house, big with paradise and mysteries, was let out for twenty-four thousand francs by Madame Nourrisson the First, and made a profit of twenty thousand francs a year – taking one year with another – when her manageress (Madame Nourrisson the Second) had been paid, for she did not run the business herself.

The paradise rented by Count Steinbock had been hung with chintz. The humble flooring, of cold, hard, red-wax-polished tiles, no longer offended the senses under a soft deep-piled carpet. For furniture, it had two pretty chairs and a bed in an alcove, before which just then, and half-concealing it, stood a table covered with what was left of an excellent dinner, amid which two long-necked bottles and an empty champagne bottle, sunk in its melting ice, were landmarks in the fields of Bacchus tilled by Venus. The eye was caught by a handsome, luxuriously upholstered easy-chair, no doubt sent in by Valérie, beside a low fireside seat, and a rosewood chest-of-drawers with a looking-glass gracefully framed in the Pompadour style. A hanging lamp shed subdued light, augmented by the candles standing on the table and the chimney-piece.

This sketch will serve to give some idea, *urbi et orbi*, of the sordid shabbiness of clandestine love in the Paris of 1840. We are so far away, alas! from adulterous passion as symbolized by Vulcan's nets three thousand years ago.

As Cydalise and the Baron were on their way upstairs, Valérie, standing before the logs burning in the fireplace, was having her stays laced up by Wenceslas. It is at such moments that a woman who is neither too plump nor too slender, like the finely-made, elegant, Valérie, seems more than ordinarily beautiful. The rose-tinted flesh and dewy skin invite the most somnolent eye. The lines of the body, then so lightly veiled, are so clearly suggested by the shining folds of the petticoat and the lower part of the stays that a woman becomes quite irresistible, like every joy when we must say good-bye to it. The happy smiling face in the glass, the tapping foot, the raised hand busily tucking up the still disordered curls, eyes brimming with grateful love, the glow of content, like a setting sun, illuminating every detail of the coun-tenance – everything that the eye rests on makes this hour a treasure-house of memories! Any man, indeed, who throws a backward glance at his youthful wild oats will remember some such charming details, and may perhaps, without excusing them, understand the follies of the Hulots and the Crevels. Women are so well aware of their power at such times that they always find in them what may be called the aftermath of love.

'Well, well! Just fancy not knowing how to lace up a woman after two years! You're far too much of a Pole, my boy! It's ten o'clock, my Wences . . . las!' said Valérie, laughing.

At this moment a malicious servant adroitly raised the door-latch with the blade of a knife, the latch of that double door on which the whole security of Adam and Eve depended. She opened the door abruptly, because those who hire such Edens can only count on a short time as their own, and disclosed to view a tableau like one of those charming genre paintings, after Gavarni, that are so often hung in the Paris Exhibition.

'This way, Madame!' said the maid.

And Cydalise entered, followed by Baron Montès.

'But there are people here! Excuse me, Madame,' said the Norman girl, in a fright.

'What! It's Valérie!' exclaimed Montès, violently slamming the door.

Madame Marneffe, overwhelmed by feelings too keen to be dissembled, sank into a chair by the fireside. Tears sprang to her eyes, and dried instantly. She looked at Montès, took in the girl, and gave a forced peal of laughter. The dignity of a woman outraged effaced all thought of the impropriety of her half-clothed state. She walked up to Montès, and looked at him so proudly that her eyes seemed to scintillate like swords.

'So this,' she said, coming to a standstill facing the Brazilian, and pointing to Cydalise, 'this is the other face of your fidelity? You, who made promises to me that would have convinced an *unbeliever* in love! – for whose sake I have done so much, to the point of committing crimes! . . . You are right, Monsieur: I cannot compete with a girl of that age, and so beautiful! . . . I know what you are going to say,' she went on, indicating Wenceslas, whose confusion was proof too evident to be denied. 'That's my affair. If I were still able to love you, after such a mean betrayal, for you must have spied on me, you must have bought every step up these stairs, and the mistress of the house, and the servant, and even Reine perhaps. ... Oh! what a pleasant thing that is! If it were possible for me to have any affection still for a man so shamefully treacherous, I could give him such reasons that he would love me twice as much! But I can only leave you, Monsieur, with all your doubts, which will soon turn to regrets ... Wenceslas, my dress!'

She took her dress, slipped it on, examined herself in the glass, and calmly finished dressing without a glance at the Brazilian, absolutely as if she were alone.

'Wenceslas, are you ready? You go first!'

She had watched Montès's face from the corner of her eye and in the glass, and thought that in his pallor she saw an indication of the weakness that betrays such strong men to a woman's wiles. She took him by the hand, going so close to him that he breathed the fatal loved scents that intoxicate lovers and, feeling him tremble and breathe deeply, she looked at him reproachfully.

'I give you permission to go and tell Monsieur Crevel of your incursion here. He will never believe you; and I have every right to marry him. He will be my husband the day after tomorrow ... and I shall make him very happy! Good-bye! Try to forget me. ...'

'Ah, Valérie!' exclaimed Henri Montès, clasping her in his arms. 'It is impossible! Come to Brazil!'

Valérie looked at the Baron and saw that she had her slave again.

'Ah! if you still loved me, Henri! In two years I should be your wife! But at this moment it seems to me that you appear in a very dubious light.'

'I swear to you that they made me drunk, false friends planted this woman upon me, and all this happened quite by chance!' said Montès.

'So it might still be possible to forgive you?' she said, smiling.

'And you will still get married?' asked the Baron, in acute anxiety.

'Eighty thousand francs a year!' she answered, with half-comical enthusiasm. 'And Crevel loves me so much that he will die of it!'

'Ah! I understand you,' said the Brazilian.

'Well ... in a few days' time, we will consider things again,' she said. And she swept downstairs, triumphant.

'I have no scruples now,' thought the Baron, standing for a moment where he had been left. 'The woman counts on using that imbecile's love to rid herself of him, just as she made her plans counting on Marneffe's death! I shall be the instrument of Divine wrath!'

Two days later, those same fellow-guests of du Tillet's who had ruthlessly torn Madame Marneffe's character to shreds were sitting round her table, an hour after she had cast her slough and put on a new woman by changing her name for the glorious name of a Mayor of Paris. Sharpening one's tongue on one's friend's reputation is a kind of treachery lightly regarded in Paris society.

Valérie had had the pleasure of seeing the Brazilian Baron at the church: Crevel, now a complete husband, had invited him in a spirit of boastful ownership. Montès's presence at the wedding breakfast surprised no one. All these sophisticated people had been long familiar with the dereliction of principle in passion, with the base compromises of desire.

Steinbock, who was beginning to despise the woman of whom he had made an angel, showed a profound melancholy that was thought to be in excellent taste. The Pole was evidently making it clear that all was over between himself and Valérie.

Lisbeth came to embrace her dear Madame Crevel, excusing herself from staying to take part in the wedding breakfast because of the sad state of Adeline's health.

'Never fear,' she said to Valérie, as she left; 'they will receive you, and call on you. Just hearing those four words "two hundred thousand francs" has brought the Baroness to death's door. Oh! you hold them all on a string with that little story; but don't forget to tell me what it is all about. . . .'

A month after her marriage, Valérie was marking up her tenth quarrel with Steinbock, who kept seeking some explanation from her regarding Henri Montès, reminding her of what had been said during the scene in the paradise; and who, not content with withering Valérie with contemptuous reproaches, watched her so closely that she had not a moment's freedom, hard pressed as she was between Wenceslas's jealousy and Crevel's enthusiasm.

Not having Lisbeth at hand now to provide her with excellent advice, she so far forgot herself one day as to reproach Wenceslas harshly with the money she had lent him. Steinbock's pride was up in arms, and he came no more to the Crevel house. Valérie had at least achieved what she was wishing for – Wenceslas's absence for a time and the recovery of her liberty. She was expecting Crevel's departure on a visit that he had to make to the country to see Count Popinot in order to arrange for Madame Crevel's introduction, and so she was able to make an appointment with the Baron, whom she wanted to have to herself for a whole day in order to provide him with those reasons that were to make the Brazilian love her twice as much as before.

On the morning of that day, Reine, estimating the heinousness of the crime she was committing by the size of the bribe she had received, tried to warn her mistress, in whom she naturally had a greater interest than she had in strangers; but as she had been threatened with being treated as a madwoman and shut up in La Salpétrière if she were indiscreet, she was hesitant.

'Madame is so nicely fixed now,' she said; 'why go on bothering with that Brazilian? If you ask me, I don't trust him!'

'You're right, Reine!' Valérie answered. 'And I'm going to get rid of him.'

'Ah, Madame, I'm very glad. That darky frightens me. I'm sure he might do anything. ...'

'Don't be silly! You should keep your alarm for him, when he's with me!'

Lisbeth came in at that moment.

'My dear darling Nanny! It's been so long since we saw each other,' said Valérie. 'I am quite miserable. Crevel teases me to death, and I haven't Wencelas now; we've quarrelled.'

'So I know,' replied Lisbeth; 'and it's because of him that I'm here. Victorin met him about five yesterday evening, just about to go into a cheap restaurant in the rue de Valois. He worked on his feelings and took him straight back to the rue Louis-le-Grand. ... When Hortense saw Wenceslas, thin, wretched and badly dressed, she held out her arms to him. .... And that's the way you let me down!'

'Monsieur Henri, Madame!' the manservant announced discreetly to Valérie.

'Leave me, Lisbeth. I'll explain everything tomorrow.'

But, as will be seen, Valérie was soon to be in no condition to explain anything to anyone.

*

By the end of May, Baron Hulot's pension had been completely freed by the successive payments that Victorin had made to Baron Nucingen. As is well known, the half-yearly pension payments are made only on presentation of a certificate that the recipient is still alive; and as Baron Hulot's residence was unknown, the payments set aside for paying off the debt to Vauvinet were accumulating in the Treasury. Vauvinet having signed his withdrawal of claim, it became urgently necessary to find the recipient in order to obtain the arrears.

The Baroness, thanks to Dr Bianchon's care, had regained her health. Josépha's kindness had contributed, by a letter whose spelling revealed the Duc d'Hérouville's collaboration, to Adeline's complete recovery. This is what the singer wrote to the Baroness, after six weeks of energetic search:

Madame la Baronne,

Two months ago, Monsieur Hulot was living in the rue des Bernardins, with Élodie Chardin, the lace-mender, who had taken him away from Mademoiselle Bijou; but he went off from there, leaving everything he possessed behind, without saying a word to anyone, and no one knows where he has gone. I have not given up hope, and have set a man to trace him, who believes that he has already seen him on the boulevard Bourdon.

The poor Jewess will keep the promise made to the Christian. She begs the angel to pray for the demon! That must sometimes happen in heaven.

I am, with deep respect and always, your humble servant,

JOSÉPHA MIRAH

Maître Hulot d'Ervy, hearing no more word of the terrible Madame Nourrisson, seeing his father-in-law married, having retrieved his brother-in-law and brought him back under the family roof, experiencing no trouble from his new mother-in-law, and finding his mother's health improving every day, became engrossed in political and legal work, swept along in the swift current of Paris life, whose hours are as full as days. Having a report to write for the Chamber of Deputies one evening towards the end of the Session, he decided to spend the whole night working. He had come back to his study about nine o'clock; and as he waited for his servant to bring his shaded candles, he was thinking about his father. He was reproaching himself for leaving the search for him to the singer, and saying to himself that he would see Monsieur Chapuzot about the matter next day, when he saw at the window in the evening dusk an old man with a fine head, his bald yellow skull fringed with white hair.

'Tell your servant, my dear sir, to open the door to a poor hermit from the desert, seeking charity for the rebuilding of a holy sanctuary.'

The apparition, in finding a voice, instantly reminded the lawyer of a prediction that the horrible Nourrisson had made, and he shuddered.

'Let that old man in,' he said to his servant.

'He will bring a stink into Monsieur's study,' the man protested. 'That brown habit he's wearing hasn't been off his back since he left Syria, and he has no vest ...'

'Let him in,' the lawyer repeated.

The old man entered. Victorin examined this so-called pilgrim hermit with a mistrustful eye, and saw a superb specimen of those monks of Naples whose habits are indistinguishable from *lazzaroni*'s rags, whose sandals are rags of leather, and who themselves are tatters of humanity. He was so evidently genuine that the lawyer, though still on his guard, rebuked himself for believing in Madame Nourrisson's sorcery.

'What do you want from me?'

'What you think you ought to give.'

416

Victorin took five francs from a pile of small change, and held out the coin to the stranger.

'As payment on account for fifty thousand francs, that's not much,' said the mendicant from the desert.

That observation removed all Victorin's doubts.

'And has heaven kept its promises?' the lawyer said, frowning.

'To doubt is a sin, my son,' replied the hermit. 'If you wish to pay only when the funeral is over, you are within your rights. I will return in a week.'

'The funeral!' exclaimed the lawyer, rising to his feet.

'Action has been taken,' said the old man as he turned to go, 'and the dead are soon disposed of in Paris!'

When Hulot, who had bowed his head, raised it to reply, the active old man had disappeared.

'I don't understand a word,' Hulot told himself. 'But in a week's time I'll ask him to find my father, if we haven't found him in the meantime. Where can Madame Nourrisson (yes, that's her name) find such actors?'

On the following day Dr Bianchon allowed the Baroness to leave her room to sit in the garden. He had just examined Lisbeth, who had been kept to her room for the past month with a mild attack of bronchitis. This distinguished doctor, who did not care to reveal his opinion about Lisbeth's case before he had observed decisive symptoms, accompanied the Baroness to the garden in order to note the effect of fresh air, after two months of seclusion, upon the nervous tremor that he was treating. The curing of this nervous condition was a challenge to Bianchon's professional skill. When the Baroness and her children saw this eminent doctor sit down and prepare to give them some minutes of his time, they politely started to make conversation.

'You must have a very fully occupied life, and very sadly occupied,' said the Baroness. 'I know what it means to spend one's whole day watching people in distress, or suffering physical pain.'

'Madame,' answered the doctor, 'I know very well the kind of scenes that you must meet with in your charitable work, but you'll get used to them in the end, as we all do. It is the social rule. The confessor, the magistrate, the lawyer, could not do their work if their sense of social duty did not override their human heart. How could we doctors go on living if we had not this detachment? The soldier, too, in time of war, has to face sights even more harrowing than ours; and all soldiers who have been in action are kindhearted.

'Moreover, we enjoy the pleasure of curing people, and, in your work, too, you have the joy of saving a family from hunger, moral depravity, and misery, and bringing its members back to work, to life within the social framework. But what consolation can the magistrate, the police officer, and the lawyer have? They spend their lives disentangling the sordid schemes of selfish individuals, monstrous parasites on society, who may feel regret when they fail, but are incapable of feeling remorse. One half of society spends its life keeping watch on the other half.

'An old friend of mine, a lawyer, retired now, used to tell me that for the past fifteen years solicitors and barristers have trusted their own clients as little as they trust their clients' opponents. Your son is a lawyer. Has he never been let down by the man he was defending?'

'Oh, often!' said Victorin, smiling.

'What has caused this wide-spread social evil?' asked the Baroness.

'Lack of religion,' answered the doctor, 'and the encroachment on everything of finance, which is just another name for organized self-seeking. Money, once, was not everything; it was recognized that there were higher and more important values. Noble disinterestedness, and talent, and service to the state, were thought worthy of esteem; but nowadays the law makes money the standard to measure everything. It takes the possession of money as the basis of political qualification, and some magistrates are not eligible. Jean-Jacques Rousseau would not be eligible!

'As inherited estates continue to be divided up, everyone is forced to think of his own interests first, from the age of twenty. And then, a young man faced with the necessity of making money, and the temptation to seek criminal ways of making it, has nothing to restrain him; because there is now no belief or religious principle in France, in spite of the praiseworthy efforts of those who are working for a Catholic revival. Everyone who, like me, observes society from the inside, thinks as I do about these matters.'

'You can have few pleasures,' said Hortense.

'A true doctor has an absorbing interest,' answered Bianchon, 'a passion for the advancement of knowledge. His devotion to it gives him courage; and of course he is sure that he is doing socially useful work, and that helps him too. At this very moment, as it happens, I feel very elated, I am rejoicing as a scientist and a medical man; and there are plenty of people who don't look beneath the surface who would think me quite heartless. Tomorrow I am going to announce a discovery to the Academy of Medicine. I am at present observing a lost disease, endemic in Europe in the Middle Ages but quite unknown here now; a fatal disease, too, which we have no remedy for in temperate climates, although it can be cured in the tropics. ... It is a fine war a doctor wages against such an enemy as that. For the past ten days my mind has been preoccupied, every hour of the day, with my patients: I have two, a husband and wife. But surely they are connexions of yours! Are you not Monsieur Crevel's daughter, Madame?' he said, turning to Célestine.

'What! Can your patient be my father?' said Célestine. 'Does he live in the rue Barbet-de-Jouy?'

'Yes, indeed,' replied Bianchon.

'And the disease is fatal?' repeated Victorin, horrified.

'I must go to my father!' exclaimed Célestine, jumping to her feet.

'I forbid it, absolutely, Madame!' Bianchon said calmly. 'This disease is contagious.'

'You go there yourself, Monsieur,' the young woman replied. 'Do you imagine that a daughter's duty is less compelling than a doctor's?'

'A doctor knows how to protect himself against contagion, Madame. The fact that you do not consider the possible consequences of your devotion suggests that you may not be so careful as I am.'

Célestine rose to go into the house and prepare to go out.

'Monsieur,' Victorin said to Bianchon, 'have you any hope of saving Monsieur and Madame Crevel?'

'I hope, but fear that it may prove impossible,' replied Bianchon. 'I find the case quite inexplicable. . . . This disease affects Negroes and native American peoples, whose epidermic structure is different from that of the white races. Now, I cannot trace any contact between Negroes, red-skins, or half-castes, and Monsieur or Madame Crevel. And though we doctors may think it a fascinating disease, everyone else finds it appalling. The poor woman, who was pretty so I am told, is well punished for it now if she was proud of her beauty, for she's hideously ugly, if indeed she may be said to exist as a human being at all! . . . Her teeth and hair are falling out; she looks like a leper; she's an object of horror to herself. Her hands are a dreadful sight, swollen and covered with greenish pustules; the nails, loose at the roots, remain in the sores she scratches – in fact the extremities are all in process of destruction, decomposing into running ulcers.'

'But what is the underlying cause of these symptoms?' asked the lawyer.

'Oh,' said Bianchon, 'the cause is a rapid change in the structure of the blood; it is breaking down at a formidable rate. I am hoping to attack the disease in the blood. I am on my way home to pick up the result of a blood analysis made by my friend Professor Duval, the famous chemist, before attempting one of those desperate throws we try sometimes against death.'

'God's hand is in this!' said the Baroness, with deep emotion. 'Although that woman has brought sorrows upon me that sometimes, in moments of madness, have made me invoke Divine justice upon her head, I wish, God knows, that you may be successful, Monsieur.'

Victorin Hulot was seized with vertigo. He looked in turn at his mother, his sister, and the doctor, and trembled lest they should divine his thoughts. He saw himself a murderer. Hortense, for her part, found that God was just. Célestine returned and asked her husband to go with her.

'If you go there, Madame, and you, Monsieur, stay a foot away from the patients' bedsides; that is the only precaution you can take. On no account should you or your wife dream of kissing the dying man! I think that you ought to go with your wife, Monsieur Hulot, to see that she does not break this rule.'

Adeline and Hortense, left alone, went to keep Lisbeth company. Hortense's hatred of Valérie was so intense that she could not contain it, and she burst out:

'Cousin! My Mother and I are avenged! . . . That venomous creature must have bitten herself. She is in a state of decomposition!'

'Hortense,' said the Baroness, 'you are not Christian at this moment. You ought to pray to God to vouchsafe to inspire repentance in that unhappy woman.'

'What are you saying?' exclaimed Bette, rising from her chair. 'Are you speaking of Valérie?'

'Yes,' answered Adeline. 'There is no hope for her. She is dying of a horrible disease, the very description of which makes one's blood run cold.'

Cousin Bette's teeth chattered. A cold sweat broke out on her skin. The terrible shock she experienced revealed the depth of her passionate attachment to Valérie.

'I'm going there!' she said.

'But the doctor has forbidden you to go out!'

'That's unimportant. I must go. Poor Crevel, what a state he must be in, for he loves his wife. . . .'

'He's dying too,' replied Countess Steinbock. 'Ah! all our enemies are in the devil's clutches. . . .'

'In God's hands, girl!'

Lisbeth dressed, took her famous yellow cashmere shawl, her black velvet bonnet, put on her ankle-boots, and, heedless to the remonstrances of Adeline and Hortense, left the house as if impelled by an irresistible force. When she arrived at rue Barbet, a few minutes after Monsieur and Madame Hulot, Lisbeth found seven doctors that Bianchon had called in to observe these unique cases, and whom he had just joined. These doctors were standing about in the drawing-room, discussing the cases. Occasionally one, and then another, of them would go into Valérie's room, or Crevel's, to note some point, and then return with some argument based on this rapid examination.

An important difference of opinion split these eminent scientists into two main parties. One man alone held that it was an instance of poisoning and suspected an act of private revenge, refusing to believe that the disease described in the Middle Ages had reappeared. Three others saw in the symptoms the results of a breaking down of the lymph and humours. The other party held Bianchon's view, maintaining that the disease was a destruction of the blood caused by some unknown fatal element in it. Bianchon had just brought the blood analysis made by Professor Duval. The methods of treatment, desperate and quite empirical as they were, depended on the diagnosis.

Lisbeth stood petrified, three steps from the bed on which Valérie lay dying, on seeing a priest from Saint-Thomas d'Aquin at her friend's bedhead, and a Sister of Charity tending her. Religion had found a soul to save in a creature that was a putrefying mass, who of the five senses retained only one, the power of sight. The Sister of Charity, the only being who would accept the task of caring for Valérie, stood a little apart. And so the Catholic Church, that blessed body, always and in all things inspired by the spirit of self-sacrifice, gave aid, ministering to the two-fold form of being, to the flesh and to the spirit, to the wicked and corrupt dying woman, lavishing upon her its infinite compassion, and the inexhaustible riches of Divine mercy.

The terrified servants refused to enter Monsieur or Madame's bedroom; they thought only of themselves, and considered that the striking down of their master and mistress was a just punishment. The stench in the atmosphere was such that, in spite of open windows and the most pungent scents, no one could remain long in Valérie's room. Only Religion watched there. How could a woman of Valérie's sharp intelligence help asking herself what interest made these two representatives of the Church remain with her? In fact, the dying woman had listened to the priest's voice. Repentance had made headway in this perverse soul, in proportion as the ravages of the disease consumed her beauty. The delicate Valérie had offered less resistance to the malady than Crevel, and she must be the first to die. She had been, besides, the first attacked.

'If I had not been ill, I would have been here to look after you,' said Lisbeth at last, after meeting her friend's dull eyes. 'I have been kept in my room for the past fortnight or three weeks; but when I learned about your illness from the doctor, I came at once.'

'Poor Lisbeth; you, at least, still love me! I can see that,' said Valérie. 'Listen! I have only one day or two left to think, I can't say *live*. As you see, I haven't a body any more, I'm a heap of clay. . . . They won't let me look at myself in a glass. . . . And I have only got what I deserve. Ah! how I wish I could repair all the harm I have done, and so hope to receive mercy.'

'Oh!' said Lisbeth. 'If you are talking like this, you must be done for indeed!'

'Do not hinder this woman's repentance; leave her in her Christian thoughts,' said the priest.

'There's nothing left!' Lisbeth said to herself, appalled. 'I don't recognize her eyes or her mouth! There's not a feature remaining recognizable as hers, and her mind is wandering! Oh, it's frightening!'

'You don't know,' Valérie went on, 'what death is, what it's like to have to think of the morning after one's last day, of what will be found in one's coffin: there are worms for the body, and what is there for the soul? . . . Oh, Lisbeth, I feel that there is another life . . . and a terror possesses me that keeps me from feeling the pain of my perishing flesh! And I used to say to Crevel, as a joke, jeering at a saintly woman, that God's vengeance took every form of misfortune. . . . Well, I was a true prophet! Do not trifle with sacred things, Lisbeth! If you love me, follow my example; repent!'

'I?' said the Lorraine peasant. 'I have seen vengeance exacted everywhere throughout creation. Even insects die to satisfy their need to avenge themselves when they are attacked! And these gentlemen,' she said, with a gesture towards the priest, 'don't they tell us that God avenges himself, and that his vengeance is eternal?'

The priest bent a mild, benign, look upon Lisbeth, and said: 'You do not believe in God, Madame.'

'But just see what has happened to me!' said Valérie.

'And where did you get this infection?' the spinster asked, unmoved in her peasant scepticism.

'Oh! I've had a note from Henri which leaves me in no doubt about my fate. . . . He has killed me. I have to die just when I want to live an honourable life – and die a spectacle of horror! . . . Lisbeth, give up all idea of revenge! Be good to that family. I have already left them in my will all the property the law allows me to dispose of. Leave me now, my dear, even though you are the only being who doesn't flee from me in horror. I beg you to go and leave me . . . I have no more than time to give myself to God!'

'She's delirious,' Lisbeth said to herself, looking back from the threshold of the room.

The most fervent affection that we know, a woman's friendship for another woman, had not the heroic constancy of the Church. Lisbeth, stifled by noxious exhalations, left the room. She saw the doctors still busy in discussion. But Bianchon's theory had won the day, and they were now only debating the best way of trying their experiment. . . .

'In any case, there will be a splendid autopsy,' said one of the opposing group, 'and we shall have two subjects for comparison.'

Lisbeth returned with Bianchon, who went up to the sick woman's bed without appearing to notice the fetid odours emanating from it.

'Madame,' he said, 'we are going to try a powerful drug on you, and it may perhaps save you. . . .'

'If you save me,' she said, 'shall I be as beautiful as I was?'

'Perhaps!' said the wise doctor.

'We know what you mean by *perhaps*!' said Valérie. 'I'll look like someone who has fallen in the fire! No, leave me to the Church. It's only God who can find me attractive now. I must try to be reconciled to him – that will be my last flirtation. Yes, I needs must try to *make* merciful God!'

'That's my poor Valérie's last flash of wit. I can see her again as she was, now!' said Lisbeth, weeping.

The Lorraine peasant thought it her duty to go into Crevel's room, where she found Victorin and his wife sitting three feet away from the plague-stricken man.

'Lisbeth,' he said, 'they won't tell me about my wife's condition. You have just seen her. How is she?'

'She's better; she says she is saved,' said Lisbeth, permitting herself the equivocation in order to ease Crevel's mind.

'Ah, good!' replied the Mayor. 'Because I am afraid that she has caught her illness from me. . . . A man doesn't travel in perfumes without running some risks. I blame myself. Suppose I lost her, what would become of me? Upon my word, children, I adore that woman.' And Crevel sat up and tried to strike his pose.

'Oh, Papa!' said Célestine. 'If you could only get well again, I would receive my stepmother, I promise you I would!'

'Poor little Célestine!' answered Crevel. 'Come here and kiss me!'

Victorin restrained his wife as she jumped up to obey.

'Perhaps you are not aware, Monsieur,' the lawyer said gently, 'that your illness is contagious . . .'

'Oh, so it is,' said Crevel. 'The doctors are congratulating themselves upon having found I don't know what plague or other of the Middle Ages that was thought to be lost, on me; and they're beating the big drum about it, through the whole Faculty. . . . It's very funny!'

'Papa,' said Célestine, 'be brave, and you will get the better of this illness.'

'Keep calm, children. Death thinks twice before striking at a Mayor of Paris!' he said, with a comical nonchalance. 'And there, suppose my borough is so unhappy as to sustain the loss of the man whom it has twice honoured with its suffrage – listen to that! You hear how eloquently the words trip off my tongue! – well, I shall know how to pack my bags and go. I am a seasoned commercial traveller; I'm accustomed to taking off. Ah! my children, I'm a man who thinks for himself, a strong-minded man.'

'Papa, promise me to allow a priest to come to see you.'

'Never!' said Crevel. 'Just think – I have sucked the milk of the Revolution. I may not have Baron d'Holbach's wit, but I have his strength of mind. I was never more Regency, Musketeer, Abbé Dubois, and Maréchal de Richelieu in my life! Upon my soul, my poor wife must be out of her mind – she has just sent a man in a soutane to me, to *me*, Béranger's admirer, Lisette's friend, the child of Voltaire and Rousseau! . . . The doctor said, in order to sound me, to see whether the illness was getting me down: "Have you seen Monsieur l'Abbé?". . . Well, I played the part of the great Montesquieu. Yes, I looked at the doctor; see here, just like this,' and he turned to show a three-quarter profile, as in his portrait, and extended his hand authoritatively; 'and I said:

> . . . Ah, that slave came to see,
> With his order displayed, but got no change from me.

His order is a pretty pun, which shows that on the point of death Monsieur le Président de Montesquieu still kept all his graceful wit, for they had sent him a Jesuit! . . . I like that passage of . . . you can't say his life, his death rather. Ah! Passage! Another pun! The passage Montesquieu!'

Victorin Hulot sadly contemplated his father-in-law, and wondered whether silliness and vanity had not just as much sustaining power as true greatness of soul. In the soul, like results seem to be produced by very unlike causes. Can it be that a major criminal's fortitude is of the same nature as that of a Champcenetz going proudly to the guillotine?

At the end of the week Madame Crevel was buried, after extreme suffering, and Crevel followed his wife two days later to the grave. So the provisions of the marriage contract were annulled, and Crevel inherited Valérie's property.

On the day after the funeral, the lawyer saw the old monk appear again, and received him without a word. The monk held out his hand in silence, and in silence Maître Victorin Hulot handed him eighty thousand-franc notes, taken from a sum of money found in Crevel's desk. The younger Madame Hulot inherited the estate at Presles and thirty thousand francs a year. Madame Crevel had bequeathed three hundred thousand francs to Baron Hulot. The scrofulous Stanislas, when he came of age, was to have Crevel's house and twenty-four thousand francs a year.

*

Among the many philanthropic associations set up by Catholic charity in Paris, there is one, founded by Madame de la Chanterie, which exists to provide a civil and religious marriage for working-class couples who are living together.

Our legislators, with their eyes fixed on the revenue produced by registration, and our dominant middle-class, with a tight grip on notaries' fees, feign ignorance of the fact that three-quarters of the working classes cannot afford to pay fifteen francs for a marriage certificate. The Chamber of Notaries lags far behind the Chamber of Advocates in practical charity. The Paris advocates, a much-maligned body, provide free legal aid for indigent people, while notaries are still unable to make up their minds to drawing up poor people's marriage certificates gratis. As for the tax, the whole machinery of legislation would have to be set in motion to induce the Treasury to relax its grasp. The Registrar's Office is deaf and dumb. The Church, on its side, claims its levy on marriages.

The Church is exceedingly revenue-minded in France. It stoops, in the house of God, to a disgraceful traffic in pew rents and chairs which shocks foreigners, although it cannot have forgotten Christ's anger when he drove the money-changers from the Temple. But if the Church finds it difficult to forgo its dues, it must be remembered that its fees, stated to be for the maintenance of the fabric of its edifices, constitute nowadays one of its resources, so that responsibility for this questionable practice of the Church lies at the door of the state.

As a result of this combination of circumstances, in times when people are much too busy worrying about the lot of Negroes and the petty criminals of the police courts to trouble about the difficulties of honest citizens, a large number of well-meaning couples live together without marriage, for want of thirty francs, which is the least sum for which the legal profession, the Registrar, the Mayor, and the Church are able to unite two Parisians. Madame de la Chan-

427

terie's organization, founded for the purpose of regularizing such unions according to the laws of Church and state, seeks out couples of this kind, and finds them the more easily because aid is given to persons in distress before their civil status is inquired into.

When Baroness Hulot had quite recovered her health, she took up her occupation again. It was then that the worthy Madame de la Chanterie asked Adeline to add the regularization of informal marriages to the charitable work she was already doing.

The Baroness made one of her first efforts in this work in the sinister quarter, formerly called Little Poland, that lies between the rue du Rocher, the rue de la Pépinière, and the rue de Miroménil, like an offshoot of the faubourg Saint-Marceau. To describe this quarter, it is enough to say that the owners of the various houses, occupied by out-of-work labourers, ugly customers looking for trouble, and men with empty pockets ready to undertake any risky job on the shady side of the law, do not dare to collect their rents, and cannot find bailiffs willing to evict the insolvent tenants. At the present time, it looks as if speculative building, which is changing the face of this corner of Paris and building up the undeveloped ground between the rue d'Amsterdam and the rue du Faubourg-du-Roule, may alter its population for the better, for the builder's trowel is a more effective civilizing influence in Paris than is generally realized. In building fine and elegant houses with a porter's lodge, laying footpaths and putting in shops, speculative builders, by the high rents that they charge, tend to drive away undesirable characters, families without possessions, and every kind of bad tenant. And it is in this way that such districts rid themselves of their disreputable population, and of the kind of dens which the police set foot in only when duty compels them.

In June 1844, the aspect of the place de Laborde and its surrounding streets was still very far from reassuring. The elegant infantryman who might chance to to wander from the rue de la Pépinière into these sinister side-streets would be astonished to find noblemen rubbing shoulders with the dregs of Bohemia. In such districts, where ignorant poverty and distress in desperate straits proliferate like weeds, there flourish the last public letter-writers, or scriveners, to be seen in Paris. Wherever you see the word *Scrivener* written up in a fair running hand, on a white sheet of paper affixed to the window of some entresol or dirty ground-floor room, you may assume with some certainty that the quarter gives shelter to a large illiterate population, and the vice and crime that result from the circumstances of the unfortunate poor. Lack of education is the mother of all crime. A crime is due, primarily, to an inability to reason.

During the Baroness's illness, this quarter – her charge as a deputy of Providence – had acquired a scrivener who had set up business in Sun Alley, so named by a kind of antithesis familiar to Parisians, for it is overshadowed on both sides. This writer, thought to be a German, was called Vyder, and was living with a young girl of whom he was so jealous that he never let her go out, except to visit a respectable family of stove-fitters living in the rue Saint-Lazare, Italians like all stove-fitters, but settled for years in Paris. These people had been saved from impending bankruptcy and consequent destitution by Baroness Hulot, as Madame de la Chanterie's agent. In the course of some months, prosperity had succeeded poverty, and religion had entered hearts that previously had cursed Providence with the vehemence characteristic of Italian stove-fitters. So it was to this family that the Baroness paid one of her first visits.

She was pleased with the scene that met her eyes at the back of the house where these good people lived, in the rue Saint-Lazare near the rue du Rocher. Above the shops and workshop, now well fitted out and swarming with apprentices and workmen, all Italians from the valley of Domo d'Ossola, the family occupied a little flat to which work had brought plenty. The Baroness was received as if she were the Blessed Virgin in person. After some fifteen minutes spent in inquiry about the family's circumstances, as she was waiting to see the husband in order to learn how the business was going, Adeline set about doing her duty as a benevolent spy by asking whether there were any unfortunate people known to the stove-fitter's family.

'Ah, you are so kind, my dear lady, you would rescue the damned souls from hell!' said the Italian woman. 'Yes, indeed. There is a girl quite near here who needs to be saved from perdition.'

'Do you know her well?' asked the Baroness.

'She's the grand-daughter of a man my husband once worked for, called Judici, who came to France in 1798, about the time of the Revolution. Old Judici was one of the best stove-fitters in Paris under the Emperor Napoleon. He died in 1819, leaving a fine fortune to his son. But the son squandered it all with loose women, and ended by marrying one of them who was cleverer than the rest, and she gave him this poor little girl, who has just turned fifteen.'

'What has become of him?' asked the Baroness, struck by a resemblance to her husband in the character of this Judici.

'Well, now, Madame, the little girl, whose name is Atala, has left her father and mother, and come to live near here, with an old German, who is eighty if he's a day, called Vyder, who does all their business for people who can't read or write. If the old libertine who bought the little girl from her mother for fifteen hundred francs, so they say, would even marry her – because he can't have long to live, and they do say that he's worth some thousands of francs a year – well then the poor child, who's a little angel, would be saved from harm, and want of money in particular, which is bound to make her go to the bad.'

'Thank you for letting me know of this good work to be done,' said Adeline; 'but I must be careful how I go about it. What is this old man like?'

'Oh, he's a very decent fellow, Madame. He makes the child happy, and he has a certain amount of common sense; for you see what he's done? He's left the neighbourhood the Judicis live in, I believe in order to save the child from her mother's clutches. The mother is jealous of her daughter, and perhaps her notion was to turn the child's beauty to some use, to make her a young madam! ... Atala thought of us, she told her Monsieur he ought to set her up near our house; and as the old fellow saw what kind we are, he lets her come here. But get them married, Madame, and you will be doing something worthy of you. ... Once she's married, the child will be free, and she'll be able to escape her mother, who would like to make some money by her, see her in the theatre, or getting on in the shocking career she's started her in.'

'Why has this old man not married her? ...'

'He didn't need to,' said the Italian; 'and besides, although old Vyder is not really ill-natured, I think he knows what's best for himself well enough to want to keep the child under his thumb; and if he married her, well, poor old fellow, he's afraid he might find himself getting what comes to all old husbands in the end. ...'

'Can you send for the girl?' said the Baroness. 'If I saw her here, I should know if there is anything I can do.'

The stove-fitter's wife made a sign to her eldest daughter, who left the room. Ten minutes later the young person came in again, hand in hand with a girl of fifteen and a half, of wholly Italian beauty.

From her father's race Mademoiselle Judici had inherited the kind of skin that seems olive by daylight, but whose pallor in the evening by artificial light takes on a dazzling quality, eyes of an almost Eastern size, shape, and brilliance, thick curling eyelashes like little black feathers, ebon-black hair, and the native dignity of carriage of Lombardy, which makes the foreigner think, as he walks through the streets on a Sunday in Milan, that the porters' daughters are all queens.

Atala, told by the stove-fitter's daughter that the great lady of whom she had heard was at the house, had hastily put on a pretty silk dress, low-cut boots, and an elegant little cape. A bonnet with cherry ribbons strikingly set off her beautiful head. The child's attitude was one of naïve curiosity, and she stood examining the Baroness, whose nervous tremor much surprised her, out of the corners of her eyes.

The Baroness sighed deeply when she saw this perfect creation of feminine loveliness that had been set in the mire of prostitution, and she inwardly vowed that she would bring the girl back to the paths of virtue.

'What is your name, child?'

'Atala, Madame.'

'Can you read and write?'

'No, Madame; but it doesn't matter, because Monsieur can. . . .'

'Did your parents ever take you to church? Have you made your first communion? Do you know your catechism?'

'Papa wanted me to do things like what you say, Madame, but Mama wouldn't let me. . . .'

'Your mother wouldn't let you?' exclaimed the Baroness. 'Your mother is very unkind to you, then, is she?'

'She always used to beat me! I don't know why, but my father and mother were for ever quarrelling about me. . . .'

'Then no one has ever spoken to you about God?' asked the Baroness.

The child opened wide eyes.

'Oh, Mama and Papa often used to say "my God" and "for God's sake" and "God damn and blast",' she answered, with a charming simplicity.

'Have you never been inside a church? Did you never think of going in?'

'Churches? . . . Ah! Notre-Dame, the Panthéon. I have seen them in the distance when Papa took me into Paris, but that didn't happen very often. There are no churches like that in the Faubourg.'

'In which faubourg did you live?'

'In the Faubourg. . . .'

'Yes, but which?'

'Oh, rue de Charonne, Madame.'

The inhabitants of the faubourg Saint-Antoine never call that notorious district anything but 'the Faubourg'. To them it is the only faubourg worth mentioning, *the* faubourg, and even factory-owners understand by the term specifically the faubourg Saint-Antoine.

'Has no one ever taught you the difference between right and wrong?'

'Mama used to beat me when I didn't do things like what she wanted. . . .'

'But did you not know that you were doing wrong when you left your father and mother to go and live with an old man?'

Atala Judici looked haughtily at the Baroness, and did not answer.

'The girl is a complete heathen!' Adeline said, as if to herself.

'Oh, there are plenty more like her in the Faubourg, Madame!' said the stove-fitter's wife.

'But, good heavens, she knows nothing – not even the simple meaning of the word *wrong*! Why don't you answer me?' the Baroness asked the child, trying to take her hand.

Atala angrily drew back a step.

'You're a silly old woman!' she said. 'My father and mother had had nothing to eat all week! My mother wanted to make something very bad of me, because my father beat her and called her names. And then Monsieur Vyder paid all my father's and mother's debts, and gave them money.... Oh! a whole bagful! And he took me away with him, and my poor Papa cried ... but we had to part! Well, was that wrong?'

'And are you very fond of this Monsieur Vyder?'

'Am I fond of him? ...' she said. 'I should just think I am, Madame! He tells me nice stories every evening! And he has given me fine dresses, and underclothes, and a shawl. I'm dressed up like a princess, and don't wear sabots any more! And for the past two months I haven't known what it is to be hungry. I don't live on potatoes now! He brings me sweets, burnt almonds! Oh, what delicious things chocolate almonds are. ... I do anything he wants for a bag of chocolates! And then my old Papa Vyder is so kind, he looks after me so well, he's so good that it makes me see what my mother might have been like. ... He is going to get an old servant to help me, because he doesn't like me to get my hands dirty doing the cooking. This month he has been earning a fair lot of money. He brings me three francs every evening ... and I put them away in a money-box! The only thing is he doesn't like me going out, except to come here. ... He's a love of a man really, so he does whatever he wants with me. ... He calls me his little kitten! And my mother only called me a little bitch, or all sorts of bad names, thief, varmint, goodness knows what!'

'Well, why, child, don't you marry Papa Vyder?'

'But I have, Madame!' said the girl, full of pride, looking at the Baroness without a blush, her brow serene, her eyes untroubled. 'He told me that I was his little wife; but it's very tiresome to be a man's wife! Well, if it wasn't for the chocolate almonds!'

'Good God!' said the Baroness under her breath. 'What kind of monster can this man be to have taken advantage of such complete and blessed innocence? To set this child on the right path again surely would redeem many of my sins! I knew what I was doing,' she said to herself, thinking of her scene with Crevel, 'but she – she knows nothing!'

'Do you know Monsieur Samanon?' Atala asked cajolingly.

'No, my dear; but why do you ask?'

'Really and truly?' said the artless creature.

'You don't distrust Madame, do you, Atala?' said the stove-fitter's wife. 'She's an angel!'

'It's because my nice gentleman is afraid of being found by that Samanon, and that's why he's hiding ... and I only wish he was free. ...'

'Why?'

'Well, of course, because he would take me to see Bobino! Perhaps to the Ambigu-Comique!'

'What a charming creature!' said the Baroness, putting her arms round the little girl.

'Are you rich?' asked Atala, playing with the lace at the Baroness's wrists.

'Yes, and no,' replied the Baroness. 'I am rich for good little girls like you, when they are willing to let themselves be taught Christian duties by a priest, and walk in the right path.'

'What path?' said Atala. 'I have stout legs for walking.'

'The path of virtue!'

Atala gave the Baroness a sly and laughing look.

'You see Madame. She is happy since she returned to the bosom of the Church,' said the Baroness, indicating the stove-fitter's wife. 'You have got married like the animals that mate.'

'Me?' said Atala. 'But if you are ready to give me what Papa Vyder does, I would be very pleased not to be married.

434

It's a dreadful bore! Do you know what it means?'

'Once you are united with a man, as you are,' said the Baroness, 'virtue means that you have to remain faithful to him.'

'Until he dies?' said Atala knowingly. 'I shan't have it too long. If you knew how Papa Vyder coughs and puffs! ... Peuh! Peuh!' she coughed, in imitation of the old man.

'Virtue and morality require your marriage to be consecrated by the Church, which represents God, and the Mayor representing the law. You see Madame – she is properly married. ...'

'Is that more fun?' the child asked.

'You will be happier,' answered the Baroness, 'for no one will be able to blame you for this marriage. You will be pleasing God! Ask Madame if she married without receiving the sacrament of marriage.'

'What has she got that I haven't?' she demanded. 'I am prettier than she is. ...'

'Yes, but I am a proper wife ... and they can call you by a nasty name. ...'

'How can you ask God to protect you, if you trample divine and human laws underfoot?' said the Baroness. 'Do you know that God keeps a paradise in store for those who obey his Church's laws?'

'What happens in paradise? Are there theatre shows?' said Atala.

'Oh, paradise!' said the Baroness. 'That's all the joy that you can possibly imagine. It's full of angels with white wings. One can see God in his glory; one can be a sharer in his power; one is happy every moment and for ever more! ...'

Atala Judici listened to the Baroness as she might have listened to music; and, seeing that she was incapable of understanding, Adeline thought that she should perhaps try a different course and speak to the old man.

'Go home, child, and I'll come and talk to Monsieur Vyder. Is he French?'

'He is Alsatian, Madame; but he's going to be rich, I can tell you! If you would pay the money he owes that horrid

Samanon, he would pay you back! Because he says that in a few months he'll be getting six thousand francs a year, and we're going to go and live in the country then, ever so far away, in the Vosges. . . .'

The memories evoked by her mention of the Vosges plunged the Baroness into a profound reverie. In her mind she saw her own village again. From this painful meditation she was roused by the stove-fitter's greeting, as he came in to tell her how his business had prospered.

'In a year, Madame, I'll be able to pay back the money you have lent us. It is God's money – it belongs to the poor and unfortunate. If I do well, one day you will be able to use our purse. I mean to repay to others, through you, the help that you brought us.'

'At the moment,' said the Baroness, 'I don't want money, I want your cooperation in a good deed. I have just seen the little Judici girl, who is living with an old man, and I would like to have them married in church, and legally.'

'Ah, old Vyder! He's a very decent chap, a man worth asking for his advice. Poor and old as he is, he's already made friends in the neighbourhood in the two months he's been here. He keeps my accounts straight for me. He's a brave colonel, I believe, who once served the Emperor well. . . . Ah! how he worships Napoleon! He has a decoration, but he never wears it. He's waiting till he has cleared off his debts, for he owes money, poor fellow! . . . I think he may even be in hiding, with process-servers on his track. . . .'

'Tell him that I'll pay his debts, if he is willing to marry the child. . . .'

'Well, that will be easily done! Why, Madame, we could go and see him. . . . It's only a step away, in Sun Alley.'

The Baroness and the stove-fitter set out for Sun Alley.

'This way, Madame,' the man said, pointing down the rue de la Pépinière.

Sun Alley – the passage du Soleil – runs, in fact, from the top of the rue de la Pépinière through to the rue du Rocher. About half way down the alley, recently made, with shops let at a very modest rent, the Baroness saw, above a shop-window screened with green taffeta curtains to a height that prevented

436

passers-by from gazing in, a sign with the words: *Public Letterwriter*; and on the door:

BUSINESS AGENCY

Petitions drawn up.   Accounts audited.

All business confidential and promptly executed.

The interior was like the waiting-rooms where Paris omnibus passengers wait for their connexions. A flight of stairs inside led, no doubt, to a mezzanine apartment let with the shop and looking out on the alley. The Baroness noticed a blackened deal desk, cardboard boxes, and a battered, shabby, second-hand arm-chair. A cap and greasy green silk eye-shade attached with copper wire suggested either some idea of disguise or an eye weakness not unlikely in an old man.

'He is upstairs,' said the stove-fitter. 'I'll go up and tell him that you are here and bring him down.'

The Baroness lowered her veil and sat down. A heavy step made the little wooden staircase creak, and Adeline could not restrain a piercing cry when she saw her husband, Baron Hulot, appear, dressed in a grey knitted jacket, old grey flannel trousers, and slippers.

'What can I do for you, Madame?' said Hulot politely.

Adeline rose, took hold of Hulot, and in a voice broken with emotion said:

'At last I've found you!'

'Adeline!...' the Baron exclaimed, in amazement. He locked the shop door. 'Joseph!' he called to the stove-fitter. 'Go out by the back way.'

'My dear,' she said, forgetting everything but her overwhelming joy, 'you can return to your family. We are rich! Your son's income is a hundred and sixty thousand francs. There is no claim now on your pension, and you only have to present a statement that you're alive in order to draw fifteen thousand francs arrears. Valérie is dead, and she has left you three hundred thousand francs. Everything has been quite forgotten. You can return to society, and you will find a fortune waiting for you in your son's house. Come, and our happiness will be complete. I've been searching for you for nearly three years, and I was so sure that I should find you that

437

there's a room prepared, all ready for you. Oh, come away from ·his place! Leave the dreadful situation I see you in here!'

'Gladly,' said the Baron, dazedly; '*but can I bring the little girl with me?*'

'Hector, give her up! Do so much for your Adeline, who has never before asked you to make even the least sacrifice! I promise you I'll give this child a dowry, arrange a good marriage for her, have her taught. Let it be said that one of those who made you happy is happy herself, and will not fall further into vice, into the mire!'

'So you're the person,' said the Baron, with a smile,'who wanted to have me married? . . . Stay here a moment,' he added. 'I must go upstairs and dress. I have proper clothes in a box up there . . . .'

When Adeline was alone, looking again round the dingy shop, she shed tears.

'He was living here,' she said to herself, 'while we have been living in luxury! . . . Poor man, how he has been punished – he who used to be elegance itself!'

The stove-fitter came to say good-bye to his benefactress, and she asked him to fetch a cab. When he returned, the Baroness asked him to take in little Atala Judici, and take her home with him there and then.

'Tell her,' she added, 'that if she is willing to put herself under the guidance of Monsieur le Curé at the Madeleine, on the day she makes her first communion I'll give her a dowry of thirty thousand francs and a good husband, some fine young man!'

'My eldest son, Madame! He is twenty-two and he adores that child!'

The Baron now came downstairs. His eyes were wet.

'You are making me leave the only creature whose love for me is anything like your own,' he whispered to his wife. 'The child is in tears, and I cannot desert her like this. . . .'

'Set your mind at rest, Hector. She is going to be settled with a respectable family and I can answer for what her way of life will be.'

'Ah, then I can come with you,' the Baron said, and he escorted his wife to the cab.

Hector, now Baron d'Ervy again, had put on a greatcoat and trousers of blue cloth, a white waistcoat, black cravat and gloves. When the Baroness had taken her seat in the cab, Atala slipped in like a snake.

'Oh, Madame,' she begged, 'let me go with you wherever you're going!... I can tell you, I'll be very good and very obedient. I'll do anything you want; but don't leave me behind and take Papa Vyder away, my gentleman who is so kind and gives me such nice things. Because I'll be beaten!...'

'Come, Atala,' said the Baron. 'This lady is my wife, and we have to say good-bye. ...'

'Her? As old as that!' the girl said artlessly. 'And shaking like a leaf! Oh, what a sight!'

And she drolly mimicked the Baroness's shaking. The stove-fitter, hurrying after the Judici child, appeared at the cab door.

'Take her away!' said the Baroness.

The stove-fitter took Atala in his arms and forcibly bore her off to his house.

'Thank you for that sacrifice, my dear,' said Adeline, taking the Baron's hand and pressing it with feverish joy. 'How you have changed! How you must have suffered! What a surprise for your daughter and your son!'

Adeline talked – like a woman meeting her lover after a long absence – of a thousand things at once. Ten minutes later, the Baron and his wife reached the rue Louis-le-Grand, and Adeline found the following letter waiting for her:

Madame la Baronne,

Monsieur le Baron d'Ervy stayed a month in the rue de Charonne, under the name of Thorec, an anagram of Hector. He is now living in the passage du Soleil under the name of Vyder. He calls himself an Alsatian, has a scrivener's business, and is living with a girl called Atala Judici. You should be careful, Madame, for the Baron is being actively searched for, on whose behalf I do not know.

The actress has kept her word, and remains, as always, Madame la Baronne,

Your humble servant,
J. M.

The Baron's return was welcomed with a warmth and pleasure which quite reconciled him to family life. He forgot little Atala Judici, for the damage caused by his life of excess had now made him subject to the rapid changes of feeling characteristic of age and childhood. The family happiness was clouded by the alteration in the Baron. He had left his children a still sound, hale man, and returned a centenarian almost, in appearance – broken, stooping, his face no longer noble. A fine dinner, hastily arranged by Célestine, reminded the old man of the opera-singer's parties, and he was dazzled by his family's splendours.

'You are celebrating the return of the prodigal father!' he whispered to Adeline.

'Hush! That's all forgotten,' she answered him.

'Where is Lisbeth?' the Baron asked, noticing the old maid's absence.

'She's in bed,' said Hortense, 'sad to say. She doesn't get up at all now, and we must have the grief of losing her before long. She is hoping to see you after dinner.'

Next morning, at dawn, Victorin Hulot was warned by his door-keeper that his house was surrounded by the Municipal Guard. The police were looking for Baron Hulot. The bailiff, who then came in, following the door-keeper's wife, presented a summons to the lawyer, and asked if he was willing to pay his father's debt. It was a matter of ten thousand francs, in notes of hand made out to a moneylender named Samanon, who had probably lent Baron d'Ervy two or three thousand francs. The young lawyer asked the officer to send the Guard away, and paid.

'Will this be the last?' he asked himself, with some misgiving.

Lisbeth, already afflicted by the family's increasingly bright circumstances, was unable to endure this latest happy turn of events. Her condition deteriorated so much that Bianchon gave her no more than a week to live. She must die, defeated, at the end of that long struggle marked by so many victories. She kept the secret of her hatred through the terrible suffering of the last stages of pulmonary tuberculosis. And she had the supreme satisfaction of seeing Adeline, Hortense, Hulot,

Victorin, Steinbock, Célestine, and their children, all in tears round her bed, mourning her as the family's angel.

Baron Hulot, on a substantial diet that he had not known for nearly three years, regained strength and was almost himself again. This restoration made Adeline so happy that her nervous shaking diminished in intensity.

'So she is to be happy in the end!' said Lisbeth to herself, on the eve of her death, as she saw the profound respect, almost veneration, that the Baron showed towards his wife, whose sufferings had been described to him by Hortense and Victorin. Her bitter resentment hastened Cousin Bette's death. She was followed to her grave by a whole family in tears.

Baron and Baroness Hulot, feeling that they had reached an age for undisturbed rest, gave the splendid rooms on the first floor to Count and Countess Steinbock, and took up their dwelling on the second. The Baron, through his son's efforts on his behalf, obtained a directorship of a railway company, at the beginning of the year 1845, with a salary of six thousand francs, which, with the six thousand francs of his retirement pension and the money left to him by Madame Crevel, gave him an income of twenty-four thousand francs.

As Hortense had obtained control of her own money during her three years' estrangement from her husband, Victorin did not hesitate now to invest the two hundred thousand francs left in trust, in his sister's name, and gave her the income from it: twelve thousand francs a year. Wenceslas, now the husband of a rich woman, was not in any way unfaithful to her; but he idled his time away, unable to make up his mind to start a piece of work, however small. An artist again, *in partibus*, he had a great deal of drawing-room success, he was consulted by many amateurs of art; in other words, he was accepted as a critic, like all such ineffectual men whose early promise proves delusive.

Each of these families, then, enjoyed its own separate income, although they lived under one roof. Made wise by so many disasters, the Baroness left all her financial business to her son; and the Baron was limited to his salary and pension, in the hope that a restricted income would prevent him from relapsing into his old ways.

By a remarkable piece of luck, however, which neither his wife nor his son could have hoped for, the Baron seemed to have given the fair sex up. His untroubled peace, which they attributed to natural causes, at last set his family's mind so completely at rest that they were able to enjoy again whole-heartedly Baron d'Ervy's many amiable and charming qualities. He was thoughtfully attentive to his wife and children, accompanied them to the theatre and into society – where he now appeared once more – and did the honours of his son's drawing-room with a delightfully gracious hospitality.

Altogether, this reformed prodigal father gave the greatest possible pleasure to his family. He was a charming old man, quite finished with life and worn out, of course, but full of sensibility, retaining only enough of his old vice to make a social virtue. Everyone naturally came by degrees to feel completely reassured. His children and the Baroness praised the father of the family to the skies, forgetting the deaths of two uncles! Life cannot go on without a great deal of forgetting.

Madame Victorin, who did the housekeeping for this large household with notable efficiency, which owed something, no doubt, to Lisbeth's instruction, found it necessary to employ a cook. The cook, of course, had to have a kitchen-maid. Kitchen-maids are ambitious creatures nowadays, busy trying to find out the chef's secrets, and ready to become cooks themselves as soon as they know how to blend a sauce. Consequently, kitchen-maids are constantly changing.

At the beginning of December, 1845, Célestine engaged as kitchen-maid a buxom girl from Isigny in Normandy, short, thick-set, with stout red arms and a common face, as heavy and dull as an occasional theatrical piece, a girl who was only reluctantly induced to abandon the classical cotton bonnet worn by the girls of lower Normandy. She was as well-furnished with fat as a wet nurse, bursting out of the cotton cloth that she wore swathed round her bodice. The solid contours of her sun-tanned coarse red face might have been carved out of stone. No one in the house, naturally, remarked the arrival of this girl, called Agathe, the kind of knowing girl that comes up to Paris from the provinces every day. The chef did not like Agathe much, because of her foul tongue – for she had been used to the company of carters in the low-class inn in which she had served – and she was so far from making a conquest of him and persuading him to teach her the high art of cookery that he despised her. The chef's attentions were all for Louise, Countess Steinbock's maid. And so the country girl thought herself badly used, and was for ever complaining of her lot; she was always sent out on some pretext or other when the chef was putting the last touches to a dish, or finishing off a sauce.

'True enough, I don't have any luck here, at all,' she kept saying. 'I'll try somewhere else.'

She stayed on, however, although she had twice given notice.

One night, Adeline, awakened by some unaccustomed sound, discovered that Hector was not in his bed near her own, for, like most old people, they slept in single beds, side by side. She lay awake for an hour, but the Baron did not return. Filled with apprehension, fearing some dreadful disaster, a stroke perhaps, she went first upstairs, to the attic floor where the servants slept, and was drawn to Agathe's room by the murmur of two voices and a bright light shining from the half-open door. She stopped in utter dismay as she recognized the Baron's voice. Seduced by Agathe's charms, he had reached the point, led on by the calculated resistance of that atrocious slut, of saying these hateful words:

'My wife has not long to live, and if you like you can be Baroness.'

Adeline uttered a cry, dropped her candlestick, and fled.

Three days later, the Baroness, who had received the last sacraments the evening before, lay at the point of death, surrounded by her weeping family. A moment before her spirit fled, she took her husband's hand, pressed it, and whispered to him:

'My dear, I had nothing left but my life to give you. In a moment you'll be free, and you will be able to make a Baroness Hulot.'

And, a phenomenon that must be rare, tears were seen to fall from a dead woman's eyes. The fierce persistence of vice had triumphed over the patience of the angel, who on the edge of eternity had spoken the first word of reproach of her life.

Baron Hulot left Paris three days after his wife's funeral. Eleven months later, Victorin learned indirectly of his father's marriage with Mademoiselle Agathe Piquetard, celebrated at Isigny, on 1 February 1846.

'Parents can oppose their children's marriages, but children have no way of preventing the follies of parents in their second childhood,' said Maître Hulot to Maître Popinot, second son of the former Minister of Commerce, and a fellow lawyer, who had spoken to him of that marriage.

THE END